We hope you enjoy this book. Please return or renew it by the due date.

You can renew it at www.norfolk.gov.uk/libraries or by using our free library app.

Otherwise you can phone 0344 800 8020 - please have your library card and PIN ready.

You can sign up for email reminders too.

BY JUAN GÓMEZ-JURADO

The Antonia Scott Trilogy

Red Queen

Black Wolf

White King

Juan Gómez-Jurado is an internationally bestselling author of thrillers. His award-winning Antonia Scott trilogy has sold nearly three million copies in Spanish, is published in twenty-one countries and is the basis for an Amazon streaming series that debuted worldwide in 2024. He lives in Madrid, Spain.

WHITE KING

JUAN GÓMEZ-JURADO

Translated from the Spanish by
**NICK CAISTOR AND
LORENZA GARCIA**

PAN BOOKS

First published in the United States 2025 by Minotaur Books,
an imprint of St. Martin's Publishing Group

First published in the UK 2025 by Macmillan

This paperback edition first published 2025 by Pan Books
an imprint of Pan Macmillan
The Smithson, 6 Briset Street, London EC1M 5NR
EU representative: Macmillan Publishers Ireland Ltd, 1st Floor,
The Liffey Trust Centre, 117–126 Sheriff Street Upper,
Dublin 1 D01 YC43
Associated companies throughout the world

ISBN 978-1-5290-9384-1

Originally published in Spain as *Rey blanco* by Ediciones B

Pan Macmillan does not have any control over, or any responsibility for,
any author or third-party websites (including, without limitation, URLs,
emails and QR codes) referred to in or on this book.

135798642

A CIP catalogue record for this book is available from the British Library.

Printed and bound in the UK using 100% Renewable Electricity by CPI Group (UK) Ltd

Visit **www.panmacmillan.com** to read more about
all our books and to buy them.

For Babs,
Because I love her

For Carmen,
For her loyalty

For Antonia,
For lending me her name

WHITE KING

AN ENDING

Antonia Scott has less than three minutes.

To other people, three minutes can seem a negligible amount of time.

Not for Antonia. It could be said her mind is capable of storing vast quantities of data, yet Antonia's brain isn't a hard drive. It could be said she is capable of visualizing in detail the entire street map of Madrid, and yet Antonia's brain isn't a GPS.

Antonia's brain is more like a jungle, a jungle full of monkeys leaping at top speed from vine to vine carrying things. Many monkeys and many things, swinging past one another in midair and baring their fangs.

Except that Antonia has learned how to tame them.

This is just as well. Because Antonia Scott doesn't have three minutes. Two men in balaclavas—and a woman with a friendly face—have abducted her police partner, Inspector Jon Gutiérrez.

Antonia Scott doesn't run after the van. She doesn't shout for help. She doesn't make a desperate emergency call.

Antonia Scott does none of those things, because Antonia Scott isn't like the rest of us.

What she does is pause.

Ten seconds. That's all the time she allows herself.

In ten seconds—eyes closed, hands braced against the wall of a building to steady her nerves—Antonia is able to:

- calculate the three most likely routes out of the city center;
- memorize everything about the van and the kidnappers;
- decide on a plan to save Jon's life.

She opens her eyes.

She dials a special telephone number. One that tells Mentor he doesn't need to speak when he picks up. Simply listen and do as she tells him.

Antonia dictates the exact words he has to send out in an APB (Inspector Gutiérrez, 10-37 Mercedes Vito, top priority), the vehicle license plate (9344 FSY), and the color (white, of course). Then she chooses one of the three possible routes. The one where the police patrol cars need to converge.

Pirámides, Madrid Río, Legazpi.

Of these three, Madrid Río is the most complicated, the slowest, the least likely, because there's always a traffic jam. Also, there's a police precinct right by the exit.

Antonia immediately rules it out.

That leaves Legazpi and Pirámides.

She chooses Pirámides. It's the most direct, the quickest, the most obvious.

It isn't an easy choice. Inspector Gutiérrez's life is at stake. When the survival of one of the three people you care most about in the world depends on you, you'd think you could make a rational decision.

But this . . . It's a coin toss.

And Antonia doesn't like that one bit.

AN APB

Ruano flicks the blinker at the last minute. Instead of going back to the precinct, he heads in the opposite direction.

"Around one last time. Do you mind?"

Irritated, his partner glances at his watch. It's late, his shift ended eleven minutes ago, and he wants to go home to his wife. But Osorio indulges his rookie partner. It's the end of the month. It's not that Ruano is behind with his fines. The idea that traffic cops have quotas is of course an urban myth.

"How many do you need?"

"Fifteen."

"No big deal. We can make that up from *double-parkers* on Carlos V."

Stopping outside the bar El Brillante in the square "for just a sec" isn't a good idea. To a traffic cop who needs to fill his quota, it's like shooting fish in a barrel. Two laps around the traffic circle, pinpoint the offending vehicle, and wait for the hungry sucker to appear. Dangling from his wrist is the inevitable white plastic bag containing a calamari roll, carefully wrapped in foil. The distinctive smell it gives off would make the stomach of any self-respecting inhabitant of Madrid rumble. But the moment a traffic cop hands the dummy a fine, his appetite vanishes. The smell is suddenly revealed for what it is: a reek of oily batter that has just cost him €200.

A crafty cop can make his quota in a single busy afternoon.

But Ruano doesn't want this easy answer. It turns out the kid's an idealist. A dreamer. In other words, an asshole. Maybe it's a hangover from his previous job. Or maybe it's simply because he's young. He'll outgrow it once he's acquired a middle-aged spread and some common sense.

What Ruano wants is to earn his paycheck. To go around catching *real* offenders. People who burn rubber down narrow streets, people who sell weed on street corners. If I wanted to catch *real* offenders, I'd have become a *real* cop, Osorio often tells him.

Whenever Ruano hears this, he looks at Osorio and laughs. The carefree laugh of the true millennial. Ruano finds everything amusing.

"Just wait till you reach my age, you'll see."

"You're thirty-seven, Osorio."

"Yeah, and here I am, still driving around with rookie cops."

"Maybe you could make more of an effort . . ."

"Maybe you could go to hell . . ."

In fact, Ruano is heading northeast. Driving from memory, on automatic pilot. They both know the route by heart. They might travel it as often as ten times a day. Countless times a year. More, if Santa María de la Cabeza weren't so slow. All the time, but especially at this time of day.

At the junction with Calle de la Arquitectura, they hear the APB on the car radio. Osorio raises an eyebrow, Ruano's face clouds. A police inspector. Kidnapped. In a white van. He opens his mouth to say something, but a loud clamor cuts him off.

Pripripri, pripripri

The screen on the dash glows prison orange. Some characters flash up in the center.

9344 FSY

The patrol car is fitted with ANPR—Automatic Number Plate Recognition. Cameras on the dash, roof, and fender scan the license plates of oncoming vehicles and run them through the police database. Just in case. You never know.

The system isn't perfect, but sometimes it issues an alert. A license number and a reason to stop the vehicle. Maybe it's stolen, or has €1,000 in unpaid fines, or contains an abducted police inspector.

"I don't get it," says Osorio. "The ANPR says it's a 'yellow Megane.' But the license plate is the one for the alert."

"Wasn't that a white van?" says Ruano, peering into his rearview mirror.

Osorio turns in his seat. A few blocks back, they passed a white Mercedes Vito going in the opposite direction. He spots it at the traffic light at Calle de las Peñuelas. From their position, they can't see the license plate.

"Call it in," says Ruano.

As Osorio is talking on the car radio, the traffic starts to move, but Ruano stays where he is. One of the drivers honks his horn, but the patrol car remains stationary.

"I'm going to follow them."

"You can't cross the median. It's too high."

Ruano drums his fingers on the wheel. The next break in the median is a hundred meters farther on. Too far.

Unit M58, confirm visual contact with suspect vehicle, over, demands the radio dispatcher.

"They're getting away."

The van is receding in the rearview mirror, and Ruano doesn't think twice. He spins the wheel toward the median and steps on the gas. The Nissan Leaf's fender shatters, sprinkling pieces of white plastic across the road, and provoking more angry honks from the cars behind. But Ruano manages to cross over into the opposing lanes.

"Unit M58, traveling southwest on Santa María de la Cabeza, in pursuit of Mercedes Vito reported," Osorio says into the radio. He releases the button and shoots Ruano a worried look. "You're nuts, kid."

"They were getting away," replies Ruano, craning his neck.

He turns on the flashing lights, but not the siren. Just enough to force the cars in front to make way for them. The traffic is congested, but the two lanes help. So does the fear of getting a fine. Madrid drivers move aside twice as quickly for the infamous blue-and-white check of traffic patrol cars than for ambulances or the federal police.

A few seconds later, they spot the white roof of the van up ahead of them.

"If they take the Acacias underpass, they're screwed. We call it in, game over. The police will intercept them at the other end."

"If they go over the bridge, calling it in won't help," says Ruano, chewing his lower lip.

Osorio sighs. The kid is right. At the far end of the bridge, the van has plenty of options. It could get lost in the endless maze of streets in the Usera or Opanel neighborhoods, and both offer several routes out of the city. Too many.

Unit M58, do not intervene, I repeat, do not intervene. We are sending patrol cars from Pirámides. ETA four minutes.

"It's a bit late for that," Osorio tells the radio dispatcher. Offhandedly, as though talking to himself.

The last set of traffic lights, where Paseo Santa María de la Cabeza crosses Calle de la Esperanza, has just turned red. The van is the third vehicle in line.

Unit M58, I repeat, do not intervene. Do not reveal your position to the suspects.

It's a bit late for that as well. The patrol car's lights, which opened their path to the van, are now reflecting off the white body of the Mercedes. Only one car stands between them.

The traffic signal bleeps more slowly, indicating the light is about to turn green. The last pedestrian reaches the opposite sidewalk. The first car drives off.

The van doesn't move.

The car in front of Ruano and Osorio honks before swinging sharply into the adjacent lane, where the other cars are driving past. Some of the drivers honk, others lower their windows to yell at the van, which still doesn't move.

Ruano looks at Osorio and grits his teeth.

"What now?"

"Give them a warning, see what they do."

Ruano presses the siren button once. The short, piercing wail fades away with no response.

"Come on, you've gotta be kidding," says Osorio, opening the passenger door.

"Where are you going?" Ruano reaches over and grabs hold of his jacket.

"Nowhere, if you don't let go of me."

Puzzled, the rookie looks at his colleague. This isn't the way he normally behaves. But then this isn't a normal alert. Ruano glances at the van in the middle of the road. Perhaps a police inspector is being held hostage inside.

"They told us not to intervene."

Osorio clicks his tongue in annoyance.

"Intervening is above my pay grade. They don't pay me enough to intervene. I'm just going to make sure they stay where they are until the . . ."

Ruano releases his grip a little. Just enough for Osorio to place his foot on the ground. His boot crunches on the asphalt. A sound that should be inaudible but which resonates in Ruano's ears, becoming a piercing, persistent echo. It drowns out the metallic clunk of the Vito's side door opening. And continues to reverberate in his head as the first shots ring out.

Ruano doesn't hear them.

He feels the thud of lead on the patrol car bodywork. He smells the stench of oil and grease from the engine, sprayed with bullets, that protects him from the shots.

He feels the air rushing in from the open passenger door, merging with the draft coming through the shattered windshield.

He is aware of shards of broken glass raining on his head and inside his uniform, scratching his skin.

He can barely see Osorio—his colleague who only a few weeks earlier invited him to spend Christmas with him and his family—*We can't leave the poor guy on his own,* he told his wife, *the more the merrier. . . .* —the lazy, kindly grump who is forever breaking his balls. Nothing more than his shoulder, protruding at an odd angle behind the torn-off door.

Ruano doesn't hear the shots or the bystanders' terrified screams or the screech of tires as the van speeds off. The echo of Osorio's boot crunching on the ground fades away after Osorio himself does, dead even before he can finish his sentence.

Part I

ANTONIA

Who guards the guards?

Juvenal

1

A JET PLANE

It's no more than a dot in the morning sky.

Dawn has yet to break when the Bombardier Global Express 7000 begins its descent from the west. It doesn't need to wait for approach clearance, because the Cuatro Vientos airport has been closed to all other air traffic.

Antonia Scott's eyes remain fixed on the jet as it lands. Oblivious to the early morning chill, she sits on the car hood waiting until the plane has taxied to a halt alongside them.

The hatch opens, and a familiar figure appears in the rectangle of light. Antonia slides off the car hood and walks toward her, one hand behind her back, ignoring the pins and needles in her legs.

"You're late," she says.

"We had problems leaving Gloucester," replies the shadowy shape.

Antonia keeps her hand hidden as she slowly ascends the eight steps. Only once she is sure the woman is the person she was expecting does she relax the grip on the Sig Sauer P290 clipped to her belt.

"You've changed your hair."

"This is my natural color. I got tired of being blond."

Carla Ortiz smiles warmly despite the fatigue and fear in her big brown eyes. She extends a hand to greet Antonia, then withdraws it at the last moment.

"I . . . I don't like physical contact," Antonia says by way of apology.

"I know. They told me. That and other things."

"Embarrassing ones, I presume."

"You presume right, dear," a voice from inside the plane says in English.

Antonia enters and crouches in front of the first seat. A crooked, bejeweled hand, cold as a bedsheet in winter, musses her hair affectionately.

"You look awful," says Grandma Scott, motioning toward the blueblack rings under her granddaughter's eyes.

"And you . . . ," Antonia replies, trying to contain the emotion she feels at her grandmother's touch.

Grandma and Marcos are the only two people whose physical contact she has ever craved. Her husband died a few hours earlier, following Antonia's decision to switch off his life-support machines after years of senseless waiting. And Grandma Scott doesn't have long to go either. This surprise journey in the middle of the night hasn't exactly helped.

Antonia studies this bag of bones wearing a polka-dot dress. The hand that isn't caressing her granddaughter is clenched around a glass containing a large whisky.

Antonia immediately notices the absence of lip smears on the rim of the glass, her grandmother's clean breath, and realizes she has lost the use of her left arm. She is opening her mouth to ask about this when a thought crosses her mind. A thought with a Basque accent and a powerful voice that is not fat.

She's gone to a lot of trouble to conceal it from you. Let her believe she's succeeded.

". . . are prettier than ever," she finishes her sentence, with an effort.

"Maybe that was true a few decades ago, dear, but now I'm pushing a hundred."

Gazing into Grandma Scott's watery blue eyes, Antonia feels her heart breaking. This could be the last time they see each other face-to-face. She desperately wants to lean over and hug her, but she can't.

"Run along, dear," her grandmother excuses her with a parting caress. "Go and do your thing. And tell me about it later."

Antonia nods and straightens up. Ignoring Carla's attempts to start a conversation, she glances around the cabin for several long minutes, noticing how her anxiety is mounting. She completes her inspection, however superficial it may be.

This is all she has time for.

She walks back to Carla.

"Any news of Inspector Gutiérrez?" the other woman asks.

"The van got away. That's all we know for now."

Scared by the thought, Carla hesitates, but finally ventures:

"She . . . she was there, wasn't she?"

Antonia nods. An awkward silence follows, the kind Antonia used to feel obliged to fill with promises. Bold, reassuring promises that, coming from other people, would be empty words.

Such promises from other people at times like this are meaningless. Not from Antonia Scott.

A promise from Antonia Scott is a contract. A contract that, if it's not fulfilled, she pays for just the same. In the inflationary currency of guilt and remorse.

That's why Antonia doesn't alleviate the silence with words such as: I will *find Inspector Gutiérrez* or I will *catch the woman who kidnapped and tortured you*. Over the past few months, Antonia has learned something about promises.

So instead, she says to Carla:

"I'm sorry about your father."

The young woman's face darkens, and she looks away.

"He was very old."

"Were you able to speak with him? Before . . ."

The ellipsis contains entire encyclopedias.

"I didn't want to, and he couldn't," Carla says with a shrug.

CARLA

The stroke Ramón Ortiz suffered a few months earlier left him a dribbling wreck. Death doesn't leave anyone off its list, not even the world's richest man. The businessman's wealth and power could do nothing to save him; it simply enabled him to pass away in pleasanter surroundings.

For her part, the rich heiress had undergone a transformation during the time she was Ezekiel's captive.

She emerged from the sewers a changed woman. All her frivolity and capriciousness evaporated in her gloomy prison. Whereas before she was selfish and needy, now she was generous and self-assured in a way at once ambiguous and unsettling. She smiled less often, but when she did, it was for real.

And, no, she never did make peace with her father. He was waiting for her by the manhole cover on Calle Jorge Juan amid a throng of photographers and journalists. She refused the hand he offered, preferring instead to lean on Inspector Gutiérrez, the man who braved a booby-trapped tunnel and took a bullet to save her life. She didn't respond to Ramón's embrace; she didn't smile or shed a single tear. In a remarkably steady voice, she thanked everyone for their support. She said she felt fine and couldn't wait to get back to work. The whole world heard her calm statement on the morning news, and the company's shares shot up by six percent.

She never spoke to her father again in private. She tried on a few occasions. She longed a hundred times to ask him why he had abandoned her to her fate. Why he didn't give in to Ezekiel's blackmail, as she would have done without hesitation had her son been the one in danger.

Her son, slumbering draped in a blanket on one of the private jet's couches, was all she cared about. To hold him in her arms again was the only thing she longed for during her captivity. She would give everything she had for him. Every last one of her thousands of millions of euros, down to the loose change in her pocket.

It was only when Ramón died—on a Saturday at three in the afternoon in the middle of the news headlines—that Carla understood everything. He was in his hospital bed, watching television, his head bobbing gently as if he were dozing off. And all of a sudden, he died. He didn't make a sound, he just went. One of the four private nurses providing him with round-the-clock care told her the details. Carla took the call at 15:08, knowing beforehand—we always know these things—that her father had just died. No sooner had she hung up than she went back to the news bulletin, scarcely registering the procession of banal events or indeed the cruel irony that she and her father had doubtless been watching the same images five miles apart.

She had just inherited a twelve-figure fortune. A one followed by eleven zeros. An absurd, impossible sum to which, when her father was alive, she had been as oblivious as she was to the news program now. Like those images, it was simply there, it existed beyond the bounds of her responsibilities and influence.

Yes, she had worked night and day in her father's company, put in all the hours she could and more. But she had done so to earn the one thing she couldn't have. Her father's respect.

She could almost see the next day's news headlines on the gigantic hundred-inch screen—almost but not quite: the screen was expensive but not a crystal ball. She saw herself in mourning attire, greeting the guests at the funeral parlor. The king and queen, of course, the prime minister, a few ministers. Other important figures: Laura Trueba or Bill Gates. All of a sudden, she had become something else. An avalanche of responsibility had cascaded onto her. The fates of hundreds of thousands of employees and millions of investors now depended on her every gesture. One misstep, one slip of the tongue, and the whole empire could come tumbling down.

This was the moment when she understood her father's betrayal.

This was the moment when she wished she could call him. Not to say she forgave him—that would be impossible—but that she understood him.

For, alongside that exorbitant sum, alongside those eleven zeros, she had inherited a steely, luminous truth in just five words:

She had not earned them.

2
DICE

"Let's go over the plan," says Antonia, moving toward the front of the jet.

Looking at this slip of a woman, nearly half a head shorter than her, Carla feels oddly envious. Antonia Scott isn't unattractive, nor is she a beauty. It isn't her looks or even her intelligence that Carla envies. It's her unswerving determination. Antonia Scott saved her life in the tunnels of the Goya subway station, and as a result, Carla is permanently in her debt.

When Antonia called her a few weeks earlier, Carla was expecting a request. Payment of some kind. Which, obviously, she was more than happy to provide.

There's no cheaper way to square a debt than with money.

But instead, Antonia Scott told her a story that made Carla sick to her stomach and kept her awake at night. A story about a mysterious woman who for want of a better name we will call Sandra Fajardo. About how this woman manipulated a mentally unstable man into believing she was his daughter. About how the two of them abducted Carla with the apparent intention of blackmailing her father. About how the bogus Sandra's body was never found.

About how everything they thought they knew was one big lie.

"I don't understand. My father's blackmail wasn't for real?"

"It was an elaborate charade," replied Antonia. "Somehow, I don't yet know how, all this is connected to me."

She went on to tell Carla about Mr. White. The man pulling Sandra Fajardo's strings.

"I don't believe it. All those police officers who were killed trying to save me. The woman at your son's school. How many lives have been lost because of this charade, as you call it?"

"Eight that we know of."

"I . . . I thought it was all over," said Carla, her voice faint with fear. She waits for Antonia to offer some reassuring words. In vain.

Then the memories come flooding back.

The diversion.

The man with the knife.

Fleeing through the wood.

The needle in her neck when she could run no more.

And afterward, her desperate battle with darkness. The friendly voice that turned out to be her tormentor.

"Do you . . . ? Do you know what she wants?"

"No. But I'm going to find out."

Before hanging up, she had given Carla very clear instructions about what she had to do if her worst nightmare came true.

Ten hours earlier, it did.

Antonia's message simply said:

SHE'S BACK

That was all Carla needed. She got up in the middle of a business dinner, muttered some excuse, and jumped in her limousine, at the same time issuing instructions to the nanny to drag her son out of bed.

The flight from La Coruña to Gloucester to fetch Grandma Scott took two hours. Leaving the airport another four. But here they were at last.

According to plan.

"No cell phones or other electronic devices. No searching on the internet for news about myself or Spain. No accessing my email accounts, no contact with anyone," Carla reels off.

"Give me your purse," says Antonia.

Carla rummages in her bag and hands it to her with a frown of displeasure. Antonia removes Carla's credit cards, her ID card, even her store cards, and puts them into an airsickness bag, which she drops into the trash can. Then she pulls a lighter and a can of lighter fluid from her shoulder bag. In a matter of seconds, Carla's life has been reduced to an evil-smelling puddle. Antonia keeps back one black metal rectangle that she slips into her pocket.

"Careful with that card, Antonia. It has no credit limit."

"I'm not a big spender. You're going to need some cash."

"I prepared that weeks ago," Carla says, pointing to an outsized Samsonite case.

Antonia doesn't bother to look inside; she knows what it contains. "Dollars?"

"Also yen, euros, and pounds."

Antonia nods approvingly.

"Where should we go?"

"If I knew that, it would put you in danger. Your decisions mustn't follow any logic. But I'll give you something to help."

Antonia places a pair of plastic dice in Carla's hand. Each side is marked with dots, and the opposite sides all add up to seven.

Carla puzzles over the dice for an instant until she understands what Antonia intends for her to do.

"Each decision, a throw of the dice. When you get where you're going, take another flight, then another. After that, travel overland for four hundred miles before catching a commercial flight. Then travel back the way you came, also overland. It'll be tough," she says finally, peering over Carla's shoulder.

Carla follows Antonia's gaze to where Grandma Scott is sitting. The old lady appears to have fallen asleep.

"Don't worry. She'll bury us all," she says.

"I don't see why that's supposed to reassure me. It's a very real possibility," says Antonia.

Only Carla's horrified expression tells her she has once again fallen foul of a metaphor. If Jon were there, he would say something to lighten things up, but he isn't. And yet Antonia doesn't apologize. Firstly, because she doesn't know how to smooth things over. She doesn't even know what that means. Secondly, because it's true, the danger is very real.

Now Sandra is back, no one is safe. Least of all Carla, one of the trophies that slipped through her fingers.

"We need to get going," says Carla, wringing her hands anxiously.

Antonia realizes she can't put it off any longer.

3

A BUNDLE

Antonia leans out of the aircraft door and waves. A tall, thin man with sunken cheeks steps out of a recently reconditioned Rolls-Royce Phantom. He is wearing a suit and tie—impeccably knotted, even after hours spent waiting in the back of the car. In his arms is a precious bundle. The other trophy that slipped through Sandra Fajardo's fingers.

"How long is this going to take?" the newcomer asks after boarding the plane.

For all that Sir Peter Scott is a diplomat, flexibility isn't one of his virtues, although he appreciates it in others. What's more, the UK ambassador to Spain is a wealthy middle-aged Englishman, and so for him, arrogance is pretty much compulsory.

The early morning chill and a night spent in a car haven't improved his manners either. He juts out his chin and looks quizzically at Carla.

"I'm sorry, I don't think we've been introduced," says Carla.

"You know perfectly well who I am, and I know perfectly well who you are. Now, if you don't mind, I'd like an answer."

Antonia shakes her head. Carla says nothing.

"It'll take as long as it takes," comes a hoarse voice from behind him.

The ambassador wheels round and meets the stern gaze of Grandma Scott. It's possible he even gulps discreetly.

"I'm sorry, Mother. I didn't notice you when I came onto the plane."

"Of course you didn't. You were too busy being rude. When was the last time you called me?"

"The responsibilities of my job . . ."

"Take precedence over your mother. You've made that perfectly clear. Now come here and let me take a look at my great-grandson."

Oblivious to the drama unfolding around him, Jorge Losada Scott has been snoring gently for the past few hours. Wrapped in a tartan blanket and wearing his Baby Yoda pajamas, he doesn't even stir when Grandma Scott uncovers his face. His cheeks are bright pink, his lips slightly open.

"He has your nose, Peter."

"Yes, he has," the ambassador says with a smile.

"Thank God he has inherited the rest from Antonia. Now lay him down on the couch before you get another hernia, my boy."

Sir Peter Scott does as he is told. The pony-skin couch squeaks as he puts Jorge next to Carla Ortiz's son. The two bundles are almost identical in size; the boys are only a few months apart in age.

"Everything's going to be fine," says Carla.

"You can't guarantee that."

"For heaven's sake, Peter," Grandma Scott scolds him. "The woman is telling you she'll do her level best. If you want guarantees, go buy a toaster."

The ambassador shifts his feet, looking first at his grandson, then at his mother. Finally he nods to the old lady and strides out of the aircraft without looking back.

After saying goodbye and imparting some last-minute instructions, Antonia joins her father beside the car. By the time she reaches him, the jet is already taxiing down the runway.

"You didn't tell me your grandmother would be there," says Sir Peter.

"She's a target too."

"I wish I'd known, Antonia."

"You should be going with them."

"Your grandmother and I cooped up together for who knows how long? What a quaint idea. We wouldn't need a psychopath to murder us."

"You'd be safer."

"Safer wandering about God knows where than in the embassy, protected by an SAS unit?" retorts Sir Peter. "I should never have agreed to allow Jorge . . ."

"Sandra Fajardo already took him once in broad daylight from somewhere we believed was safe. Do you really want to run that risk?"

Irritated, the ambassador smacks his lips. Only a few hours earlier, his daughter had called him to help her face the grim task of saying goodbye to her husband for the last time. He had gone to be beside her at once, as was his duty. He saw it as a step toward reconciliation with his daughter. Letting go of Marcos was Antonia's first step toward regaining some of her humanity. For a brief moment standing next to the heart rate monitor as the beeps became steadily slower, Sir Peter had caught a glimpse of the happy, smiling child who had rampaged along the corridors of the consulate in Barcelona when she wasn't much older than Jorge. The happy, smiling child she might have been if her life had turned out differently.

There is nothing of that child in the slip of a woman standing next to him by the runway. Her eyes are two obsidian shards.

And, even more worrying, the ambassador muses, *what she just said is true.*

"I suppose I don't want to run that risk," he admits.

"You should be going with them," Antonia repeats.

"They've already taken off."

"We can call them back."

"You're the one who should be on that plane."

"I can take care of myself."

One of her father's bodyguards emerges from the shadows where he has been waiting. Antonia remembers him well. He was the one who dragged her from Marcos's room. Six foot ten, eighty-seven kilos, and not much sympathy for Antonia. A brick wall in a suit, an elite SAS officer.

The ambassador motions toward the colossus as he opens the car door.

"Thank you, Noah."

And then toward her. So small, so alone.

"I have someone to protect me, Antonia. Day and night. You don't."

4
A RECEPTION DESK

Alone on the airstrip as she watches her father's car pull away, Antonia reflects
on his parting words.

"I have someone to protect me. You don't."

Antonia translates this as:

Raksakuḍuha.

In Telegu, a Dravidic language spoken by seventy-four million people,
the bodyguard without armor who throws himself naked into the path
of the arrow.

Antonia had someone like that. But now she doesn't. White has
snatched him from her without explanation. Only a message that said:

I HOPE YOU HAVEN'T FORGOTTEN ME. DO YOU WANT TO PLAY?
W.

A black Audi A8 with tinted windows approaches. The passenger
door opens, inviting her to climb in. For an instant and against all logic,
which in Antonia is an aberration, she expects to see Inspector Jon
Gutiérrez at the wheel. A few brief moments of magical thinking, of
crossing her fingers very tightly and wishing, wishing, wishing it were
true. The universe gives Antonia the standard response. Except that in
her case, it comes with the added shame of having permitted herself to
indulge in such foolishness.

With an annoyed frown, Antonia opens the back door and slumps
onto the seat.

"Am I your chauffeur now, Scott?"

"I need to close my eyes a minute."

"The front seat is fully reclining."

"Yes, but back here, I'm alone."

The man at the wheel turns around. Dark, receding hair, a clipped mustache, and doll's eyes that look painted on rather than real. A short camel-hair overcoat. Expensive.

"Careful where you put your feet. There's a Chekhov back there," he says.

Mentor has also spent the past few hours covering the entrance to the airfield.

"It's not a Chekhov, it's a Remington 870," says Antonia, opening one eye and nudging the shotgun with the tip of her sneaker.

"It's a loaded gun," Mentor says uneasily, twisting in his seat to reach down and remove it from the footwell. "And you know what Chekhov said about loaded guns."

"I've no idea."

"If you show one in the first act, you have to fire it in the third."

"We're already in the third act."

"That's what I meant, Scott."

After a brief tussle with his safety belt, Mentor manages to grab hold of the weapon. He places it on the seat beside him.

"How did it go with your father?"

"As well as can be expected."

"That bad, huh?"

Antonia doesn't reply; she simply stares out of the car window. A distant rumble of thunder merges with the purr of the Audi as Mentor starts the engine. Raindrops become tiny fleeting comets chasing each other across the glass.

On the M-40 beltway, near the Plenilunio shopping mall, the traffic all but grinds to a halt. Antonia notices a white van in the adjoining lane. The same make as the one that took Jon. A different model. On the middle seat, two small children are playing catch with what used to be a dinosaur and is now a shapeless green blob covered in teeth marks. The mother turns and says something to them in a serious voice, although to judge by the look on her face, she isn't really angry.

Just a normal family on an innocent trip to the mall, along with other normal families. Antonia wonders what they did to merit that life and what she did to deserve the one she has. She can find no answer, of course. Except . . .

Pothos.

In Greek, a desire for the unattainable.

Not for the first time, Antonia wishes she had a family where she could take refuge, someplace to hide. But all she has is the savage screech of monkeys in the deepest recesses of her mind. To this dubious lullaby, she falls asleep.

When she wakes, the sun is high in the sky.

She clambers out of the car, rubbing her eyes. Her bladder is full, her tongue furry. They are in the parking lot outside a soulless industrial building in the middle of a soulless neighborhood. Rejas, to the south of Madrid's Barajas airport, is an anonymous rectangle, the last blur travelers see before the cabdriver tells them that'll be thirty euros, *muchas gracias.* True, millions of people visit the mall every year: it's the biggest in the Spanish capital. And yet no one ventures much beyond the parking lot.

Nearby is a relatively settled neighborhood, but a few miles to the east, the landscape changes. The orderly buildings give way to chaos. Abandoned warehouses cheek by jowl with derelict single-family dwellings, allotments where horses are kept, unfinished office buildings. Vacant lots with FOR SALE signs hanging from the wire fences, posters where the sun has erased the reds and blacks and spewed out pale pinks and dirty grays. Posters with telephone numbers that are no longer legible and if they were would be invalid.

A place forsaken by God and his direct superiors, the urban planners.

A handful of streets named after months, where August and December are indistinguishable.

There is no obvious route leading in or out of this place, which is why Mentor chose it for the location of the headquarters of Spain's Red Queen project.

From the outside, it is just another industrial building with a fenced-off parking lot and a suitable name for an aggregates manufacturer with a corrugated iron roof and cement walls.

Mentor is sitting smoking a cigarette on the concrete steps outside the building. Going by the mound of butts between his feet, it seems he hasn't moved in hours.

"You're smoking too much," says Antonia as she walks from the car that has doubled as a bed to the steps that have doubled as Mentor's waiting room.

"My wife thinks the same. But it's never the right moment to give up."

"Why didn't you wake me?"

"You know why. You've just come back from a long mission. And you haven't slept all night."

"We can't waste any time."

"When you don't sleep, you get cranky and act like a spoiled brat."

Antonia would have yelled and stamped her feet, but has slept enough simply to heave a loud sigh and bound up the steps. Beyond the glass door—which doesn't even have a lock—is a chipped Formica reception desk, a linoleum floor, a waiting area with two armchairs that are losing their stuffing, and several magazines on aggregates. These include the current issue of the industry's official publication with a feature titled "Everything You Need to Know About Silica Sand!"

"ID, please," says the young man behind the counter.

Antonia looks wearily at Mentor, who shrugs.

"The kid is new."

"The kid is doing as he's told," the young man retorts.

"I can't waive the rules. Besides, you haven't been here for a while. He needs to know that you're you."

Antonia nods and walks over to what looks like the grubby, taped-up casing of a webcam that was already out of date before Zuckerberg founded Facebook.

Inside it, of course, is a new-generation retinal scan that causes the screen concealed behind the counter to beep.

"Good to go, sir."

"Thank you. Come along, Scott," Mentor says, motioning toward a metal door. She looks at it, but doesn't move.

"Are you through lecturing me?"

"I don't know what you're talking about."

With an irritated frown, Antonia follows Mentor to the door. It unlocks with a buzz, but when Mentor pulls on the handle, Antonia prevents him from opening it.

"You let me sleep in the car for four hours. And then that business at the entrance. You're obviously trying to tell me something."

"We've missed you, Scott, we really have."

"It would save time if you just tell me what it is."

Mentor purses his lips, trying to summon his patience.

"The message is you're not alone in this, and we need to exercise more caution than ever."

"Message received. Now, if you don't mind, we need to start searching for Jon Gutiérrez."

"What do you think we've been doing while you were asleep?" says Mentor, finally opening the door.

Stepping inside, Antonia holds her breath. She had almost forgotten how impressive the place was.

Almost, because Antonia doesn't forget anything.

5

HEADQUARTERS

The shabby reception area with its nineties furniture gives way to a bright, open space. Powerful 1,250-watt lamps hang from the six-meter-high ceilings. The lights illuminate a series of interconnected concrete structures fixed to the floor with steel girders, a miniature village. An area near the entrance serves to park the customized Audi A8s. Of the four spaces, only one is occupied. On the others, someone has taped DIN A3 photographs of successive car wrecks.

When she sees the photos, Antonia allows herself a smirk. Her gesture doesn't escape Mentor.

"It's no laughing matter. In less than twelve months, you've flushed three hundred thousand euros down the drain."

"Only a hundred thousand of that was me. The other two you can charge to Jon."

"I'm having second thoughts about rescuing him."

The first concrete module they pass is a cube-shaped structure with one enormous window. The interior is dark, but Antonia doesn't need light to know what is inside. She can recall every last centimeter of the training room. And they aren't happy memories.

She turns away and quickens her step. Stationed outside Dr. Aguado's laboratory is the MobLab, and beyond it is the meeting room block. It's a large, open space with a long table in the center and a dozen thirty-inch screens fixed to the wall.

Not a single minute or drop of paint has been spent on sprucing up the Red Queen project's headquarters. It contains nothing that isn't functional and doesn't look as if it came from the *Blade Runner* hardware store. Maybe that's why Antonia finds it so beautiful.

And yet she hasn't set foot in this meeting room for close to four years.

Mentor steps aside to let her by, but when he sees the look in her eyes and her clenched fists, he hesitates.

"When you're ready, Scott."

That doesn't seem likely to be soon.

Antonia's pulse is racing, her breathing shallow. Now that Jon needs her, she is panic-stricken. Or perhaps she is letting the panic take over because she has run out of excuses.

After all these years fleeing who she is, what she is capable of, reality has finally caught up with her. Antonia is a black belt in self-deception, but even she can acknowledge that she is torn between a desire to be back in this room and her fear of it.

Even though it's not a good idea.

Even though the man to whom she swore never to enter it again is lying in a funeral parlor with no one to watch over him.

Even though a sinking feeling in the pit of her stomach tells her she should turn and flee this concrete cage. The place that changed her forever into something infinitely superior, infinitely more hateful.

Then she looks through the open door and sees that all the screens have combined to form a single fragmented image. Inspector Jon Gutiérrez's face. His wavy hair with reddish tints, and his bushy salt-and-pepper beard. His dictionary-size square jaw. His eyes blinking in the camera flash.

Even in her agitated state, Antonia sees through Mentor's dirty trick. His ability to manipulate her infuriates her.

"Take your time," Mentor whispers in her ear.

Antonia opens her mouth to speak, but he leans in and cuts her off. His lips are practically touching her. His warm, acrid smoker's breath makes her skin crawl.

"If you're about to tell me you can't, don't bother. Whatever's going on in your head, get over it. I gave you a night to make your family safe and a morning to rest. But that's all. Because the man whose face you're looking at has saved your life more times than you can count."

Hearing this, Antonia is seized by a sudden conviction.

The heaviness in her chest lifts, her breathing slows. The monkeys in her head screech a little more softly. The beauty of convictions is that they offer us some relief.

Antonia lets out the breath she has been holding in and turns to Mentor.

"I *can*."

"That's my girl."

"You don't understand. I *can* count them. Seven times," says Antonia, entering the room.

6

A QUESTION

When she sees Antonia enter, Dr. Aguado stands up. Long eyelashes, faded makeup, a nose piercing, and a mischievous, languid look in her eyes. Currently with a glint of fear in them.

"I can't tell you how sorry I am . . ."

Aguado pauses, because in fact she has no idea where to begin. Antonia nods respectfully. She is glad to see her there.

"Let's get to work."

"Of course. Oh, I nearly forgot," the doctor says, holding out a glass of water and a small plastic beaker containing a red capsule.

Antonia shakes her head, trying not to steal a glance at the beaker.

Aguado looks inquiringly at Mentor, but he frowns at her, and she whisks the capsule away. Only then does Antonia sit down, in her favorite place, opposite the screens. As she pulls herself up to the table, the castors on the Aeron chair (the smallest size, so her legs don't dangle) make a familiar scraping noise on the concrete.

"What do we have?"

"All this," Mentor says, indicating the table in front of her.

The glass top of the table is covered with dozens of reports and photographs. Antonia leans forward to rest her elbows on the surface and scans each of the documents. Fifty seconds later, she looks up again.

"In other words, nothing."

"The license plate was false, but you already know that."

"The same number as the one on the vehicle in which the real Sandra Fajardo committed suicide," Aguado interjects.

"A sick joke, Scott?"

"She's leaving us her signature. As if it wasn't everywhere."

Antonia can't forget the way she stopped to wave at her before climbing aboard the van that took Jon. An elegant woman with a friendly face.

A friendly face only she has seen.

"No CCTV? A traffic camera? Anything?"

Mentor shakes his head. Antonia already knows the answer to her question. If there were, it would be on the table in front of her.

"We can make an e-fit from your description and within thirty minutes have it broadcast on every news channel. But . . ."

"But," Antonia says, banging the table out of frustration.

While Sandra is holding Jon Gutiérrez captive, they can't make that kind of move. There is very little they can do.

"I've sent the entire team to the Usera neighborhood to hunt for the van. Including the six rookies the National Police give us for backup, the IT team . . ."

"Even my own assistant," Aguado cuts in.

"They're driving around in unmarked cars asking people if they've seen the van."

"It's a pretty long shot."

"It's all we have, Scott. We have no photos of Fajardo, no clues, nothing. Just a dead traffic cop and another in the hospital under sedation."

The two police officers who tried to detain the Mercedes before it crossed the Manzanares River. They were told not to intervene. They were after a medal and received a hail of bullets instead.

"You've seen the ballistics report," says Aguado, pointing to the document in front of Antonia.

"Yes, 5.56 × 45 NATO cartridges," Antonia replies without looking. "Very common. Practically every soldier in the EU has been issued with them at some point in the past few decades. Not to mention thousands of police officers."

A chafing sound breaks the ensuing silence. Aguado and Mentor watch as Antonia's left hand starts to tremble again, brushing the papers.

Aguado reaches into her pocket for the box where she has put Antonia's red pill. Mentor raises his eyebrows slightly and very slowly shakes his head.

Antonia finally seems to notice the tremor and traps her wrist with her right hand. Her lips murmur a lie.

"I'm fine."

In response to a question no one asked.

Then, in a louder voice:

"We're wasting time. None of this will help us find Jon," she says, pushing the useless documents toward the center of the table, away from her twitching fingers.

"Do you have a better idea?" says Mentor.

"We need to understand what's going on. You need to tell me why you went to Brussels."

WHAT HAPPENED
IN BRUSSELS

Mentor gives in to Antonia's request and gestures to Aguado, who sends a signal to the screens from her laptop.

"This happened nine days ago. While you and Inspector Gutiérrez were on your way to Málaga, to search for Lola Moreno."

The images show a luxury hotel room. A naked man on a super king-size bed. The sheets are crumpled. The body is covered in stab wounds. There are two pairs of feet in the photograph. Those sticking out over the edge of the bed that belong to the stab victim and those dangling a few inches above it. The next photo shows the owner of the second pair. He is hanging from the ceiling fan, eyes bulging from their sockets, face contorted, tongue poking out from between his teeth.

"It's England," says Antonia.

"How can you tell? I doubt his own mother would recognize him."

"It wasn't him I recognized. It was the make of ceiling fan," she says, pointing to the tiny symbol at the bottom of the fan. "They only sell that model in the UK."

"Callum Davis, our Red Queen in England," Mentor confirms, pointing to the hanged man. "And his shield bearer, Rhys Byrne."

"Lovers?"

"Scott, you know that's strictly forbidden."

"That doesn't . . ."

"Yes, it does answer your question, in fact. And yes, they were. Not openly, but there aren't many secrets within our teams," Mentor says, looking pointedly at her.

Antonia is trying hard and failing to avert her eyes from the bulge the pillbox is making in Dr. Aguado's lab coat pocket.

"Callum and Rhys were on a rather dangerous mission. One involving a Glasgow-based diamond-smuggling ring, hardened criminals with links to the Mafia. We assumed they were the ones who did this."

"Forensics examined the scene," Aguado cuts in, "and discovered the truth was much worse."

Antonia gets to her feet and walks over to the image of her English colleague, eyes narrowed. She makes a repetitive upward motion with her arm, does some mental arithmetic, then looks again.

"Callum killed his shield bearer and then hanged himself."

"How on . . . ?"

"The blood-spatter pattern on his shirt. An almost perfect semicircle surrounded by several smaller ones. That could only happen if Callum was wielding the knife."

Aguado coughs awkwardly and looks at Mentor.

"You're right," says Mentor. "It took us slightly longer to get there, Scott. The knife wasn't at the crime scene. It turned up a few hours later on the hotel grounds. But by that time, all hell had broken loose."

Fresh images appear on the screens. They show an Audi A8 parked up on a sidewalk in a residential area. This time, Antonia doesn't need to guess. The words on the red-and-white tape, POLITIE, NIET BETREDEN, save her the trouble.

One of the screens begins to show a video taken on a cell phone. They see a dead woman in the Audi's passenger seat. She is dressed in a matching gray jacket and pencil skirt. The entrance wound is small, the size of a coin. By contrast, the damage the bullet has inflicted on exiting is enormous. The window is an abstract painting. A composition in red with a spider crack at the center, where the woman's skull has scratched the glass without shattering it.

"Lotte Janssen, our Dutch Red Queen. The car was found outside her home in Rotterdam. They arrested her shield bearer less than two blocks away. He was wandering the streets in a catatonic state, still clutching the gun."

"That's when you realized something was wrong."

"A queen kills his shield bearer. A shield bearer kills his queen. All within the space of a few hours. Yes, even we mortals managed to put two and two together, Scott."

"Don't do that."

"Do what?"

"Play Jon's role. It doesn't suit you."

Mentor plucks a cigarette from his pocket and lights it.

"I miss him, too, Scott. But we have to be prepared for the worst."

Antonia mulls this over for a few seconds. And then responds the only way she can.

"No."

"The possibilities . . . ," Aguado starts to say.

"What did you do when you found out about Holland?"

"We assembled all the team leaders for a meeting in Brussels. We were aware something was going on, but we had no intel. There were raised voices, and things got very tense. We were experiencing our very own 9/11. Nobody knew what to do. We had the Dutch shield bearer in custody, but he hadn't uttered a single word. And then . . ."

Mentor falls silent and lowers his head. Aguado averts her gaze.

"Then there was another attack," whispers Antonia.

A photo appears on the screen. Amid the smoke and rubble, Antonia makes out an ornate piece of masonry, stone carvings of saints, a door embossed with bronze. Art isn't her forte, still less Gothic art, and she doesn't recognize it right away. But eventually, she is able to connect what she is seeing to an old memory from school. A dull Friday-afternoon lesson in the drowsy late-spring heat in Barcelona. The classroom shutters are drawn, and the projector is showing an image of a twelfth-century German cathedral.

"Cologne."

"There was an explosion," says Mentor. "Two dead. Six seriously injured."

"The dead were . . ."

"I know who they were, Doctor."

Antonia looks as if she might burst into tears. Or possibly start a fistfight with someone. It's impossible to say which.

"They're hunting us down, one by one," she says, her voice choking with rage. "Everyone associated with the Red Queen project. Five dead in one day. England, Holland, Germany. What about the others?"

"The Dutch shield bearer is still being held by the police. The French one, Isabelle Bourdeau, is missing, together with her queen. Paola Dicanti and her queen were heading to a safe house in Florence, but we lost contact with them last night, we believe of their own accord."

Mentor takes a lengthy pause. He massages his forehead with his fingertips, as if trying to summon information or to chase away his despair. It doesn't seem to do much good.

"That's all I know," he concludes.

"No, it's not."

Puzzled, Mentor straightens up.

"I've told you everything I . . ."

Antonia lifts a finger to hush him.

"When you called me last night, you told me you knew what had happened in England and Holland. You said my phantom was very real."

Mentor holds her gaze without blinking.

"From the evidence you've shown me so far, you can't possibly have reached that conclusion," Antonia continues.

"I'm not sure I like your tone, Scott."

"Four years. Four years since that monster broke into my home. Four years since I first spoke to you about him. And all I got from you were condescending smiles when you weren't suggesting I needed my head examined."

"After what happened to Marcos . . ."

"'Bring me evidence. One piece of evidence and I'll believe in this killer of yours.' How many times have I heard you say that?"

"All you had were rumors, Scott, speculation."

"And what do you have now?"

"A modus operandi . . ."

"I see no modus operandi in these images. Only violence and random killings."

It's not true that in a staring contest the loser is the first to blink. The loser is the person facing defeat who looks away so their adversary can't see it in their eyes.

"Doctor, would you mind leaving us for a few minutes?" says Mentor.

Antonia nods discreetly at Aguado as she passes by her chair. She waits until the pathologist has closed the door behind her.

"And now . . . are you going to tell me what really happened in Brussels?"

WHAT REALLY HAPPENED
IN BRUSSELS

Mentor loosens his tie, reaches for his laptop, slowly lights another cigarette. He is playing for time. After exhaling the smoke from his first drag, he has run out of excuses for remaining silent.

"The Dutch shield bearer . . . talked."

"You said he was catatonic."

"For a few hours. Eventually, he came out of shock. But he still didn't want to talk."

Mentor presses a key on his laptop, and another image replaces those of the atrocity in Germany. A man with a dark complexion and chiseled features. Fiftysomething, but still physically strong.

"Michael Seedorf. Born in Suriname. Ex–military police, in the reserves. We recruited him when he was going through a particularly difficult period in his life."

"The usual procedure."

"He had recently lost his daughter. A geneticist with an exceptional academic record and a brilliant career ahead of her. She was run over by a car."

"And that's when you stepped in."

"I wasn't involved. However, my Dutch colleague did an excellent job. He helped shape a perfect relationship between Seedorf and his queen. He loved her like a daughter. They'd been working together since the beginning and had solved some very difficult cases."

"I heard she was good."

"Not as good as you, but yes, she was good."

Antonia chews her lip, waiting for Mentor to go on. He presses another button, and the screens turn black.

"You must understand we had to get him to talk, Scott."

Antonia takes a deep breath and closes her eyes.

"What did you do?"

"We held lengthy discussions with the heads of all the groups. Our decision had to be unanimous."

"What did you do?"

"Our decision . . ."

Antonia asks the question a third time.

Mentor gets to his feet, rubs his hands together, leans back against the concrete wall.

"Extreme interrogation," he says finally.

Antonia opens her eyes.

In them, Mentor sees exactly what he had feared. Shielding himself behind a euphemism doesn't work with a philologist who values precision in language above all else.

"You tortured one of our own," Antonia says incredulously.

"We did what we had to, Scott. We're under attack."

"We did what we had to," Antonia repeats with a wry, humorless laugh. She falls into one of her silences.

"Shortly before we returned from Málaga, Jon said something to me that made me think. About our job. About what we do. The detours we took to do what we had to. And do you know what I told him?"

Mentor doesn't reply.

"I told him, *Walking in a straight line never gets you very far.* Do you know who said that?"

Of course he does. Only he won't admit it.

"You did, Mentor. That was your expression. It's what we say to justify our actions when we aren't particularly proud of them. Our lies, our deceptions, our shortcuts."

"Wouldn't Jon . . . ?"

Antonia raises her finger.

"Don't. Don't even think about citing the name of the most honest and decent person I've ever met to justify what you did."

"We needed to find out what had happened, Antonia. This man killed his colleague. That doesn't come out of nowhere."

"All right. Tell me everything."

"I can't tell you any more, Scott."

"Can't or won't?"

Mentor folds his arms. He isn't about to use up what dignity he has left in one sitting. He might need some for later.

"I can't and I won't."

But Antonia is still hungry.

"Then let me tell you what happened, if I can. You just nod if I'm right. Okay?"

Mentor hesitates but realizes he has dug himself into a hole, and the only way out is to keep digging.

So he nods.

"Following the attack in Cologne, you and the other team leaders agreed there was an external threat that justified the use of torture on a member of the Red Queen project who was refusing to collaborate."

A nod.

"None of you would dare to do something like that yourself," Antonia continues slowly, thinking aloud to mask the interrogation. "Maybe *you* ordered someone to do it."

No nod.

"Or someone ordered *you* to do it."

Mentor's head remains motionless. Thank heaven for small favors.

"Okay, it just happened. It doesn't really matter," Antonia lies rather badly. "Someone carried it out. Nothing too brutal, I imagine. After all, we aren't savages. Nothing too slow, either, we're in a hurry. No sensory or sleep deprivation . . . The Flying Dutchman? Hanging upside down? Waterboarding?"

Antonia keeps listing names until one triggers a minute response in Mentor's pupils.

"Waterboarding. A classic, pretty much infallible. Tell me, did you watch?"

No nod.

"Of course you didn't. That's not your style. Your style is to delegate and await results. In that case, let me refresh your memory about how it works. The subject is immersed in a tub of water up to his chin. A towel is placed over his head. And water is poured over the towel."

Mentor lights another cigarette, affecting indifference, or possibly detachment. Antonia hasn't forgotten he was the one who taught her the basic interrogation techniques.

But she has learned a few more herself.

"The water soaks through the towel, filling the subject's nose and throat. The brain believes it is drowning, and then come the uncontrollable seizures and vomiting. The subject suffers appallingly, because he is on the brink of death, but without ever crossing the threshold. He dies for a whole minute. Sixty seconds."

Mentor is still holding his cigarette, but his hand isn't moving to his mouth. The paper and tobacco burn down into a ragged cylinder of ash that threatens to drop on the glass tabletop.

"The subject breaks down before the sixty seconds are up. Nobody holds out for longer. When they take away the towel, he spills the beans, regardless of the consequences."

"There's no cheating water," Mentor says blankly. Unaware his cigarette is about to burn his fingers.

"No, there isn't, and so Seedorf talked. Let's see if I can guess what he told you: A man contacted him. Probably by email, and then a phone call. I imagine he accompanied the first message with a show of force. A photograph or a severed finger."

"A blood-soaked handkerchief," Mentor concedes, finally realizing his cigarette has burned down. He stubs it out without looking.

"A member of Seedorf's family? His wife?"

"His mother."

"And some clear instructions. He must kill his Red Queen, the woman he vowed to protect, to save his mother, the woman who gave birth to him."

A nod.

"But he had to keep his mouth shut, which meant taking his own life. That way he'd save her."

A nod.

"And you took even that small consolation away from him. Is he still alive?"

A nod.

"What about his mother?"

Mentor's head doesn't move.

Antonia's head is spinning.

She takes time to digest everything. Not too long. Otherwise, her rage and indignation will get the better of her. And for her right now, emotion is a luxury item behind a plate glass shop window.

"My guess is White only became a suspect after you obtained that information."

A nod.

"Because who in their right mind would suspect a phantom? Someone that weird Spanish chick dreamed up? The deranged lunatic who had lost her grip on reality. Didn't you and your colleagues have a nickname for me?"

No nod. Nothing. Confirming Antonia's suspicions.

"Tell me something . . . Did you ever mention White to the other team heads? If only to make fun of me?"

Mentor, who has managed to recover a modicum of dignity, tells the truth for a change.

"No."

Antonia shakes her head. She doesn't feel hurt. Or even disappointed.

What she feels is *åselichibå*. In Oromo, a language spoken by forty million people in the Horn of Africa, the ocean of tedium created by other people's stupidity.

A vast, agonizing weariness. A sea of boredom in which to drown, let yourself go. When it's nobler in the mind not to fight but to lower your arms.

Maybe in different circumstances, Antonia would simply have left. Stood up and walked out without looking back.

But she can't do that to Jon.

Or Marcos. Or Carla.

Or herself.

And so she takes a deep breath, gets up from the table, and walks over to Mentor.

"You tortured a man into telling you something you already knew. I told you about White years ago. If you'd backed me up then, if you'd helped me find him, we wouldn't be where we are now."

Antonia snatches the laptop from him and turns the screens back on.

She starts pressing keys at top speed, retrieving images from the database, amassing them on the screens, gradually ensnaring Mentor.

The photographs from the crime scene at La Finca. The young boy who bled to death, Sandra Fajardo's first murder.

"Innocents wouldn't have died."

The disastrous police intervention in Nicolás Fajardo's apartment when Sandra detonated two bombs, one after the other.

"Police officers wouldn't have died."

The recent deaths in Holland, England, and Germany.

"Our colleagues wouldn't have died."

Fingers twitching, Antonia closes down the laptop. Mentor's sins have flooded the screens, sins of omission, for which she feels equally responsible.

"That's enough, Scott," Mentor says, his voice broken.

"No. I need one more thing from you, the most important thing. I need you to tell me how, when I succeed in rescuing Jon, I'm going to be able to ask him to come back. Knowing one day you might be willing to torture him."

Mentor opens his mouth to reply, but never gets to do so. Because just then, Antonia's phone gives two pings and starts to vibrate.

She takes it out of her bag.

Reads the message.

Starts to run.

7

A GARAGE DOOR

She disregards Mentor's yells behind her. Ignores Aguado's look of surprise as she shoots past. She hasn't time for any of that.

The Audi A8 is unlocked, the key in the ignition. She doesn't fasten the safety belt or adjust the seat, positioned for someone a head taller than her. She hasn't time for that either.

The message doesn't allow her much leeway. It contains a location and four words.

EIGHT MINUTES.
YOU ALONE.

So Antonia starts the engine and drives toward the garage door. It remains firmly shut.

Antonia digs around in the car, but the remote is nowhere to be found. And the seconds are ticking by.

Meanwhile, Antonia's phone has paired automatically with the Audi's hands-free, and Mentor's voice booms through the speakers.

"I hope you have a good explanation."

"Of course."

It's clear from the ensuing silence she isn't going to provide him with it.

"He called you, didn't he? Give me the location, I can mount an operation."

Antonia considers the options. The rendezvous destination is huge, the time frame tight. It's not a good idea.

"It's not a good idea," she says, having reached that conclusion. "Open the door."

"Scott . . ."

"White will have thought of everything. And this is Jon's life we're risking. Just for once, let me do things my way."

"The exception will be when I don't," retorts Mentor.

"Without you protesting," Antonia adds.

But it's too late, because Mentor has already ended the call. And the sound merges with the loud buzz of the metal door opening.

Antonia steps on the gas, and the car's undercarriage gives off sparks as it scrapes the exit ramp.

8

AN EXCEPTION

Mentor analyzes the situation for a few seconds, eyes closed, head resting on his fist, which is clenched against the wall, his body pressing down on it.

There's too much at stake for me to risk letting Antonia Scott do things her way, he concludes.

The decision made, his body seems to recover its equilibrium.

"Send a message to the others. Tell them to return here immediately. And don't let Scott out of your sight," he orders Dr. Aguado, who is already back in the meeting room, sitting at the laptop. A map on the screen shows the Audi A8 as a moving red dot.

9

A RENDEZVOUS

The moving red dot is doing forty miles an hour, turning corners of streets named after calendar months. It races down February, March, and December, takes a one-way street the wrong way and honks repeatedly at anyone foolish enough to speed toward it. For Antonia Scott, traffic regulations are more like suggestions, well-meaning reminders to be heeded only when you have nothing better to do, just like when Facebook reminds you it's your cousin's birthday.

She arrives at Avenida Invierno, where the speed limit is thirty, driving at a good fifty miles an hour. There are several parked buses here, but things only get complicated when she reaches Calle de Samaniego, a completely gridlocked two-way street.

Antonia bumps the two right-hand tires up onto the sidewalk. She drives along for about four hundred yards, amid angry honks (and a few envious looks) from parents waiting to enter the parking lot at the mall, cars full of kids with bursting bladders.

Antonia can't wait in line, and she doesn't want to abandon the car in the middle of the street, because she might need it afterward. So she turns sharply and enters the Aldi parking lot opposite. Antonia ignores the barrier designed to make people stop and take a ticket (her thirty-sixth traffic violation in the last seven minutes), simply stepping on the gas pedal. The metal barrier leaves a magnificent three-pronged scratch on the Audi's hood before snapping in half on the windshield.

By some miracle, no idiot has wrongfully occupied the disabled space, so Antonia parks there herself.

Eleven seconds later, when she enters the mall, she is nearly sixty seconds late. The escalators are packed with the worst kind of people. The sort who forget the escalators are there to help and not an excuse to stop and slump over the handrail until their inert bodies emerge at the other end. Antonia uses her elbows and knees to push her way through the mound of flesh.

The Café Moran is in a slightly more secluded spot, at the far end of a long walkway. Many of the franchises on the second floor have been forced to close during the recent crisis. The abandoned hulks of burger joints and pizzerias with foreign names sit immobile, like cloudy ice in a glass that once contained refreshment. Customers now eat at the cheaper joints on the first floor, next to the clothes shops and the ghastly ball pits.

Even so, the Café Moran is full. Six tables occupied by the usual kind of people who haunt such places. Antonia scopes them rapidly as she attempts to catch her breath before entering.

Three couples acting like they're listening to one another while checking their Instagram accounts, two hipsters pretending to write novels on their MacBooks, and a psychopathic killer. The last is the easiest to identify: he is the only one holding a book, not an electronic device.

When he raises his head and their eyes meet, Antonia's stomach clenches. Someone like her has seen a lot of death, a lot of corpses. At crime scenes or on the steel slab of the autopsy room. Yet there is more life in all those extinguished eyes than in the two icy-blue glinting stones lying in wait for her at the far end of the café.

This is obviously a trap. And yet she has no choice. She reasons that being in a public place gives her some protection as she steps toward the most dangerous man she has ever encountered.

He stands up when she approaches but instead of extending his hand motions gracefully to the empty chair opposite him.

"Please take a seat, Señora Scott," he says in English. "I hope you didn't have too much trouble finding the place."

Antonia sits down slowly. They both take a moment to study each other in silence.

Mr. White is about four years older than her. He has fair wavy hair and pale, smooth skin. His facial features appear sculpted in marble; you could crack walnuts on his jaw. He is sporting a navy blue three-piece suit, a white shirt, no tie, and he wears it as casually as he might a pair of pajamas. The cut of the fabric on the shoulders suggests it is tailor-made and probably cost him the price of a small car.

"I had the coordinates. The time frame made it more challenging."

"Ah yes. The inevitable race against the clock. I'm afraid that was a necessary measure. Even as we speak, your colleagues are preparing an operation to capture me."

"I gave them instructions not to," Antonia says, raising an eyebrow.

"Instructions your boss, your Mentor, has completely ignored. I estimate we have . . ."

He flexes his elbow to check his wrist. Seeing the crease of the fabric and hearing the soft rustle of his shirt, Antonia revises her opinion about the price tag on his clothes. You could buy an off-roader more cheaply. They are in stark contrast to the ugliness of his watch, which has a clear plastic strap.

". . . seventeen minutes before they are able to organize themselves sufficiently well to surround such a large area."

His English public school accent and diction are impeccable. Antonia can scarcely believe this is the same man who shot her, put Marcos in a coma, and kidnapped Jon. The man she has been pursuing all these years and who is suddenly there in front of her.

She has rehearsed in her mind what she would say to him and what she would do to him when this moment arrived. She has gone over it again and again, through long, dark nights. Dozens of lines of dialogue, a hundred different versions.

And now the moment has arrived?

Her mind is a blank.

She is confused, but also furious. She has an overwhelming urge to touch the scar on her left shoulder. A lopsided star with five jagged points where White's bullet exited her body.

Not wanting to show weakness, she resists the temptation.

Instead, she balls her fists under the table.

"I took the liberty of ordering for you," White says when the waiter arrives with their hot drinks. He pushes his book to one side to make room for his green tea. It's a nineteenth-century leather-bound volume, the gold embossed title of which is *The Dynamics of an Asteroid*. The author's name is illegible.

A cup of coffee appears in front of Antonia.

She eyes it suspiciously, then rejects as nonexistent the threat it might contain poison. She takes a sip, trying to order her thoughts, calm the monkeys, prevent her rage from boiling over, decide on a strategy.

"A latte with extra milk, the way you like it," says White.

"You seem to know a great deal about me."

"We've been silently studying one another from afar for many years, Señora Scott."

"With mixed results."

"You're too modest, señora. The mere fact you deduced my existence is already a remarkable achievement."

So far, the only strategy Antonia Scott can think of consists of:

a. smashing the saucer under her cup against the edge of the table,
b. picking up one of the shards, and
c. *slitting the throat of this supercilious, arrogant jerk.*

According to her calculations, the likelihood of Jon surviving such a strategy is 0 percent. So she restrains herself.

"It doesn't seem much of an achievement. I don't even know your name."

"Mr. White will do," he says, fanning the air with his hand.

"A lover of anonymity."

"A lover of freedom."

"I came through that door three hundred and eleven seconds ago. If you value your freedom, I suggest you get on with it."

He raises an eyebrow at such precision. After verifying it against his watch, he flashes a wry smile, showing dazzlingly perfect white teeth. It isn't a genuine smile. There is no spark or emotion in it, only muscles changing position on his face.

"What they say about you is true. You really are extraordinary."

Somehow praise from this monster terrifies Antonia more than anything else he has said. She shivers, glancing about her instinctively.

"Yes, you're right. It's too crowded, isn't it?"

He raises his teaspoon, waves it in the air like an orchestra conductor, and taps it four times against his cup.

Clink.

Clink.

Clink.

Clink.

Even before the last of the sounds has died out, all the people in the café, including the waiter, have risen to their feet and are heading toward the door, leaving behind every last one of their belongings. The action is so swift, so sudden, so unnerving and unreal that once they have left, it's as if they had never been there.

Contemplating the deserted café, Antonia feels fear, but something else as well.

A hint of admiration, for want of a better word.

It arises from the most rational part of her brain, the biggest, most dominant part. The part that appreciates the enormous amount of energy and skill involved in the sleight of hand White has just performed. And, mixed with that hint of admiration, a glimmer of gratitude.

It's better for White to think she is afraid of him. To allow the atavistic part of her brain, the smallest, most hidden part, to come to the fore, show in her eyes, color her voice with the sickly yellow of fear.

She finds this quite easy.

"Okay, White. You've made it very clear: you're in control."

White's smile broadens just a shade. It's a shade uglier, a shade crueler, yet infinitely more genuine than his earlier smile.

"At last, you've worked it out."

Antonia tries to collect herself, to buy time.

"I won't kill for you."

"Did I ask you to?"

"Then what *do* you want?"

"It's very simple. I want you to do what you do best. Solve three crimes and bring the perpetrators to justice."

10

AN ASSIGNMENT

Antonia freezes. This is the last thing she expected to hear from White.

"Why do you want me to solve crimes?"

"Isn't that what you do?"

"Exactly. And it's the opposite of what you do."

White appears to think this over. He examines the immaculately manicured nails on the end of his long, tapering fingers.

Antonia can't help remembering Marcos's hands and how she held them in hers one last time only a few hours earlier. His gnarled fingers, his square palms. A man's hands. The hands of a sculptor that lost their strength and vitality at the hands of this man.

If any hands are more unlike those of Marcos, it's these, Antonia thinks with revulsion.

"I'm afraid you have a very mistaken view of me, Señora Scott."

"You're a hired assassin who blackmails other people into doing your dirty work."

White shakes his head, clicking his tongue as if the description offended him.

"You're confusing the means with the end."

"Then enlighten me."

"You'll do that yourself, soon enough. Meanwhile, I'm afraid we're out of time," he says, checking his watch once more. "Tonight, you'll receive a message with instructions about your first assignment."

"I suppose now you're going to tell me that if I do everything you ask, you'll return my colleague in one piece."

"It sounds as if you don't trust me."

"Would you?"

White fixes Antonia with his gaze. His pupils, as tiny as two pinpoints, have a hypnotic effect. Antonia experiences firsthand what a rat must feel when confronted by a cobra.

She doesn't sense the danger from behind until it's too late.

Until she feels the muzzle of the gun between her shoulder blades and a warm, dry breath on her neck. She hears a long, drawn-out inhalation.

"You smell different when you're asleep," Sandra whispers in her ear.

Antonia feels a weight in her gut, a frozen ball of revulsion and hatred. Her feelings for White pale in comparison to the primeval feelings she has toward the woman who kidnapped her son. She sits perfectly still and upright while Sandra slips gracefully around the table and sits down beside White.

From close up beneath the café's spotlights, Sandra's face doesn't look so friendly.

She wears her dark hair, peppered with gray, scraped back as tight as a murderer's shackles.

She is still pointing the gun at Antonia.

"It's time," Sandra tells White.

He gives her an exasperated look and turns to Antonia.

"My dear lady, you'll soon be receiving the message I mentioned concerning your assignment. Obviously, I have to warn you not to try to follow us or to inform anyone as to our whereabouts. You may leave here in ten minutes. Not a moment before."

White makes to walk off, and then, as if as an afterthought, he adds:

"One last thing. To ensure you meet the challenge of my assignment wholeheartedly, I'd like to make you a farewell gift."

Antonia turns around in the direction White's finger is pointing.

She can't believe what she sees.

Slumped in a wheelchair is a figure she immediately recognizes. There is no mistaking the owner of that voluminous torso, despite the cloth bag over his head. Not that he's fat.

She is so taken aback, she barely hears White's parting shot as he disappears into the rear of the café.

"For what would Antonia Scott be without Jon Gutiérrez?"

Part II

JON

"At least I died doing something I loved."
I'd prefer to die doing something I hate.

Jerry Seinfeld

1

A CHAIR

Jon Gutiérrez doesn't like kidnappings.

It's not a question of aesthetics. As a rule, kidnappings are less bloody and violent than murders, at least in their initial phase. A kidnapping is above all an absence.

Of course, there's the violence inflicted on the victim, held against his or her will in a dark, confined space. Not to mention the pain experienced by the people waiting for news of the absent one. Every moment of waiting, every second that drags by oppresses them more and more, until their fear and anguish is transformed into a single incandescent point. A black hole of anguish and despair that sucks everything in.

None of this is what bothers Jon about kidnappings. He is used to dealing with absences (his father abandoned them when he was a child), confined spaces (he's gay), and family tragedies (he's a police inspector).

What pisses Jon off about kidnappings is when he's the one being kidnapped.

You can't walk down the street these days without someone bundling you into a van with a bag over your head, thinks Jon. *That sort of thing doesn't happen in Bilbao anymore.*

His thoughts about this are rather befuddled, as he's still coming around. His body is taking a while to eliminate the anesthetic. He can hear voices millions of light-years away (the enveloping darkness is like a tunnel). He tries to move, but nothing responds. He's afraid, yet his fear feels alien, as if on loan. A borrowed fear, identical to the one he is experiencing right now inside his own body. His throat feels rough, just as it does after an all-nighter, and his bladder is bursting.

Suddenly, the cloth covering his face is whisked away. The hood is replaced by a blurred but familiar outline.

"Did you miss me?"

"You know perfectly well you're the only one," Jon replies, coughing as he struggles to fill his lungs with air.

Despite being high on propofol and fentanyl, Inspector Gutiérrez acknowledges a sober, inescapable fact. Never in his life has he been so overjoyed to hear someone's voice as when he hears Antonia Scott's now.

She is observing Jon with apprehension. The confusion, contracted pupils, and ataxia suggest anesthetic poisoning, but also concussion, as well as a couple of other potentially lethal things.

"How many fingers?" she says, holding up her hand.

"Fifteen or twenty."

Antonia lowers three fingers and deduces that neuronal failure cannot account for such a wide margin of error. So she chalks it up to humor, a sure sign her colleague is well enough for her to continue her examination.

She reaches into her pocket for her cell phone.

"I need to warn Mentor. It's not too late for us to catch that . . ."

Jon leans forward to grab her forearm, but fails. At the second attempt, he manages to restrain her with a hand the size, shape, and weight of a paella pan filled with pebbles.

"Don't . . . don't call."

Antonia looks at him, bewildered.

"Are you out of your mind?"

Inspector Gutiérrez shakes his head.

"You'd better give me a good reason."

With great effort, Jon opens his mouth. His neck feels as if it's made of plasticine, too weak to prop up his head, which is heavy at the best of times.

"Bomb," he manages to say.

She blinks five times, at warp speed.

"Yes, that's a good reason, all right," she says.

But Jon can't hear her. He has passed out.

* * *

Antonia crouches beside the wheelchair. It's a standard fold-up model you can buy for under a hundred euros at any pharmacy or orthopedic store. Or steal from a hospital corridor for considerably less.

There's nothing under the seat or attached to the back.

The aluminum tubing doesn't look big enough to conceal anything.

So she turns her attention to Inspector Gutiérrez himself. His favorite black wool Tom Ford jacket (peaked lapels, piping on the breast, flap pockets) is creased and dirty. His once-white Egyptian cotton shirt is now a washed-out gray. Antonia frisks his torso, but all she can feel through the fabric are his muscles, bulging beneath a springy outer layer.

It's like touching steel coated in neoprene, Antonia thinks, making a rather pointless comparison.

She bends over him to continue her examination. Wrapping her arms around him, she uses her legs as a brace to shift his deadweight and enable her to reach his back and neck. Her fingertips encounter a warm, wet stickiness. And beneath it, something that shouldn't be there.

It's like touching an oil-soaked rag, thinks Antonia, this time making a more illuminating comparison. Her arm is trapped, but she's in no doubt as to what she'll find when she manages to pull it free.

An instant later, after one final tug, she has the confirmation. Her fingers are stained dark red.

With a look of horror, Antonia realizes what those animals have done to her colleague.

Even so, she is still debating with herself. She glances at her cell phone. If she alerts Mentor now, he'll have time enough to locate the nearest exit, their escape route.

Then she looks again at her bloodstained fingers.

Hesitantly, she returns her phone to her pocket, as if by so doing she is behaving beyond the bounds of what's reasonable.

And in a sense, she is.

2

AN INSPECTION

Back at Red Queen headquarters, Inspector Gutiérrez is now in the medical unit, face down on a gurney. Butt naked. Antonia and Mentor have respectfully vacated the room to give him some privacy. They are now watching everything from behind the enormous window in the concrete wall. The fact that the side of the window facing the room is a mirror doesn't help matters. It simply shows Jon exactly what they can see from the other side.

"You know I know you're there, right? And that I'm naked," Jon's voice comes through the intercom.

Embarrassed, Antonia has no idea how to respond. She has never been very skilled in social situations that require discretion, like giving up your seat on a bus, or standing in line for the restroom, or speaking to your naked colleague while he's being examined because he has a bomb implanted under his skin.

Her early years were an arid wasteland. When she met Marcos, he became her support, her strength, a sort of translator of humans to Antonia. Even when he was in a coma, she would speak to him (softly, in hushed tones, when the nurses weren't around), tell him about her communication problems. Simply by articulating them, she was taking a first step toward finding a solution.

Jon had gradually taken over that role, but he wasn't much use to her now. So Antonia turns to Mentor.

"What do people say in situations like this?"

With a straight face, Mentor gives her precise instructions.

"But it's not true," says Antonia.

Why ask what I'd do if you're just going to continue being you, says Mentor's shrug, so Antonia presses the intercom button and repeats what he told her.

"You have a lovely butt."

Jon gives a guffaw of surprise.

Short, sharp.

More like a howl of pain.

Which is what the last part of his breath becomes, when his diaphragm, serratus, anterior, and intercostal muscles pull the skin on his back, which is damn painful where they have cut into him.

Inspector Gutiérrez's skin has two incisions. One at the base of his neck, the other lower down, four inches above his belt line.

Four neat incisions in the shape of two crosses. The one on his neck is roughly three inches long, the other slightly more. The incisions have been stitched with thick black thread that has pulled open in several places. The knots protrude from the red lines of the wounds like larvae poking out of the earth for air.

Above them, a metal box attached to a robotic arm buzzes as it moves over Inspector Gutiérrez's back. He shifts uncomfortably.

"If you don't keep still, it'll only take longer."

Dr. Aguado is carrying out an X-ray examination using a portable carbon nanotube machine.

"It costs more than a hundred thousand euros," Mentor had told Aguado when she put in a request for one.

"What do we do if Scott breaks a bone, put her name on the hospital waiting list for an X-ray?"

Mentor didn't reply. Like a good civil servant, he approved the purchase. As a petty act of revenge, he chose the pediatric model, identical in every respect to the standard one, except for the vinyl wrap with bright, furry animals on it. Aguado, who is pathologically austere, cringed when she saw it but said nothing.

So far, nobody has broken any bones, but at last today, the expense seems justified.

After she is finished examining him, Aguado sprays chlorhexidine on the inspector's back, then uses an ultrafine needle to inject him with a liquid antibiotic.

"It's not good news," she says, handing him a gown to cover himself with.

She gestures toward the mirror. A few seconds later, Mentor and Antonia come in.

Jon waits, seated on the gurney.

"How is he, Doctor?" says Mentor.

"Physically, he's fine, given the circumstances. There's no concussion or significant blood loss."

"And the bad news?"

On a wall screen, Aguado displays the X-rays she has taken of Jon.

"This machine has a narrower field than a conventional X-ray, but it should give us an idea."

The image reveals the uppermost section of Inspector Gutiérrez's spine. After colliding with photons emitted when free electrons are slowed down, the Basque's powerful skeleton shows up as a shadowy negative. The bones appear delicate, ghostlike. One puff of air could reduce them to dust.

By contrast, the metal structure fastened with screws to his spinal column appears clear, solid, menacing.

"As you can see," Aguado says, pointing with her ballpoint pen, "there are two visible plates and four screws between C3 and C6. There doesn't appear to be any damage to the spine or surrounding nerve tissue. The work is crude but clean."

But as they all know, the screws aren't the problem. Mounted on them is a smallish, flat metal structure, with protruding panels welded to it. In one of the images, they can make out a wire that disappears underneath and comes out at the bottom.

"The X-rays don't reveal a lot. The surface area is small, and the majority of the elements fit onto the one panel. The screws and other bits of metal are stainless steel. No titanium or medical-grade materials, which are traceable."

"Can you tell us anything, Doctor?" Mentor asks, anxiously shifting from one foot to the other.

"I'm no expert in explosive devices. But I can identify or can guess at a few things. This," she says, pointing to the wire connected to a square on the outer face, "has a distinctive tip and looks like a GPS antenna. In fact, you can even see the serial number," she adds, indicating a series of digits.

"In other words, White can access the device from anywhere," says Mentor.

"And he wanted us to know that," Antonia says. "Otherwise, he'd have hidden the serial number."

"Does it provide us with any useful information?"

Antonia, who has just checked her iPad, says:

"You can buy them online for less than a euro. And there are hundreds of outlets."

"I can't believe that . . ."

"Before you go on," she cuts in, "you should know they use the same antenna in high-end cell phones, except that online, they sell them at cost without an Apple logo."

Mentor remains silent. Straight-faced, Aguado confirms what Antonia has said and continues her explanation.

"This solider, more opaque part is undoubtedly the explosive. It's connected to something I can't see that acts as a detonator."

"How . . . powerful is it?" asks Mentor, staying a prudent distance from Jon. Extremely prudent.

"It's too small to cause extensive damage. Whoever designed it did so in such a way that if it explodes, there'll be only one victim."

Antonia reflects silently on the way complex systems readjust. On escalation. The police buy semiautomatic weapons, criminals buy automatic ones. The police use bulletproof vests, criminals use armor-piercing bullets. You make your family and loved ones safe, and they screw bombs into your bones.

"Can't we deactivate it?"

Dr. Aguado looks at the inspector. He hasn't said a word since Antonia and Mentor came back into the room and is staring blankly at the screen.

"Maybe it would be better if . . ."

"Tell me," says Jon.

Aguado turns toward Mentor, but Jon catches her by the arm.

"I want to know what my options are."

Mentor nods his consent to Aguado. She shows them the image of the second device at the base of Jon's spine.

"They look identical, but they're not. I'm pretty sure this is a photoelectric sensor," says Aguado, indicating one of the panels. "And this thing here is a Bluetooth module."

"In plain language, Doctor," says Mentor.

"What she's saying," Antonia cuts in, unable to stop herself, "is that if she operates to try to remove either device, there's a risk it will activate the photoelectric sensor. Bluetooth works by emitting a radio signal. It has a range of approximately ten yards."

"I suspect the two are paired," ventures Aguado. "If we touch one, it will set off the other one, or both."

At that moment, Jon stands up. His bare feet make a slapping sound on the concrete floor. He leaves the room without a word.

Antonia makes to go after him, but Mentor stands in her way.

"Give him a few minutes, Scott."

She looks at him, perplexed. Jon is understandably anxious, and she only wants to offer him her support. She tries to push past Mentor, but he stands firm.

"What he has to do now, he needs to do by himself."

3

A SHOWER

What Jon Gutiérrez has to do is weep.

Jon may be sweet and sensitive on the inside, filled with fluffy, pony-print padding, but on the outside, he's still a Basque cop. And Basque cops don't cry in front of strangers. Or people they know, for that matter. *Some things are just the way they are, and that's all there is to it, for fuck's sake.*

So Jon enters the deserted locker room and heads for the showers. Undressing consists of removing the hospital gown Aguado gave him. To remove the threat under his skin is more difficult, so Jon contents himself with letting the shower run as hot as it will go. He leans his arms against the tiles and only then allows the tears to flow. Until they pour out, his tears are like a huge dog chewing at his insides, leaving behind voids, abysses filled with the unknown.

Several months go by—or possibly half an hour—while the jet of water cascades onto his neck and back. It washes over the stitches where someone has planted death inside him. Jon realizes his tears have given way to rage when he finds himself punching the side of the shower as hard as he can. Fortunately for his knuckles, the struts holding up the plywood paneling only withstand three blows before they come away from the wall.

His rage passes, or possibly the impetus that allowed it to come out, leaving him in shock. He discovers himself naked, dripping wet, with bloodied hands, his nose blocked. He washes it all away, trying to feel normal again.

When he switches off the shower and turns around, he sees Antonia.

She is sitting sideways on the changing room bench, staring at the lockers. She has the air of a churchwarden passing around the collection plate or of a waiter asking you to tap in your PIN. That look people adopt when they want to make it clear they aren't peeking.

Jon wraps himself in a towel and walks over to her.

For several minutes, they both remain silent. The lights in the locker room glint on Jon's pale shoulders, freckled like a true redhead. Antonia looks beyond them, resisting the urge to seize the two protrusions in her colleague's back and tear them out of his body.

"Aguado asked me to give you this," she says, showing him a cell phone. "And I stopped by your apartment to pick this up," she adds.

She pulls out a suit and holds it up to the light. Jon suppresses a sigh of gratitude and then, with more effort, one of frustration.

"My petrol-green Dolce & Gabbana," he says in his most neutral voice.

"I've never seen you wear it."

"Because it's not a work suit, sweetie."

Puzzled, Antonia looks at him.

"Why have a suit that's not for work?"

Jon rolls his eyes, reminding himself he has to be patient with Antonia, who dresses as if she did her shopping in a dumpster. Then he has a tussle with his clothes. He manages to slip one arm into his shirtsleeve, but getting the other one in proves more challenging. He can feel the stitches pulling, and the pain he feels is nothing compared to his fear.

Antonia, who is still watching while pretending not to, quickly grasps the situation. She stands and clambers up onto the bench.

"Be careful. You'll injure yourself, and that's all we need," Jon warns her.

She ignores him, holding out the sleeve for him to slip his other arm inside. They repeat the operation with the vest, realize the lump in his neck makes it impossible for him to wear a tie, and finally get him into his jacket. Antonia is thinking about the last time she did this: a few weeks earlier, with her son. Jon is thinking about something very different.

"A fine shield bearer I turned out to be."

"I wouldn't want any other," she replies as she finishes straightening his lapels.

"They're not exactly lining up outside your door, sweetie."

"I don't see why not."

"Maybe you're the problem."

"I'm not that bad," she says, although there's a hint of doubt in her voice.

Jon reflects, very, very slowly, that the problem isn't Antonia, the problem is what she does. And the chaos she creates around her. Scientists say someone on the planet is struck by lightning every nineteen minutes. Jon suspects that person is less than ten yards away from Antonia Scott.

That's what he thinks, but he actually says:

"No, you're not that bad."

And for now at least that's as far as Jon is able to comfort her or show his gratitude. For rescuing him and for helping him on with his clothes. Which amounts to the same thing.

"How do you feel?"

Inspector Gutiérrez makes a mental inventory: extreme nausea; a dull, persistent pain in his back despite the cocktail of anti-inflammatory drugs Aguado has injected him with; legs as rickety as a piece of IKEA furniture.

"I've felt better," he sums up.

"It's your blood sugar level. When did you last eat?"

Jon remembers it perfectly. He left home, heading for the Wok on Calle del Olivar. For what was to be his last supper in Madrid.

But in the end, it wasn't.

4

A KEBAB

Even if the world had been transformed into a postapocalyptic wasteland where cows were extinct and the chefs at Etxebarri had turned their grills into swords, Jon would still have thought twice about entering the diner outside which Antonia is parking the Audi A8.

"A kebab house? No fucking way I'm eating a kebab."

"It's the nearest place. Get out of the car. That's an order."

"You're not my boss. I resigned."

"I said get out."

Jon hasn't the strength left to argue, or to do anything else. So he goes in, vowing to himself he won't eat a single bite. Jon was a young teenager when Turkistan II opened in Bilbao (no one ever knew what happened to Turkistan I) and ever since has been revolted by those gyrating blobs of half-cooked meat. He and his friends used to make jokes about them. It was good to have something to make jokes about, given he was the butt of most of theirs. The gay hulk. But that period didn't last long, and no sooner were his friends old enough to get drunk than the kebab became an oasis of salvation in the early hours. It either kept everything down or helped you bring it up.

For Jon, therefore, the kebab was something you either poked fun at or upchucked between two garbage cans. Until Antonia sets down two paper plates on the table (one of those patterned chrome ones that always wobble) and two Cokes. He doesn't even touch the can; you have to draw the line somewhere. The meat roll, though, with its salad garnish and sauce of indeterminate color, gives off an aroma that belies its appearance, and Jon finds himself taking a first, tentative bite. Thirty seconds later, the kebab has vanished into the depths of Inspector Gutiérrez.

"You were hungry," says Antonia contentedly, still pecking at hers.

"What was that delicacy?"

"A mixture of lamb, chicken, and yogurt sauce, I think."

Jon pulls a face.

"We need to discuss your diet," he says.

"Food is food."

"Amatxo would give you an earful if she heard you say that, sweetie. *Madre mía*, I need to call and tell her . . ."

Something. Not too much. The bare minimum. Or better still, nothing, Jon reflects.

"You can't."

"You're right. She'd be a nervous wreck, poor woman."

Antonia takes a sip of her drink.

"No, I mean you literally can't talk to her. We've taken her somewhere safe."

"What?"

"A contact of Mentor's picked her up in a car a few minutes ago. They'll be out of circulation for a few days, until things become clearer."

Upset—and still somewhat uncoordinated—Jon clambers unsteadily to his feet. He whips out the brand-new cell phone Aguado gave him. Of course, no one picks up at the other end, although Antonia thinks they can probably hear his yells on the left bank of the river Nervión without any need for a phone.

When Jon comes back inside the restaurant, Antonia has to use all her powers of persuasion to convince him not to snatch the car keys from her and set off for Bilbao.

"Take it easy," she says. "It was necessary. I've had to do the same with my family."

Hearing this, Jon manages to calm down a little.

Antonia tells him about how she sent away Grandma Scott and Jorge. Jon is only half listening, as if someone were telling him about fictitious events in a far-off, distant galaxy.

"Doesn't it scare you to think of them out there, unable to communicate with you, when you have no idea where they are?"

Antonia considers her reply as she finishes her kebab. It's a question that requires weighing, measuring, carbon dating, and the use of a scale ruler.

"Yes. But it would scare me much more if they were here within reach of that cold-blooded psychopath. Sandra kidnapped Jorge once, and she'd happily do it again."

"I still can't believe she took the kid," says Jon, shaking his head. Shadowy images of the abandoned Goya subway station come back to him. Images of himself trying to avoid being blown to bits in a booby-trapped tunnel while attempting to rescue Antonia's son. He pushes them aside with a sigh. After all, he has other, much closer explosives to worry about.

"That is White's technique. He finds out a person's weakness and uses it to his own advantage."

"He's not much different from a cheap blackmailer. There's a guy in Otxarkoaga the cops know well. They call him the Banana. That bastard has a technique. He steals your car, then calls you on the phone. If you don't show up at such and such a place with five hundred euros in less than an hour, he torches your car."

Antonia grins with one side of her mouth.

"What's your favorite food, Jon?"

"That's easy. Ama's *kokotxas*."

"Your Banana has as much in common with White as this kebab has with your mother's *kokotxas*."

Jon gives his mouth a perfunctory wipe with one of those paper napkins that say THANKS FOR YOUR VISIT. He doesn't like the glint in Antonia's eye one bit, and so he chooses his next words carefully.

"I guess this crap must have disagreed with me. Because I thought I detected a hint of admiration in your voice."

"He has the most brilliant mind we've ever come up against, Jon. He's a lot smarter than me."

"He's also a killer. The guy who put your husband in a coma and who did this to me," Jon says, pointing to his back.

"All of which has a lot more merit than torching cars."

Jon scratches his wavy red hair and takes a deep breath. To fill his capacious lungs takes a few seconds and several liters of oxygen. On this occasion with aromas of reheated oil and Middle Eastern spices.

"Merit? Honestly, sweetheart, there are times when I don't get you."

Antonia folds her arms.

"All I'm saying is that his methods are more complex than those of the Banana. How else could he have operated for so long without anyone detecting him? Or rather without anyone hearing from someone who did," she says, looking away.

To say Jon is proud by nature would be like saying he's bigger than average. Jon wears his pride like a nineties bathroom, with wall-to-wall tiling and gaudy flowers.

"You have to admit your story about some phantom hired assassin was pretty incredible."

"I guess you find it more believable now, right?"

Jon receives the low blow in the place where people usually receive low blows, and in the traditional way. His neck and shoulders tense as he prepares to retaliate. He opens his mouth, gets the poison ready, but doesn't manage to spit it out. Nor does he swallow it. So it stays where it is, burning a hole in his tongue.

The two of them say nothing for a while, avoiding eye contact, with only the mind-numbing drone of the TV for company. A bunch of people cheating on each other on who knows what island hardly makes for relaxing viewing, and when Jon tires of watching the gyrating blob of half-cooked meat, he gets up and walks out.

This would be a perfect moment to start smoking, he thinks, realizing he has both hands empty. No money, no phone, no wallet, and no keys to the car parked next to him. *It's not as if there's enough time for the habit to kill me.*

5

A COMPROMISE

After a while, Antonia emerges, having said goodbye to the owner in Turkish. She approaches the car slowly, with that lost way of walking she has. As if she were floating in her own space. Jon has seen her walk like that, avoiding the slightest contact, even on a crowded avenue like Madrid's Gran Vía. Despite his predicament, when he sees her doing the same on a narrow one-way street in an industrial estate on the outskirts of the city, he's overwhelmed by a wave of tenderness and melancholy.

"Listen . . . ," she says.

"I know."

Puzzled, she stares at him.

"What do you know?"

"That we have no choice but to work together. In my case, because if I don't, they'll kill me. And in yours . . . because on your own, you'll last about as long as a *dantzari* in hell."

"And that's not very long?" Antonia asks innocently.

"I'll send you a video. As soon as I've figured out this new phone."

"Incidentally, what happened to your old one?"

"They kept it."

Antonia nods her head slowly.

"What do you remember about the past few hours?"

"What I already told the doctor, while you and Mentor were busy staring at my butt. Somebody came up to me in the street, and then everything went black. I heard people talking, but their voices were far away. Then I heard yours. That's all."

"It isn't much. Is that all you remember?"

Of course it's not.

There was also fear.

A terrible, agonizing fear.

Because, despite being sedated during the operation, Jon was partially awake. He couldn't see anything, he could barely hear. But he was conscious enough to know something bad was happening. And happening to him. He can recall trying to move his arms and legs, sending the command to his brain but not receiving a response. He can recall feeling defenseless, violated. He can recall the sound of the drill piercing his spine. The sensation of metal against his flesh, against the very foundations of his being, was deeply disturbing. An inexplicable feeling.

Painless, yet terrifying.

It's something Jon won't talk about, because he can't.

And because the best way of coping with fear is to pretend you don't feel any.

"Yes, that's all," Jon lies, more or less convincingly.

Antonia sits down beside him on the hood of the Audi. They gaze into the distance, enjoying the sunset over the roof of Ferrallas Domínguez Ltd. The dwindling afternoon light traces ominous shapes on the corrugated iron; an elongated shadow with jagged teeth advances toward them, threatening to devour them.

"It's getting dark," Antonia says. "He'll be contacting us soon with his demand."

Jon doesn't reply.

"That's what he always does. He demands something. And that something destroys you."

"How come you know so much about him?"

"I don't *know* much. I've been gathering scraps of information. Some of them are hunches. Others are calculated guesses. Nothing very useful. Not a shred of evidence that he exists. Until today."

Jon raises his fingers to the back of his neck, where there's an all-too-tangible piece of evidence.

"Something must have put you on his trail. How did you discover he even existed?"

Antonia pauses for a long moment.

"I don't want to talk about that now," she says finally.

Fine, whenever you feel like it, thinks Jon, the poison flowing to his lips once more. And again, he does his best to control himself.

"So what do we have?"

"The odds are against us. We know nothing of his whereabouts or what his intentions are."

"What do we have on Sandra?"

"Even less. Although something else seems to be driving her. Something deeply personal."

"If by *personal* you mean she's as crazy as a shithouse rat, then I wouldn't disagree."

"There's something else you don't know. It seems the two of them have been planning this for a very, very long time."

She goes on to explain how, without them knowing it, White and Fajardo have been weaving a web around the members of the Red Queen project. Sparing no detail, she calmly tells Jon what happened in England and Holland. When he hears how the Dutch shield bearer killed his queen in cold blood, his heart sinks.

"Antonia, I'd never . . ."

"Don't say anything, Jon," she cuts him off. "Have you stopped to think what you might be capable of if they took your mother?"

"I'd never . . . ," Jon repeats. A little less adamantly.

"You'd never give in to blackmail? And yet that's why you're here. Or have you forgotten how Mentor used you to bring me out of retirement? A certain video of a certain car trunk?"

Inspector Gutiérrez jumps off the Audi's hood as though it were red hot.

"That's totally different," he says, holding up an accusing finger stiff as a bridegroom's member on his wedding night. Then, as he reflects on what she has said, the finger begins to droop, before sheepishly rejoining its four companions.

Antonia watches him deflating in this way and says:

"Nobody is immune from doing anything for love, committing even the most heinous act. Love is the most powerful force on earth."

Jon stops saying, "I'd never . . ." because he has understood.

"There's no easy way out of this situation, Jon. As long as you have that thing under your skin, our only option is to play along with him."

Jon is pacing nervously in circles, overwhelmed by the urge to kick something. The only targets he can find are a used condom wrapper, a crushed beer can, the Audi, and Antonia. After weighing the options, he goes for the second-most-desirable target. The can lands with a clatter at the far end of the street.

"We can't give in, Antonia. No matter what they ask us to do, we can't give in."

"What do you suggest?"

"You could disappear," he says. "Go and find your son and don't look back."

"That would mean leaving you behind. The answer is no."

Jon nods his head, at least as far as the painful stitches will allow.

"That thing inside you has a couple of batteries. Without them, it's nothing more than a rather unsightly wound."

"Batteries don't last forever," he says, beginning to understand.

"No, they don't. So we play his game, buy ourselves time. And hope he makes a mistake."

Inspector Gutiérrez is wondering about the strategic value of hoping someone who has been elaborating a plan for a very, very long time will make a mistake. He opens his mouth to say this, but what he hears are:

Two beeps and a buzzing sound.

Antonia reaches into her pocket and takes out her cell phone.

There's no need for her to say it, but she does anyway.

"It's him."

6

A VISIT

Antonia shows Jon her cell phone. Four words, one number:

SANTA CRUZ DE MARCENADO, 3

"What's that supposed to mean?"

"He told me he wanted us to investigate three crimes. I guess this is the first."

"Not much to go on."

Antonia's phone beeps again. She unblocks it and reads the message, the screen illuminating her face. Antonia is one of those appalling people who always keeps their brightness settings on maximum. It's an unforgivable failing for which Jon has to forgive her whenever it's dark and his eyes are blinded by it. Thanks to the annoying glare, Jon can see Antonia isn't at all happy. When she shows him the message, he is even less so.

YOU HAVE SIX HOURS.
W.

"You're fucking kidding me."

Antonia sets the clock on her phone to count down from the deadline White has given them.

"Let's go to that address."

"Just like that. Because you received a text?"

"Yes, just like that."

"We could try to trace the message. Look for any clues he may have left. There were two others with him when they kidnapped me. White must have recruited them from somewhere."

"You're thinking like a cop," Antonia interrupts him. "And right now, we don't need a cop."

Jon frowns, but says nothing. He simply leans his arm against the driver's door when she tries to open it.

"What are you doing?"

"Keeping us alive. And mobile. Mentor says this is our last car."

"It's not as if we've wrecked *that* many," she sighs, handing over the key.

"*Madre mía*, how we like to play things down when it suits us, sweetie."

Even when Jon doesn't have to foot the bill, more than €300,000 worth of wrecked Audis seems a lot to him. Especially when he's the one who has to deal with Mentor. What never ceases to amaze him is Antonia's apathy toward mathematics and the means of locomotion. It's almost equal to her contempt for the highway code.

Antonia installs herself in the passenger seat. As they drive off, she FaceTimes Mentor, mounting the iPad on the dash so Jon can see it as well.

"How is the inspector?" asks Mentor.

"Well enough to drive, apparently," retorts Antonia with a shrug.

"How can I put it, Scott? If ever you need to accompany the inspector to the ER because he's been shot, I still prefer you in the passenger seat."

Inspector Gutiérrez tries in vain to keep a straight face.

"Technically speaking, Jon has crashed more cars than I have."

"Technically speaking, I don't give a damn. Any news from that bastard?"

"He made contact," says Antonia, relaying the details of White's recent texts.

Mentor tells them not to hang up while he carries out a data search. Jon half expects to hear the dreadful Muzak that call centers subject you to while you wait. But Mentor comes back in less than a minute.

"In the last thirty-five years, there's been one crime at that address. That's all the information we have."

A photograph pops onto the screen. A young woman with wavy hair and a shy smile.

"Raquel Planas Mengual. Interior designer."

A crime scene photograph appears on the screen. The details are blurry. A body draped in a raincoat. And a great deal of blood.

"Raquel was stabbed to death in Calle de Santa Cruz de Marcenado four years ago."

Hearing this, Jon wrinkles his nose.

He once took part in investigating a cold case. New evidence had emerged relating to the murder of a teenage boy in Getxo, on the outskirts of Bilbao. A bloodstained T-shirt. The owner turned out to be someone quite well known, and the case was in all the newspapers. Eight detectives from the Basque police, three National Police officers, two pathologists, and an external forensic laboratory were involved, and tens of thousands of euros.

That crime only dated back two and a half years. And yet when the detectives returned to the victim's old haunts, they found a lot of things had changed. Witnesses either remembered nothing, or their accounts differed wildly from the initial statements they gave the police.

Nothing a police officer likes less than a cold case.

"Suspects?"

"A perp."

A second photo flashes up on the screen. A man in his late thirties. Long hair, a receding chin, and shifty eyes. From the neck up, he is no oil painting, so he has compensated for this from the neck down. Ripped muscles, bubble butt, balls the size of olives. A gold Rolex that screams "I have something to prove."

All that's missing in this photo is him in a convertible, thinks Jon, who isn't very charitable toward men who kill women.

"Her husband?"

"Her boyfriend, Víctor Blázquez. The owner of a gym. With a history of domestic abuse."

"Where is he?"

"In Soto del Real jail. Serving twenty-three years. He'll be out in six, he's a model prisoner."

"It's good to know the system works."

Antonia looks at the photograph, looks at the road, looks again at her colleague, and makes a decision.

"Turn around."

"What?"

"Turn around. We're going to the prison."

"But I thought we were going to Santa Cruz de Marcenado?"

She shoots him one of those looks that tells Jon it's best not to argue. So he performs a somewhat illegal U-turn and they head off in the opposite direction. He searches for the address on the Audi's GPS while Antonia parries Mentor's objections.

"What the hell are you playing at, Scott?"

Antonia isn't sure. But a word has popped into her head.

Katsrauvsaali.

In Khmer, a language spoken by twenty million Cambodians and which boasts the world's longest alphabet, this means: he who harvests wheat when the time is ripe to harvest wheat.

"The normal course would be to go over the witness list, the case file, visit the crime scene, talk to the public prosecutor, the judge, the lead detectives. How long would that take us?"

"Too long," Mentor admits.

"It's night already. Even if we mobilized an army, dragged everybody out of bed, and lined them up, it would take days to interview them all," Jon agrees.

"And which direction do you think they would all point us in?"

Jon already knows. The same destination he has just entered in the GPS: kilometer 35 on the M-609.

"White has instructed us to solve this crime," says Antonia. "If Blázquez isn't the culprit, then who better to ask?"

"Asking a convicted criminal if he's innocent. What could possibly go wrong?" Jon says, flicking on the blinker.

"I agree with Inspector Gutiérrez. You could be wasting valuable time, Scott."

Antonia doesn't answer. It's one of the tactics she uses to show people she doesn't give a hoot what they think when she believes she is right about something. Mentor is well aware of this, which is why he resorts to the oldest trick in a boss's book: to pretend it was his idea in the first place.

"You'd better put your foot down. I'll try to make sure you have easy access when you arrive. How far are you from the prison, Inspector?"

"Twenty-eight minutes. But I'll do it in fifteen, I'm a model driver."

Before ending their FaceTime call, Mentor tells Antonia, "Pick up your phone, Scott."

Puzzled, Antonia obeys.

"And don't put it on speakerphone," he adds. "I need to talk to you privately."

"Okay," she replies, still more puzzled.

7

AN ASIDE

It's not Mentor's style to give her information he keeps from her partner. Quite the reverse.

"I need to know you're well enough to do this, Scott."

"Why wouldn't I be?"

"Don't play dumb. How long is it since you last took a red pill?"

Antonia is perfectly aware of this. She could tell him in hours, minutes, and seconds, but to do so would need her to concentrate for a while.

Once when she was little, Antonia innocently stuck her hand in the gap between the garage door and the frame. She had seen her father do it many times. A little trick grown-ups used to save themselves having to walk the short distance to the pedestrian entrance: you take advantage of a car having just driven out to access the garage via the quickest route. No sooner had her father thrust his arm inside than the closing door would start to open again.

Unfortunately, Antonia put hers where there was no sensor.

The door continued to close inexorably, trapping her hand. Her father arrived in time to stop the heavy red metal frame from severing her limb, but not fast enough to stop the pain. He drove like a maniac to the nearest hospital, where they gave her a mild sedative. In the end, it was nothing more than a nasty shock and the loss of the use of her right hand for a month. She was also left with a pale, inch-and-a-half-long scar on her forearm and an indentation in the muscle where it didn't grow properly.

And something else: whenever she heard the sound of a garage door or looked at her scar, Antonia had a vivid recollection of the pain. A jolt of electricity shot from her arm to her brain, making her flinch, no matter what she might be doing. Even after all these years.

Antonia has the same sensation when she remembers Jon throwing her stash of pills down the drain at a victim's house (and her grappling with him, trying to reach the sink where they are dissolving in the dirty dishwater). This memory dates back a few days, not three decades. And yet they are very similar: a reckless act, an unexpected outcome, an enormous, inexorable weight bearing down on her, trapping her. Or freeing her, who knows? What it leaves behind is pain and aching muscles.

"I feel fine," she replies to Mentor's question. The second lie she tells is almost as big as the first. "I don't need them anymore."

"Antonia," says Mentor—which is even stranger because he rarely uses her first name—"I've been telling you that for years. But why now?"

"I'm trying to go with the flow, not to tame the river. I'm paraphrasing, but I'm sure you remember the quote."

"Not a bad philosophy. Does it include stealing red capsules from the refrigerated chamber?"

Antonia closes her eyes and purses her lips. It's a relief they're speaking on the phone and not via video link or in person, because she's a very poor liar. On a scale of zero to president, Antonia doesn't even make it onto the scoreboard.

But she can't tell him the truth either. She mustn't. So she decides to distract his attention. She is undefeated world champion at that.

"Did someone make a mistake in the inventory?"

"Fifty red and ten blue capsules are missing, Scott."

"That's a significant mistake."

"And I'm the only one who has access to the refrigerated chamber."

"Then we know who to blame. Case closed."

"You're the only one who could get past security."

Antonia doesn't need to give much thought to her reply. Not because she hasn't daydreamed about it dozens of times in the past few days: breaking into that damn place and stuffing handfuls of capsules down her throat.

"I suppose I could figure out the ten-digit number on the digital panel. Or get hold of a copy of the actual key. I could also circumvent the biometric tests, which are practically a joke. But if I recall correctly, the security camera is an analog tape? Have you had time to check it?"

It's impossible to falsify the Serfram Cobalt analog tape Mentor has installed. You can snap it, stamp on it, cover up the camera, do whatever you want to it, but you can't change what's on the tape.

Mentor knows this.

Antonia knows this.

And he knows that she knows that they both know.

So it's stalemate. Mentor could have left it at that, and maybe he would have done so normally. To compete with Antonia Scott isn't a sprint, it's a Tour de France that consists of reaching the finishing line without collapsing. But something inside Mentor is making him nervous—stress, which lowers defenses. He can't keep quiet.

"There's nothing on the tape. But maybe I only have one suspect, Scott. Maybe you took more capsules than you should have in Málaga. Maybe you're an addict. And right now, the inspector needs something better than that."

Antonia swallows hard. When she speaks, she finds she can't do so without gritting her teeth.

"Maybe you shouldn't have injected me with that stuff when I was unstable. Maybe you got me addicted in the first place."

And then, recalling some ancestral wisdom Jon handed down to her recently, she resolves to tell Mentor exactly how she feels, with both barrels. She takes a deep breath.

"Maybe you should quit fucking with me."

8

AN ELECTRIC CAR

Mentor hangs up. He feels irritation, guilt, and shame flow to his face and hands, like a weak but oppressive electrical charge. After making a few calls to smooth the way for Antonia and Jon, fatigue lands on him like a ton of bricks.

He turns to Dr. Aguado. She still has her nose buried in the laptop, her eyes are red and dry, her hair disheveled. Not that he's in much better shape. His shirt is sticking to his skin, and he reeks of stale sweat and cigarette smoke. He is keeping going thanks to a combination of willpower, Marlboro Lights, and packets of Conguitos from the vending machine in reception. He detests chocolate-coated peanuts, but it's that or a soggy sandwich.

"Go get some rest," he says to Aguado, hoping he might take a nap himself.

Mentor is many things, but as the boss, he is always first to arrive and last to leave. It's a habit he acquired when working abroad.

"Not now. I think I may have found something," the pathologist replies.

"Really," Mentor says, thrusting his hand into his pocket in search of loose change. "Do you want anything from the machine?"

Ignoring his offer, Aguado beckons him to come over.

"Look at this."

Mentor peers over Aguado's shoulder and recognizes the Heimdal user interface, the Red Queen project's spyware. Aguado is using it to access an external system.

"What am I looking at?"

"The security cameras at the shopping mall," she says.

All Mentor can see is the time code display ticking on a black screen.

"It looks as if there was a power cut."

"There was," Aguado confirms. "Only it was intentional. Somebody hacked into the security cameras, switched them off one hour before Scott arrived at the mall, and then on again an hour after she left."

"No rest for the wicked, right?" Mentor says, rubbing his face to try to wake himself up. His stomach is rumbling. He's so famished he's seriously considering going out to grab a bite to eat at the kebab house two blocks away.

"Wait. . . . They've overlooked something."

When the security camera comes back on again, Aguado points to a parking space set apart from the others. A stationary vehicle is connected to the wall by a thick cable.

It's one of those electric models only rich people can afford. *And which, when you buy one, makes you a better person*, thinks Mentor. He has seen more than one such savior of the planet look down their nose as they pull up next to him at a stoplight.

"What?"

"These vehicles . . . are very vulnerable when they're charging. A sudden bump can destroy their batteries, and they're the most expensive component."

"So?" says Mentor, feeling slightly awkward now that his stomach is rumbling next to Aguado's ear. However, she is still furiously typing and appears not to have noticed.

"Wait a minute . . . ," she says, opening a series of new windows. *Subroutines* they're called, or so Mentor thinks he remembers from the talk on Heimdal he and the other team leaders attended.

Finally, the logo of a well-known electric car manufacturer pops onto the screen. Together with a series of instructions in Korean. This is a problem, as the geniuses who designed Heimdal forgot to install a translation app.

We pay half a billion euros for software and end up asking Google, reflects Mentor.

"I wish Scott was here," says Aguado, who has to resort to her phone to translate the Hangeul ideograms.

"Scott doesn't speak Korean."

"Not officially, but she's learned enough."

"Since when?"

"Since three weeks ago. She and I made a bet."

"Who won?"

"Who do you think?"

A side effect of spending a lot of time with an exceptionally gifted individual is that you come to appreciate their true capabilities.

Life is a lot easier when you're stupid because one of the advantages of being stupid is you don't know you are.

Mentor nods, feigning composure.

"I'm sure if we applied ourselves, we'd be equally capable."

"No, we really wouldn't," says Aguado, replacing her cell phone on the table and pointing at the screen. "This is the car's management system. And this button here activates . . ."

A video file pops up.

"The car cameras."

"I don't understand. Is this in real time?"

"While it's charging, the car activates the cameras to protect itself in case another vehicle comes too close at speed. What we're seeing is this morning's footage, taken while the car was charging."

"God bless rich liberals. And the car has saved this video file?"

"Not officially. Unofficially, it contains valuable information. And you know every programmer's rule: what the user doesn't know won't hurt them."

I didn't know that, although it's the same rule for governments, thinks Mentor, leaning forward to try to decipher what's on the screen.

A few minutes later, he decides it's the most tedious film he has ever seen, apart from one by Tarkovsky.

A total of four cameras, at the sides and front of the vehicle. In two, all you can see is the bodywork of the nearest vehicles. But another shows some movement. Every so often, somebody emerges through a door half hidden in the side of the building opposite. Mentor deduces from the clothing of the people crossing the threshold that it's an employee door to the mall.

Aguado fast-forwards to the time when Antonia and White met. They keep their eyes peeled, but the door remains closed. Nobody enters or leaves. The time code display goes beyond the moment when the meeting ended.

Nothing.

"This is pointless . . ."

"It was worth a tr . . . Wait . . ."

The door opens, but just then, a dark object blocks the screen momentarily, concealing the door.

"I don't believe it. Something's blocked the shot."

Mentor, who doesn't usually swear or utter vulgarities, on this occasion freely vents his frustration.

"It's . . . it looks like a van," says Aguado, pointing to one side of the image.

The van disappears, leaving behind only the door. It's the same color as the concrete wall, with the same painted red line.

"Rewind to just before the van arrives."

Aguado goes back eleven seconds.

"Now let it play frame by frame."

Aguado zooms in until each image appears as a thumbnail on the bottom toolbar. Slowly, she starts to press the right click. One frame, two, three.

Nothing.

"What's that?"

Mentor points to a brighter patch in the doorway.

"Wait . . ."

Aguado focuses on it, continuing to advance one image at a time. The brighter patch is there for several frames, and something is visible in the space.

"Can you make it any sharper, or is that only in crap movies?"

Aguado smiles wearily at Mentor's even more tired joke. This is probably the tenth time she has heard him say it. Mentor himself approved the budget for the edge enhancement software. Even so, he continues to find it amusing that while the technology was still in its infancy at the turn of the last century, they used it every week on *CSI: Las Vegas*.

As the filter starts to process the lighter area, a face appears.

First they see the eyes and mouth.

Nothing more than blurs in the appropriate places.

Then, as the filter repeats the process twice, three times, the features start to emerge more clearly. A half smile or perhaps a look of urgency. A slightly averted gaze. Eyebrows curved slightly upward, framing the face of a woman whom at first glance somebody might describe as friendly.

Mentor's eyes remain glued to the image until the filter has done its job. The result is a negative picture (the best way to highlight the contours of a face); even so, his reaction is as unexpected as it is dramatic.

He reaches across, presses the key combination to open the software's recent activity, and wipes everything from the past hour. The car's video file is deleted.

Aguado gazes at him blankly. Mentor looms over her, as close as someone might if he wanted to pull out one of her eyelashes. Alarmed, Aguado tries to lean back in her chair, but the way Mentor is standing over her makes it impossible.

"You didn't see that face. Is that clear, Doctor?"

His voice and manner brook no opposition.

"But . . ."

She turns around, but Mentor is no longer there. He is heading for the door, on his way grabbing his crumpled jacket from the chair where he'd left it. Before leaving, he turns to Aguado and says without emotion:

"And not a word of this to Scott."

9

A STAGE

Jon is a sophisticated guy, a guy who has a way with people. He's also very good at twisting arms—and his are strong enough to stop a cable car in its tracks. Seriously, though, the guy is diplomatic and discreet. Which is why when Antonia hangs up, he doesn't say:

"I'm going to grind that motherfucker's teeth on the sidewalk."

No, by now, Jon is experienced at dealing with Antonia, so he simply grips the steering wheel so tight he leaves finger marks in it. Then he presses the Play button on the CD player—track nine, "Physics and Chemistry." Jon turns up the volume so he can't hear Antonia's sobs. And so she can't hear him curse under his breath. Because sometimes the wounds words cause can only be healed by silence.

Jon lets time and kilometers pass while Antonia is engrossed in her iPad, going through the cold case. Two tears fall onto the bright white screen, creating a pixelated rainbow. She casually wipes them away with her thumb; they're getting in the way of her work.

The reason Jon lets time go by is because he has overheard their entire exchange. Yes, Mentor's part, too, thanks to the soundproof interior and because the volume was on loud. Antonia knows something she didn't want to tell him when he got rid of her pills, cordially inviting her to go cold turkey while she yelled, "No, no, no," à la Amy Winehouse.

She had expected to take a break after their last mission. To recover, get over her dependency, and not find herself plunged headlong into a race against time, dancing to the tune of an evil psychopath.

Jon had expected to be in Bilbao, sprawled on Amatxo's couch, digesting her *bacalao al pil pil*, instead of racing toward a prison unable to stop the damn kebab repeating on him the whole time.

Naturally, they had lots of expectations. However, the world isn't a chocolate factory where people's wishes come true. All Jon's plans, all his old aspirations have been obliterated by the wrench he feels in his neck whenever he moves his head. Now all his desires seem childish, idiotic, pathetic. Maybe that's what it means to grow up: to realize what an asshole you are.

And speaking of growing up, Antonia Scott, twelve points, thinks Jon, an unapologetic fan of the Eurovision Song Contest. The way she stood up to Mentor was awesome. By her standards, at any rate.

He'd like to talk to her about it. Find some way to congratulate her. Although he doubts she'd let him get close right now. After her emotional outburst, she will have pulled up the drawbridge again and let loose the piranhas.

There's that, and also the fact that there's something much more urgent.

"Antonia," he says softly.

She looks up from her tablet. Not at him, at the road. But Jon can see her eyes are red and puffy.

"What is it?" she says, sniffing.

"Investigating a cold case is like eating soup with a machete."

"Is that one of your metaphors?"

"It's difficult, challenging, and guaranteed to leave you needing stitches."

"I know."

"It requires a lot of resources, people, time."

"I know that too."

"You can't do it in six hours."

"Do you intend to go on stating the obvious?"

"I just wanted to be sure we're on the same page."

"While you still have that thing in your neck, we have no other choice."

"Maybe it's not a real bomb. Maybe he inserted a piece of metal under my skin to scare us, so he can control us."

Antonia takes one of her famous contemplative pauses that last precisely thirty seconds. Jon expects a lengthy explanation about the bomb's technical features. But Antonia Scott is full of surprises.

"Are you familiar with Dr. Kübler-Ross's five stages of grief?"

"Who . . . what?"

"Denial, anger, bargaining, depression, and acceptance."

A memory pops into Jon's mind. Of a black doctor talking to a yellow man wearing Y-fronts. The man passes through the five stages at dizzying speed. Not quite as fast as Jon, who has gone from smashing up the shower to denying the bomb in his neck is real.

"I saw it on *The Simpsons*," he confesses.

"Where?"

Jon lifts his foot off the gas from sheer astonishment.

"Don't tell me you haven't watched *The Simpsons* at least once this century."

She doesn't reply. Jon doesn't look, because he's afraid he might miss the turnoff, but he's sure he hears her smile.

"I'm pulling your leg."

"You're such a hoot," Jon says, flicking the blinker for the next exit. His tone is sarcastic, but all of a sudden, he feels better, in a way he can't explain.

Or maybe he can.

10

ANOTHER RECEPTION DESK

It's very late by the time he pulls into the parking lot of the López-Ibor psychiatric clinic.

Mentor knows something of Madrid's history. Obviously, not to the same astonishingly intimate extent as Antonia Scott. She reads the city like a traumatologist studies the human body. As a series of superimposed layers, where bones, muscles, organs, and skin are merely parts of one breathing, moving whole.

Mentor is an amateur compared to Antonia, but he knows a little.

For example, he knows where the money that paid for the clinic came from. That nice Dr. López-Ibor earned it from *curing* homosexuals during the Franco era. The cures included lobotomies and electroshock therapy. Carried out without the patients' consent. And extremely lucrative.

Mentor is by no means a leftist; he wears his political colors on his sleeve for all to see. But that doesn't stop him from knowing the difference between good and evil or from openly acknowledging when a building's foundations are replete with ghosts.

Even though he doesn't believe in ghosts.

Even though he's responsible for adding to their number.

We are a mishmash of inconsistencies, and it's our ability to live on that uncertain ground that allows us to flourish. No doubt such contradictions have enabled Mentor to be the person he is today.

As he locks the car door, he wonders whether the time hasn't arrived for him to pay the price. He's long been aware a reckoning is due.

He hastens toward the entrance. All of a sudden, it has begun to rain, the way it sometimes does in Madrid. With a big raindrop that chooses to land where it will make the most noise—a nearby car hood, a gutter, a traffic light. Or failing that, with fiendish accuracy in the tiny gap between your neck and shirt collar.

The first raindrop is one of these. And then the others all follow the script.

Mentor arrives at the entrance with its promise of shelter, light, and warmth, only to encounter a sliding glass door that refuses to open. He raps on the glass until the woman in reception looks up and moves her hand as though stroking an animal's back, a gesture that universally says: "*We'reclosedcomebacktomorrow.*"

Mentor pulls his detective's badge from his pocket. He always carries one on him just in case he jumps a red light. The badge is indistinguishable from a real one, because it is real, except that it's fake.

But the woman seems impressed enough to open the door in a hurry.

"We haven't called the police," she says as he approaches the desk. The woman is middle-aged and prematurely gray, and the fact she has decided not to dye her hair pleases Mentor. He smiles warmly at her despite his anxiety.

"Occasionally, we drop in unannounced."

"Visiting hours are over."

"I realize that, señorita, but this is urgent."

She closes the book she's reading. *War and Peace.*

"If this concerns the patients, you'll need to speak with the admin staff tomorrow morning."

"I love that book," says Mentor, pointing at the novel.

"You've read it?" she says, looking dubiously at him.

"Several times."

"So . . . What's it about?"

"Pretty much everything, really."

Had he said "It's about a war" or "It's a love story," she might have had a different reaction. But his reply seems to satisfy her. Her shoulders slacken a little, the lines on her face soften.

"My father gave it to me. It's my favorite book."

"You're lucky. My father was suspicious of books. He used to say there's too much knowledge in the world and too few places for it to go."

"What did he mean by that?"

"I've no idea," says Mentor.

In fact, he has a very good idea. After all, his father belonged to one of *those* families. A family that knew what was what, like the man whose building they're in right now.

She shrugs.

"So how can I help you?"

"I'm here to see a patient."

He tells her the name. Puzzled, the woman tilts her head to one side.

"Doesn't ring any bells."

"Would you mind checking the database?"

"Are you a relative?"

Mentor pulls out his ID card. His real one. It's at the back of his wallet, half buried among a stack of other more useful documents. No doubt it's expired. He doesn't recall the last time he had to use it.

"I'm the contact person."

She checks both names on the database.

"It says here she was discharged, señor."

If this were a scene from a film noir, the director would have chosen to put an ominous rumble of thunder in the tense silence that follows the receptionist's words. Sadly, real life isn't always on cue, and the thunderclap arrives a few seconds late, coinciding with Mentor's stammering reply.

"Discharged? But . . . When?"

"Over four years ago."

"That's impossible," he says, craning his neck to try to see the screen. She turns it away from him.

"I'm sorry, but it's clearly written in her file."

"Then how do you explain I'm still paying three thousand eight hundred euros a month for her keep?" says Mentor, reaching into his pocket for his cell phone. He's quite prepared to show the woman his bank account, from where the money is withdrawn once a month like clockwork. Or his private email—Hotmail, embarrassingly—where he receives a quarterly psychological evaluation from the clinic as a PDF. In them, the words *stable* and *no change* appear highlighted.

"I'm sorry, sir. If this is an invoicing problem, the admin staff will be here at nine o'clock tomorrow morning."

The woman has leaned back in her chair, on her guard once more. Her shoulders are tense, her brow furrowed.

Mentor realizes it's pointless to keep plying her with questions. But he tries anyway, without much success.

Receptionists at a mental asylum aren't required to be flexible.

When he grows tired of getting nowhere, Mentor goes back the way he came. Eleven paces to the door that closes behind him. Another thirty to his car, waiting for its owner amid the storm. Or so Mentor hopes. The rain is so heavy he can barely see in front of him. He bumps into the fender of another car before he reaches the Audi.

As he approaches the driver's side, he stops dead in his tracks.

Somebody has slipped something under his windshield wiper. It's not one of those flyers advertising the services of prostitutes that abound in his neighborhood. No, those are always four-color prints on glossy paper. To look expensive.

No, this is a humble sheet of paper, printed on one side, the side touching the glass.

Mentor raises the wiper with one hand while with the other he peels the piece of paper from the dripping windshield.

He turns it over with some difficulty, and a ball of ice forms in his stomach as he reads the first line.

It's from her.

The result of her PCL-R—the Hare Psychopathy Checklist assessment.

The sodden bit of paper disintegrates in his hands. It doesn't matter.

Mentor knows what it says by heart, the way a death row prisoner knows his own sentence. He can almost recite it down to the last comma.

Extreme egomania, entirely *focused on her own interests. Acts deliberately and unscrupulously with regard to the harm she might cause her victims, and shows no fear or anxiety when confronted with the possible consequences.*

Interpersonal facet: exploitative, manipulative, deceitful, egocentric, and dominant.

Affective domain: displays fickle, superficial emotions. Incapable of relating to others or to shared values. Exhibits a total absence of genuine feelings of guilt, remorse, or fear, although she is able to simulate these to some extent, when calm. Reacts adversely to pressure.

Behavioral assessment: impulsive, in need of strong sensations, unstable. Liable to break rules and renege on responsibilities and obligations.

RECOMMENDATION: IMMEDIATE ADMISSION.

Mentor drops this now virtually illegible testimony to his blindness on the ground. He crushes it with the tip of his shoe, plunging it into a puddle. As he does, so he glances around, straining to see through the curtain of rain.

He can't spot anyone yet senses he isn't alone in the parking lot. He hears a movement behind him, a scrape on the asphalt, possibly a foot-fall in the rain that is now overflowing the gutters. He swings around but can't make anything out. False alarm. If this were a movie, at this point, a cat would slip meowing into an alleyway, but in real life, cats don't go out in the teeming rain.

Mentor shudders, and it isn't just because of the rain. He fumbles in his pocket, drops the car keys on the ground. He has to crouch and grope for them in the dirty rainwater. When he straightens up, he imagines a pair of hands closing round his throat, a knife plunging into his back.

He imagines.

The threat he feels isn't made of flesh or steel, only fear. He manages to unlock the car, closes the door, and searches beneath the passenger seat for the Remington 870 he left there a few hours ago. Soaked to the skin and shivering with cold, close to a heart attack and barricaded in his car clutching a rifle to his chest, Mentor reflects on the mistakes he has made in his life, on how he kept sweeping things under the carpet.

On what they did next.

In fact, he barely reflects at all, because he hurriedly turns the ignition and speeds away.

Fully aware his problems know exactly where to find him.

And not doubting for an instant they will do so very soon.

11

A YARD

Jon parks near the entrance in a free space next to a Prius. He turns to Antonia.

"C'mon, sweetie."

"C'mon, what?"

"The police report. You'll have to tell me something before we go in so I'm not completely clueless."

Antonia opens her mouth to form a first syllable, then closes it again.

Here we go, Jon says to himself.

"I think it's better if I don't."

"Is there some reason, or is it just for fun?"

"If I tell you what's in the report, I'll be telling you their conclusions. And we've come here on a different mission."

"To clear an innocent man?" asks Jon with a touch of sarcasm.

"No. To do what we always do. Hunt for the truth. Which doesn't always coincide with a verdict. Besides, Jon, you aren't exactly objective toward men who beat up on women."

No, I'm not, he thinks. *And I don't give a shit.*

"So?"

"So I ask the questions, and for the most part, you observe. I don't want you jumping in with even more prejudices."

Jon isn't entirely convinced, but accepts her strategy. No sooner have they stepped out of the car than the heavens open up. They make a dash for the entrance to the patter of rain on car hoods.

They identify themselves. Today, Antonia is a police inspector, none of the elaborate covers she's used on other occasions.

A bad-tempered guard asks them to empty their pockets onto one of the grubby plastic trays before they pass through the metal detector. Jon hastily places a tray on the conveyor belt in front of Antonia. He knows she hates to touch anything that's passed through a million pairs of hands, in the same way she hates people to touch her—for reasons that are different, but the same.

"You were told we were coming," says Jon.

"Place your personal belongings in one of these," says the guard, opening a filthy cardboard box for each of them. By comparison, they make the plastic trays look like freshly blown Bohemian crystal.

"My gun as well?" says Jon, just to mess with the guy a little.

The guard's expression doesn't invite banter. His face turns even sourer when the metal detector starts beeping like crazy as Jon walks through.

Antonia and Jon exchange looks.

"I just had surgery. A steel implant."

The guard reaches for the handheld detector, rising laboriously to his feet as if he were the one just recovering from an operation.

"Where?"

"Collarbone," Antonia says.

"Spine," Jon says in unison.

"Make up your minds."

Jon pulls down his shirt collar slightly to reveal the bloodstained dressing. The guard moves the detector over the area, confirming the prosthesis story.

They follow the man out to a yard on the far side of a glass door that has a crack running from top to bottom. It's not one of those cracks caused by a sudden change in temperature but by a sudden mood change, together with the application of a size-ten boot.

"Wait here," the man says, indicating a wooden bench. It's beneath an awning but is soaking wet as the rain is now accompanied by a blustery, howling wind. Jon and Antonia stand tight up against the wall, arms folded, squinting.

At the end of the yard looms a huge concrete watchtower. All of its powerful strobe lights are blazing. Three thousand watts, color temperature 5,700 K. There's no room for warmth or lies in one of those beams, and the rain only sharpens the edges.

Antonia is fidgeting nervously.

"What's the matter?" he asks.

"This isn't a good place for me, Jon."

"Come on. You've been inside a prison before, right?"

She slowly shakes her head.

Jon has, more than once. Enough to become desensitized to it. Although he recalls the first time very vividly. The sounds, the bars, the smells. The despair.

"Relax. You'll get used to it. It's just another building. A few locks, a few guards."

He doesn't mention the inmates, for obvious reasons. But it turns out he's got the wrong idea.

"You've got the wrong idea," she says.

"So enlighten me, sweetie."

Antonia points a trembling finger at her temple, not quite touching it, as if afraid of what's inside her head.

"In here. There are monkeys in here."

Something in her voice makes Jon lay off the jokes, the quips, the funny looks. He has heard that tone before, in another deserted yard. A gray, depressing place at the British school in Madrid. The day she introduced him to her son from a distance. The day she first opened up to him.

And so Jon says nothing as the seconds stomp by in steel-tipped boots, while the wind whips swirling rain in their faces.

But she doesn't explain, and so he has no choice.

"They frighten you?"

She shakes her head again.

"They help me. They show me things. Draw my attention to details. Too many sometimes."

Another silence. Or what passes for one, amid the worsening storm.

"Don't worry, I know they're not real. They're figments of my mind. The way it processes information to enable me to make sense of it. Normally, they're calm. But . . ."

She falls silent and stares into the distance. Jon has seen that look before. The same day he asked her what they'd done to her. And she couldn't and wouldn't tell him.

"In a place like this, they become agitated," Jon suggests.

"That . . . is what I was trained for. Murder scenes, places with lots of criminals. It rouses all the monkeys."

Jon doesn't need Antonia to tell him she's never shared this with anyone before. He is overcome by a strange combination of emotions.

Pleased for her because she's been able to open up.

Hatred for the people who have caused her so much pain.

Pride at being the first to be told.

And something else, floating on top like a turd in a swimming pool.

A growing resentment toward her. Because Antonia Scott's mere existence has complicated his life to an absurd degree.

"Can't you control it?" he asks, trying to keep the exasperation from his voice.

"It's very difficult."

"Hence the pills."

"But I'm done with them."

Antonia shakes her head, wrapping her arms around her shoulders as if to hug herself. Jon, usually so keen to help her perform a task that requires two people, this time doesn't have the inner strength to force himself to force her.

"Well, as Amatxo says, it's up to you now."

Disappointed, Antonia looks away.

It must have been extremely difficult for her to make this confession. Maybe she was expecting a different response from Jon, one he's incapable of giving her right now. And isn't even sure he should. He has seen what she can achieve through willpower alone, steering clear of the chemicals.

Jon has also seen enough addicts in his time to know that other people's compassion is what feeds their self-pity.

He once came across a guy who had overdosed in an alleyway near Calle San Francisco. Face down in a puddle, the tube still tied round his arm. There was a candy wrapper next to his mouth, where a couple of cockroaches had decided to spend the night. When Jon swept his flashlight beam over the blue-and-red wrapper, they went scuttling off.

The guy's mother arrived. She cried silently and without producing any tears—she couldn't have had any left—and then, leaning on the young police officer, she said:

"If only I hadn't felt so sorry for him before."

This is why Jon says nothing now.

But that's no solution, either, because Antonia has a habit of retreating into silence, like the cockroaches in the candy wrapper.

Which is why what happens next comes as such a surprise.

"I'm going to explain to you how I feel. Pull your stomach in," she says, taking hold of Jon's elbow and placing his hand on his belly.

Inspector Gutierrez might have been less startled if she'd kicked him in the balls. He might.

"Hey, I know this suit is a bit small on me. But it's not that I'm fat," he manages to say.

"It's not that. Do as I say."

Jon does as she says.

"That's too much," she says, guiding Jon's diaphragm outward with her hand. "As if you had enough breath left for half a sentence."

Jon relaxes his stomach a little.

"Now stay like that."

At first, it's easy. But as the seconds pass, he understands what Antonia is trying to convey. It's becoming increasingly hard for him to keep his stomach taut. Suddenly, it takes every ounce of his attention; he can no longer breathe naturally and feels his enormous lungs gasping for air.

"Is it like this all the time?"

She nods. All the time. Each and every waking moment, she has to keep up her guard. That invisible muscle coiled inside her brain.

Jon is unable to feel sorry for her just then—although he will, a few hours later, at the most inopportune moment—because they're interrupted by footsteps crossing the yard.

MADRID, JUNE 14, 2013

The tall, thin man rubs his eyes from sheer fatigue. The day is nearly over, although as far as he is concerned, it ended after the second interview.

He is on the psychology faculty at Complutense University. Nowhere better to camouflage their tests and for nobody to suspect these aren't student practicals. And the setting is appropriate. A white, windowless room with temperature controls and a two-way mirror. A control cabin and loudspeakers.

"I've had enough," the tall, thin man says, still rubbing his eyes. "I'm going out for a cigarette."

"You should quit."

"It's never the right time to quit."

"There's this new technique. Acupuncture. It cured my boyfriend's habit in just three sessions."

"Didn't you say there was one more candidate?"

His assistant calls in the last candidate, not before looking at him with mock exasperation.

The tall man likes her. She is a good person. A skylark: one of those who arrive at work fresh as a daisy after running five kilometers, who always see the positive side of things and say goodbye with a big smile on their face, already looking forward to coming in to work the next day. It's hard to think of anyone more despicable.

His impression of her has improved over time. There are days when he almost doesn't want to throttle her together with the other idiots, eggheads, and oddballs who have passed through there. Over seven hundred of them.

Closer to eight hundred, in fact.

But none as promising as the second contender that day.

Candidate 794.

In the nick of time, thinks the tall, thin man.

He's well aware the big shots in Brussels were ready to give him a kick up the ass. And that pissed him off. Prior to this, he'd spent his whole life with his nose in a book. For the most part absorbing other people's ideas. Better at copying than creating. And so when they invited him to take part in the Red Queen project, he jumped at the chance, eyes tight shut. Until a few hours earlier, he had been wallowing in his failure.

But 794 changed all that.

Antonia Scott, thinks the tall, thin man. *I must start getting used to the name.*

Maybe she's the one. Maybe she's the candidate the Red Queen project in Spain needs. He has a hunch, which is something that rarely happens with him. He's not exactly known for his fertile imagination. He's more of an accountant than an artist. On a scale of one to ten, one being a tax inspector and ten Julio Iglesias, the tall, thin man would be the desk calculator.

Hunches and whisky shots have something in common: the less accustomed you are to them, the greater their effect. So he's ready to stop looking and take a chance on candidate 794.

"Can't we skip the last one?"

"It'll only take a minute. We can't have made her come here for nothing. . . ."

He nods. After all, what difference does a few minutes make? It's not as if he has anybody waiting for him at home.

"Send in No. 798."

The woman is slender. Medium height, smartly dressed. Perfectly manicured. Probably under twenty-five. Her face has a kindly look.

No, not kindly, he thinks.

Friendly.

"Good afternoon," says the tall man, pressing the button on the intercom connecting the cabin with the observation room. "I'm going to present you with a hypothetical scenario. All your answers will count toward your final score in this study. We're asking you to give it your best shot, okay?"

The woman nods.

"Fine, let's make a start," says the tall, thin man, beginning to read the text on his screen. After a week of this, he knows the opening almost by heart. "You're the captain of the oil rig *Kobayashi Maru* situated on the high seas. It's nighttime, and you're enjoying a tranquil sleep. All of a sudden, your assistant wakes you. The emergency lights are flashing, the alarm bells ringing. There's a collision alert. An oil tanker is heading toward you."

The woman remains silent, staring straight at the mirror. She hasn't removed her coat and is still clutching her bag.

"Now it's your turn," says the tall, thin man.

"Do we have a boat available?" the woman asks. She speaks hurriedly, as if she doesn't enjoy talking and wants to get it over with.

Her question takes the man by surprise.

Almost everyone asks about the boat eventually, of course. Once they realize there's no way to contact the tanker advancing relentlessly toward them and they can't avoid a collision. Once they realize the rig is doomed, they think about saving the people on it. It's the classic response to an impossible scenario: backtrack until you run out of options and all you can do is surrender.

"Nobody ever asks about the boat first," his assistant says in astonishment.

"So much the better. At least we can go home sooner."

The software has been designed to respond dynamically to the candidate's input, changing the scenario to make it increasingly challenging. Marks are also given for original answers or the capacity to improvise.

"Yes," the tall, thin man replies, pressing the intercom button. "They have a lifeboat."

"What size is it?"

Because she has asked this question now, the software generates a different question than if she had done so several minutes later.

"Ninety feet," says the assistant.

"I'm no expert about boats, but that seems pretty big to me. Do we have any explosives on the rig?"

This question is far less common.

In fact, the tall, thin man hasn't heard it asked once.

But the software has an answer for it, which he passes on, slightly bemused.

"Good," she says, after thinking it over a few moments. "In that case, I pack the prow of the lifeboat with the ton and a half of explosives and order a crew member to steer it at the side of the oil tanker heading toward us."

There's a stunned silence in the control cabin. When the assistant has collected herself, she enters this new information into the computer. Of course, the exercise is purely theoretical. Yet they both had the feeling it was completely for real.

The tall, thin man presses the intercom button but says nothing. For a few moments, only the faint sound of static comes through the loudspeakers in the observation room.

"May I ask how you reached that conclusion?" he says after a lengthy pause.

"It's simple. There are more people on the oil rig than on the oil tanker. It's the most logical outcome," the woman says casually.

Later, much later, Mentor will recall an infinite number of details about this instant.

The woman's tone of voice.

Her icy stillness.

The fact she never once let go of her bag or removed her coat.

Her eyes, fixed on the mirror.

Most of these details, nearly all of them, were more of a projection than a true memory. A rewriting of the past with the benefit of hindsight. Or with its drawbacks, such as guilt, remorse, the agony of seeing it right there in front of you, and yet being unable to alter it.

But for the moment, the tall, thin man has something quite different in mind. Because what's going on here hasn't happened before in any of the countries participating in the project.

He isn't even listening to his assistant.

"She's achieved the highest score," the woman is saying in disbelief. "According to the programmers, only one person in twenty-three million would give that response."

Two Red Queens? Could that be possible?

"I'd like to discuss a job offer with you," he says, pressing the intercom button again.

On the other side of the two-way mirror, the woman smiles for the first time. It's a mere crease at the corner of her mouth. Calculated, like all her expressions. As if she'd checked her budget and decided she could afford the expense.

"I look forward to hearing it, *Señor* . . ."

"You can call me Mentor."

12

FOOTSTEPS

"I'm the warden," says a lean, middle-aged woman with deep-set eyes as she comes up to them. She doesn't look too happy. Nor does she introduce herself by name or shake their hands. Her mouth is set in a thin, hard line.

"We appreciate you receiving us so late," Jon says, holding up his hand by way of a greeting. This is the gesture he uses when dealing with surly people, except he usually opens his police badge as he does so. The badge he has left in the boxes at security. The snap of leather as he flaps it shut helps get introductions over with.

"You're damn right, Inspector. I was on my way home, and because of you, I had to turn back."

Jon has been in this situation a couple of times. People who enjoy their quota of power and are used to giving orders in their little world suddenly receive a call one day. Not from their immediate boss, who they're used to arguing with. They have a relationship, friendly or not, and in relationships there's always give-and-take.

What Mentor does is put a call through to the boss's boss. Sometimes even higher up.

Jon wonders which string he pulled this time. Possibly the top civil servant. Or the justice minister. A polite but matter-of-fact conversation. A vague promise to remember the name of the person in question. A hasty goodbye that leaves no room for negotiation or objection.

In exchange for which we get an open door and enough bile to fill a swimming pool.

* * *

In a similar instance, Antonia had evoked a phrase used by Amazonian indigenous groups in Brazil. *When the river is full of piranhas, the alligator swims on its back.*

"From a behavioral and anatomical point of view, it's untrue, but you get the idea."

Jon did. What the expression didn't explain was what you did when the river had an alligator with a chic bucket bag and a trouser suit. An alligator you've kept from its dinner and the finale of *MasterChef*.

"It's an urgent case, señora. Please accept our apologies for any inconvenience we've . . ."

The warden turns abruptly on her heel, which Jon and Antonia interpret as an invitation to follow her.

"The sooner you're done, the sooner you leave. The inmate is waiting for you in Room Six."

They pass through several steel-barred doors. One has a guards' cabin alongside it, the others open as they approach when the warden looks into the cameras located above her.

She barely halts at each of the doors, as if she doesn't see them, as if they simply don't exist. She just keeps striding through the endless empty passageways. Her wooden-soled shoes resonate on the green linoleum with the firm, regular beat of a metronome. A rather idiosyncratic one, because for some reason her right shoe (*click*) makes a different sound from her left (*clack*).

The resulting

clickclackclickclackclickclack

is so aggravating, Jon is worried he could go crazy. A sidelong glance at Antonia, walking erect beside him and keeping pace with him, confirms it must be worse for her.

"How many inmates are there here, señora?" says Jon in an attempt to drown out the sound of her shoes.

"Why? Are you planning on dragging someone else out of bed now that you're here?"

"As I already explained . . ."

"Prison life is about *rou-tines*. Strict timetables, ironclad schedules. Discipline is the punishment. Any change, any alteration to the *rou-tine*, even if it involves somebody else, is a reprieve from that punishment."

"I thought your job was to rehabilitate," Antonia says calmly.

Without slackening her pace, the warden turns her head and glances at Antonia over her shoulder.

"Oh, please, don't spout such crap, you're a police officer."

In the awkward silence that ensues, the warden's footsteps ring out even louder. Jon decides to apologize on Antonia's behalf.

"My colleague has a quirky sense of humor."

Antonia opens her mouth to protest, but Jon gestures to her to keep quiet. Unaware of this exchange, the warden continues.

"We have over a thousand inmates, including three serial killers, eleven terrorists, eighty-four serial rapists, and sixteen pedophiles. Plus the handful of corrupt politicians you've probably seen on television playing cards. This isn't a play school, Inspector, it's a prison. Everyone here has a debt to pay."

They reach the final door. Unlike the others, this one doesn't open as they approach. This one remains firmly shut.

"This is F-block. The toughest cellblock in the prison. The dregs of society are in here. The hardest part of our job isn't keeping them locked up. It's making sure they don't kill us, or each other."

A guard appears on the far side of the security door. He has a key around his neck that he uses to unlock it. After letting them through one by one, he locks the door again and shuts himself behind the tempered glass of his cabin.

"We were told Blázquez is a model prisoner."

"That's one way of looking at it," the warden retorts with a smirk before opening the door to Room Six. "Three of my staff have had to stay late tonight to guarantee your safety. I can't afford to pay them overtime, so please be quick."

The door clangs shut behind Jon and Antonia. Chained to a metal table, the man in front of them bears no resemblance to the photograph they looked at on their way there.

To start with, he has lost all his hair. They understand instantly why he used to wear it long: his ears are two lumps of hot wax.

His body mass has suffered the same fate as his hair. Without steroids, the skin on his arms hangs flaccidly. Even sitting down, his belly protrudes beneath his T-shirt. But worst of all is his face. Jon is familiar with this jailbird "look," that of people who have learned some hard lessons. The split eyebrow, the scars on his scalp, the flattened nose. Blázquez has aged ten years.

This isn't an innocent man's face, thinks Jon. Suddenly, he's afraid Antonia's shot in the dark is nothing but one humongous waste of time. He tries hard not to look at his watch, which feels three kilos heavier and fifty degrees hotter.

"Señor Blázquez," says Antonia, sitting down opposite him. "I'm Inspector Scott, and this is Inspector Gutiérrez."

WHAT THEY DID NEXT

The walls of the room are painted black, but it's filled with light. Walls and ceiling are lined with insulating material so thick it's soundproof. When Mentor speaks through the loudspeakers, his voice seems to be coming from everywhere at once.

Candidate 798 is sitting in the lotus position in the center of the room. She's wearing a white T-shirt and black pants. She's barefoot. The air in the room is cold, although that can change at any moment. Mentor controls the temperature as he sees fit, to complicate matters.

"You have left your driving permit at home. You fail to stop at a level crossing, you ignore a yield sign, and you go down a one-way street the wrong way for seven blocks. A traffic cop is following you, but he makes no attempt to stop you. Why not?"

"Because I'm on foot," the woman responds instantaneously.

"Easy. Open your eyes."

The woman looks at the huge black screen in front of her. An image flashes across it: two groups of people are about to cross at a stoplight.

"What do you see?"

The woman's eyes scan the image at high speed, instantly homing in on the discrepancy.

"On one sidewalk, there are only men, on the other, only women."

"Too easy and too slow."

Beneath the screen is a chronometer with red digits that measures the time to within thousandths of a second. It shows 03:138. Three seconds and a hundred and thirty-eight milliseconds.

"A hundred couples live in a village. If each inhabitant has two children, and twenty-three of them die, how many people are there in the village?"

The woman is exhausted; she has hardly had any sleep. Mentor demanded she do six hours of memory tests, repeating prime numbers. She hesitates.

"Six hu . . . No. Five hundred and seventy-seven."

The numbers stop at 04:013.

"Too slow. You're not progressing fast enough."

"I need to rest!"

The woman's eyelids are heavy; she feels lightheaded. Once again, Mentor is playing with the oxygen levels in the room. For the first time, she wonders whether she's doing enough to achieve her goal. Whether she's up to the challenge. It's not as if anybody's waiting for her at home. Or that she has something more important to do.

She wants this. She needs this.

She feels sure of herself. More sure of herself than ever before.

Mentor constantly speaks to her about achieving her full potential. About being able to do things nobody else can do, to go further than anybody has ever gone before. And she agrees, as if his every word were a thought that had occurred to her first. She'd do anything to please him, earn his admiration, his praise.

But she's tired.

"If only I could—" she starts to say.

She doesn't finish her sentence. The door opens, and three men in blue overalls enter. Bewildered, the woman turns, but doesn't have time to protest. One of the men puts her in a shoulder lock and takes her down, while the other presses her head to the floor.

The third is holding a syringe.

When he enters the woman's field of vision, she suppresses a cry, halfway between relief and triumph. She knew this was going to happen. She's been begging Mentor for it for a long time. Even so, she resists, puts up a fight. Because she knows he expects it of her.

The observation room is no longer at Complutense, but somewhere much smaller and more discreet, in an industrial zone close to the airport. Mentor is talking with a small, bald, half-blind octogenarian in a plaid jacket who has the shakes. The old man doesn't look in good shape.

For a long time now, he has been slaloming downhill on the slope of life.

But age can be deceptive. This man is possibly the greatest neuro-chemist of his generation. His name would figure among the candidates for a Nobel Prize if he weren't slightly deranged.

"This is the second time you've observed the procedure. You should feel more relaxed about it by now," says Dr. Nuno, noting his colleague's unease.

Mentor presses his nicotine-stained fingers against the glass and watches as the men inject the woman. Only then does he reply.

"There are some things you never get used to, Doctor."

"Such as getting up early, correct? This is something that we hypo-tensives never manage to become accustomed to."

Mentor refrains from mentioning the subtle difference between the time you get out of bed in the morning and having to watch a human being have their brain injected with an experimental drug, even if they have proved a more-than-willing volunteer.

"You ought to be proud of yourself," Nuno goes on. "Spain was lagging behind on the Red Queen project. Those at the top were, shall we say, none too pleased with your lack of progress . . ."

As if I didn't know that.

"Then all of a sudden, you find not one but two viable candidates. You've caused a bit of a stir in Brussels, you know . . ."

That I didn't know.

"'Our Spanish Mentor is unsure of himself,' they said. They were afraid you'd decided to put forward two candidates to disguise how long it took you to find just one."

Which is partly true.

"There were rumors. Nobody had ever proposed two candidates simultaneously and with such conviction. A number of people were calling for a thorough check, shall we say . . ."

In other words, they wanted to give me a good kick in the ass.

"However, after the intervention on 794 last week—"

"Scott. Antonia Scott," Mentor cuts in.

"To me, they're numbers," says Dr. Nuno with a wave of his hand, as though dispersing candle smoke. "And numbers are what I wish to discuss with you. The early results are very promising."

Nuno has been shut away with Antonia for over an hour, carrying out all manner of tests on her. Mentor wasn't supposed to be able to listen in, but naturally, he did. He doesn't like anybody to come anywhere near his people without him being there.

Even if only to feel guilty at seeing them suffer.

"What I'm trying to tell you is that my report to Brussels will be highly complimentary. All the more so if your second candidate's results are even half as good as those of your first. Pure and simple."

"Pure and simple," Mentor repeats grimly.

He turns around. In the room, the two men have released the woman. She doesn't seem very aware of what's happening to her. Indeed, she'll scarcely recall the procedure she herself was so eager to undergo. Later on, fragments will come back, images that ignore the fact that she asked for this. They will focus solely on the pain and resentment she felt afterward. In the meantime, she remains curled up on the floor, staring into space, her arms shuddering slowly.

"They still don't know about each other, correct?"

"That's right. We have a protocol that ensures they never bump into one another. They can only access the compound accompanied. They're taken straight to the training module, where they're kept under constant supervision."

Nuno nods approvingly.

"Like in the high-class brothels in Lisbon."

"I wouldn't know. Are we done?" asks Mentor, who is keen to go home.

Nuno adjusts his spectacles on the bridge of his nose and gives a faint smile. He extracts a manila envelope from his briefcase and hands it to Mentor.

"I already have one of those," Mentor says without extending his hand. The same way someone might give the cold shoulder to those charity thugs who accost you in the street insisting you sign up to Médecins Sans Frontières.

"Not like this one."

Mentor reluctantly takes the envelope. Inside is a ring binder. As he leafs through the contents, the color drains from his face.

"This . . . is very different from the methods we're using on Scott."

"She is also a very different candidate."

"What's that supposed to mean?"

Once more, Dr. Nuno smiles.

Mentor wishes he'd wouldn't.

"You'll find out soon enough, my friend. It will certainly be . . . interesting."

13

A GUFFAW

Jon leans against the wall, positioning himself where he can see both Antonia and Blázquez. The prisoner looks from one to the other and then addresses Jon.

"What is it you want?"

"We're here to talk to you about Raquel Planas Mengual, Señor Blázquez," says Antonia.

Blázquez still keeps his head turned toward Jon.

"Why now? In the middle of the night?"

Jon doesn't reply. It's obvious what's going on.

"Look at me, Señor Blázquez," orders Antonia.

The prisoner turns his body toward Antonia. Just a fraction. Not the whole way.

"I was asleep," he says after a while.

"We're sorry to wake you, Señor Blázquez, but this is an urgent matter."

Blázquez has on a pair of presentable-looking jeans. He tries to reach into his right pocket, but the chain on his handcuffs won't let him, and so he's forced to stand up to retrieve his cigarettes. A crumpled pack of Fortunas with the lighter tucked inside.

"Raquel's dead," he says after puffing out smoke. "Where's the urgency?"

Antonia chooses her words with great care.

The slightest slipup could alert Blázquez. He might ask for a lawyer or simply refuse to cooperate. They don't have time to negotiate or anything to offer. Nor can they tell him the truth.

Mlakundhog.

In Javanese, a language spoken by seventy-five million people in Indonesia, the lightness of one who walks noiselessly on eggs.

"We're investigating a case that's related to yours, Señor Blázquez. If our suspicions are correct, we may be able to help you."

"How could you possibly help me?"

Don't say he's innocent, thinks Jon.

"I can't tell you that, Señor Blázquez."

The inmate takes another drag, reflects, then looks at Jon again.

"Don't you have anything to say?"

Jon gives such a big shrug he can feel the stitches pull on the wound in his neck.

The pain causes him to give an involuntary grimace, which Blázquez interprets as a sneer.

"You're messing with me, right? That's what this is about. Because of the complaints I've made. The letters I've sent. Well, I'm going to keep on sending them. I won't shut up about what they're doing to me in here."

"What are they doing to you, Señor Blázquez?"

"As if that weren't obvious," says Blázquez. Using the hand holding his cigarette, he makes a semicircular gesture with his thumb to point out the old and new wounds on his head.

Antonia looks at her colleague without a word.

Jon understands.

There's been a change of plan. If what Blázquez's injuries appear to suggest is true, he'll struggle to talk about it with a woman. Especially someone like him.

"Víctor," Jon says, sitting down opposite him, "are you having problems in here?"

Blázquez instantly turns toward Jon. Something about his attitude—or lack of one—appears to be screaming out for help.

Now Antonia gets to her feet and goes over to the wall. She stands with her back turned, pretending to make a call, speaking in hushed tones.

"I'm the vic," says Blázquez. "That's my problem."

Jon's unfamiliarity with prison slang shows on his face.

"The Block-F ho. The punching bag," Blázquez explains. "There's always one, you know? Always."

His hands tremble as he tries to light another cigarette. Jon goes to his aid, chasing the tip of his cigarette with the flame.

Now it all fits.

Block F is where they keep the badasses. If they don't have a weakling they can beat up on, they attack one another and end up dead. Deaths don't look good in the six-monthly review. In fact, they lower a prison's rating hugely.

Jon has heard similar stories about prisons like Basauri, Nanclares, and El Dueso, where lifers are put. Stories similar to those you might hear from a zookeeper, because there's no big difference. If you have a wolf on every block, he becomes king, and things get out of hand. If you keep all the wolves together, you're constantly checking asses for blades. Because otherwise, they end up in someone else's neck.

As a result, they keep a couple of sheep on every block. The wolves can quench their thirst for blood without it becoming a scandal. Or worse still, a headline.

"Looking at you, anyone would think you were one of the badasses," says Jon.

It's a lie, of course. But Jon can't help seeing the alpha male in the photograph superimposed on the physical wreck in front of him. Or Raquel Planas Mengual's blood on the floor.

Well, I'll be damned if this woman-killer hasn't chosen me as his savior, reflects Jon. *If so, he's up shit creek without a paddle*, he adds with characteristic finesse.

"I'm not like them, Inspector. I shouldn't be in here."

"Don't tell me. You're just an easygoing guy trying to make a living for yourself and your family. Wrongfully accused. Isn't that so?"

"I didn't kill Raquel. But I don't care, nobody cares. I just want to do my time and vamoose, you understand? But the way things are, I won't get out of here alive. They've got it in for me."

"Who are 'they'?"

"Everyone. Everyone. But especially Cuervajo from Asturias, who thinks he's a hard case. And his friend Sergei."

"Russian?"

"No way, he's from Moratalaz, he's nuts. Who cares where he's from? He and the Asturian are after my blood."

"You must have given them some reason."

"Didn't you hear what I said? They don't need a reason. It's that bitch outside who needs a spectacle. To provide some entertainment in the yard and the canteen."

"That's not a very polite way to speak about the warden, Víctor."

"Don't talk to me about polite, I've been plenty polite: 'Please, ma'am, they broke my nose. Please, ma'am, they broke my arm. Please, ma'am, help me.' Jack shit is all I get."

Jon looks at Antonia, who still has her back to them. She seems unwilling to step in. He wonders if she's even able to. He notices a slight tremor in the fingers of her left hand, despite using it to cup the other one as she pretends to be speaking on her cell phone.

"Is she your boss?" Blázquez whispers to Jon.

"My partner."

"You can tell her there's no signal in here, so she can stop pretending."

Inspector Gutiérrez looks at him open-mouthed, face as red as beetroot for borscht. Then, unable to stop himself, he laughs. It's a brief, controlled guffaw, a reluctant guffaw. The first since he's been walking around with death screwed to his skeleton. The pure, limpid sound floats for an instant in the pit of despair in which they find themselves (which matches the one inside Jon) before dissolving like a drop of water in a bucket of tar. And yet it leaves something behind. A trace of lightness.

Jon vows he will never, ever repeat to Antonia Scott what Blázquez just said—not if he lives a thousand years, or until White's deadline runs out.

Or until I have to bring her down off her high horse, thinks Jon, still smiling to himself. *Whichever happens first.*

Just then, Antonia breaks off the occasional *ahas* and *ahums* she is making into her imaginary cell phone discussion. She turns around and joins the conversation.

"Here's what we're going to do, Víctor. If you answer our questions, I'll make sure they transfer you to a 'respect module.'"

Jon looks at Antonia. He can't believe what he's just heard. His instinct is to veto the offer, but it's too late: her words have already made Blázquez's face light up. A respect module is the most coveted place in a prison. Safe, clean, where often inmates have a cell to themselves. The doors are open for two hours a day. Anybody starting a fight is sent back to a normal cellblock, so everyone is on their best behavior.

There's one small snag, however.

Which is why Blázquez squints suspiciously at them.

"You can't do it. I have a homicide conviction. And a history of domestic abuse. They won't agree to it."

Jon thinks it's a dreadful idea. The guy is said to have murdered his partner. And yet his colleague here is making promises.

"You'd be amazed."

"I want it in writing. When they move me, I'll talk to you."

"It's not that simple," says Jon, shaking his head.

Blázquez leans back, folding his arms.

"I knew it . . ."

"You'll just have to trust us."

"Go with the flow, right? They gave me that spiel more than once already."

Jon gets to his feet and seizes Antonia by the arm.

"Can we talk outside?"

Antonia angrily wrenches herself free of Jon's hold, but accompanies him into the corridor. The warden is leaning against the wall, waiting for them. She has a look of concentration on her face and is staring at her cell phone screen. To judge by the "Divines" and "Cutes" audible from her earbuds, Inspector Gutiérrez guesses she isn't exactly working.

"Have you finished already?" she asks, continuing the game.

"Not yet, ma'am. We'll let you know as soon as we have," says Jon. And then, addressing Antonia before she has a chance to remonstrate with him about the way he dragged her out the room:

"What was all that about?"

Antonia is very tense and once again has that distant, lost look in her eyes.

"Don't ever touch me again when I'm not expecting it. Especially not in here." Of course she wasn't going to let that pass. "We can't tell him the truth, Jon. That would leave us at his mercy."

"And the best way to get him to talk is to give him what you promised?"

"Why not? We came here on the premise that he's innocent."

Jon purses his lips and frowns. Doubts are still swirling round his mind.

"We don't know that. We only know what White told you. What if

Blázquez is one of White's stooges? Someone whose release he desperately wants us to secure?"

Antonia looks at Jon. Stares at the metal door to Room Six. Then back at Jon.

"Granted, the guy isn't exactly Mr. Wonderful," concedes Inspector Gutiérrez after a moment's thought.

"And even if he were, we don't have time for anything except to make it safely through the night. That's why I didn't tell you anything about the case beforehand."

I'm the one running out of time. The decisions should be mine as well, thinks Jon.

But that's not what he says, because now the stitches aren't just pulling, they're throbbing.

Antonia goes over to the warden, who is still absorbed in her video game.

"Excuse me," she says.

"One moment," the other woman replies. "I've been trying all week to get to the next level. And there's no way."

Antonia takes the phone from her so deftly the warden is still staring at her open palm before she even realizes it's gone.

"Hey!"

Antonia isn't listening. She's busy moving her finger back and forth across the screen, crushing candies. Five seconds later, she hands the phone back. On the screen, it says: LEVEL COMPLETE.

Antonia waits for the warden to pick her jaw up off the floor, then says:

"If it's not too much bother, we'd like to ask you a favor."

VÍCTOR

Raquel and I were in love. Like really in love. Well, me more than her, I guess. We met at my gym, a couple of years before . . . before that, you know what. She was living with her mom. That skinny old bitch, she was a real cow, going to Mass every day. No, we didn't move in together. Sure, she stayed at my place many nights. But we couldn't live together. No, it was because of her mother. How often? Twice a week, I guess. Yeah, at my place. Sure, we spent weekends together. All the time. She liked traveling, she liked it when I gave her presents. Her job? Up and down. She made good money sometimes, other times not so good. She was an interior designer, but the work wasn't regular. She was too dedicated to each project. No, I don't mean that. She . . . threw herself into it, you know? I used to say to her, "Raquel, you need to plan things, otherwise you lose money," but did she listen, like hell she did, that was her all over. Jealous? Me? Jealous of what? No, it was all the same to me. I wasn't her keeper. Okay, if I saw some guy at the gym ogling her ass on the exercise bike, then yeah, I'm only human, right? But . . . no, no. I didn't mean it like that. No way . . . No, I never said anything to her about it. Sure, we fought, but I never laid a finger on her. No, not that day either. She . . . She'd been acting weird. We kind of fell out, but it was no big deal. She was a bit crazy sometimes, the way chicks can be, but we didn't . . . No, look, it wasn't serious. Like when you say things on WhatsApp, and maybe you go too far. But it was no big deal. It happened on June 6 . . . we hadn't seen each other for three days. No, that wasn't strange. We'd already . . . yeah, once. She was on the rag then and acting weird the way chicks do, but I don't need to tell you that,

Inspector . . . So I figured this time around, it was the same, maybe she needed some space, time to herself. A lot of messages? I don't know . . . a few. Look, I had to show I cared. That's what she said to me. "I love you because you're like Don Quixote, ha ha ha. He's loco but he cares, ha ha ha." Yeah, she was . . . Fuck. Sorry. Yeah, Raquel made me laugh a lot. So okay, I sent her a ton of messages on WhatsApp, is that a crime? (*Silence.*) Ah, I didn't know. But hey, she messaged me back, well, that same evening, she said, "Stop by my mom's place, I need to talk to you," so of course I went. My gym is just around the corner, on Calle de Alberto Aguilera. Yeah, it's a franchise. No, I have several partners, and two investors. No, I studied physical education . . . Yeah, I put in the work, they put in the money. But I was good with people, building customer loyalty. There were lots of posh chicks, they go for guys like me with street cred. Sure, I'm from Estrecho. We're a decent bunch, maybe we didn't finish school, but we have the gift of the gab, and the chicks like that. Did I make it with them? No, no. I mean, personally, well, sure they all want to be able to say they've made it with the trainer, but no, I mean, no. Yeah, she messaged me and I went over. Sure I did, I had to show I cared.

14

A DOORWAY

At this point, Antonia interrupts Blázquez's story. In a great show of self-restraint, she has allowed him to get into the right mood, to open up, until he reaches the crucial part.

"Now I'd like you to slow down, Señor Blázquez. Give us as many details as you can."

"Okay, so I arrived at the apartment . . ."

"Before. Before that. You left the gym. Do you remember what time it was?"

"I don't have to remember. We have a clock-out system, it logs the time you scan your card. It was eight forty-three in the evening."

"All right. Now, step by step."

"I went out. I walked over to Raquel's place."

"Did you have your cell phone in your hand?"

"No, I don't think so . . . I had my hands in my pockets."

"What did you do when you got to the entrance? Did you press the buzzer?"

"I didn't have to. The porter was downstairs, the door was wedged open."

"So late?"

"They have porters twenty-four hours a day at her apartment, they do three shifts."

"I see. So you greeted him."

"No, well, yeah. I guess I nodded hello."

He's lying, thinks Jon. *For all his street savvy, the bastard's a snob.*

He sucks up to his superiors and tramples on people he thinks are beneath him.

"And then?"

"I went straight to the elevator, what else? I called it, I went up. When I got to the door, Raquel let me in."

"You didn't meet anyone on your way up?"

"No, no one."

"Did you ring the doorbell?"

"No, Raquel already had the door open. I guess she must have heard me coming."

"Describe Raquel to me."

"She has curly hair, she's quite tall, almost my height . . ."

"I mean at that moment. What did you see when she opened the door?"

"She was very pale. She didn't look good, like she was wiped out or something."

"Was she holding the door ajar or wide open?"

"Wide open. She let me in and told me to go into the living room."

"What did you do?"

"I tried to kiss her, but she pulled away. I walked into the living room. But then nature called, so I went to the bathroom."

"Before or after you were in the living room?"

"I went to the living room through one door and left by another one."

"Was there anyone else in the apartment?"

"No. It's a small place, we were alone."

"Did you walk past Raquel's room?"

"No, her room's in the middle. The bathroom is next to her mother's room."

"When you passed through the living room, did you notice anything?"

"I don't understand. You mean the couches, the dining room table?"

"Anything unusual. Anything that drew your attention."

Jon can't help but admire Antonia's extraordinary patience with Blázquez. He, on the other hand, is becoming exhausted as the minutes tick by. He glances anxiously at his watch. They've already used up four of the six hours White has allotted them. With only a hundred and twenty minutes left to live, Jon is tempted to use a more direct interrogation method on Blázquez. A style of boxing where one of the contenders has his hands tied behind his back.

As if she knows what's going through Jon's mind, Antonia spreads the fingers of her right hand, the one closest to him. She moves them very slowly up and down, barely a few inches. Jon isn't sure if she's bouncing an invisible ball or telling him to stay calm.

"No. I don't know. The TV was on."

"Any particular channel?"

"Telecinco."

"Was that unusual?"

"Raquel doesn't like television."

"What did you do after you left the living room?"

"I was heading for the bathroom when I heard Raquel in her bedroom. She let out a groan. I asked her if anything was wrong and walked down the hallway toward her."

"The one between the living room and the bedrooms."

"How do you know?"

"I saw the photos. Could you see Raquel from the hallway?"

"No, only when I reached her bedroom door. Then she practically jumped on me."

"She attacked you?"

"No. She grabbed hold of me. She told me to call an ambulance. That's when I saw blood on her hands."

"Only on her hands?"

"No. On her clothes as well. She'd been stabbed."

"Could you see inside Raquel's room from the hallway?"

"Yes. There was no one in there."

"What did you do next?"

"I called the emergency number."

"Immediately?"

"Yes, right away. I was nervous as hell, but I remember that."

"And then?"

"Raquel collapsed on the floor. And I . . . I ran."

A lengthy silence follows.

Jon tries not to move. Antonia likewise.

"Just to be clear, Señor Blázquez," she says after an eternity. "You ran out after you called the ambulance, leaving your girlfriend alone, bleeding to death on the floor."

The prisoner responds to Antonia's merciless summing up by cringing in his chair. He looks as if he wants to vanish into thin air. With the usual problems that entails.

"Why?" Jon asks.

Blázquez looks at him, looks at his hands, reaches for his cigarettes. The pack is empty, like his excuses. He scrunches it up until the cellophane stops crackling and all that remains on the steel table is a crumpled ball.

"I was scared, why do you think?"

"It's strange. The way you said that."

"What do you mean?"

"Failure to provide assistance to a person in need. Some men wouldn't be so quick to admit a thing like that."

They'd be too ashamed.

"It's been years. What I did hasn't changed. I have."

Inspector Gutiérrez has often wondered about what Víctor Blázquez has just said. About whether change is possible. And if it is, what's the motivation? Being behind bars, a beating in the showers. Or genuine remorse?

Of course, there's no way of knowing, and this is the tragedy of Jon's profession. Sadly, the police aren't the cure or the remedy. Merely the sweeper truck that picks up the pieces of something broken, pushing them to the side of the road. Allowing life to keep running as smoothly as possible.

In his first year at the police academy, whenever Jon entered the classroom, he was greeted by the same motto at the top of the whiteboard. It had been there forever, and the fading letters had to be retraced over and over. But it was etched on his brain.

Justice is to give each person their due.

During his first year on the beat, Jon came to see the motto as nothing more than a hollow phrase. Nobody could give Raquel Planas Mengual back what had been taken from her. He saw the true meaning of justice.

Justice isn't satisfaction, it's a movable truth. Because the first is impossible and the other is his job.

"Are you aware that what you've told us puts you in a very difficult situation?" he says.

"Really, Inspector, more difficult than this . . . ," Blázquez retorts, waving a hand at his surroundings.

"We're here because the possibility has arisen for us to help you. But you're not making it easy for us."

"I didn't kill her."

"Yet the two of you were alone in the apartment."

"I know. But I didn't kill her. I told the judge, I told the jury, and now I'm telling you."

"How do you explain it, then?"

"I can't," Blázquez says, shrugging his shoulders. "But I didn't kill her."

"So she stabbed herself?"

"The pathologist said she didn't."

"And you have no explanation."

"No."

"They found her blood on your body."

"Because she grabbed hold of me. I already told you that."

"What happened after you left, Víctor?"

"I ran toward the door. I said something out loud, I don't remember what."

Yes, you do.

"I went out into the hallway, I think I tripped over. I was dizzy. Honestly, I don't remember much."

"Did you take the stairs?" Antonia asks.

"No, it's on the seventh floor, I took the elevator."

Hearing this, Jon arches an eyebrow, but says nothing. It's Antonia who asks:

"Did you press the button for the elevator?"

"I pressed both. The one for the elevator and the one for the service elevator. To see which arrived first. That's when I ran into Raquel's mother. I knew it was her from her ugly white shoes. She saw me through the glass door, but by then, the service elevator had arrived. I got in before she got out of her elevator, and I went down."

Antonia jumps to her feet. She pushes her chair back so fast Jon has to grab it to stop it from tipping over.

She heads toward the door, but before going out, she wheels around in pure *Columbo* style.

"One last thing. Did Raquel own a raincoat?"

The prisoner looks at her, bewildered as much by her attitude as by her question.

"Not that I know of . . . But she was wearing one that day."

"How about you?"

"No, I didn't have a raincoat," he says with more conviction.

"That's all, Señor Blázquez," says Antonia, motioning to Jon. "Thank you for your help."

15

A SNORT

Antonia doesn't speak until she is clasping the car door handle.

"We've cracked it, Jon!"

It takes Jon a while to reply, the time he needs to catch his breath. He has sprinted behind Antonia all the way from the prison security checkpoint to the car, which was no easy feat.

She sure runs goddamn fast for someone with such short legs.

She's going that fast partly to flee the toxic environment of the prison and partly because of the manic energy that overwhelms her whenever she discovers a piece of the puzzle.

"Speak for yourself," he says, his voice ragged, as he climbs into the car and turns the ignition.

Excited and overwrought, Antonia isn't listening.

"We need to get back to Madrid as fast as possible. We're going to Santa Cruz de Marcenado."

"You don't say," says Jon, who is already heading in that direction.

When it comes to reeducating Antonia in the basic rules of human communication (such as, for example, that people around you can't read your mind), Jon follows a series of emotionally intelligent strategies, each more sophisticated than the last. In this instance, he chooses to curse her out loud.

Eighteen seconds into the treatment, Antonia manages to realize there's a problem. She takes a deep breath and succeeds in slowing her thoughts.

"I'm sorry," she says, although Jon doubts it's true.

She still seems to be inside her own head. But at least she's making the effort to pretend she isn't.

This touches Inspector Gutiérrez. He loves her sufficiently for him not to throttle her for a few more minutes.

"Let's begin at the beginning," Jon says. "You were right."

"About what?" she says innocently. Losing the points she's just earned.

Ay, Holy Mother. If this woman only knew how close she is to losing her life.

"It's obvious Blázquez didn't kill Raquel," says Jon. "Either that or he deserves six Oscars."

"I told you he was innocent. He was simply in the wrong place at the wrong time. He had a history of domestic violence. And it's possible he also hit Raquel."

"I'm saying he didn't kill her, not that he's innocent. He's a thug, a chauvinist, and a coward. Plus he's a liar. He spun us several yarns, tried to manipulate us to make himself look good, to come across as the victim," says Jon.

"None of which justifies keeping him locked up."

What sticks in Inspector Gutiérrez's craw isn't that Antonia is right. What's difficult is that not long before this, he was mad at her for something similar, but from the opposite side.

It's her attitude that hasn't changed.

Jon thinks murderers should die of fright and that cowardice is no excuse. Antonia agrees, but looks at the cost. If it means somebody is going to suffer unjustly, she'll tear up the bill.

Jon is not someone who gives up easily, and so he insists.

"Maybe Blázquez panicked, but he left Raquel to die. Or maybe he had something on him he didn't want the police to find, but the fact is he left Raquel to die."

"Failure to provide assistance to someone in need with extenuating circumstances. But he called an ambulance. . . ."

"He left her to die alone, Antonia. A woman he supposedly loved," says Jon.

In a low, solemn, drawn-out voice.

That's all he says and all he needs to say. It's the tone he'd use to talk about something unthinkable, such as a three-headed dog or wearing a navy blue shirt with a black sweater. It's self-evident.

"That's true. But he's already spent several years inside, and he's not doing too well."

"You've changed that by getting him transferred to a respect module."

"He didn't kill her, Jon."

"I know," Jon admits.

"We need to get him released."

"I know that too."

Justice isn't satisfaction. It's a movable truth. And that's our fucking job.

"Okay," he says, heaving a sigh, "so we've ruled out one person from Madrid; that means we only have three million suspects left."

"According to last year's census, Madrid has 3,397,174 inhabitants," Antonia informs him, always keen to help.

"Great, then let's do a house to house, shall we? We still have ninety minutes left to solve the murder before that bastard kills me."

Inspector Gutiérrez ends with a snort that hangs in the air between them. As the minutes he has left dip below three figures, his customary Basque sarcasm and resilience are beginning to falter.

"Jon," says Antonia after a while.

"What?"

"Trust me."

"Do you know who killed Raquel Planas Mengual?"

"No. I don't. But I know who does."

WHAT THEY DID NEXT

The test room has changed.

It's bigger now. The chair is anchored to the floor by twelve-centimeter screws. Black nylon straps hang from the ceiling. The broadest one is for her waist. The other four are for wrists and ankles. Each of them has an electrode at the tip, beyond the Velcro fasteners. The electrodes can discharge fifty volts.

Today is the tapes.

The woman doesn't care about the electrodes. Not that she remembers much about these training sessions. At the start, she sits at the table. In front of her are a glass of water and two capsules. She takes the red one as well as half a glass of water. She takes the blue one at the end. That's the one that wipes away her memories.

But not always.

For example, she remembers that a minute after taking the red capsule, two men in blue overalls hoisted her by the feet with the straps, her head hanging down.

They stand one on either side of her and start to yell in her ears. They insult her. Humiliate her. Spit at her.

Mentor's voice resounds through the loudspeakers.

"Let your mind rise above the noise."

The woman takes a deep breath and closes her eyes. She tries to close her mind to the yells and threats. One of the men has pulled out a knife and is holding it to her throat. Little by little as the drug begins to take effect, she begins to feed off the noise.

It fills her.

She focuses on the koan. An unanswerable question that Zen masters asked of their disciples centuries ago and which Mentor now poses before each session.

Her mind does rise above the noise, the commotion, her fear.

She opens her eyes.

The session begins.

An image appears on the screen in front of her. Eleven men in a line, looking at the camera. The image is on the monitor for less than a second.

"Which one has a tattoo on his neck?"

"Number three."

"Which might pose a threat?"

"Number eight. He has one hand behind his back."

"What color were number eight's suspenders?"

"Green." She falls into the trap before realizing that number eight wasn't wearing suspenders. The electric shock jolts her hands and feet, churning her insides until she almost throws up.

The tapes rise until her back and heels are almost touching the ceiling. The men shout again and shake her.

She lets out a yelp of frustration.

"Thought arises from a calm mind," Mentor cautions, "and thought is what you need to detect things. You don't even need a gun. And you certainly don't need anger. An angry mind never resolves anything. A calm one does."

"Quit the chat and get on with it," she snaps.

A fresh image appears on the screen. This time it shows numbers. Eight lines with thirteen numerals on each one.

Beneath the screen the chronometer comes on, just as the numbers disappear. The woman begins to repeat them as quickly as she can.

The chronometer stops.

09:313.

"Not a single mistake. This time, you've almost impressed me."

The tapes drop by twenty centimeters.

The rules are clear. Every correct answer, twenty centimeters down. If you touch the floor the session is over. If you get it wrong or don't answer quickly enough, you receive an electric shock and go up to the ceiling, canceling out all the progress you've made.

In the control room, Mentor realizes something that makes him shudder.

The woman hasn't stopped smiling since the session began. The sweat dripping from her brow clouds her eyes.

Only two and a half meters from the floor.

The smile is plastered on her face like herpes, and just as pleasant.

16

A MOTHER

By the time they reach the apartment building on Calle de Santa Cruz de Marce-
nado, it's almost midnight. Jon double-parks, and the two of them walk
toward the entrance.

Antonia has spent the last twenty minutes outlining the strategy
she's going to adopt. You could describe it as loosely stitched together.

"Assuming your theory is correct, we have less than an hour in
which to make her confess."

"We need to find a way to get to her."

"Any suggestions?"

"We don't have a profile or any backup; we have nothing. We'll have
to improvise."

Great, thinks Jon.

Even at night, the building Antonia and Jon are approaching is impressive. Everybody in Madrid knows it, though by different names.
The Edificio Princesa, or San Bernardo, or the home of the military. If
you're standing at Glorieta de Ruiz Jiménez, your eyes will inevitably be
drawn toward the imposing edifice studded with balconies and draped
in luxuriant vines.

Over fifty years after it was erected, the building—which has no official name—is one of Madrid's most iconic structures. Yet few people
are aware of the history behind it. The architect, Fernando Higueras,
was shunned by Francoists, who believed he was a communist, while
the communists labeled him a fascist for accepting the regime's money.
In the best Spanish tradition of forgotten geniuses, Higueras died alone

and in poverty. His masterpiece, whose staircase Antonia and Jon are now climbing, was the final nail in his coffin.

"This is where the old Hospital de la Princesa stood," explains Antonia as they reach the main entrance. "They demolished it in the seventies to build apartments for the military top brass."

Jon flashes his badge at the porter, who lets them in without a word. Not even to ask where they're going at this ungodly hour or why.

"Have the porters in Madrid lost their touch or what?"

"This place is a bit special," says Antonia, noticing his surprise.

"Have you been here before?"

"Once. To visit a contact of Mentor's. But yes, this is probably one of the few places where that badge you just flashed will open every door to you."

Hearing this, Jon's vague sense of satisfaction is replaced with suspicion—if any human being is a mass of contradictions, it's Inspector Gutiérrez. But the feeling soon evaporates.

The instant he looks up.

And he keeps on looking up as he walks.

Ironically, what you see from the traffic circle and Calle de Alberto Aguilera is the smallest part of the building. Inside, as Jon discovers, a pathway divides the block in two, making way for an enormous inner courtyard covered in balconies and enveloped in giant window boxes. The structure is made entirely of glass and concrete, circling down from the top floor to the inner courtyard, then widening out to make way for an underground garage that's open to the skies. The air, which is cold outside, is several degrees warmer in here. The traffic noise has gone, and all they can hear is the soft rustle of the vines.

"This is amazing," says Jon.

"The architect was branded a crackpot," says Antonia, opening the internal door of the entrance they are heading for.

By people shouting from out there, thinks Jon, quickening his pace. *Because nobody who has been inside this place would ever use that word.*

He follows Antonia into the building. At the far end of a short hallway lined with mirrors, there are two doors. One of glass, the other metal. An elevator and a service elevator.

Jon is immediately on guard.

"This is where it happened," he says.

Antonia presses the button of the big white elevator that is softly lit inside. It's relatively modern, no more than seven or eight years old. There's a separate button for the service lift, which is already on the first floor.

"Let's go up separately," Antonia says, opening the door to the elevator.

Jon takes the service lift—not that he's fat—and notices how different the interior is from what he glimpsed of the other one. Far less luxurious, with linoleum flooring and no mirrors.

He presses the button for the seventh floor. When he arrives, Antonia is already waiting for him.

"You took much longer," she says inscrutably.

Stepping out, they discover the doors to the apartments aren't next to the elevators but at the far end of a long corridor. Jon gazes down at the floor as he walks.

"Have you noticed?"

Jon grunts an affirmation.

Blázquez told them Raquel already had the door open when he arrived. And yet he didn't press the buzzer downstairs. Or the doorbell upstairs.

I guess she must have heard me coming.

There's thick green carpeting on the floor. The walls are clad with light oak paneling.

Jon's Italian shoes make no noise on the carpet.

And Blázquez's sneakers would make even less.

There are four doors. Two service entrances, two front doors. The two that correspond to Raquel Planas Mengual's apartment are on the right.

The doorbell has a pleasant tinkle. Quaint. Like a bronze bell, with a subtle pause between chimes.

It rings, but nobody comes to the door.

Jon tries again, calmly at first. Then more insistently. Finally, he keeps his finger on the bell, and when that doesn't work, he uses his fist. The alarmed neighbors open their door a crack, but speedily close it when Antonia waves her badge at them.

During his many years as a police officer, Jon has been able to observe a curious but surprisingly frequent phenomenon. Mentioning it to his colleagues, the smokers among them likened it to the bus that arrives just as you light your cigarette at the stop, thinking you have time.

In the same way just when you think the suspect isn't at home and you may have to break down the door, a voice comes from inside.

"Who is it at this time of night?"

"It's the police, Señora Mengual," says Jon, holding up his badge to the peephole.

"How do I know you aren't burglars?"

"Burglars don't go banging on doors and waking up all the neighbors, señora."

Confronted by this irrefutable logic, the woman opens the door a few inches, as far as the security chain allows. Jon makes to show her his credentials again, but Antonia beats him to it.

"I'm Lieutenant Scott of the military police," she says, flashing a green-and-yellow badge. "I'm here as an observer out of respect for your late husband."

Jon wonders how many badges Antonia carries around in her bag. And whether she arranges them by color. Knowing the way her mind works, it wouldn't surprise him if she'd memorized all the serial numbers, even though they're fake.

"Where did you study?"

"Toledo. Then I was with the armored corps at Badajoz."

"So was my husband."

"I'm sorry for your loss, señora."

The door closes, the chain slides back, the door opens.

"It's terribly late," the woman complains.

She's tall and skinny, brusque in her gestures. In her mid-sixties, but looks eighty. She has on a silk polka-dot dress. Jon notices she has buttoned it up wrong. From this, he deduces she was in her nightdress or dressing gown, probably in bed, possibly even asleep. The time she took coming to the door is the time she took to make herself look presentable.

"We're aware of that, señora. But this is an emergency. A matter of life and death, I assure you," says Antonia.

"Very well, come in."

Inside the narrow hallway is a side table with photographs of Raquel and a man in uniform. Jon recognizes the insignia of a lieutenant colonel. The frames are solid silver; they still have the tiny sticker on them.

A door in the hall leads to the bedrooms and the kitchen. Peering through it, Jon begins to make sense of what Blázquez told them. The apartment is compact and well designed, with very little wasted space.

If he didn't kill her and they were alone in the apartment, how the hell did it happen?

Jon turns to Antonia, who he assumes is asking herself the same question. But, from her darting eyes, shallow breaths, and the renewed tremor in her hand, he can see her brain is working overtime.

"I suppose you wouldn't be wanting tea or coffee at this hour," says the woman politely, but making it clear the answer she expects.

"Two cups of tea, if you'd be so kind," says Antonia in a bid to buy time they don't have.

The other door leads to the living room. The décor dates from the seventies. Parquet floor, ornamental chimney piece, glass dining table for when visitors stop by, which, to judge by the scuff marks on the floor, happens frequently.

At the far end is an old-fashioned television set, switched off. A DVD-VCR player. An antique *bargueño* cabinet, between two couches. Peeping out from underneath the Sunday supplements on the coffee table is a newspaper dating back several years. Further signs that life ground to a halt here a long time ago.

While the woman busies herself in the kitchen, Jon sneaks a look down the hallway. The woman's bedroom door is ajar. Her daughter's is closed.

Antonia slips between Jon and the wall. She opens the door.

An unmade bed. A computer. Dust on the shelves, the screen, the keyboard.

A floor rug is bent back where the door has caught the corner. It's an odd place for a rug.

Antonia doesn't need to lift it for Jon to know what it is hiding. The stains on the wood where her daughter's blood couldn't be removed, and never will. A scourer or other implement has left marks and taken off the varnish, making the stains even darker, especially around the joints.

It wouldn't come out even with sanding. It would have to be torn up, thinks Jon.

17

A LIVING ROOM

Antonia drops the corner of the rug, takes a last look around, and goes back when she hears the kettle whistle.

When the old lady comes into the living room carrying the tray, she finds the two of them seated on the couch. Jon leaps to his feet to relieve her of the tray.

"Were you able to pry at your leisure?" asks their hostess.

The gold-rimmed porcelain cups jingle in Jon's hand when he hears this. He sets the tray down on the table with great care. The same care they both proceed with now the game is up.

"Señora Mengual . . ."

The woman cuts short Jon's pitiable excuse just in time.

"Call me Señora de Planas, Inspector. In this house, we treasure the memory of our dear departed. One lump or two?"

"None, thank you."

"And you, Lieutenant?"

"Three, please, señora."

She serves the sugar daintily, using a pair of tweezers.

"I used to have proper sugar tongs, but they broke years ago. I haven't found another pair. Not even in El Corte Inglés."

"Limoges?" Jon asks. He knows about such things. As a child, he spent many afternoons taking tea and cake at the homes of ladies with bouffant hair because his *amatxo* loves to go visiting.

Señora de Planas nods. Her hair, dyed an impossible red, is holding up well, albeit slightly squashed on the pillow side. Completely understandable given the circumstances.

"A gift from my husband on our honeymoon. Toulouse, Poitiers, Nantes, Paris . . . We went by car and took turns driving. Our most wonderful trip together. The following year, Raquel was born, and then naturally, things became more difficult."

"Did you have your hands full?"

"My husband was a lieutenant colonel, señora. With a lot of responsibility. For a while, he was even posted to the . . . you know," she says, lowering her voice, "to the 'troubled' region."

Puzzled, Antonia blinks. Jon doesn't need much imagination to figure out where the "troubled region" was for a career soldier in the so-called leaden years. He points at his chest, and Antonia understands.

"Has it been a long time since your husband passed away?"

"Eleven years ago. He was cut down in his prime, Lieutenant. One day, he was fine, and the next, his trousers became a little loose on him. Then they wouldn't stay up at all. By the time we were able to do anything about it, he was riddled with cancer," she says, raising her hands and then letting them drop again into her lap. "Raquel . . . was devastated. As for me, well, you can imagine. He was my life, my everything. And then, she . . ."

She begins to cry. So softly, so quietly it's barely perceptible. The tears simply seep out of her like wine from an old wineskin that has lost its shape, warped by time and the sun.

"I'm sorry," she says, pulling a crumpled Kleenex from her dress pocket. She dabs away her tears. "You don't know what it's like to lose a daughter."

Jon doesn't know, but he can imagine. Back home in the "troubled region," his mother's son is a police officer. And he's all the family she has. Jon has spent many a night lying in bed staring at the ceiling. Wondering what will become of her if anything happens to him. Nights that seem to go on forever, especially after a tough day. For example, when he has to negotiate a tunnel strewn with explosives, or when he's strangled, or shot at. That sort of day. The nights that follow are never-ending. The sun comes out halfway through, but casts no light. It merely softens his nightmare's jagged edges.

A nightmare that looks a lot like the image of the woman before him, weeping alone in a bleak apartment surrounded by dusty old photographs.

"I have a son, Señora Mengual."

The woman raises her reddened eyes and meets Antonia's gaze.

"So young," she says, even though it sounds like a lamentation. "And has he broken your heart yet?"

"No, not yet," Antonia replies, even though behind her eyes are also images of dark tunnels and women alone in empty rooms.

"He will. Until then, seize every moment with both hands."

There's a silence, disturbed only by the sound of the mantelpiece clock. It is ticking, but the hands are motionless at half past six. Another indication that time has given up the ghost in this house.

"Why have you come here?"

"I think you know why, señora," Antonia says gently.

"No, I don't," she protests, shaking her head, even as she lowers her eyes.

"I think you do. I think for years you've been expecting a knock at the door. We came because you didn't tell the truth back then about Raquel's death."

The woman leans forward in her seat.

"Why can't you leave us alone? Haven't we suffered enough?"

Jon looks at his watch. Only twenty-five minutes left.

"You lied, and your lie is about to cost someone else their life."

Her face drains of color at this revelation.

"No, it's not true."

"I assure you it is, Señora de Planas."

"And I say it isn't!"

"Then tell us what really happened that night."

The woman—it's difficult not to call her old, due to her appearance—wrings her hands in her lap. She is sitting bolt upright on the edge of the couch, knees together, legs drawn up tight. The French posture, as elegant ladies in the sixties and seventies referred to it, with no hint of irony.

"If I do, will you leave me in peace?"

"I can't give you any assurances. But I promise you that if you tell us the truth, you'll feel better."

The promise rings hollow, as Señora de Planas's expression makes obvious. All the same, she sits up ramrod straight and starts to speak.

Jon is familiar with the tone of voice of victims, how they recount their sufferings. Just before they begin, they enter a state of self-induced hypnosis, a kind of numb detachment, stumbling over their words.

He detects none of this in the woman's voice. Despite her fatigue and frailty, her words follow a well-trodden path.

"I came back from evening Mass at Las Comendadoras. Around the corner from here. I went up in the elevator and I saw Víctor through the glass. He was waiting for the service elevator. But he got in before I got out, so I didn't have a chance to speak to him. I kept going toward the apartment. I was halfway down the corridor when I noticed the front door was open. I walked in, called Raquel's name, but she didn't answer. Then I saw her hand out in the hallway."

"Did you call the police?"

"No. I rushed to help my daughter. You would have done the same."

"And afterward?"

She leans back slightly.

"Afterward, everything's a blank."

"The ambulance arrived a couple of minutes later. They found you stanching the wound in Raquel's side. They attempted to stabilize her here, and then they moved her."

The woman nods, but she isn't looking at them. She is staring at a patch of wall directly in line with her daughter's bedroom.

Antonia gets to her feet and silently asks her colleague to take over. Inspector Gutiérrez nods to show he has understood.

"She bled to death on her way to the hospital," he continues, turning toward Raquel's mother.

She doesn't reply. Her gaze is following Antonia, who has walked around the couch and is heading toward the hallway.

The woman is about to say something to her. Her lips part.

"You told the police Raquel was alone when you left to go to Mass," Jon continues, doing his best to distract her, to buy Antonia time. "You told them she wanted to leave her boyfriend, that they had been estranged for some time. You said you'd been afraid for her. And that you saw him when you came up in the elevator."

"Yes," the woman says faintly. "That's exactly how it happened."

Another silence, emphasizing the lie. Only the steady tick of the clock, dissecting time without measuring it, offers a semblance of life amid the heavy, dense air. A minute passes, then another. The woman's fingers twist themselves into an impossible knot, her knuckles threatening to pierce the translucent skin.

"No. That's not how it happened," says Antonia from the hallway.

ONE HUNDRED AND SIXTEEN
SECONDS EARLIER

Antonia is barely aware of the conversation taking place behind her. She's too busy trying to make the world slow down.

After leaving Soto del Real prison, the monkeys in her head were sufficiently calm to enable her to process Blázquez's testimony. But when she enters the victim's house, the monkeys make it clear they'd only gone for a smoke.

As soon as she sees the victim's neat and tidy bedroom, her brain does its best to mess it up, make it dirty, chaotic. To return the room to its original state.

In her head

> (The monkeys clamor. The monkeys vie
> for her attention, they screech,
> hold things up for her.)

The jungle insists on taking back control.

Antonia closes her eyes and, as so often in the past, draws on her special collection of words in an effort to calm herself. She rummages in the recesses of her mind and finds not a word but a proverb.

Kkamagwiga nal ttae baega tteol-eojigo

In Korean, when the crow takes flight, a pear falls. One of the koans Mentor has taught her. The expression comes into her mind, but there's no explanation. No thread connecting it to reality. Only the obsessive, persistent repetition of the same phrase.

Why this, why now?

What am I not seeing?

Antonia opens her eyes.

She turns her attention back to the hallway. In her mind's eye, she re-creates the moment when Víctor walks through the living room and hears the groans in Raquel's room. He takes two steps forward. He comes across the victim in the exact spot where she is now.

Antonia's mind conjures images of the crime scene. They're blurred. The carpet in the hallway is different, no doubt replaced. And yet there's something. The blood on the carpet isn't right. There are splatters, but they've fallen unevenly.

And the big, ugly round stain on the bedroom floor, just a few steps away. Far from where the body fell, in the middle of the hallway. With no communication pattern between . . .

When the crow takes flight, a pear falls.

Of course, thinks Antonia. *How could I have been so blind?*

It's hard to know if the pear falls because the crow takes flight or the crow takes flight because the pear falls.

What do we learn from this koan, Antonia? Mentor asks inside her head.

That our perceptions define what we think we see.

That correlation isn't the same as causality.

The closing words of Señora de Planas and Inspector Gutiérrez's conversation reach her from the living room.

". . . you'd been afraid for her. And that you saw him when you came up in the elevator."

"Yes," she says. "That's exactly how it happened."

"No. That's not how it happened," says Antonia.

18

A MISTAKE

It isn't easy to pinpoint the exact moment when Señora de Planas breaks down. Maybe when she hears Antonia's voice from the hallway or when she sees her return with renewed confidence, her face radiating conviction. The same conviction that appears to have completely deserted their hostess, who looks as if she is propped up in her chair from sheer force of habit.

Antonia stands facing Raquel's mother. If they were both standing, Antonia would be two heads shorter. Now, she is the one towering above the other woman, forcing her to look up.

"When the police questioned you, you didn't accuse Víctor Blázquez. You simply said you saw him leave the apartment. When it was obvious nobody else was here."

"I didn't lie," whispers the woman.

"No, not about that," Antonia agrees. "Because there was no need to add anything, was there? A woman is attacked, the suspect has a history of domestic abuse. The police didn't think twice. They had their culprit, and they looked no further."

Antonia takes a step back and points at the remote control on the table.

"Of course, there were signs. The fact the television was on, for example."

"Telecinco, no less," says Jon.

Telecinco is a channel only elderly people switch on for company. Not a twenty-six-year-old who doesn't like television.

"What completely threw me was that Raquel opened the door to

Víctor. It didn't add up. It meant she was alive when he got to the apartment, pale and distressed, but alive. In the end, Blázquez incriminated himself even though he was telling the truth all along."

"He killed her," insists the woman. Increasingly distraught, increasingly broken.

"But the truth finally dawned on me when Víctor mentioned your shoes. It's always the small details that don't add up, Señora de Planas."

Stop having fun and cut to the chase, sweetheart. We only have fourteen minutes left, thinks Jon, tapping his watch a couple of times with his fingernail.

Antonia shoots him a sideways glance, but now that she has her prey firmly in her jaws, she has no intention of letting go. This is Antonia at her most terrifying. Jon can't help being reminded of the story about Mentor's dog and the ham bone.

"I don't know what you're talking about," the woman says.

Antonia ignores her.

"Of course you weren't in the apartment, but you were nearby. The truth was out there all along. How could Víctor possibly have seen your shoes in the elevator *before* he saw your face, *before* you opened the door? Very simple. You weren't coming up in the elevator. You were coming down. From the floor above, where you'd been waiting for Víctor to arrive."

Justice is a movable truth, thinks Jon. And this particular truth falls on Señora de Planas like a ton of bricks. Her shoulders slump, her lips droop to form a semicircle above her quivering chin.

"Would you like to take over, or shall I finish?"

The woman doesn't say anything. Jon doesn't believe she's physically capable of it. Antonia has to make the effort to rip off the rest of the bandage.

"Raquel came home that evening, and she asked for your help. A very specific kind of help. She told you Víctor was about to arrive, that you should wait close by and then walk into the apartment when the two of them were alone. She needed a witness. But what kind of a witness?"

Well, I'll be, thinks Jon, who suddenly understands everything.

"You went up to the next floor and waited. Your daughter sent a message and stood by the front door in her raincoat. Raquel was very pale when she let Víctor in. He thought they were meeting to make things up, but in fact, he was walking into a trap. She sent Víctor into the living room while she went to her bedroom. Then she took off the raincoat and as she did so let out a groan of pain, which Víctor heard."

"The blood in the bedroom . . . ," says Jon.

Antonia nods.

"The blood seeping from her wound had soaked through whatever she'd used to stanch it so that when she took off the raincoat, the blood spurted out onto the floor with a great splash."

Like when you fold and then unfold your arms in the shower. The water builds up and then falls in a cascade.

"Because Raquel wasn't stabbed in this apartment, Señora de Planas. Her killer attacked her not far from here. It was someone she knew, someone she wanted to protect. And she had the presence of mind to press down on her wound, put on the raincoat, and make her way home to incriminate her boyfriend."

"It wasn't like that . . ."

"Raquel probably thought she had time. That the ambulance would arrive in time to save her. What she didn't anticipate was what would happen when she took off the raincoat."

Antonia places her hands on her belly, splays them wide. Jon can almost envision the stab wound, the sudden gush of blood. Antonia goes on talking, more for herself than anything, to continue to understand. There's an air of vehemence, of triumph even as she reveals and reconstructs the truth about the events that night.

"What did she use to stop the bleeding? A handkerchief? A towel? The raincoat wasn't hers, it was too big for her, so it had to belong to her killer. But . . . the towel or handkerchief, whatever it was . . . didn't simply disappear. You got rid of it, didn't you, amid the confusion of the ambulance arriving and then the police?"

Raquel's mother doesn't say a word. But she doesn't take her eyes off Antonia. In her gaze there is fear and loathing in equal measure.

19

AN EMBRACE

Antonia smiles to herself. She knows she's won.

But she is also aware that her triumph is as far as she can go and it's not enough. She gives Jon a look he instantly understands. She's come this far, but she can't press her any further. It's his turn now.

Jon goes over to the woman. He kneels beside her, clasps her long, bony hands, which are engulfed in his.

"You didn't like Víctor much, did you? He wasn't good enough for your daughter."

Silence.

"Raquel asked you a favor, and you did the only thing you could. You helped her," Jon goes on, his voice soft and reassuring. "You helped your own daughter protect her killer."

The woman squeezes his hands. This is all the acknowledgment she can muster after years of covering up her daughter's lie, and the last request she made. Even though it was wrong and unjust, as a mother, she had gone through with it.

But this minimal confession is of little use to them.

Time is running out. And they still lack the one thing they need.

The *who*.

But before the who . . .

"Why did she do it?"

"Because he hurt her. Maybe Víctor didn't kill her, but he pushed her into the arms of the man who did. He abandoned her, Inspector. He abandoned her."

Jon's eyes show a glimmer of sympathy. Not approval, sympathy. The correct amount. After all, it goes with the job. Part of being a police officer is to find sympathy for everything—even for yourself, if you're lucky. It enables you to take on board the suspect's actions, to gain their trust so they keep on talking. It enables you to follow your hunch and make the following kind of statement because it will draw out the response you need:

"He cheated on your daughter."

"With a client at the gym. When Raquel found out, she broke up with him."

"And started seeing someone else."

The woman nods slowly.

"We need his name."

"All I know is that Raquel was in love with him."

"He's the person who stabbed your daughter."

"Raquel said it was an accident. He couldn't help himself."

Inspector Gutiérrez understands things that Jon cannot accept. He understands there are recesses in the human soul where it's possible for words like the ones he has just heard to come to the surface.

And be believed.

This is also part of his job. To accept the hidden places, the impulses in a person's understanding that make it possible for two contradictory propositions to exist side by side in the same sentence. "I love you so much that if you leave me, I'll kill you," or "It was an accident, he couldn't help himself," come from the same place. From the fault line between the two tectonic plates along which we humans construct our beliefs. We call such constructions love, family, friendship. What do you do when the plates shift in opposing directions . . . Nobody knows beforehand, nor should they be too quick to condemn with hindsight.

Goddamn fucking empathy, thinks Jon, partly to draw a line under the matter.

"We need to hurry, señora. Somebody's life is on the line here, and we're running out of time," says Antonia. Her voice has taken on a steely tone. "We need you to give us the man's name. Now."

"I don't know who he is," the woman repeats, shaking her head. "I don't know."

Antonia checks the time.

Eight minutes.

She is starting to show signs of becoming agitated—almost like a human being—pacing around the room, arms akimbo. Going over in her mind what they have.

Suddenly, she stops in her tracks.

She's remembered something important.

Something they don't have.

"Raquel's cell phone. They never found it. The police assumed Víctor had taken it, but he didn't, did he? Raquel gave it to you, and it was you who sent Víctor the message on WhatsApp, asking him to come up."

"I want you to leave my home," says the woman, freeing her hands from Jon's clasp and getting to her feet. "I'm calling my lawyer."

"Good idea, señora," says Jon.

And then adds in a show of street know-how:

"You can use your daughter's phone."

The oldest trick in the book: name the hidden object and wait for the suspect's eyes to drift inevitably toward it. Every drug dealer knows it, so Jon used to search the place where they *didn't* look.

Sadly for Señora de Planas, she's never dealt drugs. She lacks the pushers' guile.

She only takes her hate-filled eyes off Antonia for an instant.

It's enough.

Antonia follows the direction of her mistake (the bisecting line between her and Jon) to the piece of furniture right behind her.

The cabinet.

If anything symbolizes Madrid's moneyed classes—or those who would like to be—of the last four centuries, it's this kind of *bargueño* cabinet. An ornate piece of wooden furniture with lots of small drawers standing on four legs. Originally designed as a safe place to store papers and other documents concerning family finances. The cabinets were usually made of hardwood: ebony, mahogany, citronella. Inlaid with tortoiseshell, bone, and ivory. The oldest examples can fetch millions at auction, to the dismay of the nephews and nieces who inherit them. In their ignorance, they consign these "horrors" to the trash, and replace them with functional shelving units in IKEA's KALLAX series, sixty-nine euros, doors not included.

Antonia has no idea if the cabinet is an original seventeenth-century antique or a cheap early-twentieth-century reproduction, popular among social climbers of the time. She has no eye for such details, and they don't particularly interest her.

What does interest her is the cabinet's hidden purpose. One that's been forgotten in an era when money is stored in bits of data, but which meant something when it was minted from precious metals. She begins to pull the drawers out one by one, stacking them on the floor. She ignores the contents: Faded books of matches, mini photo albums, a collection of postcards. A 1998 income tax return.

"Hey, what are you doing?" the woman yells.

Too late. Antonia finds what she's looking for when she pulls out the right-hand bottom drawer. From the outside, the interior walls of the cabinet appear equally deep. But careful inspection reveals that the left-hand side is several inches shorter.

Reaching inside, Antonia feels something sticking out: a rope handle. She pulls on it, and a drawer two inches broad by eight long slides out. The ideal place to hide valuables: a bag of gold coins, a wad of banknotes . . .

A cell phone with a Hello Kitty cover.

She holds up the phone. It's a Samsung Galaxy, several years old. There's little doubt who it belonged to.

The phone has been carefully wiped with a cloth, but there's a stubborn coppery stain on one button.

"The battery's dead," Antonia announces, pressing the On/Off button.

"We have a charger in the car," Jon says. "Quick, let's go."

"Please don't take it with you," the woman begs, her voice quaking. She is standing between them and the door. "It has all her photos on it."

Jon suppresses a stab of compassion. He wonders how many times the woman has switched on her daughter's phone to pore over those images—late at night, blinds down, the door double-locked. She probably has no idea how to delete them and nobody to ask to do it for her.

"We'll return it to you shortly, señora."

Antonia walks around her, heading for the door, but Jon doesn't follow at once. He thinks of his *amatxo*, wherever the hell she is, and how this woman is the embodiment of her, like an ominous ghost of future Christmases. He decides to spend a few precious seconds with the woman and embrace her. As he does so, he can feel how close her bones are underneath her meager, sagging flesh. She doesn't return the gesture—a proud life won't consent to frivolity in the last few yards—and yet Jon feels her body absorb, receive, and accept it.

He whispers comforting words in her ear that only she can hear.

Then he trots after Antonia.

20

A CELL PHONE

"Six minutes," Jon says, glancing at his watch.

"Relax. We won't gain anything by getting anxious," Antonia replies, pressing the Down button a dozen or more times.

The elevator is rapid, but Antonia's brain outstrips it. She's already figured out how to access the phone if it is password-protected.

"We plug it into the charger in the car, sync it with my iPad, and use Heimdal to hack into it. That way we'll be able to see Raquel's final messages."

"You realize you're talking in the plural, right?"

"Of course, when I refer to the team, I always talk in first-person plural."

Totally impervious to sarcasm, thinks Jon. He, too, tries pressing the button to the first floor to see if he can make the elevator go any faster.

"Have you thought about how we're going to tell White we've solved the crime?"

"He'll call," says Antonia.

She leaves out the *I guess*. In Antonia Scott's vocabulary, that expression is as taboo as the word *sphere* is for a flat-earther.

"Everything's going to be okay," she adds with a smile. It's one of her good smiles. The kind that makes a dimple appear on either side of her mouth, forming a perfect triangle with the cleft in her chin. The kind she doesn't give many of these days.

It's a shame Jon doesn't see it. Considering how much he loves Antonia's smiles, with their ten-thousand-watt charge and their ability to light up the whole room.

Jon doesn't see it because he's too busy saving her life.

This is what happens in one and eleven-hundredths of a second:

Traveling at nine hundred meters per second, the elevator door is no match for the first volley of bullets that destroys it even before the elevator has reached the ground. The shooter is well aware the glass cubicle and the outer door of the elevator act as shields that slow down or deflect bullets. That's why the first salvo is short and sharp, a gentle pull on the assault rifle trigger that fires a total of five rounds.

The first two shatter the outer doors as they open. The next two hit the steel frame. The bullets are crushed, lose most of their piercing power, and ricochet down the gap into the elevator shaft.

The fifth opens a hole in the door large enough for a coffee table. It narrowly misses Antonia Scott's head before burying itself in the glass behind them, creating a giant spider's web.

Antonia has missed losing the organ that makes her the most intelligent person on the planet by little more than an inch.

She doesn't owe that inch to the hand of fate but to that of Jon Gutiérrez. Because, split seconds before the elevator reached the first floor, he glimpsed a shadowy figure reflected in the hallway mirror, armed with a high-caliber rifle.

Jon instinctively grabs hold of Antonia's jacket and thrusts her behind him to shield her. He pushes her downward so that Antonia dodges the bullet, but her mouth slams into the handrail. She narrowly avoids breaking her nose, and even more narrowly losing her front teeth, but the blow is hard enough to fill her mouth with blood.

By now, they have heard the report of the first shots, although they scarcely register them. Antonia because she's writhing in agony (anyone who's been hit in the philtrum will know why), and Jon because he's busy trying to remove his service revolver from its holster with one hand while using the other to keep Antonia behind him.

So the one and eleven-hundredths of a second conclude and the nightmare begins.

"Stay behind me!" Jon yells as he feels Antonia start to struggle.

Jon tries to flatten himself against the side of the elevator, but that's not easy. The cubicle barely provides half a meter of cover, and the angle to the shooter's position isn't ideal.

When you have no barricade, use a bullet as cover, Jon remembers from his time at the police academy. Great advice when you're sitting in a classroom discussing tactics. Not so great when you're scared witless and have to pull in your stomach so it doesn't protrude beyond your cover.

Extending his arm a fraction, Jon fires at random through the door opening. Three bullets that only help the shooter locate his position and the angle of fire.

Halfway along the corridor to the foyer is a small recess behind which their attacker is barricaded. Along the opposite wall are the mirrors that have saved Antonia's life, at least up to now.

The *up to now* needs emphasizing, because Antonia seems hell-bent on getting herself killed. To judge from the way she is struggling at any rate.

"Get off me!" she yells, although with her mouth full of blood, it sounds more like *geomih*.

A fresh volley smashes through the gaping hole. Jon hasn't heard the *click*, but he knows their attacker has switched from automatic to manual. The shots—three, this time—are consecutive, but there's a deliberate pause between each of them.

Of course, Jon isn't consciously aware of these details. He feels them instinctively in his bones. It's the result of twenty years of training, which didn't end when he joined the Red Queen project. Once a week, four times more often than before. However, there are things his training doesn't cover, and that's when he has to go with his instinct.

The bullets hit the corner of the elevator near them, showering him and Antonia with broken glass. No sooner has the echo of the third bullet died away than Jon leans out far enough to return three more shots. This time, he aims at the recess their attacker is using for cover, tearing out big chunks of plaster but barely scratching the concrete. It does, though, buy them a few precious seconds.

He would find it easier to take aim if he did not have to restrain Antonia.

"Will you keep still?" he says, pinioning her against the side of the elevator.

Antonia inhales, gulps blood, and manages to make herself understood through the pain, the adrenaline, and the fear.

"The cell phone," she says.

Jon looks down at the floor, and his blood runs cold. Now he understands his colleague's efforts to wriggle free.

With the first volley, Antonia dropped Raquel Planas's phone.

A yard away amid a heap of glass and metal debris lies their sole hope of solving the case before the deadline runs out—something Jon senses is imminent.

Why can it never, ever be simple? thinks Jon.

"Keep still," he orders again.

"I need to get it."

Jon fires once. Their attacker returns fire almost instantaneously.

Four shots in quick succession just as Antonia is straining to reach her arm out from beneath where Jon has her trapped. A shower of sparks falls on them as one of the bullets smashes the lights in the ceiling. Antonia yelps in pain and snatches away her arm.

They hear the far-off wail of a police siren, and Jon realizes the clock is working both for and against them. If only he can keep Antonia still long enough to allow him to hold off the shooter.

"I can reach it. Just a bit farther."

"Antonia . . . leave it," says Jon.

She looks at him and sees something in his eyes she's never seen before. Or maybe she has, but failed to recognize it. Jon is asking her to trust him just as he has trusted her all the months they've been together.

Antonia closes her eyes and keeps still.

Jon gives a crooked smile.

Maybe I'll die, but I'll take this bastard with me, he thinks.

There's no time for a battle cry, so he contents himself with a low, guttural rasp as he leans halfway out of the elevator. He empties the five remaining bullets in his clip at their attacker's position. The shooter shrinks back, returning fire at random, but the sirens are closing in.

Jon, who has pulled back to reload and catch his breath, waits for another attack, but none comes. The only sound he can hear are the shouts of the police on the far side of the inner courtyard.

He considers for a moment whether to peer out to see what's going on, but before he can make his mind up, three things occur simultaneously.

One, Antonia's cell phone rings, but Antonia doesn't pick up because

Two, she's on her hands and knees trying to salvage Raquel Planas's cell phone from beneath a layer of shattered glass. She looks at Jon despairingly as she holds it up. The phone has taken a direct hit, and the half she isn't clasping between her fingers is dangling from a wire. But the really terrifying thing is

Three, Jon has started to hear beeping noises very close to his ear, together with an unpleasant vibration beneath his skin that reverberates down his spine, rattling his teeth.

The time is up.

White has just activated the bomb in Jon's neck.

21

A BEEP

No. No. No.

Antonia looks at Jon. She is still on her knees holding the remains of Raquel Planas's cell phone between her bloodstained fingers. The half that was dangling has just plummeted onto the broken glass with a crunch.

The flickering light in the elevator ceiling casts a ghostly sheen on Inspector Gutiérrez's sweaty skin. He looks as wan as a quarantined vampire.

"Antonia . . ."

She looks at him, racking her brains. Not an easy task with the incessant ringing of her phone and the ever-more frequent beeps.

"Calm down. I just need to . . ."

Her sentence is cut short by someone yelling.

"Hands in the air! National Police!"

Antonia is still on her knees when a uniformed officer appears in the hallway, trampling the spent cartridges left by the fleeing shooter.

Jon is standing with his back to the officer, gun in hand.

Frozen.

"I won't say it again!" the officer yells, before saying it again: "Hands in the air!"

"Jon," says Antonia, raising her hands.

Jon doesn't reply. Fear is making his muscles seize up as the beeps in his neck grow more insistent. His face is tense, his jaw clenched. Only the fear in his eyes is glinting like diamonds in a spotlight.

Antonia turns toward the officer. She doesn't like what she sees. A nervous rookie, his finger on the trigger. A deadly combination.

"Officer, I am Inspector Scott, and this is Inspector Gutiérrez; we're with the National Police. Badge numbers 27451 and 19323," Antonia reels off.

"First, throw down your weapon, then show me your badges," the officer replies, gun still trained on them.

"I can show you . . ."

"Keep your hands in the air!"

"Officer, we have a bomb scenario here. Step away immediately and set up a three-meter perimeter."

"Throw down your weapon!"

"Officer," Antonia says again. Unsure how to make her voice sound authoritative, she finally decides to adopt the advice of the master: "Quit fucking with me. If you don't obey my order this minute, as of tomorrow, you'll be directing traffic in Albacete. Is that clear?"

Antonia must have hit the right note because the rookie finally reacts. He points his weapon at the ceiling and steps back, speaking into his walkie-talkie.

Antonia's cell phone starts to ring again.

She reaches into her pocket.

She picks up.

"Deadlines are made to be met," says White. His voice is harsh and unpleasant, simmering with rage.

"It would've been easier if you hadn't sent one of your hit men to kill us."

There's a tense silence at the other end. Betraying a note of bewilderment.

"I'm afraid I don't follow you, Señora Scott."

"Caucasian male, tall, in a balaclava, jeans, and a black leather jacket. Armed with a Colt Canada assault rifle. A C7 or C8 Carbine model, I couldn't see properly, it was dark and we were under fire. Obviously, this occurred prior to the deadline running out. Do you have anyone working for you who fits that description?"

Another silence, tenser and more prolonged.

"No. Not at this moment. Although I must say I didn't rule out their making an appearance."

"A disgruntled ex-employee?"

"Nothing of that kind. But I'm afraid they're not playing on our team."

"You and I aren't on the same team, Señor White."

"Is that what you think? Well, you'll change your mind soon enough. I'm still waiting for the result of your first assignment."

"Raquel Planas's boyfriend didn't kill her."

"Easy. You found that out hours ago. Probably after reading the police report, correct?"

"I had my doubts," Antonia admits.

She realizes White is flattering her ego, and also notes her own involuntary response. She senses the trap and so continues talking.

"The victim was in a relationship with a third person, somebody she met when she and Víctor Blázquez were breaking up."

"His name."

"Someone she fell in love with and who for some reason stabbed her." Antonia is speeding up as she talks. "She persuaded her mother to help her conceal her attacker's identity."

"His name," White repeats.

"But her plan backfired, her wound was more serious than she thought . . ."

"I take it you haven't discovered his name."

The beeps in Jon's neck accelerate, becoming one long, continuous, deadly protest.

"This isn't right, you evil bastard!" yells Antonia.

"No, it isn't."

Doing her best not to give way—to tears or rage—Antonia seizes Jon's left hand. The one that isn't wrapped around the gun Inspector Gutiérrez has decided to hold on to in a final show of dignity in face of the inevitable. But Antonia's best isn't enough.

"Are you crying?" White says after a pause.

"You know perfectly well I am," she retorts.

"Is Inspector Gutiérrez really so important to you? Or are you crying simply because you've failed? Think hard before you respond."

Antonia wonders which of the two choices is correct. She knows how she ought to feel, what the right answer should be. Yet she doesn't give it. Confused about how she feels, she scours her vast memory palace until she finds the right word.

Fa'atanmaile.

In Samoan, the dog that sees its reflection in a mirror. The feeling you have when you recoil at your own image because you don't recognize it as you.

She takes a deep breath and replies.

"Both."

For several interminable seconds, White seems to be weighing up the truth of her response.

"I believe you," he says finally. "So I've decided to delay the punishment."

For a split second, Antonia wonders if she has heard correctly.

"Why?"

Another silence. And then:

"My reasons are mine alone. Now get some rest. I'll be sending you another assignment shortly."

"Thank you," says Antonia.

She realizes how stupid this is as soon as she says it. A knee-jerk expression of courtesy, a vestige of good manners—or Stockholm syndrome—out of place in a life-and-death situation like this.

White lets out a brief, loud guffaw totally devoid of humor.

"Don't. You still have to pay the price for your failure. Only now you will do so in installments. And with interest."

He hangs up.

The beeping stops abruptly.

Antonia and Jon stare at each other. They have tears in their eyes.

They both turn away, so as not to see them.

Part III

SANDRA

*To conceive a thought—just one, but one that would
tear the universe apart.*

E. M. Cioran

1

A MATTRESS

It's almost three o'clock the next morning, and Jon is still tossing and turning in bed.

He's neither fully awake nor asleep. He's vaguely conscious of his body's heat and weight on the state-of-the-art mattress. Far superior to the one he has at home. Clad in boxer shorts, with the tangled duvet at his feet, he finally gets into a comfortable position an hour after he has crawled into bed. He drifts off, but doesn't quite fall asleep.

This is partly because he woke up at three the previous afternoon after nine hours' sleep. Waking up so late and going back to bed so soon afterward isn't Jon's thing.

Partly also because he's haunted by images of what has happened in the past few hours.

The prison.

The widow.

The elevator.

The beeps, still ringing in his ears.

And what happened afterward.

They had lots of explaining to do.

Too much.

First to the police about the shooting. The bare minimum, but it was stressful. The authorities take a keen interest when an exchange of fire involving high-caliber weapons takes place in a building full of army officers. Even if nine out of ten of them are retired and the rest receive threatening leaflets with headings such as "Your time is up," "Welcome to God's waiting room." *Well, maybe not those exact words, but close enough*, thinks Jon, who fears old age more than he does bullets.

But less than he does bombs.

Pronouncing the word *explosives* in a building filled with military personnel didn't help reduce the police's curiosity. Bomb disposal experts showed up, but they didn't have Mr. White's imagination. They searched everywhere except beneath Inspector Gutiérrez's skin while he waited, draped in a blanket, clutching a reasonably decent cup of coffee, and gazed into space. Or at the nearest piece of it—namely, a flower bed in the inner courtyard, planted with hydrangea and wisteria just coming into bloom.

Jon sat quietly in a corner, while all around him the night flapped about as crazily as a bird on fire.

Paramedics treated the porter for a concussion, after the intruder had knocked him unconscious. A dozen forensics personnel ran around like headless chickens, a bunch of irate detectives darted back and forth. Jon left the public relations to Antonia. Never a good idea under normal circumstances.

Or under any circumstances.

Jon barely paid attention to their conversation. Or rather, it reached him through a veil, like when you put your head underwater in the bathtub and somebody yells from the adjoining room. He listened with detachment to the snatches that reached him, with that indifference the world bestows on those who have had a close brush with death. Not when he knocks on your door but when he squats in your house, taking it over, changing the locks, and blowing you kisses from the window.

There was an occasional raised voice, disbelieving looks, as well as a few audible whispers, such as: "Who is this crazy woman?"

Then Mentor arrived—and with him the calls to those higher up—after which the questions petered out. More reluctantly than usual due to the address, the situation, and the number of retired regimental commanders in pajamas shouting contradictory orders from their balconies.

At last, Mentor went over to Jon, frowning when he saw the state he was in. And probably also because he was close enough to catch a whiff of him. Inspector Gutiérrez was immersed in a cloud of sweat and adrenal burnout. Neither of them very pleasant odors.

That would never bother Antonia, thinks Jon, realizing his job had its perks.

Further, briefer, and more straightforward explanations followed. Antonia and Jon traveled in Mentor's car to the Red Queen project's headquarters. There they both took showers and retired to a special module where people could sleep. The rooms weren't big enough to swing a cat in, but at least Jon could rest—with the help of a sedative carefully administered by Dr. Aguado, together with his antibiotics.

They woke after lunch.

There was a meeting.

They exchanged a few words.

They realized they were totally screwed.

"To sum up," Mentor said after a lengthy, brooding silence, "we don't know who killed Raquel Planas because her phone was destroyed. Did we find anything on the cloud?"

Aguado shook her head.

"And we don't have the faintest idea why White ordered you to solve her murder," Mentor continued.

Antonia shook her head.

"We've ruled out any possible link between White and Víctor Blázquez," said Mentor. "Who, for the time being, is the sole beneficiary of our efforts."

Jon shook his head.

And that was the hardest part.

In view of Señora de Planas's confession, the authorities had no choice but to do something to change Blázquez's situation. Probably with a call to the original detectives in charge of the case: firstly, to remind them they'd botched the investigation, basing it entirely on prejudice, and had convicted an innocent man; secondly, to offer them the chance to redeem themselves by presenting the public prosecutor with their new "conclusions." This would cause a lot of red faces, a great deal of upset, and Señora de Planas would almost certainly be handed down a two-year sentence. Meaning she wouldn't spend a single day in prison, because in Spain a sentence of two years or less is automatically suspended.

True, they'd been faced with a four-year-old cold case. Something that at best normally required vast amounts of time and resources. And at worst was impossible.

They had resolved it in six hours.

And yet . . .

They had no sense of triumph.

Justice is a movable truth, thought Jon. *It's also the only game where everyone's a loser.*

"And not only that," added Mentor, "a third party is now involved. A mysterious shooter, with firearms experience and a military assault rifle. We know nothing about their identity, their motivation, their relationship with White, or why they tried to kill you. All we have is a general description of them."

"We also have the images recorded on cell phones from people's balconies," Jon points out, always keen to help.

"Yes, of course. Six videos recorded by septuagenarians, which, bearing in mind the quality of the phones, the light conditions, and the steadiness of their hands, have resulted in a delightful blur," says Mentor, pointing to some fuzzy images on the meeting room screen.

"Have you made any headway here?" asks Jon.

"None whatsoever," Mentor says, quickly and emphatically, glaring at Dr. Aguado, whose lips remain sealed. "No new leads. Which means that once again, we're at the mercy of whatever White orders us to do. And our only strategy is to wait."

"In eleven out of twelve cases, that's the best course to follow," says Antonia in an attempt to give credibility to a statistic she has evidently pulled out of her ass.

"So, zero suspects, zero positive IDs, zero clues. Is that a fair reckoning, or have I overlooked something?"

Antonia, Jon, and Dr. Aguado nod as one.

"In other words, we're totally screwed," concludes Mentor.

Jon agreed with Mentor back then, and he agrees with him now.

They've done their best at Red Queen headquarters to ensure that the bedrooms—more like cabins in that sea of concrete—although basic, are well appointed. Jon's mattress and pillow, for example, are made of the best-quality visco latex, or memory foam. Not only does it support your neck, it "memorizes" the shape of your body, as well as adjusting to your weight and body temperature. Jon wonders if the pillow will also retain the imprint of the lump on his neck where the bomb is.

He wonders how long the bed's memory lasts. For instance, if the bomb exploded right now. If it went off in his neck and shards of metal and bone pierced his brain stem, killing him instantly. Would the pillow retain his shape after his heart stopped beating? Would Antonia see his outline when she came into the room?

Jon imagines two paramedics carrying his body on a stretcher. Then, a bit more realistically, he makes that three. Not that he's fat. Lifting him and carrying him the short distance, less than twenty yards, to Dr. Aguado's lab. The pathologist would examine what was left of him after the explosion, rummage around in his brain, desperately trying to find a clue among the fragments. Sorting through the pieces of what until a few moments before had been Jon Gutiérrez. Still warm to the touch.

Antonia would of course weep for him. Then she'd throw herself into a single-minded quest for vengeance. Or maybe she'd plunge into one of her depressions, shutting herself away in her loft for another three years.

With Antonia Scott, you never know.

She can surprise you when you're least expecting it.

For example, when she hammers on your bedroom door at 3:26 in the morning.

Jon opens it to find Antonia standing before him in her underwear. Clothes in one hand, sneakers in the other, cell phone in her mouth.

He takes it from her when he realizes she's trying to speak.

"A text message came," she says as soon as he frees her mouth. "Thirty seconds ago."

Jon looks at the screen while Antonia pulls on her clothes out in the corridor.

CALLE CISNE, 21.

"Where's that?"

"I don't know," she says, grappling with her shirt buttons.

Jon tries to endow the first word he utters with all the archness he can muster, which is not inconsiderable, given the hour and the fact he's still half asleep.

"*You* don't know a street in Madrid, sweetheart?"

"Madrid has 9,187 streets, Jon. I can't memorize them all."

Antonia blinks, creating a dramatic pause while she pulls on her jeans. She has a pillow mark on her cheek, her hair is mussed up, her face pink.

"I mean, I *could*. I just haven't. Google it!"

Jon clicks on the app.

"Have you told Mentor?"

"I forwarded him the message."

The app opens, and within milliseconds, the signal links up to the satellite tracking system. It locates Antonia's phone, shows a map of the area around the airport, and gives the distance from there to Calle Cisne, 21; all in less time than it takes to read fifty words, say.

"Show me," she says, buckling her belt.

Jon turns the phone around to show her the location. She studies it for one and a half seconds.

It suddenly occurs to Jon why Antonia would do something so bizarre as to go out into the corridor half naked and give him her phone for him to find the address. It occurs to him the instant she says:

"Get dressed. I'll wait for you in the car."

She runs off barefoot, but with enough of a head start.

That crafty son of a gun . . .

WHAT THEY DID NEXT

"She's not ready to start yet, Dr. Nuno."

Unaware that her future will consist of causing untold pain to a great many people, the woman on the other side of the glass is concentrating hard on arranging a series of numbers into logical sequences. She has electrodes taped to her head and is wearing nothing more than a hospital gown.

"How long has she been in training?" asks the doctor, even though he knows this only too well.

"She and Scott have both gone over the recommended time. But I can't get her to control her emotions. It's very frustrating."

"How has she reacted to the drug?"

Dr. Nuno stretches out a hand lined with varicose veins that look like a storm of purple lightning. He takes the sheet of paper Mentor is holding out to him.

"Her results are excellent. Even better than Scott's."

"And yet I can't manage to stabilize her. The pills have proved useless."

Nuno clears his throat and takes a deep breath. Mentor senses a lecture coming. This isn't the first time he has a strong urge to call security to restrain the man, lead him to a dark alleyway, and discreetly make him disappear. He could do it. And nobody would protest.

But Nuno remains silent. As if he has lost the thread of what he was about to say. Or something inside him has made him keep quiet before it's too late.

When he finds his voice again, something has changed. It no longer bobs along on a river of sarcasm. It's gone down an octave. He sounds more honest. Contrary to expectation, this alarms Mentor even more.

"A few years ago, I took part in an experiment that changed my perception of the world. What I'm about to tell you is in the public domain; you can easily look up the experiment. Not my personal conclusions, though."

Nuno leans up against the wall as if he has the weight of the world on his shoulders.

"Fifty subjects took part in the experiment: twenty-eight men and twenty-two women. We strapped them to a chair. Only tight enough to ensure they looked at the screen. Then we started to show them a slideshow. Images of cakes, chubby babies, fluffy puppies. We played cheerful, upbeat background music. Louis Armstrong, someone called Katy Perry, the kind of things young people like. Do you have one of those?"

Mentor hands him a cigarette. Nuno cups his trembling hands, and Mentor is afraid he might burn him as he lights it. The doctor takes a puff before continuing.

"In among the cute pictures we inserted extremely violent graphic images. Bodies maimed in car crashes, photos from murder scenes, festering wounds, facial disfigurements. The worst kind of death and carnage you could find. And believe me, we spared no effort."

Something in Nuno's tone makes Mentor shudder. Imagined horror is always worse than the real thing. Moments later, this turns out to be prophetic.

"The subjects exhibited classic signs of stress. Increased heart rate, raised blood pressure, sweaty palms. What we didn't expect is what happened next."

The doctor contemplates the tip of his cigarette, which is slowly burning down. He blows on the ash. It falls to the floor, exposing a glowing ember that tinges his furrowed face orange in the semidarkness of the control room.

"The images appeared randomly. A violent image might pop up after fifteen, six, or thirty positive ones. There was no preestablished sequence."

"Didn't the algorithm take into account the subject's reaction?" Mentor asks.

"Pure chance. White noise."

Nuno drops his cigarette to the floor. He doesn't crush it or grind it under his shoe. He simply steps on it and allows physics to do the rest.

"The amazing thing was that, after several hours of the experiment, some of the subjects began to show signs of stress *just before* they were shown the image."

"That's impossible," says Mentor. "What you're talking about is . . ."

Nuno shakes his head.

"It wasn't an isolated case. Seven of the fifty subjects—two men and five women—displayed the same anticipatory response, eighty-four percent of the time."

"That can't be right, Doctor. It would be like predicting the future."

"Absolute nonsense, my dear fellow. You spend too much time watching that garbage called television. No. What happened inside the subjects' brains was that their cognitive abilities started to become enhanced. In other words, their intuition."

"Intuition is when I see someone stumble and I predict they're going to fall down the stairs. But this . . ."

"Who the hell do you think you are? You haven't the faintest idea about anything relating to the brain, my friend," says Nuno. When the doctor loses his temper, his Portuguese accent becomes more conspicuous, more singsong. It takes the sting out of his reproach. "Neither do I. Nobody does."

Mentor lets what he's just heard sit for a while.

"What became of the experiment?"

"It was halted."

"But . . ."

"Our methods were considered unethical. We were using trauma to modify the participants' brains. Many suffered nightmares for weeks."

A prolonged silence follows.

"There were threats," confesses Nuno. "Serious words were bandied about."

"How serious?"

"Torture. Mengele. That sort of thing."

Quite rightly, Mentor thinks, swallowing hard.

Both men turn toward the glass. In the room beyond, the woman has started a fresh raft of tests. But she doesn't complete the exercises.

Instead, she gets to her feet, rips off the electrodes, paces around in circles like a caged animal.

"Scott is nothing like this one," says Nuno. "They're both highly gifted. But they are different. Hence, the . . . special methods I've devised for her."

It finally dawns on Mentor what the doctor is saying. Not all at once, like a knife in the back or a door in your face. No: it reveals itself gradually, like an object you feel in the dark for hours, trying to discover what it is, until it dawns on you that what you've been holding is, quite literally, a turd.

All this son of a bitch wanted was to experiment on her. To carry on what he was unable to finish four years earlier.

"You're a bastard, Nuno."

"For the first time ever in the life of the Red Queen project, we had two candidates. A replacement. It was worth a try," Nuno says with a shrug. "When you're so old even the flies won't settle on you, in exchange you acquire a certain indifference."

Mentor looks at him, shocked by such coldness. He hopes that if he stares long enough he'll detect a glimmer of culpability in the doctor's eyes.

"This woman had something. An inner configuration I thought would protect her."

"What are you talking about?"

"You mean you haven't seen it? Take a good look at her, Mentor. A close look. But not the way you've been looking at her up to now, like a piece of meat to use for your own aggrandizement. Both of us were mistaken, each in our own way. And now you have to make a decision."

Nuno leaves the room.

Mentor stays behind, observing the cigarette end the doctor stepped on. A thin plume of acrid smoke is still rising from the blackened tip.

In the end, you can't trust a thing, thinks Mentor.

2

AN ADDRESS

Jon manages to get dressed in record time and reaches the car while Antonia is still tying her sneakers. Too late. She's already behind the wheel. And Jon was stupid enough to leave the key in the ignition.

"I'll drive carefully," Antonia swears when she sees him standing there, probably trying to decide whether to drag her out.

"Respecting the speed limit?" says Jon, because it's not the same thing.

"Respecting the speed limit."

Against all his better instincts, Jon believes her. Instantly. He realizes in an extraordinarily lucid way as he walks around, opens the passenger door, and buckles his seat belt that his cerebral cortex has been rewired to trust Antonia Scott blindly. Just as his body has done in order to protect her. Not without reason, part of him rejects this unconditionally servile attitude. Not without reason, but not maturely, either; there's something childish, petty, and selfish about rejecting his own reason for being there.

He slams the door shut to banish the thought.

"Hasn't he sent another text?" asks Jon, pointing to her cell phone on the dash. For Jon, this is the most pressing question. For the first of White's *assignments*, he had given them the address where a crime had been committed and then a follow-up text with the amount of time they had: six hours. So when Jon asks if there was another text, he's asking how much time he has left.

There may well be two kinds of people in the world. On the one hand, those who wish to know the exact hour of their death and feel tormented by the need to know. With a big pork chop and a couple of beers inside him, Inspector Gutiérrez would have slapped the table without a second thought and declared himself one of them. Ninety-eight kilos of the hundred he weighs are made of pure Basque pork crackling. Plus skinny-dipping in a local river in midwinter and beating the crap out of anyone who even contemplates insulting his *amatxo*.

And yet.

It's just possible the other 2 percent, curled up in bed in postcoital lethargy, would think twice about it being best not to know.

"Just the one," says Antonia, starting the engine.

Jon discovers that not having a countdown, not having to watch the numbers grow smaller and smaller, produces a huge sense of relief.

Having a bomb screwed under my skin works wonders for self-discovery, thinks Jon, making a mental note to thank Mr. White for this at the first possible opportunity.

However that may be, Bilbao is Bilbao and cops are cops, says the exasperated voice of the Basque pork crackling.

"That's just great. Do we at least know what this is about?"

"Not yet. Mentor is onto it. But when he finds out, I want to take the lead."

There's something about the way she says this that gets up Jon's nose.

Not her actual choice of words but that they vibrate on the same frequency as her conversation with White. Jon couldn't follow it all. He doesn't know much English and watches TV series dubbed. But he grasped enough: a *both of us* that has been whirling round his mind since the previous night.

"This is just a game for you, isn't it?"

"Is that what you think?"

"I think you're enjoying it, yes. Even if you won't admit it to yourself."

Spoken so crudely, this sounds offensive, however much Jon tries to avoid it. But it's the truth, and now he's said it.

I've got every right to be angry, for fuck's sake.

So if that's the case, why do I feel so bad?

Antonia lapses into one of her thoughtful pauses, which takes them to Avenida de Logroño and several more avenues beyond. Just as it seems she's finally made up her mind to speak, the phone buzzes.

Mentor's voice comes through the hands-free.

"I have the info. Cisne 21 is a private residence. According to the land registry, a couple bought the plot and self-built on it ten years ago."

"What else?" Jon wants to know.

"That's it," says Mentor. "I have nothing else on that address."

"What about the rest of the street?"

"I've checked that out too. The nearest report of a serious crime is a homicide and suicide involving an elderly couple back in the nineties."

"How far?"

"Six blocks away."

Jon shakes his head. It seems too distant—in time and space—for this to be a simple error.

All of a sudden, his eyes open wide as he realizes what's going on. Why they haven't yet received the text with the countdown.

There's an expression on Antonia's face Jon has learned to recognize. Glassy-eyed, jaw clenched. The expression that shows her brain is spinning around faster than normal.

And that she's reached the same conclusion that he has, only a few seconds earlier. That's why she's driving within the speed limit, glancing repeatedly at him, waiting for him to free her from her promise.

Because no crime has been committed at Cisne 21.

Not yet.

"It's your call," Antonia says, hand on the gearshift.

Jon nods, clutching the handgrip.

"Mentor," says Antonia. "Tell the National Police to send a patrol car to that address, with the siren on. We're heading straight there."

"Why do I . . . ?"

Jon cuts off the call to avoid unnecessary distractions.

Taking a deep breath, Antonia counts down from ten. She seems to be sitting more upright, her shoulders raised. And her eyes no longer look glassy but have become two laser beams. She engages sixth gear and presses her foot to the floor, drawing a roar of approval from the V-8 engine. Just like her, it seems to have been waiting for the chance to unleash its full potential.

At this time of night, there's very little traffic on the freeway.

Even so, as they speed along at over 180 kilometers an hour, the few other vehicles on the road look like fixed obstacles, walls they could crash into.

"Six minutes."

Jon doesn't have Antonia's superhuman powers of calculation, but he knows that's a big ask.

"It's twenty-one kilometers, sweetheart."

"Exactly," says Antonia, swerving to avoid a truck that seems to have appeared from nowhere (in fact, from the merging lane) and accelerating still more until the speedometer shows two hundred kilometers an hour.

The previous night, Jon hadn't seen his life flash before his eyes. *Thank God*, he thinks, *it's bad enough to die without having to do it watching Spanish cinema.* The terror produced by having such a close brush with death had been different. A kind of tunnellike darkness. Both his body and his eyes had stopped responding; he could barely take in what was happening.

The panic he feels now, knuckles white from gripping the strap, feet rooted to the car floor, is totally different. Now everything he sees around him—the streetlamps, other vehicles, the barrier so similar to the one Antonia crashed through a few months earlier—looks like a threat.

Identifying the different kinds of fear. Something else I owe to Mr. White.

"What stage of fear am I in now?"

"What are you talking about?" says Antonia, keeping her eyes on the road.

"That Dr. Kubrick of yours. The stages of grief. Denial, anger, all that stuff."

"Kübler-Ross. And for the record, that theory is now seriously questioned."

Jon stifles a guffaw of astonishment.

I don't believe this. A double joke, although inadvertent. But even so, thank heavens for small victories.

"I may yet live long enough for you to make me laugh, sweetie."

Although, things being as they are, he thinks as their car nearly brushes a Golf that seems nailed to the asphalt, *I have my doubts.*

NINE MINUTES EARLIER

Happiness comes in small packages.

So says the mug a work colleague gave her as a birthday present a couple of weeks earlier. Aura thinks about this as she sips her herbal tea. It's the sixth one the woman has bought her. With ironic intentions, she thinks.

Even though she doesn't yet know it, being determined to finish the drink in this mug is what is going to save Aura's life tonight.

Aura has a tendency to forget her mugs next to the microwave, in a corner of the living room table, as well as other strategic places in the apartment. She spends several minutes every morning searching for these tokens of her absentmindedness, which she has left three-quarters, half, and frequently, to her shame, completely full. The idea is to collect and empty them before the cleaner arrives and scolds her with a sardonic smile and an "Ay, señora" that Aura finds deeply embarrassing.

Her search usually ends with the creation of a small collection near the sink. The mugs, with their pastel-colored slogans partially hidden by the string and brand tag of herbal tea, remind her of a police lineup from the movies, where each person holds up a board with a number on it.

Happiness comes in small packages.

That night, happiness comes from the novel that keeps her up late—she has to reach the climax—and the cup of rooibos she's determined to finish although it's gone stone-cold. Unlike her. As always before her period starts, her body is making insistent demands on her. Jaume hasn't been much help. He came home exhausted from the office and after dinner lay groggily on the couch, then barely made it to their bedroom to put his pajamas on before collapsing.

The nearly eight-year age difference between them—she is forty-three, he is fifty-one—is beginning to show. He can still perform all right, but a certain lack of urgency is already obvious, an incipient softness.

Aura wonders how long it will be before they start sleeping in separate beds. They still love each other—the critical mass provided by sixteen years of marriage, a mortgage, two adorable kids—and are reasonably happy. Sometimes blissfully so. Aura can't find a single reason why she shouldn't spend the rest of her life with this man now snoring beside her under the quilt. Their marriage isn't perfect—whose is? But the threats to it come from outside. Problems at work or in the extended family or when the world is simply turned upside down. But they love each other, and that's more than a lot of people can say.

None of which, however, resolves Aura's immediate problem, which is that—to quote her friend Monica—she's like a bitch in heat. Monica has three children, zero husbands, and a more-than-healthy libido. In fact, it was Monica who gave her the toy Aura is desperate for right now.

"It solves all your problems. Thirty seconds. Wham, bam, thank you, ma'am."

At first, Aura had felt a bit ashamed. She'd never been exactly prudish about sex. No more than normal for a conservative-leaning family that prided itself on being modern. A private school, but conversations in the bathrooms. Yet it's some distance from there to getting a Satisfyer as a birthday present in the middle of a Brazilian-style steak restaurant with free caipirinhas at the bar.

When she opened the package and saw what it was, she closed it at once, her cheeks bright pink. But the other five women guests—two work colleagues, a cousin, Aura's sister—recognized it immediately and began to praise its benefits so openly and naturally that for a moment Aura felt a stab of frustration at being a bit old-fashioned. So it *was* okay nowadays to talk about these things. In her own defense, she claimed that from the description on the box, she thought it was a vacuum cleaner.

Even so, she put it in her bag and forgot about it. Until a couple of days later, one Saturday morning when the girls were at tennis lessons and her husband was playing golf—she remembered her gift. She took a shower and gave it a go. She applied it as illustrated, only to be disappointed for the first twenty seconds. Then all of a sudden, *whoosh*, off went the fireworks.

It's not that she's crazy about the gadget—in her mind, she immediately made the comparison between a lobster paella and rice in a bag—but Aura is a fund manager in a private bank, with an average of 8.32 percent annual profit for her clients, so she knows added value when she sees it. Which takes us to her next problem. Because she keeps the blessed thingamajig in her gym bag in the downstairs bathroom, far from prying eyes and unfortunately from the bedroom. For a moment, Aura thinks she'll stay where she is, come what may—*Ha ha!* she laughs to herself. So as not to have to get up, because she's cozy in bed, spellbound by Dan Brown. He's her favorite author because he's been publishing the same novel over and over for twenty years. And Aura gets a six-figure bonus every year because she knows the value of the predictable.

In the end, the urge is too great for her.

Happiness comes in small packages, with a lithium battery, she says to encourage herself.

It's the best decision of her life, courtesy of Mr. Wonderful. Suck on that, reality.

Aura slides one foot out of bed, careful not to wake her husband. She feels her bare big toe tingle as she searches for her slippers. The underfloor heating is designed to save electricity at night. She doesn't find the slippers and can't be bothered to bend down and look under the bed, so she decides to go barefoot.

This is the second-best decision of her life, thanks to her laziness. Suck on that, willpower.

She steals out of the bedroom, walks past those of her two daughters, and reaches the staircase. This is the house's pride and joy. Beautiful steps with a zebrawood veneer, a visually striking wood that's expensive to import—*A bit less if you cheat a little*, the carpenter told her.

The cheating involved paying cash and avoiding bothersome invoices. Thanks to this, Aura and Jaume could afford a fine hardwood staircase. *And it doesn't creak*, added the carpenter.

The third-best decision of her life, thanks to tax evasion. Suck on that, civic responsibility.

Aura is halfway down the stairs when she realizes something is happening.

Something bad.

There's an important difference between people who live in an apartment building and people who live in a house. The former develop a sense of closeness, of familiarity. They have neighbors above, below, and on either side of them. Most likely opposite them too. Their habits, their movements take account of this.

So do their perceptions.

Aura has always lived in a house. First her parents' and now this one. Sixteen years living in the same place creates a number of certainties. A sense of her surroundings. The temperature, the light, how far away the walls are. It's all an extension of her own body.

She doesn't hear anything. In movies, there's always a creaking sound, a noise from the floor above, a telephone ringing and a voice asking if you know how the children are—*from inside the house!*

Even so, Aura knows something isn't right. She can feel a breeze on her bare ankles that shouldn't be there. Because it comes from the door to the garden, and she always makes sure she locks that door. Every night for the past sixteen years. If she didn't, she wouldn't be able to sleep. She creeps slowly back up the stairs. Step by step. The wood doesn't even creak once (*cheat!*) as she heads back to the main bedroom.

Part of her (*the rational, civilized, serious part*) tells her not to be hysterical, she must have forgotten to close the door, the garden and door alarms haven't gone off, she's been affected by all the thrillers she's read, she should go back to bed.

The other part pummels Jaume's shoulder until he wakes up with a start.

"What's wro—"

Aura covers his mouth with her hand and raises a finger to her lips. For a brief moment, Jaume thinks she has woken him to have sex—he can see the lusting look in her eyes as he emerges from sleep, but Aura is too frightened to put that at the top of her mental inbox. She is dimly aware of a couple of new messages, but they're buried below the one that says in red capital letters: **THERE'S SOMEONE IN THE HOUSE.**

Aura mouths a version of this message and waves her hands until Jaume blinks and reacts, throwing off the quilt and getting out of bed. He goes to the dressing room and searches until he finds an old golf club that's been there for ten years, just in case something like this happens.

Seen from the outside, standing there in his pajamas, with his middle-age spread and receding hairline, holding a golf club in his hand, he could look ridiculous. Aura has her own view about it. She feels a very precise desire, born of fear, adrenaline, and the state of her hormones. She tells herself that as soon as this false alarm is over, she's going to screw her husband like there is no tomorrow.

Jaume advances down the corridor, brandishing the club. Aura follows him: in a clear sign of the times, she has grabbed her phone. At the slightest hint of danger, she'll press the emergency number. Not before. Aura's biggest fear still is of making a fool of herself. It comes from her conservative education, from being the middle sister. Whatever.

Maybe if she'd called immediately, things would have been different.

It's hard to know, and that's the bummer.

The intruder appears at the top of the stairs: a shadow all in black. Neither of them has heard him. The problem with wood that doesn't creak is that it doesn't discriminate against armed men who invade your home.

Jaume's reaction is instinctive: he cries out and swings the golf club, hitting the stranger on the shoulder. Once, then again. The intruder gives a yelp of pain and surprise and raises his arm to protect himself from a third blow just as Jaume launches it. The golf club splits in two near the club head, which rolls across the floor and drops through a gap in the stairs.

There is no mathematical formula for bravery, no type of equation of the sort *taking stock plus daring multiplied by lack of awareness equals x*. But if there were, one of its variables would have completely altered now. It's one thing to go out onto the top-floor landing in your house armed with a golf club to confront a possible burglar. It's quite another to confront an attacker with a hunting knife when all you're holding is a broken bit of aluminum and plastic.

Jaume recoils, colliding with Aura, who is pressing the emergency call button.

"What do you want? Get out of our house!" Jaume screeches, panic-stricken.

Behind him, he can hear Aura giving the operator their address, but what he really wants is for her (and him) to run away and lock themselves in the bathroom. Except that right then, their bodies are all that separate the attacker from their daughters' bedrooms.

"I've called the police," Aura declares triumphantly, holding up her cell phone. As if invoking the name of the Supreme Authority could act as a protective shield keeping evildoers in their place, which is outside the homes of Decent People With Jobs Who Pay Their Taxes (Almost Always).

The incantation doesn't appear to have worked on the intruder, who advances toward them, rubbing the shoulder where Jaume hit him. His left hand is holding the knife, which is the most dreadful thing Jaume has ever seen. A length of metal, serrated close to the hilt, curved and pointed at the tip.

Jaume is sure he's seen one just like it before. The image flashes through his mind. Of himself sitting on his parents' living room floor, eating a sweet roll, transfixed by the sight of a bare-chested, muscular hero plunging an identical-looking knife into an evil Vietcong soldier. All his schoolmates coveted one, and his parents gave him his just in time to show it off on a school trip. But that knife was a cheap plastic imitation that soon ended up in the trash.

The one being waved in front of him is real. The most real thing he has ever seen.

The stranger says nothing. He doesn't open his mouth, simply takes one step and then another until his face becomes lit up by Aura's reading lamp, which is still on.

"No. You . . . Why?"

The assailant doesn't respond, but draws back his arm and lunges at Jaume, who narrowly dodges the blow. As he does so, he knocks Aura to the floor. She barely notices when the cell phone flies out of her hand. Her only thought is to get as far away as possible from the two figures locked in a struggle in the middle of the landing.

Jaume is tall and relatively strong, but even Aura—who has only ever seen violence at the movies, without paying it much attention— can see he's no match for the man with the knife. The fight her husband is putting up can only offer him a brief respite from the inevitable outcome.

At that moment, Aura would give all she had for a few paltry seconds. Her house, cars, credit cards. Everything just for a few extra moments until the police arrive. Jaume has hold of his attacker's arm, but not for long. The man punches him in the head and neck and manages to free the arm with the knife. He plunges it into Jaume's stomach, pulls it out, then stabs him a second time.

Jaume's resistance ends there. Aura looks on in horror as her husband begins to vomit blood—no, he *spouts* it as if his mouth were full and he couldn't hold any more. He falls to his knees, and his body starts to jerk as it slumps to the floor. Aura hears the sound of breaking bones that conjures images of traumatologists. Crutches. A spotless white plaster cast her daughters will spend some time doodling on.

In another life, another universe.

As her husband collapses on the wood floor, all Aura can think is how quickly it all happened. How little time he managed to buy her and their daughters.

The intruder—*Now a murderer, now he's a murderer*, thinks Aura— is leaving nothing to chance. He seizes his victim by the hair with a gloved hand, tugging his head back to expose his throat. He slides the knife blade under Jaume's right ear, and draws a semicircle to his left. He keeps hold of Jaume's hair until he's satisfied with the incision he's made, then simply releases his grip, leaving gravity and the laws of physics to finish the job.

Don't scream. Don't scream. Don't scream. The girls mustn't see this, they mustn't see him, they can't come out, they can't, no, don't let them come out.

Aura tries to clamber to her feet. Her arms are extended across the wall separating the doors of her daughters' two bedrooms. For a brief moment, she sees herself opening one door and running into the room to protect at least one of her children. But that would mean abandoning the other to her fate. The temptation is vast, immense, overwhelming.

She has been attracted to a lot of things in her life. Sex (without any great drama), money (without prejudice), and drugs (without excess). All of them more or less fleeting. And beyond all those, the most awkward, most constant, and hardest to overcome, the attraction of food (the most pernicious, the one she knows she shares with all her female friends).

But all of those put together are nothing compared to her irresistible, overwhelming, and brutal desire to open these two doors. On the other side of ten centimeters of wall, her daughters are tucked in, fast asleep in their beds. Their small, fragile bodies beneath their duvets, Amanda's nightlight still on, Patricia's switched off because she's older. Their hair still smelling of shampoo from their baths, their mouths half open, their lips shiny.

Aura needs to get into those rooms to protect them, embrace them. She needs it more desperately than she's ever needed anything in her life before. And yet she can't. She can't because there are two doors. It's an impossible choice, so she stands between them, arms splayed, back against the wall, pushing with her feet to stand up straight. In a last pathetic bid to act as a shield, to buy them a few more seconds until the police arrive.

The intruder raises his head and looks at Aura. He steps over Jaume's body. Now he's within arm's length of her. His watery blue eyes alight on the doors—the girls' names written on them in cheap wooden letters—then turn back to Aura.

He raises a gloved hand to his lips. Points first to one door then the other, and finally at her.

Aura understands.

Aura nods.

She shuts her eyes tight, clenches her teeth. When the blade sinks into her stomach, Aura stifles the urge to cry out.

(don't scream don't scream don't scream)

Telling herself this pain is her daughters' salvation, it is happiness, it is time, it's Patricia at her graduation; it's Amanda achieving her dream job. She sees them both in years to come, being happy, in exchange for her renouncing a last embrace, giving up her life in silence, without making a sound, without waking them, in exchange for this pain, this pain is

(unbearable)

life, hold on, hold on, hold on . . .
Just before everything goes black, she hears the sirens.

3

A PIECE OF LEGO

The Audi reaches No. 21 Calle Cisne surprisingly unscathed. *It's a Christmas miracle*, thinks Jon, even though it's almost March.

"Sweetie, if you carry on like that, they'll end up putting points back on your license."

"What license?"

Jon looks across at Antonia, realizes she's being completely serious, and takes a deep, deep breath to calm himself before he speaks.

Which he doesn't manage to do, because Mentor—who's blessed with this gift—interrupts with a call.

"A police alarm has gone off at your exact location," he says.

"Have you sent a unit?"

"I did the moment you told me. It must be about to arrive."

"In that case, send an ambulance as well," Antonia instructs him somberly.

She ends the call and steps out of the car. From outside, everything appears quiet. It's a modern-looking house: Corten steel, flat roof. A stone-and-aluminum fence, with a door to the property via the garden. It's locked.

"What do we do?" asks Antonia.

Inspector Gutiérrez hesitates. There exists a long-standing debate among the forces of order in cases like this. Whether to go in with a bang or on tiptoe. If the suspect's still inside and they give themselves away, the homeowners could get hurt.

Besides, we've had enough drama lately, thinks Jon. *The last thing I want is to warn an armed intruder that I'm going in.*

"Slow and steady."

"You perform the honors, then," says Antonia, signaling the lock.

Jon returns to their car and fishes out his old picklocks and something else out of the glove box. He rejoins his colleague, who shines her cell phone flashlight while Jon puts to use the skills he learned one evening from Luismi some eight or nine years earlier. *Locks on garden gates are as easy as pie*, Luismi told him. *And if it's a spring lock, they open if you just look at them.*

This one is a spring lock, but Jon is no Luismi, so it takes him the best part of a minute to open it. He feels a pang in his stomach as it occurs to him he might set off the alarm; he has seen the Securitas Direct plaque right underneath the entry phone.

"No alarm, no bother," says Jon, looking at Antonia, who had been expecting the same thing.

"They don't seem like the kind of people who'd put the sign there for fun," she says, her brow furrowing.

"Here, take this," Jon tells her, holding out the other item he took from the glove box.

It's the holster containing "Antonia's" Sig Sauer 290. Quotation marks because although officially the gun is hers, she refuses to accept it. *Well, it can't be mine, sweetheart; it's so small I can't even get my finger into the trigger. Take it. I don't want it, you have it,* and so on all the time.

"I don't need it."

"Take it, or you're not going in."

Antonia grudgingly takes it, knowing that next she'll be going to the car trunk and putting on her bulletproof vest. To avoid this, she hurries toward the house, with Jon cursing her under his breath. He has to be content with the fact that at least she has a weapon. With only the light of the moon and some distant streetlamps to go by, they're glad the owners laid white marble slabs, even if it's only a short distance.

He comes to a halt halfway there.

The front of the house is dotted with enormous windows three meters high that look out onto the front garden and the living room. One of the windows is a door.

Open.

Far off, a police siren starts to wail.

So much for not making any noise, thinks Jon.

"Let's wait," he whispers to Antonia.

She nods.

In situations like this where the element of surprise is lost, it's best to wait for backup. That's what all the manuals say. Swap surprise for numerical superiority.

Then she looks down at the ground. Something next to the door runner draws her attention. She bends down to get a better look. It's a small piece of molded yellow plastic. On one side there's a half-torn-off sticker. On the top there are four round pegs. On each of them is written *LEGO*.

A few months ago before Christmas, Jon had accompanied Antonia to Sarasús, a toy shop close to her apartment, to buy a present for her son, Jorge. The assistant had explained all there was to know about LEGO and its DUPLO range. The pieces were twice the size so kids couldn't swallow them. Recommended age: one to five.

Nobody had said anything about young children being in the house. Antonia drops the piece of LEGO and charges inside.

So much for caution, thinks Jon.

Nothing for it but to follow her. He walks very slowly, trying not to bump into anything. He takes the small flashlight out of his jacket pocket and shines it in front of them. There's something terribly unnerving about entering a strange house in the middle of the night knowing you could come up against an assailant. Every shadow becomes a threat, every corner hides a weapon pointed at you, every portrait on the walls looks down at you with a burglar's greed, a rapist's lust, a monster's voracity. Jon finds himself holding his breath. He walks on the outer edges of his feet rather than his heels. His ears are pricked for the slightest sound or whisper.

Then they hear a noise on the floor above.

A thud and glass smashing.

Jon pushes past Antonia, forcing her behind him, and starts up the staircase. Which, Jon notices, is very fine. Extremely tasteful. And the wood doesn't creak, he thinks as he plants his foot on the first step.

There are seventeen of them altogether.

The blood appears first on the fourteenth, staining almost all of it. It streams down onto the thirteenth, before splashing on number twelve and dripping to the living room floor.

Inspector Gutiérrez can't help but tread in it. He crouches down at the top to check that the landing is empty.

It isn't. There is a man's corpse gushing blood down the stairs. Farther on, a woman lies in a heap on the floor, a deep wound in her stomach.

Then Jon hears the gurgling.

Antonia whizzes past him, reaches the woman, and turns her on her back. Then she presses down hard on the wound.

"Is she alive?" whispers Jon.

"Only just."

Jon strides past Antonia and continues along the landing. A lamp in the main bedroom gives off a dim triangle of light in which some reddish tracks are visible. Jon doesn't need an expert in blood splatters like Antonia to figure out which way the killer went.

Despite this, Antonia gestures in that direction, doing her best to staunch the woman's wound. The victim appears completely gone: her eyes have rolled up, but she's still breathing.

Jon returns shortly afterward with bad news.

"He smashed one of the windows and jumped down into the garden. I'll tell the cops to . . ."

Antonia shakes her head and gestures to him to lower his voice.

"You'll do nothing of the sort. Call Mentor and tell him to order the cops to stay out. We've contaminated the crime scene enough as it is. Only the paramedics should be allowed in."

The sound of the police siren has reached the house and then dies away. They can hear voices outside, and the police radio. In the distance, an ambulance wail, more urgent and insistent than the police's.

"Stay with us," Antonia whispers to the woman.

Jon, meanwhile, follows Antonia's instructions; when he's done, he goes to check on the little girls. He opens each door a crack: the rooms are untouched, and the girls seem to be sleeping normally. Completely unaware that when they wake up, it will be to a world totally unlike the one they're used to. They'll wake up to a nightmare.

They're young, thinks Jon. *They'll get over it. But at what price?*

When the paramedics arrive, Antonia moves aside to let them get on with their work. While they're trying to stabilize the woman, she goes up to Jon. Her hands are covered in blood; so too are her T-shirt and jeans.

"He told me I'd pay for it. With interest," she says, voice cold, her eyes icy.

Frightening eyes.

"How do you know that . . . ?"

"He sent me a text. As we were coming in. My phone was on silent, but I saw the message on my watch."

She pulls up her sleeve—it doesn't matter now, the jacket's already ruined—and shows Jon her wrist.

YOU HAVE SIX HOURS.
W.

4

A PHRASE

The rest of the night is chaotic, dirty, and confused. A psychologist and a relative take away the two girls. Getting them out of the house is a complicated operation. It takes more than ten people, including two firefighters, to extract them through their respective windows to ensure they don't see the landing or come into contact with the horror even for an instant. Antonia stays out of the removal; Jon is the one responsible for ensuring that at least the girls won't have mental images that oblige them to remember an event that will anyway be a turning point. They'll never see their father again. They'll probably never return to this house.

At least they can avoid the toughest part, thinks Jon, looking around him when he reenters the property. The kitchen with its top-of-the-range fittings—NEFF, Gaggenau—the covered swimming pool—the house reeks of money from top to bottom. They may not be superrich like the Ortiz or Trueba families, people for whom money is a concept, not a reality you have to fight for. But it's obvious the girls will want for nothing.

Then Jon thinks this over and realizes he isn't fooling anybody. And since he's the only one listening, that makes it twice as bad.

They will want for everything.

There'll be a hole they will never fill.

Human beings are stories, and the story of that woman and her daughters can only be told as a tragedy. They will grow, live, and be reasonably happy. If they're lucky. But there will always be a void that will devour everything, a bottomless pit that will swallow all happiness and light.

Inspector Gutiérrez knows something about guilt, although compared to his colleague, he's a novice. He finds Antonia at the foot of the stairs, waiting patiently for Dr. Aguado to give her permission to go up. Thanks to Mentor's efforts, forensics and the examining magistrate have allowed them a couple of hours' head start. For now, the house is out of bounds to everyone but the three of them.

"They're safe," says Jon, gesturing toward the street, where the lights on the patrol cars are slowly gyrating.

Antonia doesn't respond. She simply stands there, arms folded. A bundle of guilt and rage compressed into a meter and a half.

"I know what you're thinking. And you're wrong," says Jon.

"He was in the house when we got here. If only . . ."

"He stabbed the woman and left her when he heard the sirens. Do you know why?"

"He figured she'd bleed to death before they arrived."

"And that didn't happen because we were already outside. You saved her life, Antonia. You drove like a lunatic, broke into the house, tended her wound."

"What did the paramedics say?"

"Nothing," Jon lies.

In fact, they told him the odds were not good for her. Word for word. But he sees no need to add fuel to a fire that Antonia is already piling logs on.

"One minute. If only we'd arrived a minute sooner . . ."

"Sweetheart," says Jon, who's becoming impatient. "If my mother had wheels, she'd be a bicycle."

Antonia lowers her head.

"It's always the same story. No matter what we do, what we achieve. In the end, at night, we remember the ones we couldn't save."

Jon knows this is true. But they have no choice, they have to carry on.

That's what his *amatxo* would say. Jon can't stop thinking about her. He wonders where she might be and if she remembered to take the moisturizing cream for her legs, because they get very dry.

He wonders how he might reassure Antonia but can't think of anything intelligent or profound. *Take a deep breath and carry on* isn't exactly one of those phrases you find in capital letters on the internet next to a black-and-white photo. But it's all he has, so he offers it.

"All we can do is take a deep breath and carry on, angel."

Antonia manages to raise her head and attempts a timid smile.

"I'm sorry. I usually talk to Grandma Scott about these things."

"I can wear rollers if you want, sweetie."

"Grandma Scott wouldn't be seen dead in rollers, and besides, they wouldn't suit you."

Humor bounces off her, thinks Jon.

WHAT THEY DID THEN

Nuno leaves the room, but Mentor stays to study the woman. Her hospital gown is open at the back, showing her underwear. Black sports bra and underpants. She has straw-colored hair and hard-to-define eyes, possibly gray. Her skin is a strange dark color, unhealthy looking. She is as lean and muscular as a competitor in a twenty-kilometer walk.

Observing her, Mentor realizes something for the first time. Her vast intelligence is different from Antonia's. She has the cunning of a trapped animal, of a wolf that scents the weakest sheep. Ironically, this isn't what terrifies him. What scares Mentor most is realizing that the radical difference between Scott and her lies somewhere far deeper.

It's a question of willpower.

Antonia Scott keeps going even after she's run out of road. When she's reached the cliff edge and is plunging into the abyss. Antonia simply refuses to hit the ground.

This woman, on the other hand . . .

"I'd like to ask you a question," says Mentor through the loudspeakers.

She continues pacing in circles, but turns her head sharply toward the two-way mirror. She's still moving, but her eyes are fixed straight ahead, like a mongoose's.

"The day of your first test, you gave me a most unusual answer. I'd like to know how you concluded you had to make the decision you did."

"There are more people on an oil platform than on a tanker," she says, breathing heavily.

"Yes, that's what you said then," recalls Mentor. "Now tell me the truth."

She comes to an abrupt halt. Her breathing is increasingly rapid. She can't get enough air into her lungs. If he hadn't left the control panel, Mentor would see that the oxygen levels in her blood are dangerously low. In fact, he doesn't need to see, because it's obvious she can barely stay on her feet.

"Are you playing with the air supply again, Mentor?" she asks hoarsely.

"Isn't the brain a marvelous machine? A two percent variation in oxygen to the hippocampus, and the executive functions become impaired. For example, the ability to lie is diminished."

The woman leans against the mirror. Her sweaty forehead is pressed up to the glass; her left fist pummels it feebly. Even so, Mentor flinches. If it weren't for the twelve millimeters of glass between them, they could virtually kiss each other.

Or she could kill me, Mentor realizes.

In many ways, it's as if he's seeing her for the first time. Without the veils she has draped about herself or those he has attempted to drape.

"It was the quickest way to win," the woman says, panting.

"Finally, a true word," says Mentor, pressing the button that releases oxygen. There's a slight hiss in the pipes in the ceiling. It will take a few seconds to fill the thirty cubic meters of the room.

"It's not the one you wanted, is it?"

"Neither I nor the families of the eighty crew members on the tanker."

"It was only a theoretical exercise!"

"One you didn't hesitate over for an instant."

"There's no glory without corpses. Regretting it would be like regretting peeling an orange."

"Would you do anything to win?" says Mentor, a shudder running down his spine.

Mentor barely reacts when she slumps to the floor, half unconscious. He is still troubled by his own failure. Perhaps that's why he doesn't hear the last words she utters. Whispered with what remains of her breath to the hard, cold concrete.

I'd do anything for you.

Two men in blue overalls enter the room and walk over to her.

They've come to pick her up off the floor. Help her. Lead her out of the room.

She has forfeited her place on the Red Queen project.

None of this happens.

She knows the veil has fallen. That she no longer needs to restrain herself. To hide. Mentor has seen her true colors. To some extent, it's a relief. A liberation.

The moment has come to tear away the mask completely.

When the first of the two men places his hand on her shoulder, she plays dead, forcing him to lean in closer. Then she reacts.

She yanks his wrist until his neck is level with her mouth. She lunges at him, sinking her teeth into his throat, ripping his flesh. She doesn't manage to take a bite out of him, but the wound to his throat is severe. He can't scream because she's destroyed his larynx. He's busy trying not to choke, raising his hands to the gaping, bloody wound.

While this brief slaughter was taking place, the other man froze.

It's one thing to tie up, gag, and insult a defenseless woman for a scientific experiment

(and a pretty good wage in the midst of the crisis, I mean, where would I find another job at my age that even gives me time to go home and help the kids with their homework)

it's quite another to watch her sink her teeth into your workmate's throat.

He only reacts when she turns toward him. There's next to no blood on her mouth, just a trickle running down her chin and onto the white gown. What terrifies him are her eyes, the pupils tiny as pinpoints.

This is when he turns and runs for the exit. He has almost reached the door handle when something jerks him back. Not far, just a few centimeters. He lifts a hand to his neck, where the woman is throttling him with the electrode cables. He falls backward onto her, struggling to free himself. In vain. One cable snaps, but the others evade his groping fingers, cutting into his neck. As he tries to stand up and get away from her, he merely increases the pressure around his neck. In the final moments before he loses consciousness, blue tongue protruding from his mouth, he's aware of her feet braced against his shoulders to ensure she finishes the job.

When three more men burst into the room, she's still intensifying the pressure on his throat. She's exhausted, but she hasn't let go.

Or stopped smiling.

5

A CRIME SCENE

"Whenever you're ready," comes Aguado's voice from the top of the stairs. It's a few minutes later and all the lights in the house are on. The staircase looks like a still from *American Psycho*, with the blood drying on the micro-cement floor. Aguado's plastic suit only adds to the illusion. The pathologist has covered the problematic stairs with more plastic sheeting.

To judge by the few markers Aguado has placed, there is not much to see on the landing. The killer's shoe prints, bloodstains, and little else.

Antonia Scott has her own way of doing things. She ignores Aguado's little orange plastic triangles and relies on her training.

She takes in every detail of the crime scene. She studies each element in turn in an endless loop, homing in on:

The staircase banister, where one of the struts is slightly damaged.

The position of the body, face down with the arms underneath the torso.

> *The pajama, the defensive wound, thecutsthedamagetothefaceitsverycloseandthatrequiresanexplanationthatsenough-please...*

"She's going to need one of these," Aguado whispers to Jon, who is standing a safe distance from her.

She shows him a small metal box.

"I'll take care of that, Doctor."

He snatches it from her nicotine-stained fingers. Dr. Aguado usually has a strong tobacco smell, but in recent days, it has solidified, almost as though she is wearing it.

"Aren't you going to give her one?" she asks, surprised.

"Not if I can avoid it. She had a crisis in Málaga, but she sorted herself out."

"It's not the first time. Listen . . ."

The doctor seems to want to tell him something, but Jon cuts her short.

"She'll come out of it on her own."

"I don't think that's the best solution, given . . ."

Aguado doesn't finish her sentence: there's no need. Jon knows what she means.

Given your life depends on it.

"I trust her."

"I see," she says, drawing out the syllables. "It's your call."

What Aguado's skeptical, educated voice actually seems to be saying is, *It's your funeral, you fool*, but even so, Jon has no qualms. Or very few. Okay, a lot, but he bites his lip like a true champ.

He has no intention of betraying Antonia.

More important than staying alive is staying human.

"I trust her," he says again, largely for his own benefit.

6

TWO STAIRCASES

Right now, the person keeping Jon awake at night doesn't inspire much confidence.

She stumbles, props herself against the wall, buries her head in her hands. She isn't exactly a picture of stability, outside or inside. Her breathing is heavy and rapid, and she seems on the verge of a panic attack.

She counts to ten, breathing out between each number, descending one step at a time, toward where she needs to be, toward darkness. Only she can't reach it.

The koan doesn't really work. Words no longer tether her to anything.

You have to find your story, Mentor had told her. *Your story. Somewhere between rage and serenity.*

In Málaga, she didn't descend a staircase, she crossed a bridge. She found her story by remembering her mother. Traveling to a place within herself she'd never been to before. She came back wounded, but stronger.

She doesn't want to go to that place again. The pain is too great, too fresh. Ever since this kicked off—and Antonia is pretty sure that was when Jon entered her life—her peace ritual, her sacred three minutes a day, has become a rare luxury. And in recent days, impossible. Serenity is not an option. A sense of guilt dogs every step she takes. Sometimes she feels if she turned around fast enough, she'd see them all behind her. The string of corpses she has left on the ground as a result of her clumsiness, her incompetence. Because she wasn't strong enough.

And maybe that's the problem, she thinks, stuck on her mind's staircase, only two steps from darkness. *Maybe I've got this wrong. Maybe Mentor has as well.*

Then she does something she's never done before.

She turns back.

There are no longer eight steps behind her like before. Now there are more, many more. And the staircase isn't straight, it twists up in a spiral, growing narrower as it does so.

Antonia starts to ascend.

She opens her eyes.

All at once, the world slows down. The tingling in her hands, chest, and face dissipates.

As she takes a last big gulp of air, she realizes the monkeys inside her head are almost silent. It's not the same as a red pill—nothing could be. But she can't remember having felt this

(sane)
serene for
(ever)
a very long time

She turns to examine the crime scene. And starts to see:

"The killer came in through the garden door. There's a pressure sensor, so he must have disconnected the alarm. Unless they forgot to switch it on, which I doubt. Doctor?"

"I'll check," says Aguado.

Antonia doesn't respond. She's still in her bubble, visualizing every single detail of the crime, almost like rewinding a film in her mind. Or rather, doing another take, because she moves the characters around in her mind until they fit the facts.

"He climbed the stairs, and that's where he encountered the husband. What's his name?"

"Jaume Soler. The woman is called Aura Reyes."

"Jaume attacked the intruder with the golf club. The intruder must have protected himself . . ."

Antonia raises her arm and moves to one side. Then she bends down and picks up the golf club Aguado has already bagged up and labeled. She studies it closely.

"He's left-handed. He raises his arm to protect himself—it's the same one with which he's holding the knife."

"How . . ."

"From the marks on the shaft of the club. Then the killer and Jaume struggled. One of them was pushed against the banister."

She points to the damaged strut.

"It was only a very brief struggle. A man who's half asleep and out of shape hasn't a chance against a trained killer."

Antonia looks down at the body on the floor, then at the wall where the woman's blood has left a smeary semicircle on the acrylic paint.

"He was the target," says Antonia.

"It could have been the woman."

"He stabbed the man first, then turned on her."

"Possibly to get rid of the threat the man posed."

Antonia points to the lateral wound on the corpse. The tear in the pajama jacket is relatively small, despite the huge loss of blood.

"Look at the intercostal incision. I reckon when you do the autopsy, you'll see he didn't even touch a bone."

"I agree. This is the work of a professional. A perfectly aimed thrust," says Aguado.

"Hers was . . . different. A first wound to the stomach? Not something a professional would do. So he was the target. She was . . ."

Jon, who has remained silent all this time, listening closely to the exchange between Antonia and the pathologist, chooses this moment to intervene.

"The dessert. He was toying with her. But we appeared."

He doesn't add *so we saved her life after all*, because he's not in the mood to listen to Antonia deny it. Even so, he lets the phrase hang in the air for her to cling on to.

Antonia nods grimly. Her eyes are on fire.

If Jon didn't know better—because he's been watching her like a hawk—he'd suspect her of taking a red pill. But no. This time, it seems she's done it all by herself. Her hands are still shaking, her head bowed—maybe to try to listen to those monkeys of hers or to get away from them. But at least this time she hasn't run away or blamed herself.

Small victories, thinks Jon.

"Possibly. But we arrived too late," she says, pointing to the dead body.

And a few defeats, thinks Jon.

"Can we turn him over?"

The pathologist nods and bends over the body. With the expertise of someone who has flipped dozens of corpses, she slides her forearm under the victim's chest to make a lever. She uses the other to pull the pelvis toward her. The dead man turns over.

Jon also stoops and looks with horror at the terrible, gaping wound in the man's neck. It's like a second mouth in the wrong place. An obscenity that offends the sight and another sense as well. Common sense.

It's hard to look at the man without averting your eyes, but Jon does just that. When he turns his head, he finds Antonia crouching right beside him rather than in her usual position, looking down from a great height.

So Inspector Gutiérrez finds himself centimeters from the disaster. A privileged witness to the confusion and surprise in Antonia's eyes as she stares relentlessly at the dead man's cold, unmoving eye sockets.

"No," she says.

Antonia straightens up without adding anything more and moves off into the main bedroom. Jon and Dr. Aguado exchange glances. She gestures to him, and so Jon follows Antonia, who is standing in front of the window.

Even from the hallway, he can see she's still trembling. He goes over to her, treading firmly on the parquet floor so as to avoid startling her. He stands beside her and peers through the glass. The window faces east, so the bed is bathed in the early morning light. To Jon, who detests the slightest amount of light when he's resting, this is plain weird. But then he'd sleep inside a gas tank if he could.

The sun hasn't yet risen, but the sky outside is turning from indigo to magenta. The officers out in the street huddle in their coats and stamp their feet on the ground to ward off the cold. The handful of nosy neighbors have scuttled back inside their houses.

Antonia's breath condenses on the glass in a faint cloud, a semicircle almost identical to the one made by the woman's blood on the wall behind them. It's something neither Jon nor Antonia will ever realize.

"Well, are you going to tell me why Antonia Scott was so surprised? She who normally looks at dismembered bodies without raising an eyebrow?"

Jon casts the line and waits.

A minute goes by.

Two.

"Take your time. It's not as if we're in a hurry," says Jon, nostrils flaring.

Antonia goes on staring out of the window, arms folded. When she finally starts to speak, she does so exasperatingly slowly, as if she were digging each word from a past buried under a ton of rocks.

"I was so surprised because that man has been dead for four years."

THE DEAD MAN
FOUR YEARS EARLIER

"You haven't even tried the artichokes."

Antonia looks at her husband, at the empty tray, and at her husband once more.

"There are none left," she says, unable to follow.

Marcos smiles. It's a gentle, slightly wry smile. The sort you give when you see a child avoiding, by a miracle, putting their fingers in a socket or when a TV competitor gives an obviously wrong answer. "Shall I order another dish?" he says, knowing full well what the answer will be.

"No, I'm not really hungry."

Marcos looks at his wife and then at the empty plate of *callos a la madrileña*, then back at his wife.

"It's a mystery how you survive on so little."

Antonia is vaguely aware that Marcos is teasing her. In recent days, they've barely had time to be together, so she makes the most of the moment. When he extends his hand across the table, she takes it and squeezes hard. She can't hurt him this way: Marcos's square hands are tough and calloused, as if they were sculpted in the same stone he works with every day.

"This one's on me," she says when the waiter brings the check.

"No, me," Marcos replies, trying to snatch it.

It's an old game they play.

Ever since they began seeing each other, they've fought over who gets the check. At first, it was a matter of principle for Antonia because

Marcos comes from an affluent family. So does she, but since she cut all ties with her father, she's had to fend for herself.

Nowadays, Antonia has a five-figure monthly salary, so she can compete with Marcos as an equal. His parents are no longer alive, but they left him the building where the couple live.

The rents from the other apartments bring in a tidy sum each month, even after all the expenses are paid. The tenants are mostly hipsters, willing to pay premium rents—and then some—so they can live as close as possible to the center, its bars that sell craft beers, and cafés that look good on their Instagram posts.

This enables Marcos to dedicate himself to sculpture, which is his passion. Art absorbs and fulfills him, and he is improving by leaps and bounds. He's already had two pretty good exhibitions; every indication is that his career is about to take off. It also leaves him time for his son, which is the important thing, especially since Antonia keeps odd hours and often spends periods away from home. Because of her work as a police "consultant." Work that intrigues Marcos, but which he never asks her about, because Antonia has made it clear she won't tell him a thing.

Marcos has learned to understand this aspect of his wife. It drives him crazy, but he knows it's part of what makes her unique. His reticence has to do with the essence of his profession: to extract beauty from the world, however hidden it might be at first sight.

It's said of Michelangelo that one day he found a block of Carrara marble in the work yard of Florence Cathedral. He was twenty-six at the time and not afraid of challenges. The slab of rock was covered by weeds and was thought to be cursed. The sculptor Agostino Di Duccio had made an enormous hole in the marble, then abandoned it. Five meters of marble that nobody wanted.

For months, Michelangelo stared at the block. He walked around it, sat on it, even put his ear to it. Students and priests walked by, looking at him as if he were mad.

One day, he picked up a chisel and set to work. He didn't have a plaster model or any sketches. He simply started chipping at it. After a week, he asked for a wall to be built around the marble block. He needed privacy for what he was about to do.

It took him four years.

Finally, Michelangelo announced that in a few hours the walls could come down. The whole of Florence gathered in the yard and beyond, intrigued but certain the young sculptor had failed. Workmen knocked over the bricks of the wall. And for the first time, the world beheld his *David*. The greatest masterpiece not only of the Renaissance but also perhaps in the entire history of mankind.

Speechless with astonishment and admiration, the bishop of Florence went up to Michelangelo and asked him how he had managed to create something so perfect. Michelangelo shrugged and said:

"David was in the block of marble, I simply had to remove what was inessential."

Marcos isn't Michelangelo, but he shares the same profession. And knows that it's from the most challenging blocks that the most beautiful sculptures are hewn. His love for Antonia is boundless precisely because it isn't easy. Because it takes effort, because it's noble but satisfying. Because, like him, Antonia gives herself wholeheartedly. That's why he loves her madly. Even if sometimes she drives him out of his mind. Like now, for example.

She won't stop looking at her watch, even though it's an hour before the nanny has to leave.

"Jorge is fine. Relax. Let's have an ice cream."

Antonia shakes her head.

"I have to make a couple of calls. Do you mind going on ahead of me? I'll make it up to you."

Marcos sighs, but can sense she's in a weak position and so uses it to negotiate in his favor.

"That depends."

"On what?"

"If '*make it up to you*' has a hidden agenda."

"Of course not, what kind of hidden agenda?"

Antonia stops when she sees the gesture Marcos is making with the first finger of his right hand and the first finger and thumb of the left one. She smiles, scolds him, and blushes, all at the same time. Seeing this stirs Marcos's heart and other muscles as well.

"Tonight, we can talk about polysemy," says Antonia, giving in, "if you have any new words for our special dictionary."

"I have one, from Latin. I'll explain it later."

Marcos gives her a kiss, says goodbye, and heads for the exit. Antonia stares after him, a faint smile still on her lips. It vanishes the moment he has left. She takes a little metal box from her jacket pocket and picks out one of the red pills she carries for emergencies. She bites the capsule to release the bitter powder, then sprinkles it under her tongue so the mucosa will absorb the cocktail of chemical substances quickly into her bloodstream.

She waits a moment while the world around her slows and she can focus on the danger behind her back.

"I hope you know who and what you're messing with," she says out loud, without turning around.

The person at the table behind Antonia gets up and sits in the place Marcos has just left free.

"With your permission."

"You didn't need it to follow us all the way down Calle de Preciados or when we went shopping. Or when you gave the waiter a tip so you could sit at that table," says Antonia.

The man must be forty-five or forty-six years old. He's tall, with broad, prominent shoulders. A Catalan accent. He has a small goatee, eyeglasses, and the timid, myopic gaze of people who spend too many hours in front of a screen. An accountant perhaps. Clearly not trained for violence. In Antonia's mind, the danger level goes down from threat to concern. She was right to let him trail them for hours without informing Mentor. She sensed from his manner that he only wanted to talk to her. But that he couldn't do so in front of Marcos.

"I could have sworn you hadn't seen me," the man says. "You really are as impressive as people say."

"What people?"

"Everyone. At least all those who know about Valencia."

Antonia observes him a little more closely.

He's definitely not an accountant. The shirt is expensive, good quality. The cuffs are slightly shiny around the buttons. The jacket is comfortable, but he doesn't wear it for work. He sits at a computer, yet the material shows none of the characteristic signs—the telltale bulge of jackets that are hung up or the bagginess of being draped around the chair back. He only wears it to go out. No necktie. His nails are manicured. His hair neatly cut.

"I don't know what you're talking about."

"We both know perfectly well what I'm talking about."

"What I'd like to know is your name."

"I've come to talk to you about what you need to know, not what you'd like to know."

With that, the strange man begins to tell her a strange story that's plainly bogus. About a professional hit man. An extraordinarily dangerous individual.

"He can make any murder look like an accidental death. Even the most complicated. He's worked in America, the Middle East, in Asia. . . . For the past few months, he's established himself in Europe."

The man passes her a photo. When Antonia makes no effort to take it, he sets it down on the table in front of her. Between the glass of water and the sugar bowl.

Taken from a distance, it shows an elegant man aged about thirty-five. Wavy fair hair. He's about to get into a car. Antonia thinks he looks similar to the Scottish actor in *Moulin Rouge*, but it's hard to tell because the image is blurred.

"It's the only existing photo of him. In fact, he doesn't know it exists. If he did, he wouldn't have stopped until he killed everyone who'd seen it. He has something of a theatrical bent."

"Why are you telling me all this?"

"Because this man is a devil, Señora Scott. He's implacable and has superhuman intelligence. Only someone like you can stop him."

"Me? But I'm an English philologist."

"What you definitely aren't is an actress," the man says, rubbing his stomach. He must be famished, he can't have had time to stop for a bite if he's been following them all day. They're on the roof terrace of one of Madrid's finest restaurants, and at four o'clock in the afternoon in mid-June, sunny Puerta del Sol is living up to its name.

Antonia raises a finger, and one of the waiters hurries over. Soon afterward, he returns with a bottle of water for the man and a coffee for her.

"I still don't understand why you've been trailing me all day. Why not go to the police?"

"Señora Scott, the mere existence of this . . . being, to call him something, is the reason why the Red Queen project was created in the first place."

Definitely works in computing. But not an executive—the speech and mannerisms don't fit. An engineer, a consultant, Antonia deduces. He has a Barcelona accent. *Maybe one of the people involved with the new tool they started testing prior to Valencia? The technology is in Barcelona.*

"It's not smart to use those two words in public."

"I'm desperate. I need your help. And believe me, when I tell you what I know, you won't refuse."

Antonia leans across the table.

"Tell me, then. I have fifty minutes before my son has his tea. Start with your name and how you're linked to the Red Queen project. And no lies. If you really know who I am, you'll know I'll check."

The man leans back to avoid being so close to Antonia. He glances over his shoulder. The tables are emptying as people finish lunch. There's no longer anybody near him.

"No . . . not here," he objects. "We can speak some other time. Think about what I've told you."

He rises clumsily to his feet, knocking the back of his chair against the one behind. Then he leaves without looking around.

Antonia stays where she is, thinking about the strange encounter that's just taken place. She doesn't say anything until the waiter comes to whisk away the empty bottle of water. She stops him, picks up a napkin, and takes hold of the neck of the bottle, carefully avoiding touching the lower part, where the man has left his fingerprints.

7

A TICKET

"And that was everything," says Antonia, who has been staring out of the window all this time.

Outside, day has broken over the horizon. It promises to be one of those icy Madrid mornings. Not a cloud in the sky, not a hint of warmth. Jon isn't the first to think that in a Madrid winter the sun cools rather than warms.

"And you never saw him again?"

"No. Two days later, White broke into our apartment and left Marcos in a coma. He almost killed me; the rest you know."

No, thinks Jon. *No, I don't know the rest.*

I know nothing about those three years. About what you did or how low you sank.

I know nothing about how much you lost along the way. Or what you are regaining now. Because piecing you together is like doing a fucking jigsaw puzzle without the photo on the box. In the dark and with my hands tied.

I don't know, but I will. As you always say. If you let me. If you'll only let me.

Jon wants to shout at her. To embrace her. He wants to be a thousand kilometers away with a beer—and without a bomb on his neck.

But the world isn't the outlandish Willy Wonka's marvelous factory. The only ticket you're sure to win isn't a golden one, and it doesn't take you to a magic place with rivers of chocolate but to a very different one.

And Jon's ticket has an exit time that's drawing ever closer.

"I understand why you didn't want to tell me this before."

"Two days, Jon. I had two whole days' warning. And even so . . ."

"You didn't do anything because you thought they were a madman's ravings. But you did get his fingerprints, didn't you?"

"Yes, but I was told he was dead."

"Well, it seems he wasn't."

"We'll come back to that. First, let's find out who the victim is. What's most important is to discover who killed him, not my link to him," says Antonia, moving away from the window.

"That's where you're wrong."

Taken aback, Antonia turns, a strange expression on her face.

She cannot remember Jon ever having spoken like that before.

"Your brain. The way it works . . . it's programmed to follow the evidence," says Jon, pointing to her head. "To analyze it and come to conclusions. You're trying to fit together in your mind everything we're experiencing, all this craziness."

Like me with you.

"Piece by piece, by color. But the *whats* and *hows* are distracting you from what matters most."

Antonia pauses and looks down at the floor, as though the answer were somewhere between her toes.

"Okay. The *why* is what matters most."

"It can't be a coincidence that the man who told you about White four years ago is now dead. Didn't he say White was so concerned to remain undetected that he eliminates all those who know of his existence?"

"Are you suggesting White killed him?"

"It makes no sense. If he killed Soler to cover his tracks, why order us to solve the murder?"

"A murder he knew was going to happen. Remember, he just gave us the address to start with. It was only when we were there that he sent the second text."

"It's still crazy."

"So is this part of his game?"

"That's a circular answer: he killed Soler because he's playing with us. It leaves out the most important question: Why?"

Jon raises a fingertip to his lips—the way he always does when he's about to make a profound statement:

"I haven't got a fucking clue."

* * *

Antonia rubs her face, drags her fingers through her hair—without improving the mess—and eventually comes out with the Scott variation of what Inspector Gutiérrez has just said.

"We'll work with what we have. Time is running out."

8

A NUTCRACKER

When they return to the body, they find Dr. Aguado packing up her things. Jon has always been fascinated by the myriad bits and pieces the pathologist always carries with her. Measuring rods, scale rulers, magnifying glasses, cameras, jars containing all manner of powders, chemical products and reagents, plastic bags, and empty receptacles of all sizes. He finds it fascinating that she's mastered all these elements but is still more impressed by an apparently trivial detail. Whenever she finishes her work, she puts everything back into her two steel cases without leaving behind so much as a single paper clip. An incredible feat anyone can appreciate if they've ever purchased something made in China, taken it out of its box, discovered it doesn't work, and tried to put everything back in exactly as they found it.

"I'm just about done here. The crime scene's been processed, so I'll leave the rest of the house to the forensic team, though I doubt they'll find much."

"It's a professional job," agrees Antonia.

"Something went wrong. Otherwise, he'd have killed them in their beds without all the fuss."

"Maybe the woman saw something," suggests Jon. "We need to talk to her."

"She's in the ICU at La Zarzuela hospital. I asked Mentor to put a guard outside the door. If she saw the killer, he might want to finish the job. Meanwhile, I'll go back to headquarters and get everyone working on this. Let's see if we come up with something."

"Thanks, Doctor," says Antonia.

* * *

After a few minutes separately inspecting the house—as dull and conventional from a police point of view as from any other—they converge in the doorway of Jaume Soler's study. It's a surprisingly somber place. A shelf full of programming language and software manuals. One in particular catches Jon's eye.

"It looks as though the guy wrote books too," he says, taking it out and showing Antonia the cover.

Deep Learning and High-Level Programming Languages, by Jaume Soler, Ph.D., it says on the cover. The illustration is a drawing of a brain made up of ones and zeros.

There are no more books by Soler but a bunch of family photos. The biggest hangs on the wall near the desk. A picture of the couple's wedding day. Jaume appears much younger dressed as a bridegroom, a goofy look on his face. *All grooms look goofy, but this takes the cake*, thinks Jon.

It's hard to tell how happy a marriage is from photographs, but in his years as a cop, Inspector Gutiérrez has developed a certain knack for it. A knack that doesn't seem to be working properly, because he can't reach any conclusion from what he's looking at. Señor Soler has one of those faces that makes it impossible to tell whether they're concealing intelligence or ulterior motives.

And this freaks Jon out.

He'll soon discover how right he is, but for the moment, he's too preoccupied by something else that jars.

"I don't get it. If this guy is so into computers, why isn't there a single Funko on his shelf? No Ghostbuster figures, not even a sad old Darth Vader. . . . What's wrong?"

"I thought you didn't like clichés."

"What clichés do you mean?"

"Stereotypes. Like saying gays always dress like freaks."

"Honey, I'm *literally* wearing a bright green Gucci suit. Thanks to you, I'm practically expiring in this horror."

Jon realizes too late this could refer to something other than Antonia simply having picked out his party clothes instead of his usual sober work suit. He instantly regrets having opened his big mouth, but happily Antonia's customary deafness to sarcasm comes to his rescue.

"To me, it looks elegant."

"Not for a crime scene. Especially not when I'm the victim."

He takes a deep breath and looks around him.

"I don't know, sweetheart. This guy doesn't seem on the level to me. Something here doesn't quite fit."

Antonia is rummaging in the filing cabinet next to the desk. Her hands in their latex gloves appear to be randomly pecking at the different items she finds—most of them items of stationery.

"From a heuristic point of view, intuitions are data that hasn't been processed rationally but can leapfrog logical thought processes to produce a cognitive result."

Jon mulls over what she's just said.

"I wish I understood you."

Antonia in turn mulls over how to translate for Jon what she's just said. She can't find the words in any language but thinks of a personal experience she confided to him. The only living person apart from her grandmother who knows about it.

"Maybe," she says slowly, as if she still finds it difficult to talk about, "you also have a monkey pointing things out to you."

Jon has no difficulty understanding this. The problem is the monkey doesn't appear, the study isn't very big, and the only bit they haven't examined is the desk. A mahogany top resting on two stainless steel trestles. A state-of-the-art model you can raise or lower simply by pressing a button. On it is a laptop on a metal base, two thirty-inch monitors, and a keyboard.

Antonia switches on the computer and is faced with the login screen. She stares intently at it, then strides out of the room. Puzzled, Jon follows her to discover she's stopped the forensics team carrying out a stretcher upon which they've placed an enormous black bag.

"Hold on a sec," she tells them.

She runs to the kitchen island, rummages in the drawers, and reappears with a long metal object in each hand.

"A nutcracker? What do you want with a . . ."

Antonia doesn't respond but unzips the bag and pulls out the dead man's right hand. The reason for the nutcracker becomes clear when she holds up the dead man's right index finger at the level of the middle knuckle and presses down with all her might. At first, nothing happens. On her second attempt, there's a dull, unpleasant crack. Like opening a pistachio wrapped in a slice of ham.

"Oh."

This is all Jon says. An interjection sufficiently ambiguous to mean anything on the broad spectrum running from:

Oh, so that's what the nutcracker was for.

To:

Oh, you're crazy as a coot.

By the time it comes to using the other object she brought from the kitchen (fish scissors), Jon doesn't need to look. He can't anyway, as he's busy trying to stop the forensic team hurling themselves at Antonia. Somewhat vigorously, grabbing one by the shirtfront and another by the arm. Luckily, they're more accustomed to lifting petri dishes than three-hundred-kilo rocks, so Jon copes quite well. At least until Antonia severs the finger from the corpse and returns to the study, leaving Jon with the awkward task of explaining.

"Look, the thing is . . ."

9

A FINGER

When Jon returns to Jaume Soler's study some ten awkward minutes later, Antonia is sitting absorbed by what's on the computer. The finger is lying abandoned on the mahogany desk, as is the Touch ID to activate the login.

"Can I ask you a favor?"

Antonia gives what sounds like a vague grunt of agreement.

"Would you mind not mutilating victims' bodies without warning me beforehand? If it's not too much to ask."

Another vague murmur.

Jon walks round the desk and stands behind her. Once the temptation to throttle her has passed—which takes a while, as with Antonia, it's a sensation that lingers like a deodorant—he concentrates on what she is doing.

Antonia has accessed the computer archives and is opening folder after folder, trying to find something that doesn't look like gibberish.

"Do you understand any of this?" he says.

"No. They're strings of code, project archives, but nothing I can follow. Do you know anything about programming?"

"I used to program Amatxo's VCR to record her favorite afternoon TV program. Does that count?"

"I'm afraid not," Antonia says, turning back to the screen.

"If we're looking for a motive for his murder, we could start with the traditional one: money. Why don't you search your magic fascist satellite and leave the suspect's computer to me? I'm as likely to understand it as you."

Antonia grudgingly yields the chair to him, then picks up her iPad and opens the Heimdal app. A few minutes later, she looks up and shows Jon the dead man's current accounts.

"Wow, they weren't doing badly, were they?" says Jon, giving a whistle when he sees the balance.

A few cents short of €2 million.

"You can say that again," says Antonia.

"Do we know where the dough comes from?"

"There are regular monthly transfers of fifty thousand euros from the same foreign company. Let's see if I can find out who they are."

Antonia struggles with the app while Jon is engrossed in the computer. Normally for both of them, these qualify as tedious tasks. Under pressure from the countdown hanging over their heads, they become unbearable. Jon can't help glancing every few minutes at the corner of the screen where the clock is inexorably advancing toward the new deadline White has set them.

This level of anxiety makes it a lot harder to stay focused. Jon's mind wanders for a moment, leading him to make a strange reflection. His life can be summed up not just by the few remaining minutes he has but also by the unspoken words. All those that will stay inside him having never reached their goal. Some would enable him to get a last few home truths off his massive chest to certain people.

Then there are the others.

Words that heal, that save.

To Amatxo, first and foremost.

To Antonia as well.

To himself, who needs them most of all.

We always tell ourselves that tomorrow is another day. That we'll have time to fix things. Until we don't.

Antonia throws her iPad onto the desk in a gesture of utter exasperation. This is so unusual for her that Jon turns to look at her with alarm.

"I can't take any more," says Antonia.

"Don't quit on me now, for God's sake, sweetie."

Antonia shakes her head and leans on the desk.

"There's nothing here. I've found the company that makes the transfers on the island of Jersey. A tax haven. Beyond that, nothing. It's as if it didn't exist."

As so often when he needs to think, Jon scratches the back of his neck. Except that this habitual gesture of his now becomes a stark reminder of the threat hanging over him as his fingers come up against the lump in his skin and the bump of the incision. He pulls his hand away.

"I'd suggest we go home and sleep on it, but we're running out of time."

"I know. I know. And I feel it's all right there in front of us. And has been ever since . . ."

Jon usually hates the face Antonia has just pulled. The one that says, "You've given me an idea, even though you haven't a clue what it is, and right now, my mind is working so hard I won't bother explaining it to you." On this occasion, though, his sense of relief is more than understandable.

Antonia picks up the iPad again and starts typing furiously.

"The payments start four years ago."

"Before or after your encounter with him?"

"The first is one month after. Do me a favor and open the calendar icon."

The icon is clearly visible in the toolbar. A double click and it opens, showing the current calendar month. Each day is filled with notes and strange terms.

ASSEMBLE BLOCK 34HCV

CLEAN UP ERRORS STR.SUBSTRING

"I don't understand any of it."

"Me neither. Go to four years ago."

Jon scrolls back until he reaches the month in June that changed everything.

"That's the day he and I met," says Antonia, pointing to the eleventh.

There are no entries on that day. Strange for a man who has filled all the others with notes.

Only one other day is blank.

A week prior to that.

"Do you know what day that is?" Antonia asks in a whisper.

Jon knows he's heard that date before. All of a sudden, he can hear Víctor Blázquez's voice:

It happened on June 6 . . .

"That's impossible," says Jon. "Do you think . . . ?"

"Let's search his emails."

They look through everything, but find no leads. Almost all the emails are in the spam folder. Ads or offers of millions from people in Africa who've inherited a fortune, the usual stuff. Soler's inbox contains only emails from relatives, telephone or electricity bills . . .

"No, he's too clever to have left any trace there. Where do you men hide what you don't want your partner to see?"

Jon hesitates a moment, then says:

"In a folder called MISCELLANEOUS that contains another called BORING STUFF, and inside that a third that says CONTAINS NO PORN."

"Try in photos."

Jon returns to file finder and filters the search to show only folders with images.

"There are hundreds of them."

"Put them on gallery and scroll through," says Antonia. She's very aware they have only sixty minutes remaining.

"This is no way to work," complains Jon.

The folders appear on the screen, all of them apparently identical. Until one catches Antonia's eye.

"Stop. Open that one."

The folder she's singled out has nothing distinctive about it apart from a small lock icon in one corner.

The folder's name is GRAPHIC RESOURCES.

"I suppose that could be the same as MISCELLANEOUS," Jon says, double-clicking on the icon.

The folder won't open. What appears instead is the Touch ID. Antonia picks up the dead man's finger from the desk and places it carefully on the sensor. A red light blinks in the top corner.

"What the fuck is it doing now?"

"The sensors function by detecting the electricity in our bodies. That's how they read the fingerprints. The longer you're dead, the less electricity."

"Is that how you stole the red pills?" asks Jon, all innocence.

"Did you notice Mentor was missing any fingers?"

"I don't go around counting people's knuckles."

"And I don't go around stealing pills. I didn't need to," says Antonia, still struggling unsuccessfully with the sensor.

"If the coffee machine at the precinct refuses your euro coin, you rub it on the side of the machine, and it works," suggests Jon. Partly to help and partly to piss her off.

Antonia stares at him, lowering her head slightly as though considering the idea. Then she moves the fingertip toward Jon's jacket sleeve.

"Hey!"

Ignoring his protests, Antonia rubs the finger on the material. She quickly presses it on the sensor and is immediately rewarded with a green light.

"Static electricity. Good call."

Jon doesn't have much time to curse, because the folder opens, revealing its contents to them.

Reveal *is the word*, thinks Jon when he sees this display of skin, buttocks, sexual organs, and mammary glands.

Fifty-four photographs.

The same woman appears in all of them. In all the usual positions. *Sexting* it's called. Her face is visible in only a few of them. But one is enough. Jon opens it to confirm what they already know.

I knew this guy was hiding something.

Buck naked, looking suggestively into the camera, is Raquel Planas.

"It looks as if we've found her killer. A bit late, but we're doing good. Fucking awesome," says Jon, thumping the desk exasperatedly.

WHAT THEY DID THEN

When it comes down to it, life in an asylum isn't so bad. Nights hardly exist. The drugs they stuff down your throat—by force the first few nights, then slightly less violently as your spirit starts to break—make you disappear. They get rid of dreams, nightmares. The endless half sleep from the moment when you closed your eyes until your bladder took over has gone. Instead, there's a thick, heavy black curtain. And when you awake, drapes of dark velvet still hang from your eyelids.

You truly understand death when they induce that dense, muddy sleep. You understand what it is to disappear into the void. To cease being.

This is the first time the woman has slept. In her previous twenty-three years, she can't remember a single night of pure relaxation, of authentic calm.

Thanks to the distance and emotional numbness the medication produces, she starts to analyze her life before. Not during the absurd therapy sessions the psychiatrists impose on her, where she simply remains silent and withdraws inside herself. No, she does it during the moments when they leave her sufficiently alone, when they park her in a corner of the communal area, strapped to her wheelchair, along with the other guests. That's what they call them.

Something in her has changed, and she's only aware of it now.

Sleep masks her needs. The logic of life demands we sleep. Which is what normal people do. They may go to bed eyes moist with tears: desperate, drowning, defeated. Longing to pay back a hundredfold the people who made them suffer.

Yet when they wake up, nothing is like it was the night before.

It has become yesterday, a memory. Many of us sense there's something wrong with reality, with everything around us. With the system, other people, ourselves. Yet life bribes us, it buys our silence with the gift of sleep.

She, on the other hand, doesn't forget, can't forget. She counts the nights, long as snakes. Her hatred doesn't wane with the dawn. On the contrary: every sleepless night, every waking nightmare—her eyes half closed, conscious of the weight of the sheets on her body, the cold sweat between the nape of her neck and the pillow—only serves to feed her resentment.

In the asylum, she has for the first time discovered the value of sleep. Of the *nonbeing* that resets everything, that interrupts the workings of hate.

Day by day, she's being transformed. In a general sense, it's no big deal. She still sees other human beings as objects, disposable as a piece of toilet paper, crushable as a cockroach. Nothing exists except for her. That hasn't changed. Only now she feels somewhat serene faced with the inevitable.

One day, one of the orderlies—the same one who usually paws her boobs for several minutes while he straps her to her bed at night—forgets to fasten her left arm to the chair. She looks with complete indifference at the lump of flesh going from her elbow to her fingertips. During her early days in the asylum, she had constantly wished an opportunity like this would arise.

Now days have turned into months. Her belly is full, her brain is fogged up. She's gained weight. Her hair is a mess, her skin dull and greasy. She doesn't recognize herself in the mirror.

Nor her arm hanging lifeless, untethered at the wrist. Fleetingly, she considers sending it an order, the order to move, to take off the other restraint. In her mind, she sees images of herself running to the orderlies' room, seizing one of them by the neck, and using some object—a ballpoint would suffice—to threaten him, force him to unlock the door.

It would be easy. But she can't muster the strength or the motivation.

One night, the bad dreams return.

It's not gradual. It simply happens. A single nightmare in the early hours. And she can no longer sleep.

The next day, she's exhausted, anxious, writhing about. The orderlies look at her once more with caution. They thought she'd been tamed, but now they're on their guard again. She hasn't harmed them in a long while, but they seem not to have forgotten.

She also takes note. Dissembles. And waits.

The following night, she can't fall asleep.

She takes the pills they give her without protesting. Opens her mouth wide to show she's swallowed them, while the nurse checks every corner with a flashlight.

She can feel them gently descend her throat. Occasionally, one gets stuck halfway, producing a horrid, sticky sensation. But they always work.

Not this time.

She lies still in the bed while they restrain her. Tonight, the orderly who gropes her isn't on duty. She's glad, because she doesn't think she could have controlled herself. They close the door, and she closes her eyes.

It's her hearing that enables her to discover a previously hidden world. At night, the asylum is transformed. She hears soft moans through the wall. And on the other side, someone is groaning: she listens to her neighbor masturbate. Although she has seen her by the light of day—a repulsive woman who often pukes all over herself at mealtimes—the combination of panting, rubbing, and squelching sounds arouses her slightly. Fortunately, the sensation is only fleeting.

Minutes, possibly hours, go by, until she hears footsteps in the corridor. They're accompanied by a strong odor of disinfectant and the repetitive metallic rattle of trolley wheels. She notices the left wheel is out of kilter and wonders how she can tell. She also thinks she hears music from a pair of headphones. She doesn't recognize the orderly's voice—it's someone she's never had dealings with. They are singing something to themselves surprisingly in tune (*your body and mine / filling the emptiness / rising and falling*).

It's a catchy song. She promises herself she'll check it out someday. In her previous life, she loved music—it was a wall she raised against people's stupidity.

With the refrain in her head, she descends a step into sleep. Just one. She's halfway between the harshness of wakefulness and the black peace of nothingness. A place inhabited by monsters, sown with drag-ons' teeth. She spends the night there, stumbling as she flees, unable to sleep or completely wake up.

The next morning, her hatred is back.

The memories return after lunch.

They're given food at 12:30. Bland pasta, a dollop of rice, uniden-tifiable meat, green Jell-O, depending on the day. The cutlery is flimsy plastic to avoid temptation. One of her arms is freed, but today, she pretends she's completely out of it, which she is sometimes. One of the female orderlies reluctantly spoon-feeds her, wiping her chin when she remembers to do so.

After the meal, she watches television. With a full stomach and the soporific drone of the TV, the sound turned low, the communal area is a quiet spot, where the inmates' snores and belches ring out.

Then the news program comes on. The latest bulletin is from Va-lencia. Aerial views of the city hall square. A dense column of smoke rises from the building, almost obscuring the palm trees. The fountain is turned off, the streets are blocked. The forecourt is crammed with police vehicles. Patrol cars, huge trucks with satellite dishes.

The female presenter's voice-over speaks of a miracle. Of hero-ism. An unknown member of the forces of law and order has saved hundreds of lives. A blond waitress in a light-colored uniform with a name badge talks to the camera, hair disheveled, face streaked with soot.

"She saved my life. Wherever she is, I just want to thank her."

Now the TV images show the police cordon. Beyond it, officers are shouting, giving orders, rushing about. For the briefest of moments, a figure appears in the background. It's only a flash, but the woman has been trained to recognize faces and take in the smallest details.

Her response is instantaneous. She sits up in her chair, opens her eyes, lets out a short, savage bark. The orderlies all turn to look at her. One of them puts his hand behind his back where he keeps his extend-able baton. No, they haven't forgotten. Neither has she: the bruises made by the steel and polypropylene baton on her buttocks, shins, and back. Sometimes with no provocation. So she shrinks down, lays her head on the armrest, narrows her eyes to two slanting lines, and watches closely what's being said on TV.

The woman by the dark car doesn't appear again. But she has recognized her.

Her rival.

She always knew there was someone else. The efforts made to control her movements in the compound, the existence of a second training room she never used even though she passed it every day. Always in darkness. Always empty. Hers was farther on, at the other end of the building.

Despite being constantly watched, she had managed one day to evade them when she went to the toilet. She had spied on the other woman through the glass in the training room door. A slender figure, with straight, black hair and green eyes. Fascinating. The other woman. Another like her. Someone special, unique. Someone with almost supernatural intelligence, able to see what nobody else saw, do what nobody else could do. That's what Mentor had told her.

A few seconds later, the fascination turned to hatred when she did the math and realized two of something is worth less than one of that same thing.

Her hate turned to scorn—far more dangerous than hate: hell hath no fury like a woman scorned—when she heard Mentor's voice through the loudspeakers.

"You can't tame a river, Antonia. You have to give in to the current, make its power into your own."

"To control by giving up control? That makes no sense."

"Not everything makes sense, and it doesn't have to. Give in to the current, Antonia."

Antonia. He addressed the Other Woman by her name. Softly, affectionately.

None of the brutality and disdain he showed her.

She returned to the bathroom with the blood pounding at her temples; in her mouth, a taste of rage and iron. Without realizing it, she had bitten her lips and cut her palms from clenching her fists so tightly. She wondered if he would notice anything when he came to give her training. For hours, she fantasized with this possibility. That he would enter the room, take her in his arms to embrace her, ask her what was wrong.

It didn't happen.

The news bulletin ended, the afternoon went by, night came. They locked her in her room once more, shackled her. She closes her eyes again.

"You look a real mess, don't you?"

The voice sounds near, inside the room. She sits up the few inches her shackles will allow.

The light filtering through the barred window leaves a darkened corner in the room. Tonight, the shadow is even denser, its shape seems to have changed. This is where the voice is coming from. Steely, self-assured. Speaking in English, a language she is fluent in.

"Who are you?"

"Goodness me, what an accent. We're going to have to work on that too."

She squirms on the bed. She's not afraid—she never is—but she feels threatened. And whenever she faces a threat, she responds in exactly the same way. Like a wild animal.

"What do you want?"

"That question isn't important right now."

She stops struggling against the shackles—the leather, steel, and a ton of padlocks make it a fruitless endeavor—and pauses to think. She learned something from her training. To please the voice emerging from the darkness. The voice controlling her destiny. She has understood the power behind that faceless voice. In the future, a perversion of that power will help her cause Carla Ortiz immense suffering. Now it's useful in a different way.

If who he is, or what he wants, isn't important . . . then what's important is the only thing she knows about him. That he's somewhere he shouldn't be, without having been spotted or having made sure it didn't matter. That and the extremely unlikely coincidence that her medication has stopped working.

"What's important is what you can do."

It takes the man a long while to say this. So long she's on the verge of falling asleep, believing she has dreamed this strange presence in her room. Madness, always lying in wait.

"Who would have thought it?" he says eventually. "After all these years on my own. You and I are going to achieve great things together."

She can't help letting out an exasperated snort.

"I've heard that one before."

"I'm nothing like your old Mentor."

"I was called upon to fight on the side of the angels. It didn't work out," she says, her chains rattling against the bed frame.

"This call is from the other side, my dear," says the man, rising to his feet.

Sandra considers this for a moment. Finally, she decides she likes it. If she's to be cast as the villain, then so be it. Villains always make more interesting characters anyway.

When the man stands up, the light from the window hits him squarely in the face. He has fair, wavy hair and soft, pale skin. He looks a bit like the actor who played the father in *The Impossible*.

"I'll wait for you in the car with the engine running," he says, heading for the door. "Don't be long."

"Wait. Aren't you going to untie me?"

He turns around and throws a ballpoint pen onto the bed. It bounces off the sheet and rolls almost to within reach of her right hand.

"If you are who I hope you are, you don't need me to."

10

A VISIT

"Do you have a theory? Because we could do with one right now."

"I don't like working with theories. You end up forcing the facts to fit them."

Inspector Gutiérrez grimaces as he tries to keep up with Antonia along the hallways of La Zarzuela hospital. It's no longer a question of agility but of exhaustion. The antibiotics as well as the stress have left him groggy, and he hasn't had a decent meal in hours. On top of which, he only has fifty-nine minutes left to live. So he has no intention of slowing down.

"It's obvious you haven't read a newspaper in the last ten years. Don't you know that the thing nowadays is to tell people what they want to hear?"

"I don't understand. Information is either true or false," says Antonia, swerving to avoid a nurse scurrying down the hallway.

"You just don't get it. What people think now is: *How can it be wrong if it's what I think?* Maybe your Mr. White is one of those."

"He's not *my* Mr. White. And the profile doesn't fit."

"All right. So you tell me what facts we have and I'll come up with the theories."

Jon attempts to mask the anguish in his voice. He doesn't succeed, but at least he tried.

Antonia seems distant, as happens when she's busy doing what she does. Weights, wheels within wheels, measurements. Almost grudgingly, she does as Jon asks.

"We have the murder of Raquel Planas four years ago. We know from her mother that the killer was her lover."

Antonia turns into another corridor, following the blue arrow and the sign that reads INTENSIVE CARE UNIT. "The lover is a computer engineer who happens to turn up dead four years later."

"Don't forget he followed you in the street."

"I'm not forgetting it. A week after Raquel Planas's death, Jaume Soler contacts me, asking for help. And I . . ."

She breaks off, and Jon doesn't insist.

"Three years later," Antonia continues, "you come on the scene. We have to capture a killer who is kidnapping and blackmailing very prominent people. That killer was a mere puppet in Sandra and White's hands."

"A ruse to hoodwink you."

"In hindsight, the whole modus operandi reeked of him. We know that now. Sandra vanishes, not without first warning us that White was back."

"And while we were busy down in Málaga, he attacks the Red Queens in other countries."

"When we return, he abducts you. And sticks that thing in your neck. Makes us his puppets to investigate three crimes. Raquel Planas. Jaume Soler."

That's all.

It's not insignificant.

It's not enough.

"That wasn't much help," Jon says with a sigh.

"No," Antonia admits. "We have fifty-seven minutes left before the next deadline. And our most urgent task is still to solve the crime."

Jon agrees with that.

The fear he felt in the elevator hasn't completely evaporated. It's just moved somewhere else. From his barrel chest, it has descended into his guts—gripping him, freezing him, preventing him from thinking. It's a heavy, growing sensation, a cold, sticky acid, increasing in volume and density, even as the time he has left slips away.

Jon has never had a diagnosed panic attack, but if he were to describe his symptoms to a psychiatrist, that's probably the term they'd employ. Before prescribing him half a pharmacy. Of course, Jon would prefer to be blown sky high than visit a shrink. Because Bilbao is Bilbao and cops are cops, et cetera.

At the entrance to the ICU, they run into two obstacles. The first has the build and look of a policeman, and he steps aside when Jon shows him his ID.

The second, much smaller and wearing a hospital uniform, turns out to be a duty nurse who has no intention of letting them through. Jon has to use all his charm and smooth talk to get her to allow them in. It's a matter of life or death, you see.

The nurse only agrees after Jon and Antonia promise to wear overshoes, plastic caps, masks, and gloves.

"How is the patient?"

"Providing there's no infection, she'll survive. She has a perforated intestine, but narrowly missed having her liver punctured."

"Is she conscious?"

"She came around a short while ago. She's still very weak and is dosed up with morphine."

"But she's able to talk."

"Five minutes."

As if we had more time.

"Don't mention her husband, okay?" the nurse shouts after them, before the pressurized doors close behind them.

The inside of the ICU is a grim, hostile place. Everything around them is either sterile, noisy, at death's door, or in a hurry. These refer respectively to the air, the machines, the patients, and their nurses.

Even through his mask, Jon can tell Antonia is in a bad way. Her eyes are flitting about, and she's clutching her stomach again.

"What's . . . ?"

"Please, not now. We can talk about it later."

Inspector Gutiérrez puts his concerns for his partner on the back burner because by now they've reached Aura Reyes's bed. Separated from the others by a privacy screen a meter and a half high, the victim is connected to a monitor and a drip. She blinks as they approach.

"Who are you? Where is Jaume?" she says in a croaky voice.

Jon sits on the bed to make himself smaller and less intimidating, and Antonia sits alongside him.

"Señora Reyes, we're from the police. I'm Inspector Gutiérrez, and this is my colleague Antonia Scott."

The woman is staring into space somewhere above their heads. But when she hears the word *police*, something readjusts inside her as the pieces click into place—the odor of disinfectant, the dull ache from her wound, the inconvenient drip in her arm—and she realizes she isn't waking from a nightmare that will fade as soon as she gets up to prepare the girls' breakfast.

"My daughters. My daughters!" she screams, trying to get up.

Jon gently places his hand on her shoulder to prevent her from moving and doing herself an injury. He scarcely has to press down at all—she's as weak as a kitten.

"The girls are fine. They're safe and sound with their grandma. They won't be going to school today, they'll spend the morning watching *Frozen II* and some episodes of *Peppa Pig*."

"I want to talk to them."

"Later, señora, I promise you. We haven't much time. We need you to answer a few questions first."

"I said I want to talk to my daughters!" insists Aura, with the closest thing to a yell that somebody who has narrowly escaped death and still bears the finger marks on her neck can muster.

Jon is forced to waste precious seconds finding the grandmother's telephone number. He finally manages to put the two of them in touch. They have a brief conversation. The girls are oblivious to what's happened and respond gaily; their voices sound incongruous in such a situation. There will be time enough for them to learn the truth. And yet somehow her daughters' blissful ignorance has an anesthetizing effect on their mother. Her body relaxes; her eyes start to wander over the ceiling once more.

"Señora Reyes, we need to ask you some questions. It's important."

"Now I want to talk to Jaume."

Her fresh request sounds completely different. Urgency has given way to something else. The expression of a wish, perhaps. Jon is vaguely aware she's speaking through a cloud, a bank of fog that muffles her voice.

Don't mention her husband, the nurse had warned them.

But they need to rouse her from the daydream into which she seems to have lapsed. Time is running out for them. So Jon gets ready to give her the bad news. It won't be the first time. Along with paperwork, it's the part of their job that cops hate the most. Worse even than the possibility of being shot. Like taking a cold shower, the kind of interaction with reality that doesn't improve with experience. You can do your best to soften the blow, but sooner or later, you have to turn the tap on; sooner or later, your skin comes into contact with the icy water; sooner or later, it runs down to your scrotum.

"Señora Reyes—" Jon starts to say.

"Jaume is dead. There was nothing we could do. I'm sorry," Antonia cuts in, with all the subtlety of a flamethrower.

Dammit, woman, Jon curses.

Aura Reyes doesn't react. Her face is a blank sheet of paper, her eyes don't move. The only sign she's still alive is the constant beep of the heart monitor.

This is where Inspector Gutiérrez's experience comes in handy. Jon has seen this kind of reaction before. The survivor's face remains intact while the information penetrates their conscious mind, gradually transforming the blank sheet. It's like setting fire to that piece of paper. It starts timidly, hesitantly, in one corner. A line of flame you can blow out with one breath. But then as it advances, it becomes unstoppable, revealing the truth beneath.

Aura starts to tremble; she bursts into tears.

After a few seconds, Jon says:

"We're so sorry, but we really must find his killer, Señora Reyes."

"What . . . what do you want to know?"

Aura's version is brief, it doesn't tell them anything they don't already know. She got out of bed, sensed there was someone in the house, warned her husband. This kind of story nearly always contains an unbearable moment (in Aura's case, when the killer slashed Jaume's throat) and an agonizing regret (in Aura's case, not calling the police immediately).

Inspector Gutiérrez makes a vow—like someone swearing to go to Lourdes on his knees if the Virgin will make his legless child whole again—that he will visit this woman to calm her, help her get over it, to make her realize there was nothing she could have done to change her fate. For Jon, who only has fifty minutes to live, it's the kind of vow you can make with impunity. Because in fact you're pretty sure the child won't grow a new pair of legs, and because who wants to crawl on their knees to a grotto in the South of France anyway.

"Do you know what your husband did for a living? Who he worked for?" asks Antonia when she sees the woman has stopped crying.

"He's a consultant. He . . . he programs computers. Something for the government, I think."

"For the government? Are you sure?"

"He doesn't like to talk about his work."

Her descriptions are too abstract. Jon signals to Antonia to move on. The clock is ticking. So she decides to go back to the previous night.

"Tell us about your attacker."

"I don't remember much. He was . . . he was dressed in black and wore a kind of mask. Like for skiing."

Antonia doesn't have time for any of the usual procedures. She can't get an Identi-Kit picture or sift through stacks of photos of known criminals.

"Was his face covered?"

"No. He was . . . I don't know, I think he was fair-haired. A little older than you," says Aura, pointing to Jon. "But less . . ."

"Even thinner," he says in a flash.

"I didn't get a good look at him. I'm sorry."

"You need to leave now," says the nurse, appearing from behind the screen. "The patient is exhausted."

"Just one more question," says Antonia.

"Don't make me have to call security, officers," the nurse threatens.

Antonia ignores her and turns back to Aura, who is showing signs of exhaustion. Her wounds, her grief, and the interview have sapped her strength. But Antonia can't leave with things as they stand. Empty-handed.

"You must have seen something that struck you as unusual," she says, almost pleading.

After reflecting about this for a moment, Aura replies:

"I had the feeling my husband knew him."

"What makes you think that?" asks Antonia, leaning closer to her.

"I don't know. When the man attacked him, my husband said something. I don't remember exactly what. *Not you, wait*, or something like that."

11

A DOWNHILL SLOPE

"It's impossible. We're not going to make it," says Jon desperately.

The nurse ended up kicking them out of the ICU. So now they find themselves in the hospital parking lot. With no leads, no fresh information. Rudderless.

Antonia calls Aguado, who informs her there's nothing new. They're following up all the data they have, but so far, they're getting nowhere.

Antonia doesn't need to tell Jon the upshot of the conversation, because her face says it all.

"We're not going to give in," says Antonia.

"We're out of time."

"We have thirty-seven minutes. Until they run out, we're going to carry on doing what we do. You hear me?"

Jon says nothing.

He walks the few steps to the Audi and sits on the hood. Emerging into the pale sunlight, the cold air, and the breeze rustling in the dry leaves, he has realized something:

How terribly tired he is. That's all he can think about. How tired he is.

Like everyone aged forty-four, Jon has experienced all kinds of tiredness. The kind that drains you to the point of insomnia. The kind that makes you want to cry. And the kind that leaves you sad, extremely sad.

This tiredness is none of those.

It's a tiredness beyond tears, beyond sadness. It's a numbing, painful weariness that clings to his flesh and bones.

"I'm done, sweetie. Try to understand."

Antonia looks at him, puzzling over what he means. A word pops into her head.

Karōshi.

In Japanese, death from exhaustion.

The word is vulgar. Uninspired, crude. When Marcos suggested it, she stowed it at the back of the closet, like one of those gifts from a mother-in-law who means well but has no taste.

She discards it and carries on searching.

Dharmanisthuya.

In Kannada, a Dravidic language spoken by forty-four million people in India, the relief of the downhill slope. The sensation an exhausted walker has when they come to a downward stretch of the path.

Antonia hasn't much to offer Jon: everything is stacked against him. All she can give him is the opportunity to keep fighting to the last. Deny him the chance to think. Propel him down the hill. Offer him the relief of the slope. If that's all there is, at least it'll lessen his anxiety and fear on the final straight.

So she takes out her cell phone and makes a call. A call she never thought she'd make. Someone from her past who definitely isn't expecting her to call.

So much so he doesn't answer.

We'll just have to go see him, thinks Antonia.

"Listen, Jon. I've had an idea."

Inspector Gutiérrez turns his head very slowly and looks at her with surprise. They have no strings to pull. None. At least none that would bring results in so little time. All Jon's exhaustion asks is for him to lie down and wait for death. Or maybe find a bar and eat a ham roll he'll never fully digest.

"If you're not coming with me, at least get off the hood," says Antonia.

Jon moves a leg, then his foot, fills his chest with air—this takes a while—and stands up with a heavy sigh, the sort that change the wind direction.

Why am I even doing this? he wonders, glancing at his watch. Why carry on when you know it's futile?

Because he's scared, and that makes him ashamed.

Because Antonia still matters to him.

Because the way a man goes under matters.

Because when the worst happens in thirty-seven minutes, he refuses to give this bossy little know-it-all any reason to reproach him. No way.

So he gets up.

For whatever reason.

"Sweetie, I hope you're not making me waste my time," he says, forcing a grin. "Because in my last thirty-seven minutes, I wouldn't mind eating a sandwich."

12

A CLASS

The police headquarters in Pinar del Rey is fifteen minutes by car from La Zarzuela hospital.

The way Antonia drives, she cuts the time by half.

"The only thing I can think of," she says, speeding over the bridge across Avenida de Burgos, "is for us to find out why they killed him. Maybe then I can negotiate with White."

"Have you ever thought this could be a motiveless crime?"

"The problem with motiveless crimes is they don't exist. We just can't see it."

Jon leans back in the passenger seat, flinching helplessly when Antonia overtakes a car that's overtaking another car. The columns of the La Paz bridge pass so close to their side-view mirror, he can see the grains in the concrete.

Don't look. Don't yell. Don't object, thinks Jon. *If she kills you, it'll be while trying to save your life. You're in no position to be asking favors.*

"Do you know what really pisses me off? That he hardly had any emails on his computer. That's totally weird. Who doesn't communicate by email these days?"

"You and me, for example," says Antonia. "People who have a job they need to keep secret."

Jon thinks about what Antonia has just said and puts it into the context of everything they know until now.

"Are you telling me Soler didn't just know about the existence of Red Queen? He may have played an active role in the project?"

"That's what I suspected four years ago. But when they informed me he was dead, he had a different identity."

Turning your head to look at Antonia in astonishment isn't a good idea when you're dizzy, exhausted, have a bomb in your neck, and are traveling in a car at almost two hundred kilometers an hour. Jon has to struggle to keep down what little is left in his stomach.

"What do you know about my former partner?" Antonia asks him, to take his mind off things.

"Not a lot. Only what Mentor told me."

"What exactly?"

Inspector Gutiérrez may not be the most intelligent man in the world, but he's not next to the subtlest woman on the planet, so he instantly realizes what Antonia is doing. Still, he decides to play along.

"That he was an insufferable hunk. And that you two got on famously."

"Yeah, that about sums it up. He's also very smart, capable, and an overachiever."

"Is that who you've had on automatic redial since we got in the car?" says Jon, pointing to the cell phone on the dash and the number that never picks up.

"You'll meet him soon enough."

It's absolutely not a good idea to drive into police headquarters at two hundred kilometers an hour, both because of the security barrier and the officers with assault rifles posted at the entrance. So they impatiently wait their turn in the line of cars. In the meantime, Antonia looks up something on the internet, reads and memorizes it. Then she calls Dr. Aguado to see if she's made any progress.

None.

Next on the list is Mentor. Who has no good news, but does have something bad to report.

"It's the Dutch shield bearer. A few hours ago, he was found in his cell. He hanged himself."

There's no reaction from Antonia. Nor does she end the call. She sits, gazing blankly somewhere between the windshield of the Audi, the endless line of cars, and the barrier.

"Before you hang up without saying goodbye . . . ," Mentor begins.

Antonia supposes he's going to add something about the shield bearer, but it's not that.

"Some years ago, I confessed I envied you," Mentor says slowly, almost in a whisper. He sounds on the verge of tears. "I was about to ask if you remembered, but of course you do. You remember everything."

"I remember," says Antonia. "Just before you injected me with whatever it was."

"Well, it's no longer true."

He hangs up.

Without really knowing why, Antonia thinks Mentor has just asked her forgiveness.

It takes them six precious minutes to reach the entrance to the building. Antonia asks some questions at reception, then drags Jon along endless corridors until they reach one of the training rooms in the west wing. Another three minutes.

Thirteen minutes left.

The two of them burst into the room—painted a sickly green color, walls plastered with motivational posters. There they find thirty-four very bewildered rookies in tracksuits and an even more puzzled police officer on the platform in front of a blackboard covered in diagrams, the Spanish flag, portraits of the titular king and the one on the run.

Their reaction turns to annoyance when Jon announces:

"Off you go, kiddies, it's playtime. We need to talk to Teacher."

The students slowly stand up to leave while their teacher turns to the intruders indignantly. He takes three steps forward and bends down:

"This is out of order, Antonia," he hisses.

"Inspector Gutiérrez, may I present Chief Inspector Raúl Covas," she responds.

Jon doesn't react. Right now—doubtless reinforced by the stress he's under—he's experiencing Stendhal syndrome. Or more exactly, its sexual equivalent. Chief Inspector Raúl Covas, Antonia's former partner, her first shield bearer. Fiftyish, a meter eighty, reddish-brown hair, gray eyes, and shoulders to die for. Jon stares at the chief inspector's body like someone looking at the map of Disneyland, unable to decide which attraction to jump on first.

Now there's a reason for living, he thinks.

"I thought the last time we met, you assured me it would be the last." Covas ignores Jon and talks directly to Antonia, not quite able to hide the tension in his voice.

"Raúl, we're in a big hurry. A colleague's life is at stake. I need to talk to you."

Hearing this, Covas's face relaxes a little.

"What is it you want?"

"Four years ago, I gave you one final assignment. I want you to tell me everything you remember about it."

13

A WAIT

She has never liked waiting.

Who does?

Of course, if in the behavioral assessment of your psychopathic diagnosis it reads, "Impulsive, in need of strong sensations, unstable. Liable to reject norms and fail to meet responsibilities and obligations," it means you'll like waiting somewhat less than most. Waiting irritates her, confines her in a strange limbo between inaction and action.

As usual, she chews her hangnails.

And as usual, it hurts. She realizes it's a bad habit. As usual.

Sitting in the car in the deserted street, music blasting on her AirPods—Michael Jackson's *Thriller*—it occurs to Sandra she's done little else but wait for this moment ever since White freed her from the asylum.

It's curious how pure, unadulterated happiness leaves no residue in our hearts, whereas the troubled waters of sadness leave their mark on everything. Each day Sandra has been waiting for this moment has been filled with anxiety and agony, a complete waste. It's true she has learned a great deal from him. Skills that were missing from Mentor's handbook. For example, how to stab someone at the base of the skull with a fork. Plunging it into the soft flesh up to the handle until it reaches the medulla and kills instantly. She has already been able to put this into practice on two occasions, both of them special moments she treasures with great satisfaction and recalls from time to time. One at a gas station in the early hours. No great challenge, apart from having to avoid the CCTV and other modern inconveniences. Another in a lonely house chosen at random in a town chosen at random. The only reason for these two murders: her personal development . . .

She has also learned how to handle and detonate explosives. Not as close-up and intimate as sharp objects but fascinating nevertheless. She was taught by a tedious old Hungarian guy the size and shape of a metric cube. The Hungarian had lost half his left arm—against all the odds from sticking it out at the wrong moment while driving as drunk as a skunk; it had limited his professional opportunities to teaching. He had passed on to her all his dirty tricks, the astonishing secrets of someone who uses physics and chemistry to cause the maximum possible damage. She had relished each small discovery, with the subtlety and cold cunning that were part and parcel of the trade. Of course, the cherry on the top had been to blow up the Hungarian himself at the end of her training. The old fellow took it surprisingly sportingly. Despite being tied to a chair, in the midst of his whimpering, he made a couple of suggestions about the detonator and the stick of dynamite tied around his neck.

Naturally, there were some real assignments. Not as many as she'd have liked. All the time, she had the feeling White was treating her like a puppy on a short leash.

I'm surprised he doesn't put me in a kennel at night, she'd often think.

Even so, White exercised a strange spell over her. Sandra frequently sought to oppose him, to discover his limits, to make him angry. In a moment of extreme need, she had even tried to have sex with him. None of her approaches, outbursts, or excesses had brought any results. Occasionally, she tried to sweet-talk him the way you entice a cat through a fence. But most of the time, he simply remained impassive.

Which is a more effective means of control. Sandra has found this out from the negative side of the equation. But she discovered something else about White, after asking him time and again why he was helping her.

"I have a selfish motive," he had told her. "And that's a good thing for you because they're the only ones you can rely on."

Selfishness is something Sandra understands. When White finally began to elaborate the plan that had begun with Ezekiel, she adopted the name she now has.

She also understood that her own revenge, her personal goal, was secondary. An extra in a much grander plan.

She's still willing to play the game a bit longer. While it suits her. After that, things will change.

Spotify stops because she has a call.

She picks up by tapping her earbud.

"Carry out my instructions," White orders.

"The time you gave her isn't up yet."

"I'm changing the rules."

That can only mean one thing, thinks Sandra.

"Has she already figured it out?"

"She will in a matter of minutes. Then she'll go straight for you. Scott is even more brilliant than I imagined." White pauses and then adds: "I didn't expect her to reach this point so quickly."

Sandra knows why he has said this. White never utters a single word that isn't premeditated. She knows why he's praising her rival, the woman she detests above all else. He believes this way he can provoke her, motivate her, arouse feelings of rage and frustration in her.

He doesn't realize it's unnecessary. That she has an endless supply of both fuels.

That's my secret, Cap. I'm always angry.

White is devilishly smart. But so is she. While he believes he's controlling her, she has been playing her own game. While he thinks he's waving a red rag in front of her, he doesn't realize he's also revealing something about himself. . . .

I didn't expect her to reach this point so quickly.

It's true. The plan Sandra is about to execute is the fourth in a list of options. Months earlier, while he was setting up the pieces to force Scott out of her solitary loft, and when he had everything in place for the game to begin, he hadn't even considered it.

Which means the genius is fallible.

That's the thing about control: it works both ways. To be able to pull on a puppet's strings, you have to tie them to your own fingers.

And one day, you may find it is the puppet's turn to pull.

Sandra smiles and says nothing, choosing to let him believe he has succeeded in provoking her with his praise of Scott. She waits for him to speak. A little tug on the string.

"You'd better get going. This is what you've been so looking forward to."

"You bet," says Sandra, still smiling.

She hangs up. She checks her two guns again, adjusts her raincoat, and steps out of the car. Turning up the music in her earbuds, she starts walking toward the plot of land at the end of the street.

There's nothing special about it.

Yet another industrial unit, with a fenced-off parking lot, the name of a respectable aggregates manufacturer: a building with a corrugated iron roof and cement walls.

14

A QUESTIONNAIRE

Meeting an ex is always an emotional experience, even if you weren't romanti-cally involved. To do so thirteen minutes before a bomb explodes in your new partner's neck is even more of a challenge.

Which is why, while they were waiting to enter the building, Antonia took a few seconds to do a bit of research. Google soon took her to a questionnaire in *Telva* magazine: *How to meet your ex and not make a fool of yourself*, which seemed to contain some relevant advice.

Point 1: Pretend it's a casual encounter.

This bit has already been sabotaged by them bursting into the class and the eighteen missed calls, so Antonia moves quickly on to number two.

Point 2: Behave naturally.

"Those fingerprints on the bottle I gave you so you could find out the identity of the man who came up to me when I was with Marcos. What do you remember about them?"

The chief inspector straightens up, turns around on the platform, and smooths the three or four hairs on his head that are out of place.

"Not a lot. Didn't I give you the file?"

Point 3: Don't let them see that you're anxious.

"Yes. But I need to know what you can remember. It's very important, Raúl."

Covas smiles—a small wrinkle of disdain appearing on his cheek—and he looks Antonia up and down. Because he's much taller and on the raised platform, it's as if he's a floor above her.

"I thought you never forgot anything."

Antonia has rejected this myth so often she's grown weary of doing so. Especially considering the state she was in when she made the request. Alone in her hospital room. A week after the attack on Marcos and her. Raúl came to visit. She asked him to go to her place for the glass bottle (currently wrapped in plastic in a drawer in his desk) and check the prints on it.

Raúl took another week to get back to her. By then, Antonia had practically stopped speaking. The pain and guilt had grown inside her like a weed, invading everything. She could barely move her left arm and was drugged to the eyeballs on tranquilizers. Bullet fragments were still in her body, tearing her apart, while she waited for a second operation.

So Raúl handed her a piece of paper, made a couple of suggestions, but that was all. Antonia barely took any of it in. By then, her descent into the hell of depression and suicidal thoughts had begun.

However, Antonia adheres to

Point 4: Avoid drama.

and simply says:

"Raúl, please. This is extremely serious."

"Okay," he says after a pause. "I didn't discover much. I checked the prints as you asked. The man was called Enrique Pardo. He was a bank employee who'd been out of work since the financial crisis. He threw himself on the subway tracks a day before your husband was shot. That meant I immediately ruled him out as a suspect."

The next point in the questionnaire suddenly becomes relevant:

Point 5: No reproaches.

Because maybe Antonia feels slightly betrayed by the way Raúl left her in that hospital room as a hopeless case and pursued his own career. Of course, he may regret it and have resentments of his own. The selfish, simplistic, childish ones men often have. So Antonia tries not to let her voice betray her emotions and to ask a question from a strictly professional viewpoint.

"So, how do you explain that he was murdered early this morning?"

"What? No . . . that can't be right," stammers Covas.

"Perhaps the subway train was moving as slowly as this conversation," says Jon, holding up his watch to Antonia in desperation.

"He wasn't called Enrique Pardo, and he didn't jump on any tracks. His name was Jaume Soler, a computer consultant possibly linked to the Red Queen project. Where did you get your information from?"

"Are you insinuating I didn't do my job properly?"

"It wouldn't be the first time."

"You're wrong. I went down to the morgue myself to check."

Jon can't bear it any longer. He looks at his watch: only eight minutes left. He feels as if he's suffocating, so he takes off his coat and jacket and opens the window next to the chief inspector's desk. The Spanish flag barely flutters, but the slight breeze is enough to bring some color back to Jon's distraught face. Resting his arms on the windowsill, he cranes his enormous neck in search of oxygen. The stitches on his wound are clearly visible from there.

Antonia looks at her partner. She shares his anxiety, urgency, despair.

"You yourself went down to the . . ."

She stops.

So does the world.

How blind I've been, she thinks.

Karışkırkira.

In Kyrgyz, a language spoken by millions of people in Central Asia, the wolf disguised as a rocking chair you've been sitting on for ages without noticing it. The feeling of being a total idiot because what you're looking for has been right under your nose from the outset.

Antonia gazes at Jon's wound. It's even more conspicuous now the swelling has gone down and it's no longer covered in blood. She concentrates on the sutures. Longitudinal. Done with a straight needle. With two proximal and distal supporting sutures. An excellent, virtually flawless job, known in medical circles as a horizontal mattress suture.

And at one end, a butterfly knot.

Tying such a small, perfect knot is very fiddly.

And Antonia Scott has only seen one person do it. With supreme skill.

How blind I've been, she repeats to herself.

"Who attended you at the morgue?"

Chief Inspector Covas doesn't remember her name. But he can describe her. He's always had a good memory for attractive women.

INTERLUDE

A STOPWATCH

There are only a few seconds left before everything comes to an end. Jon shows Antonia the countdown on the stopwatch.

The end of everything, thinks Jon.

They clasp each other's hands tight.

What a vulgar, pitiful death.

Jon wants to look Antonia in the eye; he wants to say goodbye to her.

But he stares at the stopwatch.

He can't help it.

Six seconds.

Five seconds.

How stupid, he thinks once more.

Four seconds.

Three seconds.

To die staring at a stopwatch.

Two seconds.

One second.

Nothing.

Jon lets go of Antonia's hand when, after a few moments in which the air stops moving, he realizes—with an inexplicable feeling of disappointment—that the countdown was never meant for them.

Part IV

MR. WHITE

Hell is truth seen too late.

THOMAS HOBBES

1

A FRIENDLY FACE

The man at reception smiles. Grudgingly, but he smiles. After all, the woman has a friendly face. No one suspects a friendly face like hers.

He sees no reason to reach for the gun beneath the counter—a fourth-generation Glock 17—because the woman looks harmless. She has drops of rain on her coat, more in her hair. That explains why her shoulders are hunched, her hands thrust in her pockets.

She's not the first lost visitor to come into the building for directions or simply out of curiosity. Every week, there are at least a couple. In front of the receptionist—next to his cell phone and a battered old keyboard—there's a well-thumbed leaflet in a plastic cover with phrases to distract the attention of snoopers. They're seldom necessary: it's usually enough to grunt "No idea," or "It's my first day," or "There's nobody here now."

The receptionist has been on the job for two months. He's fresh out of the police academy and imagined something far more exciting when he graduated. Like the majority of personnel on the periphery of the Red Queen project, all he knows about this place is that it's an undercover operation led by the National Police, and he'll be transferred after a brief stint with a glowing recommendation.

He's also been told to be discreet, not to discuss his work with anyone, and to send strangers packing. Apart from the support people, he only answers to the four people who carry an ID with a red border. Impossible to mistake them: one is the boss—the gray-suited fifty-year-old who keeps sneaking out for a smoke. Another is the small woman who's only been there a couple of times and is probably some kind of scientist. A third is the big, if not fat, Basque inspector, whom he gets on with. Because he's friendly and because he tries so hard to hide being gay.

The last person he has to answer to is standing next to him, looking for something in her bag. She's nice, the pathologist. And a looker, too, with her long blond hair and the piercing that does something for her.

He's tried asking her on a date a couple of times, but she's always politely turned him down. He's beginning to think they don't play on the same team, but he's willing to give it another go. Maybe this weekend, as there's a new movie on at the mall. Aged twenty-three, his long years of experience with women tell him none of them can resist a movie and pizza at Gino's. Who could?

The other woman is by now only a couple of steps from the counter. She hasn't greeted him or opened her mouth. She simply smiles as she nods to the rhythm of a music only she can hear.

Now the desk officer can see her better, she doesn't look so friendly. "How may I help?" he asks.

The woman stops at the counter and takes her hands out of her pockets. A gun in each of them. The man doesn't know they're both Sig Sauer P226s, because he's not that well informed about firearms, and because when he sees them, his stomach flips with fear and surprise. His hand makes to grab his own gun but never gets that far. The shot doesn't come from in front of him, but he doesn't realize that.

For some reason, the world has decided to tilt on its axis. The counter—his only horizon for eight hours a day—suddenly rises to vertical from his right, taking the floor with it.

That's odd, he thinks before everything turns black.

Dr. Aguado returns the still-smoking gun to her bag. Fifteen years working with corpses has taught her a sad truth. To make a person takes a lifetime's hard work. To destroy one only takes the slightest pressure on a trigger.

This is the first time she's created a potential client for herself. She'd been turning this moment over in her mind for weeks, afraid she wouldn't be up to it. That she'd back out at the last moment. That the defense mechanisms society implants in us—a conscience, religion, empathy—would take over and prevent her putting a bullet in the brain of this rookie cop while he was distracted looking at Sandra.

It didn't turn out that way.

In the brief moments that follow the gunshot, with the smell of cordite still filling the reception area, the pathologist examines inside herself and sees no great changes. Nerves, of course, and the urge to pee, but no trace of the major fracture in her soul she'd anticipated. Killing closes one door and opens others. In Dr. Aguado's mind, there appears a fleeting vision of the reality of God, his true nature. There's no need for any microscope or forceps to discover the side of him we can see, his infinite creativity; it's enough for us to stroll through a wood or to see a platypus swim.

The Creator's other side, his infinite and criminal indifference toward his creation, is harder to comprehend. Some idea of it can be had from looking at a photograph from Auschwitz or Mauthausen, but that's only a vicarious, secondhand appreciation. You have to press the barrel of a gun to the left temple of a young, healthy, and rather dim-witted young man and pull the trigger. During the second that follows, you wait for the earth to open up, the flames of hell to rise, and a purifying fire to descend from the heavens and consume your sinful flesh.

It doesn't happen.

It's then you see God's true face without any intermediaries. And you realize he doesn't give a damn.

"Bravo, Doctor," says Sandra, taking out her earbuds as she goes over to her.

Aguado's hand is trembling.

"Calm down, Doctor. Now's not the moment to be afraid. That comes later."

The pathologist thrusts her hand into her pocket.

"The cylinders are in the ventilation system," she says. "I've asked everyone to wait for me in the meeting room."

Sandra nods and gives a knowing smile.

"What about . . . him?"

"In his office."

"Bravo," Sandra repeats, replacing her earbuds. "You can leave now. But don't forget to make that call."

She pirouettes and heads for the entrance.

2

A CYLINDER

There's an unwritten law of memory whereby we store places that were important to us with certain errors of scale. We only need return to our childhood bedroom or the college lecture theater to realize they're much smaller and more ordinary than we had imagined. We ourselves may not have grown an inch, but this place from our past will inevitably have shrunk.

The same is true of the place where you were once mercilessly tortured, as Sandra discovers when she enters the Red Queen building. The threat, the darkness, the fear, and the trauma have diminished. They have become her.

On her way to the meeting room, Sandra passes by the training module without so much as looking inside. Rather than go around the MobLab stationed next to Aguado's laboratory, she turns sideways and edges between the two in order to avoid being seen through the meeting room door. Without breaking step, still humming to herself.

You'll count the nights as long as snakes, she sings softly, hardly doing more than shaping the words with her lips.

When she reaches her goal, she circles around it and crouches in front of the air-conditioning system. There are the two green-colored cylinders with their letters and warnings, and the skull and crossbones sticker, black on a yellow background. Aguado has done her part. All Sandra needs to do is turn the knobs.

She walks around the other side of the apparatus and goes over to the door. Peers through the glass. Inside are thirteen people around the conference table, looking bored. None of them realizes she is placing a chain through the door handles and securing it with a heavy padlock. Nor do they seem to notice a wispy, orange-colored cloud seeping through the ventilation grille. It's one of the Hungarian's inventions, a mixture of ethyl bromoacetate and mustard gas. He wasn't proud of it, though. *If it doesn't explode, where's the fun?* he used to complain.

Sandra loves to have fun but is also practical. When you're playing at home and you have several months to plan an attack on the forces of law and order, you can really go to town on the details—as she did when she prepared the double explosion against the team trying to rescue Carla Ortiz.

In this case, playing away and with very little warning, you have to skimp on the details and get the job done.

I'll knock on the door, we'll hide and throw stones just to be bad, she hums, leaning on the door.

From inside, she hears the first cry of alarm.

She feels the desire—the urgent, all-powerful, physical desire—to peer through the glass to see with her own eyes the result of her efforts, but it's still too soon. Some of the people inside could be armed, and she doesn't completely trust the thickness of the glass. So she waits a while longer, imagining the scene.

The ones closest to the air-conditioning vent will have been the first to notice something, because the symptoms start with the tongue. It swells up until it feels twice its normal size, and you have a strange taste in your mouth.

Surprise gives way to panic when you realize it's increasingly difficult to breathe as the poison passes through your airways and into your lungs. By the time your eyes start to sting and your brain is depleted of oxygen, you can no longer cry out.

Those who yell are those farthest away, when they see your face has turned a strange reddish color and you rip open your shirt to try to get some air. In the most extreme cases, the nervous system takes over, causing you to claw at your own throat with your nails, until your vision goes and you slump to the ground.

By now, those closest to the first victims have run to help them, to ask what's wrong, bend over them. This is the worst thing they could do: the gas is heavier than air. They're the next ones to collapse, falling on top of the first victims, crushing them with the weight of their writhing bodies and hastening their deaths.

Those farthest away, closest to the door, still have a few precious seconds to react, especially if they were on their feet.

That's what they do.

Sandra feels someone push at the door, at first forcefully, then with mounting desperation. One blow, two, three. The chain holds, although she miscalculated the distance between the links, and the person pushing must be quite a strong man.

The door opens a crack.

Not enough of the poison is able to seep through the gap to be dangerous in this open space six meters high. Even so, Sandra notices the hint of an odor.

Acid, metallic, corrosive.

It smells like the liquid used to clean firearms. When the nitrobenzene runs down the barrel, dissolving any traces of carbon, gunpowder, and copper.

Sandra reluctantly takes a couple of steps back. Her eyes have sprouted a few tears. Nothing serious. More distressing is her disappointment at not being able to enjoy the spectacle. She can't possibly watch through the glass, so she keeps one eye on the door while with the other she looks at the playlist on her phone. She puts the song she's listening to—track eleven of the disc—on a loop. Because it seems the most appropriate.

The banging on the meeting room door has ceased. By now, the people inside must either be dead or in their final spasms, a pink froth bubbling from their swollen, bloodied lips. The froth is in fact the mucous membrane of their own lungs. She would have liked to get a closer look, but she can't, thanks to the guy pushing at the door, and her own miscalculation about the length of the chain. But this is no time for self-criticism.

To the sound of a duet between electric guitar and drums at the start of the song, Sandra goes back to the gas cylinders and shuts them off. This way, at least she'll be able to take a quick peek inside the room as she leaves the building. Scant consolation—seeing the ball in the net is less satisfying than seeing it go in—but she'll have to settle for that.

She straightens up just in the nick of time.

The shotgun blast smashes the air-conditioning unit in the exact spot where her head had been only a second before. Instead of piercing her skull, it tears a hole in the flap of her Burberry raincoat—a special cashmere-and-silk edition that cost over €4,000.

Sandra is filled with rage, more so than if her head had been blown off. After all, if that had happened, she wouldn't have noticed the mess. She reacts instinctively, hurling herself to the floor and returning fire.

3

SINS THAT COME BACK TO HAUNT

Mentor takes cover behind the MobLab. The front of the van absorbs the impact of Sandra's shots. The 9 mm bullets destroy the windshield, the right front tire, and one of the headlights. Mentor knows then he's screwed. Because he's had little training in using firearms, because he's lost the surprise factor . . .

And that crazy bitch knows exactly what she's doing. After all, I taught her.

Cowering, he curses his own stupidity over and over.

Less than two minutes earlier, he was leaving his office for the vending machine when he saw Sandra at the meeting room door. He saw the chain and put two and two together. Sliding along the wall, he reached his car and grabbed his shotgun from the passenger seat.

At that moment, he felt the temptation—the urgent, compelling physical temptation—to run for the exit and put distance between himself and her. There was nothing to stop him. He glanced in that direction and then back inside the building. There, in the act of murdering almost all his team, was the fruit of his sins. The thing he'd swept under the carpet that was now crawling back out, more powerful than ever.

He cocked the shotgun.

After all, we know what Chekhov said about guns, he thought before running headlong toward her, the fruit of his sins.

Right now, barricaded behind the MobLab, Mentor regrets not running for the exit. He regrets having missed his mark—an easy shot at her back. He regrets many things, but most of all, the fact he left his cigarettes in his coat. It's obvious he's going to die in the next fifty seconds, and what pisses him off most is not having one last puff.

On the other hand, I'm going to stop smoking forever, he thinks as he edges counterclockwise round the MobLab.

There's no way he can make a run for it. From what he supposes is Sandra's position, she can easily cover the entrance and the path to his car. His only chance is to set a trap for her, get behind her.

There's a narrow space between the van and Aguado's lab (*I hope she's not in there, that she managed to escape*), big enough for a body to edge through sideways. The width of the enormous wing mirror at least.

If he can slip in there, he might still stand a chance. Even if Sandra decides to come around the same side of the van, she'll find the shotgun barrel pointing straight at her disgusting, friendly face.

Not even I could miss at that range, thinks Mentor.

Thrusting the gun in front of him, he slips into the gap. It's a fifty-fifty life-or-death gamble. But that's only counting the possibilities he has thought of. Mentor hasn't even considered she might shoot at his ankles from under the van. The thought flashes through his mind when it's too late, when he's already wedged in the narrow passageway of metal and cement. He has no choice now but to press on. One meter. Two meters.

When he's halfway along, close enough to the wing mirror to touch it with the shotgun barrel, he hears her laugh.

A laugh as piercing as a knife blade.

Sandra goes on laughing some more as if it's bubbling out of her, un-stoppable. It's the kind of laugh that comes from somewhere far away and could make you lose your mind.

Mentor feels an icy fist ram into his insides, scrape his guts, get stuck in his windpipe. She's right behind him.

And when they wonder who it was, we'll say no, no, it wasn't your friends, they're all gone, Sandra sings softly.

"Please . . . ," says Mentor, closing his eyes.

A drop of sweat, or perhaps a tear, trickles down his cheek to the corner of his mouth. A delicate taste of salt finds its way to his tongue. He tries to swallow and succeeds only with difficulty.

"Solve this one," says Sandra in a passable imitation of Mentor's voice during their training sessions. "You're in a very confined space, your weapon pointing forward. There's no room for you to transfer it to your other hand, and your enemy is right behind you. What do you do?"

Mentor of course doesn't reply. So she takes a step forward and presses her pistol into his armpit. He can feel the cold metal through his sweaty shirt.

"There's nothing I can do," he says.

"Too easy and too slow," says a gloating Sandra. She jabs the gun barrel into his axillary nerve. A jolt of unbearable pain runs through Mentor's body. The muscles of his left arm contract. He drops the shotgun with his right. A warm wetness fills his crotch. Not entirely a result of his pain reflex.

"Go ahead and shoot, for fuck's sake."

Sandra clicks her tongue disapprovingly. As if the mere idea he could get out of this so easily offended her.

"Do you know something? All I needed was for you to love me. But you never even saw me. You never discovered who I am."

"You're a mistake. That's what you are. A mistake from my past."

Sandra laughs once more.

A different kind of laugh this time.

A simpler one.

Almost childish.

She leans in until her face is pressed up against his and lowers her voice. Now she's an old friend whispering a secret in his ear.

"Yes, you're right. But a mistake from a lot earlier than you imagine."

Before shooting him in the head, she gently sings him the song's refrain.

After shooting him in the head, she straightens the thinning hair on his brow.

"I'd have done anything for you."

4

SEVEN SNAPSHOTS

Neither Jon nor Antonia will recall with any clarity the next few hours of their lives, apart from a series of three-dimensional snapshots, moments frozen in time, disconnected from one another.

1. Jon compulsively presses the Call button on the car phone. Antonia is driving along the hard shoulder at the M-40 exit. Their left side-view mirror takes off the one on a car that came too close. A cloud of shattered glass, plastic, and wires hangs in midair.

2. Jon switches on the police radio—hidden under the dash—just in time to hear the call to all nearby units. His hands form an incredulous equilateral triangle around his temples. It's the kind of thing Antonia would normally notice, but not this time.

3. Two police vans and a fire engine are stationed at the exit to the camouflaged Red Queen headquarters. They're waiting for instructions that never come. The blue lights of their sirens cast phantasmagoric shapes on the front of the anonymous building. Antonia, with Jon following in her wake, heads for the entrance, ignoring the yells of the police.

4. A firefighter, face covered by a mask, slams his axe into the chain blocking access to the meeting room. The links fly through the air, and a faint, orange-colored cloud wafts through the open door. The bodies have long stopped twitching in their death throes, but several still have their faces turned toward the door. As if they hadn't yet given up all hope.

5. Antonia kneels down to close Mentor's eyes. Her fingers brush against his eyelids. The paramedics have left his shirt unbuttoned after confirming he's dead. One of them is talking to Jon a few meters away. Jon's face is a picture of despair. The paramedic's lips are thrust out as though poised to give a kiss as they form the fourth letter of the word *impossible*.

6. Antonia weeps, one forearm leaning against the Audi, her left hand clinging to Jon. He tries to console her, but his eyes are on the gurney carrying away his boss's dead body. The rain comes down harder, and the plastic wheels throw up tiny droplets as they fall into cracks in the sidewalk.

7. Antonia's phone rings. Sniffing hard, she pulls it out of her pocket. Jon is still looking the other way, so it takes him some time to turn around. Antonia dries her tears with the back of her hand, incredulous when she sees who the caller is.

5

A PHONE CALL

Antonia answers the call.

"Are you calling to beg for forgiveness?"

"No, I know I won't get that," says Aguado. "Not in this life at least. I'm calling to say goodbye."

When like Antonia you're unable to analyze your own feelings properly and communicate them; when what for others is blindingly obvious is for you a jigsaw puzzle, then you develop coping mechanisms. But none of them are capable of assimilating and processing what she feels at this moment. The jumble of emotions overwhelms her.

"How could you do it? How?"

"Because I had no choice. He has me trapped. Just like you."

Antonia can't help herself, and suddenly, everything that's been building up inside her over these last dreadful minutes comes flooding out. All the answers that have fallen into place, the tiny cogs in the enormous machine that finally fit together.

"For a long while now, right? It was you who gave Covas a fake report saying Jaume Soler was dead. Did you also tell Sandra about White, or was it the other way around? Did you manipulate the evidence in Laura Trueba's house, Sandra's first crime?"

"I'm afraid you're right about a lot of it."

"When I was obsessed with finding her, with using her to get to White, what did you do? You stole the red pills from that chamber 'to help me.' And I'm sure you also suggested to Mentor it would be perfect for us to investigate the Málaga business. To keep us busy while White prepared his masterstroke . . ."

Antonia only stops talking when she feels Jon's hand on her shoulder. She's leaning on the Audi in the rain. Her hair is dripping wet, her soul in pieces. Jon's hand is soothing, a gentle relief that allows her to stay grounded in reality.

"He won't let me tell you any more. I'm sorry."

"So why did you call? Did he ask you to? I guess this is another move in his game."

At the far end of the line, the pathologist stays silent. Antonia can almost hear her making excuses, justifying herself. Someone who has gone this far can't have many scruples.

"I did it because he asked me to."

"And for that reason today, you killed a dozen people."

"I'd kill two hundred if he ordered me to. Without a second thought."

"What does he have on you, Aguado? How did he manage to blackmail you?" Antonia asks, desperate for the tiniest bit of information.

"I'm not going to tell you that. But I'm sure you can imagine."

Yes, Antonia can.

In fact, the details aren't important. A girlfriend, brother, a mother perhaps. Whoever White is threatening in Aguado's life, it only confirms what Antonia already knew. No one can escape from committing even the most dreadful act for love. Love is the most powerful force that exists.

"You could have come to me. I would have helped you."

"Using . . . how did the inspector describe it yesterday? Your brain programmed to follow the evidence?"

"Together—"

Aguado interrupts her.

"You have no idea what he's capable of. How he can anticipate everything. No matter how carefully you plan something, he's already a step ahead of you. No one can defeat him, Scott. Not even you."

Antonia shivers, and it's not just because of the rain streaming down her hair, trickling into the neck of her blouse and soaking her back, her bra, and continuing down to the white, smooth skin at her waist. No, this cold springs from within.

"The odds were stacked against me from the beginning, weren't they?"

"He made you believe you could defeat him. You're nothing more than a kite caught in a gale."

"What about you? Do you think he's going to just let you go now? Knowing everything you do?"

"That's the deal we made."

"He'll kill you," Antonia warns her.

"Maybe."

Antonia's voice lowers to a whisper.

"Pray that he does. Because if he doesn't, I will. I'll find you, Aguado. You'll pay for what you've done."

A gentle whisper uttered by a tiny, half-broken woman. A minuscule speck in an indifferent universe, her voice scarcely disturbs the rain and the March wind. But the rain and the March wind know nothing. Aguado does. That's why an ice cube rolls down her spine. She'll have to live the rest of her life knowing she is the target of that vow.

"I have no doubt you'll try. Goodbye, Antonia."

6

A BREAKDOWN

When Aguado hangs up, Antonia explodes.

If Antonia were someone else, someone who had to struggle with the emotions she's now busy processing—for example, the person closest to her right now, who happens to be Jon Gutiérrez—she'd probably do it by kicking over a trash can. Shouting and stomping on it until it's reduced to a piece of plastic an inch or two thick.

For Antonia, it's not that easy.

She is suffering both the agony of loss and the torment of her own blindness. But above all, the betrayal of her trust.

When people let others get close to them, there's usually a reason. Sometimes this closeness happens gradually, almost imperceptibly. But regardless of how slowly it happens, there's always a decisive moment. Something that changes the label that person's face has in our personal archive. Whether it's a work colleague, a neighbor, or somebody you met on social media, there's always something. A gesture, a look, a few words. A shared laugh, a joint insight. You don't always remember it clearly or consciously, but if you make an effort, you can retrieve it. The exact day, hour, and minute when the inscription under their photo changed from *acquaintance* to *friend*.

For Antonia, who has very few of the first and still fewer of the second, who has an inexhaustible memory and an unhealthy capacity for analysis, such moments are unforgettable milestones.

With Mentor, it was one day after her training, very early on. She was sweaty, exhausted, and unsure of her own abilities. Feeling, like all truly intelligent people, something of an impostor. He came over to her with a towel and said:

"I envy you."

That was all. A single sentence. Sincere and real; disconcerting as only the truth can be. There are huge quantities of idiots in the world who think they're intelligent, capable of managing the national soccer team, performing open-heart surgery, or solving the immigration problem. They come out with irrefutable answers on each of these topics in only a few minutes. Truly intelligent people have doubts about everything and everyone, but above all, about themselves.

With those words, Mentor changed the inscription under his photo. Antonia still hated him—and continues to do so, because of all his lies—but in the way you hate someone who's inside the tent, not spitting from outside.

And Inspector Gutiérrez? Oh, that's easy.

As they were leaving Laura Trueba's office and Antonia saw her own pain reflected in the face of another mother, Jon was there. He went with her to see Jorge at his school. He didn't ask too many awkward questions, which for Jon was quite an achievement. What he did was make her Spanish tortilla. Antonia even forgave him for adding onion. Not that she was aware of the taste—like everything else, the tortilla tasted of cardboard—but you can't disguise the texture of the tiny bits between your teeth.

Antonia, who couldn't boil an egg to save her life, is acutely aware of such small acts of love. Of the value inherent in a gesture apparently so minimal as to cook for another. It leaps out at you, like those joke boxes with a paper snake hidden inside them. You're as calm as anything, and then *pow!* a ton of love smacks you right in the face.

It was the tortilla that changed the inscription under Jon's photo. And it kept changing until there were no more left. The progression from *stranger, colleague, friend, family* ended in a three-letter word: *J, o,* and *n.* For Antonia, that says it all. *Jon.*

And Dr. Aguado?

Antonia thinks back to the first time they met, in Laura Trueba's house. She was just a technician, excited because she had read Antonia's file. Curious to get to know the freak responsible for what happened in Valencia. In awe of her, or so Jon had told her afterward.

The inscription beneath Aguado's photo changed a few days later.

When Antonia was facing one of her darkest moments. When Ezekiel escaped following a difficult and eventually fruitless chase. Antonia was trying painfully to make sense of all the puzzling aspects of the case. She knew for sure this killer was a different kind of animal from any she had dealt with hitherto. She was right, of course, but for the wrong reason.

That moment of doubt and uncertainty, that early morning of sleeplessness and unease, found her sitting next to Marcos's bed. Clutching his right hand and staring at the wall while she listened to the beep of the heart monitor in the burgeoning hospital silence. Eyes misty with tears: desperate, drowning, defeated. Longing to pay back a hundredfold the people who made them suffer.

While she was in this weakened state, Aguado had called. Her voice at the other end of the line was like a lighthouse, a rope Antonia could cling to in the midst of the waves. Exhausted from smoking and tiredness, hoarse from her allergy, or vice versa. Loneliness turns the soul into a dried-out sponge that's grateful for any liquid that drips onto it.

Aguado had lied to her while she was holding her husband's lifeless hand: all the time she had been conniving with the people who had laid him low in that hospital bed!

Somehow this was the worst insult of all.

All these thoughts flashed through Antonia Scott's mind in the moment between when Aguado hung up and she pulled the cell phone away from her ear.

The telling of it takes a lot longer.

As we were saying, when Aguado hangs up, Antonia explodes. The agony of loss, the torment of her own blindness, the betrayal of trust. There is no word in any language capable of expressing this breakdown in Antonia's brain and heart.

Her body decides matters for her. Her stomach heaves once, then a second time. At the third retch, Antonia brings up what little is in her stomach onto the Audi's side window.

Jon, who was on the point of stamping on a trash bin, exchanges violence for kindness—he takes a freshly laundered handkerchief from his pocket and offers it to Antonia—and swaps fury for regret—specifically at having left the car window open.

"The evil bitch," Antonia says between splutters and retches. She spits, but her mouth still tastes of what just passed: of loss, blindness, deception. Mixed with the bile, she finally comes up with a word.

Desperation.

She accepts Jon's handkerchief and cleans her lips and chin.

"You can keep it, sweetie," says Jon quickly when she makes to return it to him.

"The evil bitch," she repeats, balling her fist around the handkerchief and pounding the car roof.

"Don't overdo the swearing, angel," Jon needles her. "You have to find the happy medium."

"How can you joke at a time like this?" says Antonia, turning around and pummeling Jon with her fist. She hits him on the chest with every last ounce of her strength, with the expected result. Arms open, he absorbs the blows, giving her time, offering himself, waiting. When she has finished, when all her anger has dissipated and only sadness remains, he prevents her falling as she collapses against him. It's only then that he ventures to put his arms around her and allow her streaming eyes and nose to complete the ruin of his dry cleaning.

7

A GETAWAY

"They're waiting for you inside," says Jon when Antonia finally pulls away from him.

She dries her eyes, sniffs loudly, and uses the handkerchief once more. She opens the passenger door, but seeing the mess she's made of the upholstery, she reconsiders and sits in the back.

Jon taps gently on the window.

Antonia lowers it.

Jon props himself against the door.

"The crime scene is clear. We need to . . ."

"We're not going back in," she says without looking at him.

"But, Antonia . . ."

"No. We know who the culprit is."

"But, Antonia . . ."

"Who's in charge in there?"

Glancing back over his shoulder, Jon realizes he doesn't know the answer.

"I don't know. There was some officer arguing with a guy from the National Intelligence Agency. An examining magistrate is also on the way."

"Exactly."

Jon suddenly understands what's going through Antonia's mind. They used to arrive at any crime scene through the back door, without asking anyone's permission. If a problem arose, they simply made a phone call. A few minutes later, as if by magic, all the barriers came down, all the obstacles were smoothed over.

The problem is that the person who made those calls is now lying on the concrete floor of their headquarters, in a pool of his own blood.

"We can't leave him all alone in there, Antonia."

She looks around her at all the strangers coming and going from the building, the unknown faces, the strobe lights. The chaos that will engulf them if they don't play their cards right.

"We're not investigating this crime scene, Jon. We know the victims, we know who the killers are. We're now persons of interest."

"But . . ."

"If we go in, we'll never get out. They'll put us in an interview room, and it's not as if we have any time to lose," she says, pointing to his neck.

"So what do you suggest?"

"That we lie low for a while. I need to think."

Inspector Gutiérrez drums his fingers on the car roof as he considers what Antonia has said. Unfortunately, she's right. Without their customary protector, they're nothing more than a humble, *officially* suspended functionary and an out-of-work philologist.

"They'll look for us anyway."

"We'll have to go rogue for a few hours. It won't be the first time."

Jon smiles through his weariness and walks around the car. He sits at the wheel and peers over his shoulder at the back seat.

"Where to, Miss Daisy?"

Antonia stares back at him with a bewilderment bordering on helplessness.

"Forget it," says Jon. "I know the ideal place for a woman of your caliber."

8

A TOBLERONE

The Repsol service station on Avenida de Aragón, opposite the Vehicle Inspection Center, may not appear in the Michelin Guide or have won any stars on Tripadvisor, but it has top-quality packaged cholesterol. It even has the new Toblerone filled with Funduk, which is all the rage. Antonia takes the twenty-euro note Jon hands her and scoops up all the chocolate bars she can carry. She sits eating them on a bench so close to the restrooms she can hear the toilets flushing.

Jon, meanwhile, cleans the car. He vacuums the interior, wipes it down thoroughly, and sprays it with air freshener until it smells of vanilla-scented vomit rather than just plain vomit.

Once he's finished, he goes inside to see what he can find that isn't lethal. A glance at the counter confirms his worst fears: the food is so bad you can see the streptococci running for cover. In the end, he resigns himself to feasting on a dried-out steak roll, which looks like the least repulsive choice on the establishment's vast menu.

"If Mentor could see you eating that . . . ," says Antonia.

Jon removes a piece of gristle from his mouth to be able to reply.

"If he hadn't gotten himself killed, we wouldn't be here, hiding out."

"You're doing it again," says Antonia after a prolonged silence.

"Doing what?"

"That thing you do. It's not funny."

"Sweetie, you wouldn't know funny if it kicked you in the butt. And anyway, jokes are a coping mechanism for pain."

Antonia pops the last triangle of Toblerone in her mouth and chews it slowly as she solemnly considers what Jon has just said.

"Do you think you could teach me?"

"No."

Jon crumples the red-and-white napkin from the roll, tries to throw it into the nearby bin. He misses, bends down to pick it up, brushes the last crumbs from his jacket, and goes over to Antonia, who is still waiting expectantly.

"Don't give me that look. I can't teach you that."

"You taught me to swear."

"That's different."

"Why?"

"It just is. Because pain and humor. Only you can be in control of those things."

"I don't get it. Would you make a joke if I died?"

Jon, who has spent sleepless nights fretting over just such a possibility. Who has pushed her out of the way of a speeding off-roader. Who has her to thank for being shot at several times. Who has jumped from a roof to save her, as well as a number of other things that are beside the point, thinks about how his heart would break if this slip of a woman with greasy hair vanished from the face of the earth.

"I'd be laughing before your body turned cold," he says very seriously.

Antonia bursts into laughter. Which is an event as infrequent as Halley's Comet. She has a wonderful crystalline, harmonious laugh, which is contagious. Even so, Jon considers it his sacred duty to keep a straight face.

"What's so funny?" he says through gritted teeth.

"The algor mortis. The postmortem body temperature. Calculated using the Glaister equation. In a very specific way."

"Which is?"

"A thermometer up the anus."

To hell with Jon's sacred duty.

He laughs.

He laughs with all his might at the frailty of existence, at thermometers in anuses, at his own defenselessness.

Jon laughs, and Antonia laughs with him, until they're both crying with laughter.

"I don't want to become even more alone," she says.

"I know."

"No, you don't, Jon. There's something I haven't told you."

And Antonia explains what she was doing the night he was abducted. What she was on her way to tell him when Sandra drugged him, shoved him in a van, and took him away.

How she made the hardest decision of her life. To disconnect the machine keeping Marcos alive.

She tells him how much his body had atrophied in recent months. His limbs had shrunk, his skin had become opaque and flaccid. The medical diagnosis was plain. The doctors had given up on him years before. No chance, they'd said. Antonia refused to believe them. She turned her back on reason because she was too proud to admit a mistake she couldn't put right.

"Then I met you, and you changed everything," she tells Jon.

She tells him how he reconnected her to life. To the possibility of making a mistake. Of being wrong. She doesn't talk about her daily ritual, her sacred three minutes. About what keeps her sane. Because there are recesses of the soul that can't be shared, however much you want to and however much you trust the other person.

She explains what it meant to feel alive again only to see everything she loved destroyed or endangered.

"First Marcos, then Jorge, then Mentor. Now you."

Jon listens to her story without a word.

When she has finished, he tells her one of his own.

"I know what it means to feel you're to blame for all the world's ills. I have a friend who ran off into the hills when he was eight. He took two slices of sausage, half a loaf of bread, and half a wineskin of Fanta Orange. All because a kid at school told him his father had left home because of him. Before he'd been away two nights, the Civil Guard pulled him out of a sheepfold. Where, had it been up to him, he would have stayed forever."

Antonia thinks this over for a while, then looks tenderly at Jon.

"Look, I'll tell you. That friend was me," he explains.

"I'd already guessed."

"You really are the smartest woman in the world," says Jon with a hint of irony. Then he turns serious. "But you don't have to be the loneliest."

Antonia gives a timid smile of thanks and gets to her feet.

"Can I know why you're telling me this now?" asks Jon.

"Because you left your phone in the car."

Inspector Gutiérrez pats his pocket in surprise.

Then he notices Antonia doesn't have her shoulder bag either.

He looks out at their car, parked ten meters or so away near the car wash.

"I don't get it."

"That was very personal. I didn't want him to hear it."

Jon rewinds. Back to the moment when he woke up in a wheelchair without his phone. He spools forward. To the moment when Aguado gave him a new handset with the same number.

He adds those two moments together, mixes in the nebulous certainty that White seems to know where they are at every moment.

That he's always a couple of steps ahead of them.

As though . . .

"Fuuuuuuck!"

"Exactly."

"Has he been listening to us right from the start?"

Antonia nods slowly. Allowing Jon the time to reach his own conclusions. She can be considerate. Sometimes.

"Using my cell phone mic?"

Another nod.

"Maybe mine as well. I've left everything in the car: my iPad, cell phone, and watch."

Jon shakes his head incredulously.

"How long have you known?"

"I suspected it from the beginning. Because I would have done exactly the same. But I've known for sure for a while."

"Since when?"

"Aguado repeated something you said to me at Soler's house. 'A brain programmed to follow the evidence.'"

"You and I were in another room. There was no way she could have overheard," says Jon.

"I think she did it on purpose to warn us, without White knowing."

Jon takes a deep breath and exhales with a sigh so powerful it stirs the dead leaves on the ground, as well as a candy wrapper and one of those bits of paper you clean your hands with after filling up with gas.

"That doesn't exonerate her in any way."

"No, but I think in the end, she wanted to help us."

"Wait a minute," says Jon, who is still assimilating this fresh information. "That means. . . . if you knew from the start he was listening to us . . ."

"I didn't tell you because you'd have given the game away, Jon."

"But, sweetie, you don't know *how* to lie," the inspector says, coloring up. "You're the worst liar I've ever met."

"And you don't know how to hide your emotions."

Checkmate.

The sly boots.

Jon has to admit that if he had known, with everything they've gone through, everything they've suffered, and given his personal history of confrontation—of going in fists flying—with regard to the obstacles he has come across in his life, possibly he would have given the game away.

For whatever reason.

"So all those things you said about having no idea where we were headed, or what to do next, was . . ."

". . . to a large extent true."

"To a large extent," he echoes her gloomily.

"I have a hunch about what's going on. In part at least."

"And you aren't going to tell me, are you?"

"If you already know, why ask?" says Antonia, looking at him in all innocence.

9

A MESSAGE

Antonia returns to the car. This time, she sits in the passenger seat, which is tolerably clean. Not that the smell would bother her anyway.

When Jon gets in beside her, he has to pick up the cell phone from the seat. Putting it back in his pocket, he feels a combination of fear and disgust for the device that used to bring him so many good things.

Well, some good things. Like Grindr, for example.

Inspector Gutiérrez realizes Antonia was right all along. It's impossible to forget there's a third person in the car with them, another pair of ears. It's the same idea as in the show *Big Brother*: however much they try to sell it as reality TV, it's all playacting. So he decides to say as little as possible. Because of course the bomb at the back of his neck really is impossible to forget.

"What do you think will happen now?" he asks Antonia, trying to sound natural. In other words, worn out, tired, and scared to death.

"He'll get in touch with us. He still has to give us the third address. The third crime to solve."

"Do you think that sick bastard . . ."

Antonia opens her eyes wide and flaps her hand at him.

Jon tries to rein in his emotions. Yes, it's impossible to forget you're being overheard by the same person who only has to press a button to end your life.

". . . might provide us with the answer?"

"What do you mean?"

"When we tried to find out who killed Raquel Planas, we couldn't.

When we were looking for Soler's killer, we discovered Soler killed Planas."

"You have a point," says Antonia after a moment's reflection.

"Maybe what you said just now is right. There's no way we can win this game."

"Jon, we already knew everything was fixed. He's a psychopathic killer, not the Supreme Court."

"No, what I mean is he never intended to set this thing off," says Jon, pointing to his neck. "Not before now, I mean. I don't know what comes next, but I suspect what he really wanted was to bring us to this point."

"I don't know. I really don't know," says Antonia. "Right now, I'm too tired, too drained, too overwhelmed. As long as you have that thing there, I'll do whatever he asks. There's no other solution. And you'll do what I tell you."

Inspector Gutiérrez listens to her skeptically, not quite sure what to make of what he's just heard.

It turns out Mr. White can interpret Antonia better than he can.

Jon can't help smiling. All of a sudden, the ever-present, all-powerful White has lost some of his power to intimidate. Because if he hadn't known his phone was bugged, Jon would have shit himself when he heard

(two pings and a buzz)

on Antonia's cell phone, just as she finishes speaking. With the perfect timing and synchronicity of a Hollywood film editor.

Jon, whose addiction to cinema is boundless, became hooked one day on a documentary about the work of Skip Lievsay on *The Silence of the Lambs*. How he managed to mix the sound so the voices of the actors in one scene began to be heard before the previous scene had finished. It's the omniscience of the narrator, who knows what's going to happen before we do as spectators, that creates the feeling of menace. In fact, Jon wasn't afraid White was listening to them. He was afraid he was omnipotent.

But he isn't. He's a guy with a microphone.

We can deal with him. Okay, so he's smart. Maybe even smarter than Antonia. Maybe he has everything planned.

But if in the end I have to choose, if I have to take him with me, I will. And that's a power he can never match, thinks Jon.

Antonia, meanwhile, has picked up her phone and read the message.

Her face falls.

She shows Jon the screen.

Jon's face falls too.

This time, they don't need to search in Heimdal for the crime that took place at that address. Or set up their GPS to help them find it.

Because she knows only too well what crime took place there.

Because the address that just flashed up on her phone is the one she knows best in Madrid.

MELANCOLÍA, 7

Antonia Scott's home address.

10

A LOFT

They reach the top floor and find themselves outside the loft door.

Green. Ancient. Its paint flaking.

Open. Wide open.

Jon carefully pulls out his gun and stands in front of Antonia.

He had gotten her out of the bad habit of leaving it open months ago.

Not that much has changed inside her apartment. It's almost bare and has nothing worth stealing. Apart from a nice fake rubber plant in the hallway.

Jon advances down the hallway, both hands clutching his gun. The kitchen is empty and dark. So is Marcos's old studio.

The only thing that appears from the living room is the barrel of a pistol. It's pointing directly at Jon's right temple. Jon returns the compliment, aiming into the darkness.

Two steps farther on and he sees Sandra's smiling face, as inviting as a rat's dinner.

"Inspector," she greets him.

"Psycho-bitch," he greets her.

"I suggest you put your gun away."

"You first, darling."

Sandra exaggerates her smile until it becomes an impossible grimace.

"My pleasure," she says, concealing the gun in her raincoat. She holds up her empty hands like a magician who has just put the dove back in the hat. She all but bares her forearms for him.

"Jon."

A word of warning from Antonia in the doorway, but Jon still has his gun raised. The barrel is inches from Sandra's face.

A slight pressure would be all it took.

A gentle pull on the trigger, and we'd eliminate a piece of vermin from this world, thinks Jon. *A police killer.*

The temptation—urgent, all powerful, physical—tenses all his muscles. His arm is as stiff as a soccer crossbar. The whole Bilbao Athletic team could swing from it. The muzzle of his gun visibly pulses in time with his heart.

Sandra sees this, but her smile doesn't falter. If anything, it becomes twisted, almost lascivious. She takes a step toward Jon and bends forward to the gun. For a split second, the look in her eyes leads Jon to think she's not all there, that Sandra is going to stick her tongue out and run it along the barrel. But what she in fact does is press her forehead against it.

Inspector Gutiérrez feels a vibration running from the tip of the gun to his wrist, as if he can sense her craziness through the metal.

"You don't dare," Sandra whispers, snakelike. "I've just killed your boss and all your colleagues. But you don't dare, do you, fatso?"

Now you've done it, thinks Jon.

But he doesn't pull the trigger, because a small, white hand is laid on the black, oiled metal. Very gently and slowly, it forces him to lower his weapon.

Jon turns his gaze from Sandra's venomous, mocking eyes and follows the direction Antonia is looking in. She is quaking with rage.

Outside, the sun is going down.

In the living room, Mr. White is sitting in the middle of the floor in the lotus position. Fortysomething. Wearing black pants and a white T-shirt. Barefoot. In front of him is a brown leather folder, tied with a red felt ribbon.

"Come in, Señora Scott," he invites her in English. "Come in and close the door."

"No," says Jon, pushing in front of her.

"Inspector, your subconscious is so near the surface I can see the periscope coming up," White says in clumsy, drawling Spanish.

He shows Jon a small device he's holding. Like the old-fashioned ones used to open garage doors. Jon has a very clear idea of what this one is for. A strong itch in the wound on his neck accompanies this realization.

"Be so kind as to step outside, would you?" adds White, seeing Jon hesitate.

"Nothing will happen to me," says Antonia, skirting around her colleague.

Before closing the door behind her, she has some final words of advice for him. She nods in the direction of Sandra:

"Try not to kill her, Jon."

"I'm not promising anything."

Antonia turns and confronts White.

"That place is mine," she says in English, pointing to the exact spot on the floor where she always sits.

White gives no sign of having heard but points to the floor in front of her.

"Please, sit down. Make yourself at home."

A wave of fury suffuses Antonia's face. The last time she and White met, she went through a similar process. She needs to calm the monkeys, prevent her rage spilling over, decide on a strategy.

On that occasion, she had no weapon. This time, she has her P290 in a tiny holster barely concealed inside her jacket.

She moves her arm toward it. Only slightly.

"This is quicker than a bullet," says White, raising the hand holding the remote.

Antonia knows he's right. She doesn't even bother doing the math, although numbers followed by a string of zeros flash before her. It's not humanly possible for her to grab her weapon and put a bullet in White's head before he presses the button to kill Jon.

Caught between anger and common sense, Antonia has no choice but to lower her arms in front of her again.

White enjoys seeing her change her mind at the last minute. Like someone watching a well-trained dog.

After all, we prefer most animals in cages, thinks Antonia, reflecting on her monkeys.

She sits down very slowly opposite White.

The room looks strange from this angle.

Which is exactly what he wants.

Speaking of monkeys, quite a crowd is gathering. To screech at her, warn her against the man sitting opposite her. She's inundated with details that impose their own daunting conditions.

"Take a deep breath," White tells her. "You and I have reached the endgame. And no one likes that to be rushed."

Antonia has no difficulty detecting the menace in his voice. But something that ought to increase her anxiety has the opposite effect.

"What are you doing in my home?"

"I thought it was about time we had our first meeting," he replies with a shrug.

"Do you have some malfunction in your memory as well as in your prefrontal lobe?"

White shakes his head disapprovingly.

"That old bias. A weakness in my limbic system, in my prefrontal lobe, is what made me into a psychopath. Born evil. Devoid of empathy. Is that what you think?"

"I'm quite sure of it."

"I won't even deign to discuss the matter with you, Señora Scott. But I'm glad you brought it up. A few years ago, someone else said the exact same thing to me. The only person who dared. Things didn't go too well for him."

"What is it you want, White?"

"Actually, the doctor—for he was a doctor, you see—well, I taught him a relatively swift lesson. I kidnapped his little girl and left her nanny's body in the basement. That was all it took."

Not for the first or last time, Antonia relives the anxiety and fear she felt in the subway tunnel when Jorge was in Sandra's hands.

"This time, you won't be able to touch him."

"Well, that's debatable," says White, opening the folder on the floor between them. He takes out a photograph and lays it in front of Antonia.

No.

It's not possible.

11

A THEORY

Antonia stares at the photograph for a few seconds. Taken in the street with a telephoto lens. Despite the distance and the blurred image, the faces are unmistakable. An old lady in a wheelchair, another woman, and a child.

"The Las Flores Hotel in San Salvador. An oasis of peace in a strife-torn country where life is cheap. I have a contact in the Mara Salvatrucha gang. They would charge me six thousand dollars to kill the boy. For the two women, probably nothing. When it comes down to it, the biggest expense for all services is transport. *Where you shoot once, you can shoot three times, dude,*" White concludes.

His attempt at a Salvadorean accent is somewhere between passable and lousy. Even so, it's enough to make Antonia swallow hard.

"We've done all you asked of us."

White joins his fingertips to make a little roof.

"Ah, but that's not quite true, is it? You didn't manage to solve the first case in time. Or the second one. And your debt has been slowly increasing, Señora Scott."

"You killed twelve people," says Antonia, trying unsuccessfully to hide the fear in her voice.

"I'm afraid that was down to my assistant. She had an account to settle with her boss. A disgruntled employee—you know what they're like."

Antonia's emotions change as rapidly as the lights on a dance floor. Fear, anger, hatred, suffering. Again she feels the urge to slip her hand behind her back. She could save the lives of Jorge, Carla, Grandma Scott.

At the price of Jon's life. One against three.

But the math doesn't work for her.

"As I was saying, teaching you a lesson has taken me a bit longer than with the doctor. But you're an exceptional case, Señora Scott. You've made me reassess everything I know, really you have."

"What is it you want?" whispers Antonia.

"I hope I'm not boring you. If I am, please say so. Look, I have a theory. A little idea that first came to me years ago when I was studying at the university. A professor explained that emotions are changes that prepare us for action. And I thought . . . if we stimulate the right emotions in the subject, we can control their actions from outside. Like . . ."

He waves the remote a second time.

"That's an abomination," Antonia says in disgust.

Although at the same time, and she'd never admit this out loud, she's fascinated.

White realizes this. He has noticed Antonia's voice is a bit higher. Her pupils slightly dilated. This encourages him to go on talking; that's the weakness of genius. It needs an audience.

"That's what my professor thought. Eleven days later, he killed himself in front of his wife and children. I struggled a bit; it was a clumsy first effort. But it was also my *eureka* moment. I remember it fondly."

"Archimedes used his discovery to save Syracuse. You did it to make money."

"As I told you a few days ago, you're confusing ends and means. I don't use my research to make money. I make money to further my research."

"It's all the same. The point is you've found a method for sowing evil," says Antonia, who doesn't dare ask but needs to know.

"More than one. I discovered there are a specific number of personality types into which humans fit like gloves."

"People aren't bits of clothing."

"Your friend outside, for example, is a typical Type Three. I wager if I ordered him to come in here, I could make him blow his brains out in"—he consults his watch ostentatiously—"let's say seventy-four seconds."

"Oh, I wouldn't bet against Jon Gutiérrez, Mr. White," says Antonia, her eyes narrowing.

"You're the one who's betting against his life, Señora Scott. I don't wish to appear presumptuous, but I think you've enjoyed this little chat of ours."

Antonia blinks incredulously several times.

"Do you really think you know me?"

"No, actually, I don't. This should have ended eight months ago when we took your boy. After all, it was a very simple idea."

"All those theatrics about a serial killer, about Ezekiel. You think that was simple?"

"The idea, not how it was executed," admits White. "But it turned out you didn't fit any of the categories. Who would have imagined you'd risk your child's life to save that of a stranger?"

Antonia can't, won't, shouldn't respond to this. Because this is the question that feeds the nightmares that eat her up inside. And not just at night. Incredibly real dreams where she doesn't arrive in time to save Jorge.

She can see what White is trying to do. Manipulate her emotions by reminding her she's a mother. And she is. But she's lots more as well.

"You chose duty. And I have to admit, it worked. You definitely won that battle."

"I intend to win this one too," she says, though her voice quavers.

White studies Antonia for a few moments. At first, genuinely intrigued. Then more pensively.

He shakes his head.

"No. Actually, you already know you've lost," he says dismissively. "It's your pride talking, but your intelligence has more weight."

"What is it you want, White?"

"You already know. I want you to investigate the crime committed here."

"And you know perfectly well who the author of that crime was," says Antonia, gritting her teeth.

"I do, indeed. You're the one who refuses to see it, Señora Scott."

Hearing this, Antonia freezes.

"I realize you've been blaming me for years. But now I'm asking you to delve into that extraordinary memory of yours."

Antonia has no difficulty summoning that nightmare.

12

A NIGHTMARE

Marcos is in his small studio. The chisel draws sharp clicks from the sandstone. *Antonia is painfully aware of what is going to happen, because it's happened a thousand times before. She isn't in the living room in front of a heap of papers with lines of inquiry, reports, photographs. She's standing beside him, peering over his shoulder at the sculpture he's working on. It's a seated woman. Her hands are on her thighs, and she is leaning forward in an aggressive posture that contrasts with her serene face. There is something in front of the woman that makes her want to stand up, but her legs are still trapped in the stone. The chisel hasn't yet managed to free them. It never will.*

The doorbell rings. Antonia wants to stop Marcos going to the door, to tell him to continue working, to allow their lives to go on undisturbed. But her throat is as dry and dusty as the stone chippings on the floor. She hears herself—that other woman, that stupid, ignorant woman with headphones who turns up the music—shout something, and Marcos leaves his hammer on the table next to the unfinished sculpture. He puts the chisel in his white apron and goes to the door. Antonia, the real Antonia, the Antonia who is looking on, who knows what is going to happen, wants to follow him, and she does, but slowly, too slowly, so she doesn't see him open the door or see how the stranger and Marcos start to struggle. By the time she reaches the hallway, the two men are on the floor. The chisel is already sticking out of the stranger's collarbone; his blood has stained Marcos's apron, and yet he manages to fire off two shots. One speeds through Antonia, the real Antonia, the one waiting in the hallway, and hits the ignorant woman still in the living room with her headphones on, the music going full blast, still gazing at the papers splayed in front of her. The shot glances off the side of the wooden cradle where Jorge is asleep, changing the bullet's trajectory enough so that it doesn't enter Antonia's body from the front but hits her in the back and exits through her shoulder. A benevolent trajectory. Without fatal consequences: just a few months' recuperation. And perhaps a fresh coat of varnish on the cradle.

The other shot isn't so kind. It hits Marcos's frontal bone, which the doctors will have to remove a large chunk of to allow the brain to expand as it tries to heal itself. Apparently after ricocheting off the wall. Apparently because Marcos threw himself on the stranger. The nightmare is never clear about this. It always ends with the report of the second shot echoing in Antonia's ears.

13

A WORD IN BULGARIAN

Antonia opens her eyes.

White is studying her closely. As motionless as she is.

"What do you know about the intruder who burst into your home, Señora Scott?" White asks softly.

"He rang the bell. He had a gun. Marcos attacked him with the chisel."

"Wasn't the man's blood on your husband's apron?"

"A few drops. There was no viable DNA. They said it was because of the chemical products on the apron."

"Who said that? Who did the analysis?"

Antonia pauses, thinking over the implications of what White is suggesting.

"I . . ."

"You don't know how to use a DNA sequencer. That's normal: neither do I. That sort of manual task is for inferior minds. Your job is to know who to trust. I repeat: Who did the analysis?"

"Someone from Mentor's team."

"He was the one who gave you the report. Who told you it was a dead end, isn't that so?"

Antonia is gripped once more by conflicting emotions. The shock gives her another free tour of the most interesting parts of her psyche. In an open-topped double-decker bus. It goes around the Confusion traffic circle, the monument to Rage, and Betrayal Square. The bus is filled with the people in her life, all looking about and pointing, taking selfies.

When she recovers, her pulse racing faster than ever, the blood pounding in her temples, her breath jagged, she senses White's hand on her forearm. It's as cold as a fish fresh from the slab.

Strangely, Antonia is so lost she doesn't pull away from the contact.

"I can ask Inspector Gutiérrez to come in. I think he still has some of those blue pills that help you at moments like this," says White, his kindness cloying.

Antonia feels the need—physical, urgent, imperative—to accept. But there are boundaries she's no longer willing to cross.

"You already made sure I'd never have to go without that poison. But I won't give in to it again."

"Ah yes, Dr. Aguado. A most useful collaborator. Partly thanks to her profession. I've never known a pathologist who believes in God or the soul. It makes them very easy to manipulate. Reliable."

Hearing this helps Antonia recover her composure somewhat. She pushes White's hand off forcefully.

"You may have been able to manipulate Aguado at will. You probably prevented them from analyzing the attacker's DNA, and concealing Soler's fingerprints. But none of that proves you didn't kill my husband."

White exhales loudly through his nose, shakes his head like a parent who can't believe his child still hasn't learned to use the toilet.

"Correct me if I'm wrong, Señora Scott, but isn't it up to the prosecution to prove the charges? What happened to 'innocent until proven guilty'?"

Antonia leans forward and jabs her finger in White's face.

"Are you trying to tell me it was pure coincidence you were pursuing Soler in Madrid exactly when Marcos was shot?"

"I can't believe you're so close and yet you still haven't reached the proper conclusion. Perhaps I chose the wrong Red Queen after all . . . ," White says with a shrug.

"Believe me, I've often wished that bullet had killed me, White. That you'd finished me off like you did all the others."

"There you go again, skirting around the solution. Once again ignoring my motives and my nature. I have to admit, I'm very disappointed."

"Your motives . . . ," whispers Antonia.

The world comes to a halt.

So does Antonia.

Kuklenlĕva.

In Bulgarian, a person who throws lions at the puppeteer.

Antonia closes her eyes and disappears for a few moments into her inner world. All the pieces of the jigsaw appear before her. The monkeys howl desperately and point to them. Antonia yells at them to be quiet inside her head.

And for the first time, she organizes the pieces in a logical order.

- Jaume Soler, a high-level computer consultant, asks her to help him escape from White's clutches.
- Raquel Planas, Soler's lover, murdered *before* Soler seeks out Antonia. Her boyfriend is falsely accused.
- She and Marcos are shot in their own apartment.
- Jaume Soler starts receiving substantial payments from a mysterious offshore company based in a tax haven.
- Someone conceals the evidence from Marcos's murder and leads the devastated Antonia to believe Soler is dead.
- Three years later, Ezekiel appears. White's first attempt to control Antonia, which fails.

And here they are again. Playing a second game of chess after the first one ended in stalemate. With three interconnected crimes that take them right back to the beginning.

To this same room.

Kuklenlĕva.

The only piece of the puzzle she never thought of, the only one she was never even capable of imagining is suddenly there at the center of the image. A huge hole toward which all the other pieces inexorably point.

Kuklenlĕva.

The image the pieces of the puzzle form in front of Antonia in her strange, complex inner world is a chess figure. Incomplete, white in color. Missing only one fragment.

That's what is fascinating about puzzles. When there's only one piece missing, the others outline its exact shape.

The shape of this piece is rounded, with a cross on the top.

The white king.

Kuklenlĕva.

In Bulgarian, a person who throws lions at the puppeteer. Given that the word Bulgarians used for their currency was *lĕv*, or lion, it's not hard to understand.

This process has lasted only a few seconds. A lifetime for Antonia Scott. But when she emerges, something has changed. The nature of the air is different. Its previous oily density seems to have lightened. Night has replaced day in the room and White hasn't switched on the lights, and yet they can see each other perfectly in the semidarkness.

Perhaps for the first time.

White is smiling—a strange, almost respectful smile.

"It was a privilege to witness that."

Antonia takes a deep breath as she averts her eyes. She still hates him with every fiber of her being. And yet something has changed between the two of them.

"All this time . . ."

He nods his understanding.

When Marcos was attacked, Antonia decided the implacable, mysterious killer had to be the one responsible for her husband's death, the one who had destroyed her life.

White undoes the top three buttons of his shirt. He pulls back the fabric on the left side to reveal a patch of perfect skin. His chest muscles are well defined, his taut neck forms a perfect triangle with his muscular shoulders.

But there's a scar on his left shoulder. An irregular five-pointed star, twisted where the skin had decided to close over the wound.

A scar where Marcos stabbed him with the chisel just before White opened fire.

A scar that's smaller but not dissimilar to the one Antonia has on her own left shoulder, caused by White's bullet.

"The queen is the most powerful piece on the chessboard," says White. "But however powerful a chess piece is, one mustn't forget . . ."

". . . there's always a hand moving it." Antonia finishes his sentence for him.

"Exactly. So now you're a step closer to solving the crime, aren't you?"

White's expression hardens once more. Antonia hasn't for a second forgotten who she's talking to, but his mask had momentarily disconcerted her.

The truce is over.

"You held all the trumps from the start, White. All I ever did was run wherever you wanted me to."

To exhaust us, undermine our self-confidence. Kill all our colleagues. Cut our links with the police. Destroy the Red Queen project.

"Why did you go to so much trouble?" asks Antonia.

"To complete your education. And now, finish the job. Solve the crime."

"It would be simpler if you just told me who contracted you."

"Yes, perhaps. But less interesting. Instead, I'm going to answer the question you put to me in the elevator. The answer is staring you in the face."

Antonia stretches out her hand and opens the folder from which White took the photograph of her family in San Salvador.

Inside is another black-and-white photo.

Even though it's nighttime, Antonia recognizes the street and the Solers' house. If the shot had been taken a bit farther to the right, it would show the living room window. Perhaps with Jon Gutiérrez about to appear in the frame.

What it does show is a man standing beside a powerful motorbike parked behind a dumpster. Thirty yards or so from the house. He is wearing jeans and a black leather jacket. He's carrying a helmet, and his face is turned slightly toward the camera.

"Our Sandra would make a good *paparazza*. It wasn't an easy image to obtain, at night and while moving. You came this close to catching him," says White, holding up his thumb and index finger, a fraction apart.

Antonia doesn't see White's mocking gesture: her eyes are glued to the photograph of the man she clearly recognizes even in the dark.

She tries to speak, but her throat is dry.

"Of course you would have arrived at this same point long ago if you hadn't been dealt marked cards," says White.

Antonia shakes her head, refusing to believe what she's looking at.

"No."

"I assure you I don't come cheap, Señora Scott. Far from it. Very few people can afford my fees."

"You're lying."

"I guess there's only one way to prove it, isn't there? So, get started."

Antonia rises to her feet and turns away from White, but before she reaches the door, his voice rings out.

"Let's increase the stakes. No police. No outside help. Just you two. Do I make myself clear?"

Antonia nods, still with her back to him.

"Excellent. Oh, by the way, I know how much you enjoyed my previous two countdowns, so . . ."

Two beeps and a vibration.

A message appears on Antonia's cell phone.

YOU HAVE THREE HOURS

14

A FIRST MISTAKE

Jon is driving. Antonia is too nervous, too much on edge. Her head is in chaos; her body craves a red pill. Only the fact that White was waiting for her to relapse has prevented her from hurling herself at Jon and snatching the box from his jacket pocket. She can see the outline of it through his suit material.

Just knowing the pills are there ought to make her life more difficult. Like a child forced to go on a diet for his own good, who presses his nose against a cake shop window. And yet the opposite is true.

"Are you going to tell me what went on between you two?"

Antonia doesn't reply. She takes out her iPad and makes a quick search on Heimdal. Out of the corner of his eye, Jon can see a map with various points marked on it.

Inspector Gutiérrez is well aware that when his colleague is in this mood, it's best to give her space.

"At last. At last he's made his first mistake," she says after a while.

"His second mistake."

Puzzled, Antonia asks:

"Which was the first?"

"His first," says Jon, raising an eyebrow, "was to mess with us."

Antonia looks at him, eyes narrowing to slits.

"How long have you been waiting to say that?"

Jon thinks for a moment.

"How long were you with your pal White?"

"About twenty minutes."

"So let's say ten minutes. In my mind. I spent the rest of the time thinking up ways to kill that bitch."

"Violence isn't the solution," says Antonia, focusing on her iPad once more.

"It's obvious you've never hit hard enough, sweetheart. Your other pal spent the whole time staring at me without saying a word. She does a great job playing the main creep's sidekick."

"She's not my pal. Anyway, you should be pleased. Right now, it could be her sitting here beside you."

Jon has to wait for the next stoplight twenty meters farther to be able to turn to Antonia and give her his *whatthefuckareyoutalkingabout* look.

"I'll explain later. The important thing is we have a chance, Jon."

Inspector Gutiérrez hasn't forgotten he still has the phone Aguado gave him in his pocket. He has to muster all his self-control to reply naturally.

"I really would like to know where we're going and what we're doing."

Antonia's face darkens.

"We're going to the worst place on earth. Before that, I want to make a stop somewhere. Turn right at the end of Calle de Atocha."

Then, without further explanation, she starts to rummage in the glove compartment.

Whatever you say, princess.

15

A TRAFFIC COP

Ruano is parked opposite El Brillante bar when the universe offers him an unex-pected gift.

Until a minute earlier, there was no indication this would happen. His new partner is a pleasant, quiet type. Even more of a rookie than him. Ruano is teaching him how to make up his quota of parking fines on the sly. You just wait for someone to double-park and pop in for a takeout, and *pow!* a ticket.

"This is too easy," says the rookie when they catch a third driver. Some idiot with a green Mini who, to top it all, was uninsured and hadn't passed the vehicle inspection test. The police crane has just towed the car away.

"Oh, you should've seen what it was like before they introduced the new parking rules. That was a real . . ."

No sooner have the words issued from his mouth than Ruano realizes he sounds like an old veteran reliving past battles.

The doctors didn't want him to return to work so soon, but Ruano insisted he was fine. That if he stayed at home, he'd end up going crazy or shooting himself. So here he is. Doing the rounds with a new partner only a few days after Osorio's death.

Concealing the PTSD symptoms from other people is simple. He's always been a quiet, reserved sort. Hiding them from himself is more of a problem. Every time he closes his eyes, he's back at the shoot-out. The door of the Vito opens, the bullets slam into the police car's bodywork. Osorio's wife shakes her head in disbelief at the news, grabbing hold of him angrily, telling him to stop lying, how can her husband be dead, she's pregnant, and this can't be happening.

That wasn't the best day in Ruano's life. Even though in his previous job he'd seen some terrible things. Two missions to Afghanistan, one to Somalia. Right afterward, he joined the municipal police thanks to the places reserved for ex-army personnel. Easy job, good pay, decent pension. Nothing too complicated.

Even so, whenever he closes his eyes, he can feel the lead hitting the bodywork, smell the oil and grease from the bullet-riddled engine, feel the breeze coming in through the open passenger door, the shards of glass showering his head. He sees Osorio's dead body slumped over the open door.

So he doesn't close his eyes much.

Not that he could have done anything. This is Madrid, not a Liam Neeson movie. He emerged unscathed from the shooting with only a few scratches from the glass that left no marks. He wasn't even eligible for a wage hike for being wounded on duty.

The only thing he was eligible for—a few weeks' rest—was the last thing he wanted.

So here he is, dishing out fines.

What Officer Ruano cannot imagine when he sees a black Audi A8 pull up next to them is the unexpected gift the universe is about to bestow on him.

"You can't park here," he says through the open window. He signals for them to move on, a gesture that irritates drivers the world over.

The side window of the Audi goes down, and the face of a cute woman appears. Let's not exaggerate: she's no beauty. But she has something. Despite the bags under her eyes as big as hammocks and the messy hair.

"We're colleagues," she says, flashing her National Police badge at him. The driver leans over and does the same. "Inspectors Scott and Gutiérrez."

"Hey there. What can I do for you?"

"We have a favor to ask. We need two municipal police cars to park outside a specific address."

"A request like that has to go through control," says a perplexed Ruano.

The woman fixes him with her strange green eyes. *Piercing* is the word that comes to Ruano's mind, if you can say that about eyes, he thinks.

"It has to do with Osorio, Officer. I suppose you get my drift."

Ruano is a millennial, but he's nearly thirty, and so belongs to that generation that still used the expression *holy shit* before *WTF* became universal. This is a moment when neither expression seems strong enough.

"What . . . what exactly do you need?"

"We've identified the whereabouts of two suspects. One is a forty-year-old male, fair, wavy hair, elegant suit. He's with a blond female wearing a raincoat, aged approximately thirty. We have reason to believe they'll be at this address in two and a half hours' time," says the female inspector, holding out a piece of paper.

Ruano takes the note, reads it, and looks the woman in the eye. She nods slowly.

"We need two cars outside the building. If you see the two suspects enter, don't intervene. They're both extremely dangerous. Only make a move when they come out."

"Inspector, I have to call this in. We need to speak to control, and talk to . . ."

"No. If you do that, they won't show. Our only chance of apprehending them is if you do *exactly* what I'm asking."

Ruano thinks of Osorio. Of the nightmares that come even when he's wide awake. He thinks of Osorio's unborn child.

"I'll do as you ask, Inspector."

"Discreetly," she insists.

"Discreetly."

Ruano stares at the Audi's rear lights as they disappear around the traffic circle heading north, then begins to make a list. There's no time to lose.

Life is too *valuable to be left in the hands of fate*, thinks Antonia, watching in her rearview mirror as the figure of Officer Ruano dwindles in the distance. *Although to entrust it to a seventy-seven-word message isn't much better.*

16

A TOWER

Of course it all had to end with a gigantic dick, thinks Jon, peering skyward.

"This won't be like in Rascafría," says Antonia, also looking up. "No fireworks."

"They don't have to be in the plural. One is enough," says Jon, stroking his neck. The stitches on the incision are pulling more than ever. All of a sudden, Jon wishes he had some of Amatxo's moisturizing cream with him.

In front of them looms Torre Espacio. One of the four towers on Paseo de la Castellana. Two hundred and twenty-four meters high. Fifty-six floors. The fourth-tallest skyscraper in Spain. A steel, glass, and concrete monstrosity, standing alongside the other three tallest buildings in the country. A monument to a bygone age, a mausoleum, an aberration, depending on who you're asking.

To Jon, it just looks like a gigantic dick.

With certain advantages. For starters, one main entrance. With maximum security. No side access, no parking. A real rattrap.

"Are you sure White will show up?"

"Yes, I'm sure. This is his moment of triumph. What he's been working toward for years. To break my will and prove his theory is infallible."

Jon looks again at the entrance to the building, and all the official cars filling the street outside. Mercedes, BMWs, Audis, all of them black or gray, some with pennants. Almost all have diplomatic plates.

"We ought to flood the place with cops," he says, more to himself than to her.

"I can't take that risk," says Antonia, shaking her head.

A couple of days earlier, Jon's next question might have been ironical. Filled with reproach, drama, rancor. Now, after all they've been through in the past few days, it has a different tone. Verging on tender.

"Of losing the game?"

"No, Jon, of losing you."

Jon curls his lips in surprise. He wasn't expecting that. He's not sure whether Antonia even considered the possibility of losing before today. Or of not sacrificing whatever was needed in order to win, which is tantamount to the same thing.

We're in complete agreement on that score, sweetie.

Even so, the countdown is still ticking, and Antonia's plan doesn't entirely convince him.

"Remind me again of what we're going to do."

"We're going up. To talk to him. To get him to confess."

"And that will be enough for White to consider you've completed the task."

Put like that, it sounds simple. A mere bagatelle.

Jon glances at Antonia, imagining what must be going through her mind at that very moment. All the decisions. The dilemmas. The tremendous bravery to confront a truth that will completely alter everything she thought she knew about herself.

Not who she is, of course. Because Jon knows other people's actions can't change that.

He'd like to tell her all this, to be able to comfort her somehow, but he's never been particularly good with words. Choosing the right ones, using them to heal, to provide the necessary strength in a few syllables. That's not Jon Gutiérrez's style. Nor is it what he's learned in life.

"Thanks for being here, Jon," says Antonia, looking him in the eye.

Jon smiles, because in the end, that's the most important thing in life. Ninety percent of work consists of being with the people you need to be with. The other 10 percent you make up as you go along.

"There was nothing on TV today. Shall we go?"

Antonia removes her shoulder bag and throws it into the Audi's open trunk, together with her watch and cell phone.

Jon does the same. He empties his pockets, only taking with him his badge and gun. But when he makes to leave his phone, Antonia gestures to him to keep it.

Jon doesn't get it. The phone allows White to hear everything they say, so leaving it in the car would be to make him deaf as the endgame is played out. But Jon isn't about to argue with Antonia; he knows she must have her reasons.

If nothing else, at least he can try to protect her. He takes the bullet-proof vest from the trunk and holds it out to her.

"Put this on, sweetheart."

"They won't let us in wearing those."

Jon looks at Antonia, then at the vest, and at the entrance to the tower. Bites his bottom lip. Repeats the process a couple more times and concludes she is right. He drops the vest.

"Don't worry, this won't end up in a shoot-out," she says. "This is very different."

I'm not sure whether to believe you, thinks Jon, slamming the car trunk shut.

17

A PARTY

The reception desk is at the far side of the enormous vestibule with a travertine marble floor. A thirty-foot-long shiny glass countertop in a futuristic design. Behind it, half a dozen coincidentally young and attractive receptionists (there's one token male).

Coincidentally, he's the one Inspector Gutiérrez heads for.

"We need access to the seventeenth floor," he says, flashing his badge.

"Are you on the list?"

"It's a police matter."

The attractive young man flutters his long eyelashes.

"I'm afraid that won't be possible without authorization, sir. As you know, there's an important event taking place here today," he says, pointing with his pen at the entrance, where a group of latecomers in cocktail attire are swiping their cards through the scanner.

"Check my name," says Antonia, showing him her ID.

The attractive young man is seated on a high chair that, coincidentally, allows visitors to see the receptionists' legs. It also gives them a vantage point from which to carry out a thorough visual check on visitors that would be the envy of any nightclub doorman.

Jon is painfully aware of their deplorable appearance. He in his scary crumpled petrol-green suit. Antonia in her casual jacket, still with vomit stains visible on it despite her desperate attempts to brush it clean in the gas station. They aren't exactly the image of glamour.

"As I say, this is a private event," the young man repeats.

"I'm on the permanent list," insists Antonia.

The long eyelashes blink incredulously, but he plays along, if only to put this pair of down-and-outs in their place.

Jon and Antonia can't see the result that flashes up on his computer screen, but they don't need to. The eyelashes open wide in self-explanatory amazement.

"I'm awfully sorry, Señora Scott. Here's your card," says the receptionist, handing her an oblong piece of plastic.

"And one for my companion," says Antonia.

As they move away from the counter toward the turnstiles, Jon is still relishing the *youhavenoideawhoyou'retalkingto* moment.

"Just occasionally, life offers you special moments," he says to Antonia as they join the line of dolled-up guests.

"It's not as if we have too many left," she replies, glancing at the clock beyond the turnstile.

Although the elevator is full, Jon and Antonia have plenty of room to themselves. Everybody else is crowded round near the door to get as far away as possible from them, and her in particular. Mainly due to the stench of vomit.

The brief journey up to the seventeenth floor is so swift it leaves an empty feeling in their stomachs when the elevator reaches its destination and glides to a halt.

"Enjoy your evening," Jon calls out, himself enjoying the disapproving looks of the other occupants, who are busy competing to see who can be quickest to get away from them.

They leave the elevator and wait for the other guests to swipe their cards at a second turnstile. Bursts of music reach them from beyond the interior doors. Jon recognizes the lyrics

> They will not force us
> They will stop degrading us
> They will not control us

from "Uprising" by Muse, spilling out of the reception room together with colored lights and the sound of a hundred loud conversations.

"He had to choose tonight of all nights, didn't he?" says Jon, glancing at the automatic doors flanked by two women guards with stiff smiles.

"It's no coincidence. With White, nothing is."

Jon shrugs stoically. It's not as if he has time to complain.

"You know what they say. Let the end of the world find you dancing."

"Who said that?"

"A neighbor of yours who sings much better than this group. Come on, let's go in."

They head for the turnstiles, the women with their stiff smiles, and the door they're guarding. A door over which hangs a banner declaring in two languages:

64th COMMEMORATION
OF COMMONWEALTH DAY

The banner is just above a steel plaque welcoming visitors to the

BRITISH EMBASSY

A SOIRÉE

Antonia Scott doesn't like parties.

It's not a question of aesthetics. This one is taking place in the reception room at the embassy, an open, contemporary space (refurbished five years earlier by the only English interior designer who doesn't have abominable taste). It's festooned for the occasion with all the flags of the Commonwealth in general and the United Kingdom in particular.

The lighting is soft, and the effect of the red and blue LED lights dotted all around is to turn the guests into ill-defined shapes with identical features. Which favors most of them, who find themselves in that golden age between maturity and decomposition. After all, this is an embassy, an annual reception, and the guests are a select bunch—which in English means they're rich and snobbish.

None of this is what upsets Antonia Scott about parties, because she's accustomed to dealing with VIPs (she is the British ambassador's daughter), people approaching liquefaction (she speaks with her grandmother a lot), and rampant jingoism (she's a functionary).

What Antonia Scott hates about parties is the sheer number of people there.

Antonia's brain is used to drawing invisible lines (ones she's almost unconscious of) through the space between where she is standing and where she is aiming for. These invisible lines usually avoid any obstacles that pose a threat to her personal preferences. Dirty, harmful, or dangerous objects. This includes lampposts dogs have peed on, dumpsters full of trash, and 100 percent of the human race.

This party is crowded, so it's quite complicated to get from one point to another—which you haven't properly defined yet, because you're still looking for someone—without bumping into another person.

Antonia wastes a few seconds attempting to do just that. To trace a route through all those moving bodies, hubs of small talk, vanities, false smiles, and rented tuxedos. And on the way steering around the coincidentally attractive young waitresses pirouetting with trays filled, sadly, with English delicacies.

Antonia tries and fails. Antonia changes tack. She strides toward the drinks table besieged by a gaggle of guests not yet sufficiently drunk, a somewhat bewildered Inspector Gutiérrez tagging along behind.

"Excuse me," says Antonia, pushing one of the waitresses aside.

She puts one foot on a beer crate, the other on two wine cartons; a third step takes her onto the table, where she knocks over a line of tall glasses with half-melted ice cubes in them. The domino effect produces a nasty sludge that slops across the white linen tablecloth and ends up all over one lady's white dress. As Botox has long since robbed her of the ability to register emotion on her face, her voice steps in to squeal her dismay.

"That dress was way too short for a formal occasion like this anyway," Jon says, to silence the screeching woman.

Oblivious to the drama she has created, Antonia is now a foot or two above all the heads in the room. Every party looks depressing when seen from above. The merrymaking at eye level turns into a sea of bald heads and expensive hairdos. All of which turn toward the crazy woman who has just climbed onto the table.

Antonia spots the man she is looking for at the far end of the room, next to a tiny platform where a DJ in a sequined jacket is trying to liven things up, with varying degrees of success.

"Come on," she says, leaning on Jon for support as she steps back down.

Inspector Gutiérrez acts as a human icebreaker to clear a path through the crowd until they reach the side of the stage. The huge loudspeakers and a couple of tall tables have created a kind of clearing. In the center, Sir Peter Scott, the United Kingdom's ambassador in Spain, is listening—slightly stooped and clearly bored—to the rant of a plump man waving his hands in the air.

"Antonia?" says Sir Peter when he sees his daughter appear from behind Inspector Gutiérrez's vast frame. "What are you doing here? Is Jorge back already?"

Antonia advances toward him . . .

"Father," she greets him, with a slight nod.

. . . as she sweeps past him and heads for the man waiting patiently a few feet behind, arms folded at waist level in front of him. Six foot six, eighty-seven kilos, and none too pleased to see Antonia. A brick wall in a suit, elite training, an SAS officer, Sir Peter's personal bodyguard, and head of embassy security.

"Noah Chase," shouts Antonia, looking up at him and trying to make herself heard above the loudspeakers. "I'm arresting you for the murder of Jaume Soler and the attempted murder of Aura Reyes."

The big Englishman looks with bewilderment at Antonia, Jon, and then at the exit. His square jaw quivers slightly; his unshakable confidence of a few moments earlier collapses like a house of cards.

"I . . ."

He makes to raise his right arm toward the bulge in his jacket, but immediately finds his wrist pinioned by Inspector Gutiérrez. The bodyguard struggles to free himself, but he might as well attempt to escape from a bear trap.

"Don't make a scene, darling," says Jon, slipping his free hand inside the man's jacket. The pistol slides out of its holster and disappears discreetly behind the inspector's back.

"What the hell is going on here, Antonia?" says the ambassador, managing to escape his tiresome guest.

"I don't have time to explain, Father. We need to detain this person."

The ambassador looks at his daughter as if she were speaking to him in incomprehensible slang. He only seems to react when Jon twists his bodyguard's arm behind his back and starts to frog-march him toward the exit.

"Antonia, may I remind you we are on the United Kingdom sovereign territory. You have no jurisdiction here," he insists.

"The arrest may not be valid," says Antonia with a shrug. "Your government may even refuse to waive Mr. Chase's diplomatic immunity because of the convention between our two countries. But by then, he will have told us everything we want to know. And it will be all over the media."

Sir Peter looks at Chase, who for all his elite soldier's muscles looks like a teddy bear in Jon's hands.

"You can't do this."

"I have someone to protect me," says Antonia, pointing to Jon. "You don't."

The ambassador purses his lips at his daughter's jibe.

"Maybe we should talk somewhere quieter."

19

AN OFFICE

Almost fifteen years earlier, the British government decided to sell for €50 mil- lion the enormous building that had been its embassy in the Almagro neighborhood for four decades, and move to ultramodern offices occupying floors seventeen through twenty-one in the Torre Espacio. Sir Peter had himself overseen the purchase of the new diplomatic headquarters and its installation, with the promise in the midst of a recession it wouldn't cost Her Majesty's government a single pound.

At times like those—not so different from ones that soon followed, after a brief period of optimism—such a move aroused a great deal of suspicion. The ambassador, a man so upright and honest he used his ballpoint pens until they ran dry, was determined not to allow the slightest shadow of doubt over his role. He invited three different media outlets—the BBC, *The Sun*, and *The Guardian*—to check the accounts in real time. It turned out there was a deficit of £85,274, the result of a mistake in the furnishings budget.

The ambassador called together the media, who had audited the process, and in their presence airily signed a personal check for the exact amount that had gone over budget.

That is the sort of man Antonia's father is.

Sir Peter's office is on the eighteenth floor, right at the heart of the embassy. The floor below is a reception area; the ones above are offices and administration. The eighteenth floor is all thick-pile fitted carpets and hardwoods from the colonies to remind the visitor England once possessed a huge empire.

Antonia follows her father to his enormous office, situated in a corner of the building. Inspector Gutiérrez is behind, holding on to Noah Chase. Now they're away from the crowded room, the bodyguard has regained some of his composure and isn't making things easy for Jon.

Entering the office, Antonia's heart skips a beat. She's only been here a couple of times before, always on urgent business. The most recent occasion being after the attack on Marcos, when she tried to explain to her father her theory about an invisible assassin. Her father's response had been to take custody of Jorge from her.

But the reason her heart skips a beat isn't a result of—or isn't exclusively a result of—the circumstances of her last visit.

It's because of the décor.

Not the armchairs or the original Chippendale desk. Or the teak-paneled walls or the vast window stretching from floor to ceiling. Or the marble pedestal table with one slightly wonky leg, the result of Antonia toppling it over when she was playing hide-and-seek as a little girl.

No, it isn't because of any of this, although it doesn't escape Antonia's attention that the only piece of furniture the ambassador has kept from his days as consul in Barcelona is precisely the one she damaged in a moment of carelessness. Her father has always known how to send a pointed message.

No, it's the painting.

Antonia can't recall the artist's name, nor does she think she ever knew it. But she remembers perfectly the long hours she stood posing for him. A thin, haughty man who didn't smile once.

The painting shows Sir Peter on a two-seater couch. Beside him, legs together pointing at the viewer, a beautiful woman smiles a warm, mysterious smile. Paula Garrido has her face turned toward her daughter. Little Antonia is six years old, has shoulder-length hair, and her eyes are greener and have more sparkle than they do now. And yet she isn't smiling. There's a sadness in her expression, a foreshadowing of what would happen the following year, of the illness that was already consuming Paula without any of them knowing. Three human beings frozen in what was perhaps the last happy moment in their lives, captured on canvas with rather inelegant brushstrokes and a mediocre color palette. And yet it still creates turmoil in her heart when she enters the office, even though she had prepared herself for it.

"Is that you?" asks Jon, bundling Chase down onto a chair. The marble table shakes on its bronze feet; the chair creaks with the body-guard's weight.

"Be careful with the furniture, Inspector. Believe you me, you wouldn't be able to pay for any repairs."

Jon is about to answer back but changes his mind when Antonia makes a gesture to corroborate what her father has just said.

"Before we begin," says Sir Peter, "I have to inform you my office is protected against any electronic surveillance. Important security matters are discussed in here."

"We're not recording our conversation, Father," Antonia says. "We simply want you to know what this man has been doing behind your back."

"Noah? That's absurd. You have no proof that . . ."

Taking the photo of Chase from her jacket pocket, Antonia tosses it onto the eighteenth-century desk. Even though it's nighttime, the spatters of blood on his face are clearly visible. As Sir Peter discovers when he picks up the photograph.

"Taken minutes after he killed Jaume Soler, a computer consultant, and stabbed his wife. She's in a serious but stable condition. She's already identified him as her assailant."

The last bit is a lie, but it'll happen anyway, as Antonia can see from the way the color drains from Chase's face.

"Noah, is this true?" the ambassador asks with alarm.

The bodyguard shifts in his chair and finally folds his arms, averting his eyes from his boss.

"There was no other way," he confesses before finally turning toward him, guilt etched all over his face. "I couldn't allow him to get to us, sir."

20

A CRIME

The ambassador stares at his bodyguard for several seconds, then looks away.
But this offers only fleeting relief. His daughter is still confronting
him. Thoughts are swimming behind her eyes like fish under green ice:
unreachable.

"I don't know what you think you know, Antonia, but I can assure
you . . ."

"No," she says.

It's a categorical no, but at the same time gentle, almost tender. Antonia shakes her head and smiles as she says it. It's a refusal full of
weariness, of nostalgia. There's nothing worse than to long for what
never was.

"It's not what I think I know. It's what I do know."

"Antonia . . ."

She ignores him and continues speaking. The lights in the room
seem to dim about her as she starts to tell her story; her face is the only
bright spot in the surrounding gloom.

"Four years ago, a computer consultant, Jaume Soler, was approached
by an independent contractor named Mr. White. He threatened to destroy Soler's life by revealing to his wife that he had a lover. When Soler
refused to play ball, White killed the lover and pinned the blame on
him."

She takes a deep breath. Her voice cracks a little.

With pain.

With anger.

"Unfortunately for us, Soler turned to me to try to escape from

White's clutches. But all he achieved was for White to come to our apartment to shoot Marcos and me, intending to cover his tracks. After that, Soler capitulated and gave White what he wanted. However, something went wrong. I don't know exactly what happened, but White was wounded; I suspect he was being followed. One of his employers intervened and walked off with the prize. My intuition tells me this was Chase himself. After all, he's been with you a long time, hasn't he, Father?"

"Antonia . . ."

Again, she ignores the voice coming from the darkness.

Now only she exists.

Only the story exists.

The undeniable truth, revealed by all the evidence, clues, threads they've been untangling over the past few days.

"What did Soler have that was so valuable? And how did he know about the existence of the Red Queen project? The answer to both questions is incredibly simple: Soler was one of the Heimdal programmers."

Antonia shakes her head slowly. Even as she speaks, she is still piecing together the story.

"Not the main one; he wasn't talented enough for that. But he was sufficiently involved to be able to get his hands on a copy of the source code. Because that's what's so brilliant about the Heimdal program. Even if an enemy agent got hold of a terminal that has the program installed, without the source code, without being able to connect to the central computer, it would be worthless."

The ambassador pulls a chair away from his desk and sinks down on it, legs trembling. Antonia doesn't react but continues with her tale.

"It's so easy to see MI6's hand in all this. Who else would have the funds to pay White's exorbitant fees? Who else would need an external contractor, to ensure none of their agents would be involved in an operation on foreign soil and against their own allies?"

"We're running out of time, Antonia," Jon reminds her.

She glances at the huge wall clock—a Bennett that still has its original hands—and reluctantly speeds up.

"So Her Majesty's Secret Service paid for the operation. But they never got what they wanted. Someone made sure of that."

"Believe it or not, we all want what's best," says Sir Peter bitterly.

"The root of all the world's ills is that nobody can agree on what that is."

"Of course not. You made sure your government never got what it wanted. But that didn't stop them. They went on paying Soler all this time to get a clean, uncorrupted copy of Heimdal."

"That program can hack into any computer. Break almost any code. Heimdal means an end to all privacy. It's too powerful to be left in the hands of so few people, Antonia," says the ambassador, trying hard to stay upright on his chair, to maintain his dignity.

"In other words, the power has to be spread around," Jon clarifies.

"The UK government wanted their own copy of Heimdal. As security. And for their own ends. Without their European partners—who were increasingly less their partners—finding out what they did with it," says Antonia, going over to her father.

Sir Peter shrinks back in his chair when Antonia leans over him, both hands on the desktop.

"How long have you known?"

"About what White is after? Since we were in Soler's house."

From the far side of the room comes an exasperated snort and some swearing in Basque that Antonia doesn't entirely understand.

"What I didn't know until today was that you were involved in all this."

"I had to obey orders," Sir Peter says, lowering his eyes.

Antonia has heard this before. It's very convenient to have a loft where you can store all your guilt.

"There's such a thing as free will. Take your bodyguard, for example. When he saw we were closing in on Soler, he tried to kill us. Of course, he wasn't following your orders. I guess he acted out of a sense of duty. Or he was trying to protect himself."

The ambassador has nothing to say to this. He doesn't look at Chase. Nor does he explode with rage when he discovers what he did. Because in reality, Antonia isn't talking about Chase.

"Since Soler was of no use to you, you decided to have him killed."

Her father remains silent. Antonia looks at the wall clock again.

Their time has all but run out.

"Four years ago, Soler gave White the source code," she goes on. "Chase intercepted it and handed it to you. But you never passed it on to MI6. That was one order you didn't follow."

The ambassador straightens up a little. His eyes are moist, and his voice quavers.

"After what happened to Marcos . . . I couldn't go ahead with it."

"After what happened," Antonia echoes him blankly.

"I had no idea he'd go after you, Antonia. You have to believe me."

Antonia smiles once more. There is no happiness or joy in it. Her smile is as sad as the lone teardrop that rolls down her left cheek.

"You brought a killer into our lives. A cruel, ruthless psychopath. He killed my husband. When I told you about him, you made me think I was crazy. You stole my son from me."

"You weren't the target!" says the ambassador in self-defense, clenching his fists.

"Somebody was," says Antonia, shaking her head. "The fact it was your daughter who suffered rather than another person doesn't alter what you did; it only makes it even more painful."

"I couldn't have known."

"Give it to me."

Sir Peter looks up when he hears this.

"What?"

"You know what. There's no more time, Father. Give it to me. He's about to arrive. I can get us all out of this mess, but you have to give it to me. Now."

The ambassador opens his mouth to respond, but doesn't manage to do so. At that moment, the office door opens.

A man in a jacket and tie appears in the doorway.

He's a member of the embassy security staff. Antonia remembers him: shaven head, earpiece. An inscrutable expression on his face.

His expression is very different now.

"Thanks for the guided tour," a woman's voice says behind his back.

He takes a step forward, half stumbling, half pushed.

Before his other foot touches the ground, a shot rings out.

He crumples to the floor. Where there was once a life, now there's Sandra. She enters the office, her smile as deranged as ever.

Strolling in after her, calm and elegant, is Mr. White.

"You heard your daughter, Ambassador," he says, pointing a gun directly at Antonia's head. "I strongly suggest you listen to her and give her what she's asking for."

21

A WORD IN YAGHAN

For a moment, everyone looks on, paralyzed.

Mamihlapinatapai, thinks Antonia.

In Yaghan, a language spoken by a nomadic people in Tierra del Fuego, the beached eye.

A look people exchange when they're waiting for others to start something they all want but none dares initiate.

Then the spell is broken.

22

TWO PAINTINGS

"There are too many people in here," says Sandra.

She aims her gun at Chase and pulls the trigger once more. The explosion echoes off the teak panels; a red bloom appears in the center of the bodyguard's chest. He slumps back in his chair. Jon starts to take out his own weapon but discovers the barrel of Sandra's gun inches from his face.

"Please, Inspector. Very slowly, just with your fingertips."

Jon swallows and obeys with gritted teeth. Unbuttoning his jacket, he hands Sandra his pistol, who makes it disappear in the folds of her raincoat.

"Where were we?" asks White, taking another step toward Antonia. "Oh yes. Ambassador, would you oblige?"

"I can't," says Sir Peter.

White doesn't find the ambassador's tone sufficiently convincing, so he goes right up to Antonia and presses his gun to her temple.

"Of course, you're perfectly within your rights to refuse. I'm afraid the consequences will be plain enough."

"Don't do it, Father," says Antonia.

The Glock's metal barrel doesn't appear to move. There's only a faint swish and a dull thud. Antonia's head jerks back, and a red rectangle appears on her forehead where White has struck her with the gun. A trickle of blood runs down her face, speeds up around the eye socket, and follows the same damp route taken by the tear Antonia shed a few minutes earlier.

"I suggest you do the opposite," says White with an icy look.

Sir Peter struggles to his feet.

"What do you plan to do with it?"

"Nothing that concerns you, Ambassador. But, in honor of our former business relation, I can tell you there are various interested buyers. Not the most respectable people. In short, I'm about to become fabulously rich. No more consultancy work for me."

"So in the end, you're nothing more than a common thief," Antonia says, turning to look at White.

Moving past her, White stands on the far side of the desk close to the enormous window, where he can cover everyone with his gun.

"I'm hurt, Señora Scott. I have to admit, I'm hurt. Deeply offended that you don't imagine I'll keep my own copy of this little toy. On a modest scale, nothing like what Beijing or Moscow would do with it. But sufficient to enable me to continue working in what truly interests me."

White opens wide his cold, dead eyes, already savoring his victory.

"And now, Sir Peter, if you'd be so kind . . ."

The ambassador turns toward the picture hanging above his desk. Three feet high by eighteen inches wide, it shows two dead, dried-out trees, with a misty waterfall in the background. A reproduction, of course. The original watercolor is in the Tate Gallery in London, less than six miles from where Turner painted his watercolor in 1802.

Which is just as well, because this reproduction is merely a door mounted on two cleverly disguised hinges. When pulled open, they reveal a safe.

"A timeless classic. Be very careful when you open it, Ambassador."

Sir Peter taps in the combination, then holds his fingerprint against the red sensor on the side of the door. It opens with a metallic click.

"Forgive me, Antonia," he says, plunging his hand into the safe.

In the next second and a half, seven things happen.

Sir Peter starts to spin around, holding the pistol concealed inside the safe. His tense face shows a kind of calm determination.

Sandra, who had a better view of the safe, swivels her gun from Jon toward the ambassador. A savage, guttural growl rises from her throat.

Seizing the moment, Jon grabs from behind his back the pistol he took from the bodyguard. Jaw clenched in rage.

Sandra tries to correct the aim of her weapon, swinging back to point at Jon's head and squeezing the trigger. Her arm is slow to react, her face reflecting her disbelief at not checking that the inspector didn't have another weapon.

Mr. White fires. The bullet smashes into the side of Sir Peter's skull. As White does this, there is not the slightest hint of emotion on his face.

Jon Gutiérrez doesn't have time to aim properly but pulls the trigger three times, firing at random. An earthquake occurs in his inner ear from Sandra's shot, knocking him off balance.

Antonia Scott yells and leaps forward to try to stop Jon's fall as his head strikes the pedestal table. In her exceptional brain, Antonia is glad she damaged one of its legs an eternity ago, because thanks to that, the marble top collapses with Jon rather than snapping his neck.

23

A FINAL PROBLEM

Antonia looks about her, analyzing the outcome of the previous second and a half. She has to control three competing emotions:

- A gut-wrenching sadness at seeing her father lying between the bureau and the wall, his head blown off.
- An insane joy at seeing Sandra breathing her last, raincoat soaked in blood, a look of incredulity on her face.
- Tremendous concern at seeing Jon, eyes closed, on the floor, menacing beeps coming from his neck.

"That just leaves the two of us, Señora Scott," says White.

Antonia ignores him and goes to check her colleague's pulse. Inspector Gutiérrez is out for the count, but his heart is beating strongly and regularly.

"Please don't be tempted to reach for your colleague's gun or for the one on the floor by the desk," White warns her. "May I remind you I'm not just pointing a weapon at you."

Antonia turns toward him.

White is waving a small device he has in his left hand. The size and shape of an old-fashioned remote control for a garage door.

"That's useless in here. My father's office is protected by signal jammers," says Antonia.

"It's a good thing I added a Bluetooth connection that operates on a different wavelength."

He presses one of the buttons on his remote. A sustained beep issues from Jon's neck.

Antonia rises to her feet, her face an admission of defeat. White observes her triumphantly. It was always obvious she wasn't a woman who liked to lose. But what pleasure could he get from defeating someone who did?

"Would you be so kind as to take the hard disk from the safe?" says White, motioning with his gun.

Antonia skirts the desk and feels inside the safe. Behind a stack of papers and folders she finds a rectangular shape, lined with red rubber.

With her left hand, she holds it up to show White.

With her right, she whips out her own gun from behind her back.

"Well, I never, Antonia Scott with a weapon. That's a novelty," says White with a smile.

"I won't let you take this," says Antonia. "Even if you kill us. Millions of people would suffer."

White glances with amusement at his rival's weapon.

"You're not the best shot in the world, Señora Scott. If you pull the trigger now . . ."

Antonia does. Again and again, until she empties the magazine. Six 9 mm bullets hit the big window, making six holes several feet from White.

". . . you're bound to miss."

The P290's slide has jammed, reducing it to a useless piece of junk. Antonia drops the gun and walks around the desk toward White.

"You'll never make it out of here, White. Why don't you surrender?"

"Surrender? When I'm holding all the aces?"

White reaches for the hard disk. Antonia looks down at Jon, unconscious on the floor, his neck still emitting the deadly beeps. She hadn't bargained on him being out of action when it came to the endgame. So she'll just have to rely on Officer Ruano.

"Not all of them," she says.

White gives a nasty, rasping guffaw.

"Haven't you learned yet I'm always four steps ahead of you, Señora Scott? I know you've asked some municipal police officers for backup. In fact, I know everything you and the inspector have been saying right from the outset," he says, leaning forward to show her his earpiece.

Antonia doesn't respond or move. She simply looks at him, the disk in her outstretched hand. Still a few feet away from him.

"How convenient for your plan that this skyscraper only has one entrance," White continues. "But you didn't count on it having a roof big enough for a helicopter to land on."

Antonia nods and laughs.

Ha. Ha.

A sarcastic laugh, not loud but sufficiently powerful to force its way through the grief, rage, and fear choking her.

"What is it you find so funny?"

Antonia shrugs.

"That you've lost, only you don't know it yet," she replies.

White's eyes narrow.

"And why, might I ask, is that?"

"Because every day, I devote three minutes to thinking about suicide," says Antonia.

Before finishing her sentence, she hurls the disk drive at him. As White instinctively dodges, he bangs his back against the window.

Thickened glass designed to be unbreakable.

But not to withstand the impact of six 9mm bullets, plus a body weighing eighty kilos. Huge cracks appear in the center of the window.

Not enough to break it.

At least not until Antonia launches herself headlong at White, ramming into him at waist height and holding on as tightly as she can.

The glass shatters with a crash.

White drops his pistol as he tries desperately to stay on his feet and free himself from Antonia, but it's too late. The window gives way under their weight, and their two intertwined bodies topple into the void.

24

A REFUSAL

It takes four seconds to hit the ground when you fall from the eighteenth floor of a building.

Four seconds may seem an infinitesimal amount of time.

Not to Antonia Scott.

In four seconds—eyes closed, clinging on as tight as she can to White's belt as she plummets—Antonia is able to:

- Calculate the speed they are traveling at (this depends on the square root of the length of time it takes to fall). With every second, they fall past twice as many floors as in the previous one, due to the acceleration caused by the only true religion: the law of gravity;
- See that as he's falling, White presses the button to activate the bomb in Jon's neck, unaware that his Bluetooth has a range of less than fifteen meters and that by now he is too far from his target;
- Experience a strange feeling of peace knowing that, come what may, she will have saved her friend.

That's all she can manage, because even Antonia Scott has limits. Only her indomitable will refuses to accept them.

This indomitable will prevails even after there's no more road. When she has toppled over the edge of the cliff and is in free fall. Even then, Antonia simply refuses to crash into the ground.

At the last moment, she opens her eyes.

She can't see a thing.

The world is a speeding blur. Made up of wind, darkness, the nothingness she's heading toward.

But even as she plummets, Antonia Scott simply refuses to crash into the ground.

What White's body and hers do is crash into Hortaleza Fire Station No. 11's giant inflatable rescue cushion. The one she specifically mentioned to Ruano in the note she handed him in the car only three hours before:

> *Ignore everything I've said up until now. Go to Hortaleza Fire Station No. 11 and commandeer their anti-suicide inflatable mattress as well as some assistance. Unfold it on the corner of the building closest to the Torre Espacio newspaper kiosk, exactly two yards away from the wall of the building. And in exactly two hours and fifty minutes, not a moment sooner, inflate it to 92 percent. Then you can arrest the man who killed your partner.*

Ruano had followed Antonia's instructions to the letter. Exactly seventy-seven words, but carrying them out wasn't easy. Ruano had to argue for over an hour with the fire captain in charge of Hortaleza Fire Station No. 11 before he agreed to use his extremely expensive piece of equipment for what seemed like a hoax. As well as enlisting the help of eight other firefighters to transport and spread the 371 kilos of rubber and canvas, calculate how long it would take to inflate it, and in addition an expert to judge when it was sufficiently hard. In the end, they succeeded in having the cushion ready moments before two bodies leaped into the void from the eighteenth floor of the skyscraper, to the astonishment of the fire chief and his men.

Antonia doesn't have it easy either.

Even with the anti-suicide jump cushion.

Even though she is clinging to White to make their mass as compact as possible.

Even though she has often anticipated such a moment during her daily three-minute sessions.

Nothing has prepared her for anything like this.

The shock is brutal, terrifying.

At the first bounce, White's stomach slams her in the face, crushing her nose and filling her mouth with blood, spraying tiny scarlet droplets everywhere.

The force of the impact hurls their bodies almost six meters up into the air.

They come apart and cross over in midair.

Antonia's forearm breaks as it hits White's face, fracturing the killer's cheekbone. He instantly passes out.

When they fall back onto the cushion, the second bounce throws them together again, in an untidy embrace that ends with them both in the middle of the cushion.

Bruised and battered, but alive.

Before she in turn loses consciousness, Antonia sees Officer Ruano's handcuffs being snapped on White's wrists.

She would like to add all kinds of warnings, advice, words of caution.

But it's impossible.

Darkness closes about her.

EPILOGUE

A CONVALESCENCE

After that, things became rather dull.

Antonia ended up in the hospital. She needed an emergency operation that same night to reset the bone in her arm. It turned out she also had three broken ribs, which were unbearably painful. Despite all the doctors' best efforts, she refused to take any painkillers.

Instead, she began making phone calls as soon as she woke up. Her first task—to find Aguado—was unsuccessful. The earth had swallowed up the pathologist. Antonia decided to leave that for later.

Her second task was much more important.

She would have gone herself to sort out the details, but there was a police officer at the door to prevent exactly that. Mentor's absence complicated things a lot, but Antonia isn't one of those who give up easily.

The purpose of her calls—interminable and exhausting for those on the receiving end—was to put in place specific procedures to prevent White from escaping.

"I can assure you that . . . ," was how every conversation began.

"And I can assure you that if you don't obey my instructions to the letter, you and your family are all at risk."

In the most reluctant cases, Antonia forced a contact of hers in Inland Revenue to call them. Even the most law-abiding among them gave way faced with that threat.

"You're a cruel woman. But we'll do as you say."

"That's good, because I have another suggestion. Only one food delivery a day. To be left in the outer room. When the first door has been closed, open the second one. At no time are any of the guards to be in direct contact with the prisoner. Is that clear?"

"Yes, ma'am. What a woman."

"That way, you may succeed in keeping him locked up for five weeks," Antonia said, following a rapid calculation, "while we look for a more permanent solution."

"What do you mean perm—?"

Antonia hung up without saying goodbye. She had another call, one she'd been waiting for with her heart in her mouth.

"Good morning."

"I got a message in reception saying I should call this number," said Carla Ortiz.

"How did you know it wasn't a trap?"

Antonia hadn't dared to agree to any method of contacting Carla after her flight to keep her family safe, not even a password; none of them seemed secure enough. She had told her, "I'll find you," genuinely believing she could, although she hadn't the faintest idea of how.

Once White had told her they were in San Salvador, it had been a lot easier. She had left a message at reception in their hotel because it was very late when she called. But she had added a detail that would remind Carla of that fateful night in the subway tunnel.

"Apparently, the person who left the message said they should draw a duck under the number."

"Did they do it properly? Most people don't know how to draw."

"It was recognizable, apart from the fact it was smoking a cigarette," laughed Carla. "I think there are two people here who want to talk to you. But before that, give me the good news."

"You're coming home."

"It's all over?"

"It's all over."

Carla breathed a huge sigh of relief and passed the telephone to Jorge.

"Mama! I flew in a plane! They showed a movie. It's my favorite now. Do you know which one it is?"

Antonia told him she didn't but would be delighted to find out.

* * *

And Jon?

Inspector Jon Gutiérrez woke up in the hospital, more confused and hungry than with a sore head. The first thing he did was ask after Antonia and Sandra. When it was confirmed the first of them was alive and the second dead, his appetite came to the fore. Several male nurses had to come and restrain him from going down to the hospital cafeteria for a sandwich, bawling, "I'm perfectly all right, it only skimmed my head." He refused to taste the insipid dishes he was offered, eating no more than apples and yogurt, the only things he wasn't suspicious of.

In the end, it was Antonia—arm in a sling, underwear showing through the hospital gown—who ended up going to a nearby restaurant to get him some decent food.

"Five eggs and three sausages," said Jon without emotion when he opened the restaurant's plastic box.

"I thought that's what you'd like. If you want, I can go and get something—"

Antonia broke off when she saw Jon begin to devour the eggs, tears in his eyes.

The operation to remove the two explosive devices from his spine was less complicated once they'd deactivated some of White's booby traps. Even so, Antonia arranged for a neurosurgeon to be flown over from the United States to be present during the procedure. There were seven people in the operating theater, and nine experts assisted them online from different parts of the planet. When the last screw dropped into the steel bowl with a satisfying metallic clunk, there was a general sigh of relief that Jon was never aware of.

Nor did he understand much during his subsequent conversation with the surgeon. What with the effects of the anesthetic and the fact that the man was speaking in a foreign language, Jon only understood a few phrases. Something about him having been imprisoned but that now he was finishing a soon-to-be-published book. Jon thought the guy must be making fun of him, but thanked him warmly in his best Basque English. Apart from his *zenkiu, zenkiu very much*, he doubted the doctor understood much either.

They kept Jon in the hospital a few more days. And he had an unexpected visit. His beloved *amatxo*, who had broken her lifelong vow never to cross the invisible frontier of the river Duero. She entered his hospital room glancing suspiciously at Antonia. She sent her home: "Run along now, you must be tired, my girl. I'll look after him, you take care of that arm." Extracting a lunch box full of *kokotxas* from her bag, and a loaf of bread—from Gorka's bakery, you know Gorka, he's Maider's second cousin. A really handsome boy, I think he's single, you know, in case you feel like leaving your very important job in Madrid and coming back to your land and your family, stranger things have happened. And he said: Do you happen to have a photo of Gorka, Amatxo? And she said: Actually, I do. And Jon gawped at the Facebook page of the Gorria Bakery, next to the Basarrate subway station. And at Gorka, smiling for the camera, a big baguette in each hand.

And Jon was filled with a terrible, inconsolable nostalgia. He grasped Amatxo's hand and pulled her toward him, kissed her on the forehead, and said something to her.

Something that made Amatxo incredibly happy.

And they both burst into tears.

A FRESH START

Antonia Scott only allows herself to think of suicide for three minutes a day.

For others, three minutes can be a negligible amount of time.

Not for Antonia.

The three minutes when she thinks of ways of dying are *her* minutes. They're sacred.

In the past, they were what kept her sane; now they're her Escape key. They organize her thoughts. They remind her that no matter how difficult the game becomes, she can always end it. She always has a way out. She can attempt anything.

Now she lives these three minutes almost optimistically. They have saved her life. She speculates with them like someone who's bought a lottery ticket and mentally spends the first prize the night before the draw.

Like a teenager thirsty for the magic moment of her first kiss.

These minutes are sacred. They remind her that, however painful it may be to fall from a great height, you have to have climbed up there first.

Which is why she really, really doesn't like it when, a floor below, footsteps she knows only too well interrupt her ritual.

Antonia is certain someone is coming to say goodbye.

And she likes that even less.

* * *

Jon Gutiérrez doesn't like stairs.

That's why he decides to take the elevator to Antonia's loft.

But he gets out a floor below. To keep the tradition going. To get some exercise. To give her fair warning.

He takes his time going up the last four steps, because of the commotion of the past few days, his exhaustion, and because he's not used to it.

Not that he's fat.

He crosses the threshold—the door is wide open, green, flaking, obviously ancient—and walks to the end of the hallway.

Antonia Scott is sitting in the lotus position in the middle of the room. Staring at him with surprise.

"Have you come to say goodbye?"

"I came to tell you that a couple of days ago, I got a call. Offering me a job."

"Ah," says Antonia.

Jon draws out the moment. It's great for once not to be on the receiving end of Antonia Scott's awkwardness.

"I found it quite hard to understand them. Their Spanish was dreadful, and I don't speak a word of French."

She stares at him blankly. Not putting two and two together. Another novelty: it's a day of miracles.

"Are you going to France?"

"For Chrissake, sweetie. That's not the only country where they speak French."

Nothing. Not a flicker. Nothing more than her neutral, expectant face. Which, with time, effort, and generosity, one might accept as being human.

"They were calling from Brussels."

"Aha," says Antonia. Still not catching on.

"The heads of the remaining teams are relaunching the Red Queen project. There'll be fewer resources. Less money. Not as many countries involved. But they still consider it strategically important."

"I'm pleased for you. Brussels is a beautiful city."

Jon smiles to himself. For all her intelligence, she still doesn't realize what this is all about.

It'll probably take time.

"I accepted the job, of course. All I asked in exchange was for them to allow me to put forward a candidate for another job that's come up."

"Jon, unless you explain to me what—"

"It wasn't easy," he cuts in. "They needed someone who had experience in the project, who'd passed all the security checks, and was management material. And suddenly I thought, hey, I know just the person."

Jon steps to one side.

Behind him in the hallway is Raúl Covas. Fiftysomething, six feet tall, auburn hair, gray eyes, and shoulders to die for. Less pronounced in a suit than in uniform, but even so . . .

"Scott," he says, tilting his head.

"Inspector Covas," she responds, like somebody summoning the devil.

"Not anymore. You can call me Mentor."

In Antonia's mind, there appears the key point, the most important of all the ones in the *Telva* magazine questionnaire:

Point 6: Never go back to your ex. Regardless of what you think, there are a million things that will go wrong.

Antonia gets to her feet, circles the room a couple of times, and stops under the skylight at the far end.

"Come here a moment, will you, Jon?"

Jon goes over to her, all innocence.

"Yes, dear?"

"You do realize he's an idiot, don't you?"

"You said he was really smart."

"Not that kind of idiot."

"Brussels has approved him."

"Yes, but I don't."

"That's different, sweetie. Brussels approves of your results. But they're a little"—he slides his right hand parallel to the floor, fingers splayed—"so-so when it comes to your initiative, or more precisely, your excess of it. And something they called *bullé purle veicúl espesió*."

"That's unfair," complains Antonia. "It's two for you and one for me. And we didn't write any off this time."

Mentor takes a sheet of paper from his pocket and starts to read.

"Sixteen thousand euros for a new paint job, new side-view mirrors, a shopping mall barrier . . ."

Antonia looks at Jon and shakes her head despairingly.

"I have to hand it to you. They needed an ass-kisser and a professional yes-man. You've chosen the best."

"I've got a great eye."

"What about you, Jon?"

"Me?"

"Haven't you had your fill of blood, crime scenes, and violence?"

"Enough to last a lifetime," Jon admits.

"And you want more?"

"Hell yes."

Antonia smiles. Her trademark ten-thousand-watt smile.

Mentor hands them a ring binder containing a sheaf of papers.

Another mystery, of course.

"So what are we waiting for?"

It's Jon's turn to smile and extend his hand. Antonia offers him the file, but he shakes his head. Amatxo didn't bring up a fool, no sirree.

"What do you think? For you to give me the keys to the car, sweetheart."

DISCOVER THE ANTONIA SCOTT TRILOGY

Juan Gómez-Jurado's Antonia Scott Trilogy is an internationally bestselling serial-killer-thriller series set in the Red Queen universe. Now an Amazon Prime series.

RED QUEEN

You've never met anyone like her . . . Antonia Scott has a gifted forensic mind; her ability to reconstruct crimes and solve baffling murders is legendary. When police officer Jon Gutiérrez comes to her to solve a murder, Antonia is forced out of her solitary apartment to solve the case before tragedy strikes again . . .

BLACK WOLF

Antonia is called upon to work for the Red Queen project once again, this time to track down a mafia figure's wife after he is brutally murdered. But she must get to her before her mysterious rival, a contract killer known as the Black Wolf, does . . .

WHITE KING

The Red Queen project is under attack, and at the centre of it all is the dangerous Mr White. Jon Gutiérrez, Antonia's protector and the only person she trusts, has been kidnapped. Antonia must play Mr White's game if she is to keep him alive – but will she succeed?